Readers love
EM LYNLEY

I0669285

24-Karat Conspiracy

"…an excellent story for a hot summer evening if you want to get lost in romance and suspense."

—MM Good Book Reviews

"Thank you, EM Lynley, for creating such an adorable, interesting, and cool couple."

—Inked Rainbow Reviews

Sex, Lies & Wedding Bells

"Kieran and Jaxon together totally sell this book and they have some amazing moments."

—Joyfully Jay

"I thoroughly enjoyed this book, with its twisty middle that leads to an unexpected HEA based on the way the story begins."

—Happy Ever After (*USA Today*)

Dirty Dining

"…this is a very sexy, and almost edgy story that had me wishing for the HEA from about the middle of the book, but that kept me waiting for it right up until the last page."

—Sinfully… Addicted to All Male Romance

"…I think this was a fun, smoking hot story, with great characters."

—It's About The Book

By EM LYNLEY

Bound for Trouble
Dirty Dining
Hostile Takeover
One Marine, Hero
Out of the Gate
Sex, Lies & Wedding Bells

THE DELECTABLE SERIES
Brand New Flavor
Gingerbread Palace
An Intoxicating Crush
With Shira Anthony: Lighting the Way Home
Spaghetti Western

PRECIOUS GEMS SERIES
Rarer Than Rubies
Italian Ice
Jaded
24-Karat Conspiracy

Published by DREAMSPINNER PRESS
http://www.dreamspinnerpress.com

ONE MARINE, *Hero*

EM LYNLEY

Published by
DREAMSPINNER PRESS

5032 Capital Circle SW, Suite 2, PMB# 279, Tallahassee, FL 32305-7886 USA
http://www.dreamspinnerpress.com/

One Marine, Hero
© 2015 EM Lynley.

Cover Art
© 2015 Reese Dante.
http://www.reesedante.com
Cover content is for illustrative purposes only and any person depicted on the cover is a model.
Photo courtesy of the author and Vertical CFI Helicopters, Hayward CA

ISBN: 978-1-63476-383-7
Digital ISBN: 978-1-63476-384-4
Library of Congress Control Number: 2015905841
First Edition August 2015

Printed in the United States of America
∞
This paper meets the requirements of
ANSI/NISO Z39.48-1992 (Permanence of Paper).

To the men and women who have served this country, and the people who love them.

Preface

EM Lynley after her first helicopter lesson.

THE SEEDS of this story are scattered far in the past.

I've never followed politics much, but like nearly everyone around the world who watches international news, I had a strong image of the President of the United States getting into a green-and-white helicopter on the South Lawn of the White House and being whisked away to attend to some vital presidential business. I had a vague notion of the helicopter being called *Marine One*, but beyond that, I never thought much about it.

That changed when I was lucky enough to get a job at the White House Council of Economic Advisers. Though the offices are located in the Old

Executive Office next to the White House, we were part of the White House complex. It was a thrill to be so close to the inner workings of Washington.

Even more exciting were the perks that came with the job, including attending any ceremony on the White House lawn, including welcoming receptions for visiting heads of state where the president and the foreign leader would inspect US troops and color guards and military bands.

But I will always remember the first time I received a phone call from my boss's secretary telling me to head out to the South Lawn to wait for *Marine One* to land. Everyone in our department who wasn't in a meeting or facing a deadline would head downstairs and across the yard to the White House and wait on the South Lawn waving little American flags the staffers handed out. To one side was a row of press with cameras, ready to catch the helicopter landing and the president as he stepped down, waved to everyone, and then walked inside.

Despite repeating the same process every time, it was always a thrill. There is a lot of ceremony around nearly everything the president does, and even in the age of the Internet, the press corps need to be on hand to photograph and film it.

Flash forward to the fall of 2014.

October brings Fleet Week to San Francisco. A dozen ships, even more aircraft, and tens of thousands of sailors and Marines. I love visiting the ships during Fleet Week. This year I visited the newly commissioned USS *America*, an amphibious assault ship. I didn't know quite what that meant until I arrived. Basically, this ship serves as a support base for Marine units to stage an attack.

After making my way past displays of armored vehicles and light assault vehicles (tanks, to the rest of us), I arrived on the lower deck, where a number of helicopters were displayed. Pilots and members of the air crew answered questions from visitors. I was listening to other people (mostly men) asking questions, when it hit me that helicopters were a hell of a lot more interesting than I'd realized.

In fact, a helicopter pilot would make a fantastic main character for a book.

Up on the flight deck, about a dozen smaller helicopters were on display. Now I started taking notes and asking my own questions. To my surprise, the pilots were really thrilled to answer questions, talk about the capabilities of their aircraft, and even let visitors climb inside a few different ones. I happily spent about three hours moving between Cobras, Hueys, Super Stallions, and more. I took a lot of photos and, of course, asked how I could get to fly on a Marine helo. (The answer is, you can't. Even the pilots' families can't get on board, partly for security reasons and partly because the demand would be incredible.)

By the time I got home, I was dying to include a Marine pilot in a story.

And that's when I got the idea of writing about a former combat pilot who comes home to fly *Marine One*, ferrying US government officials around and dealing with the drastic transition between those two jobs.

Which is when my real research began, up to and including taking a few beginner's helicopter flying lessons to know exactly what it feels like to pilot one of these fascinating rotary wing aircraft. I was immediately hooked and definitely would love to take more, maybe even get a helicopter pilot's license.

What that means is that you just might see another story starring a helicopter pilot.

I hope you enjoy the taste of the inner workings of Washington and the White House in *One Marine, Hero*. I've been lucky enough to attend White House holiday parties and other staff events, and it's such a pleasure to share these incredible experiences with readers.

—EM Lynley, May 2015

Chapter 1

BEAU HAD never received a letter from the president of the United States before.

Matthew "Beau" Beaumont stared at the elegant cream envelope he'd found propped against his monitor when he settled at his desk on this blustery Wednesday morning in late September. He picked it up and flipped it over, running his fingertips across the raised seal on the flap. He'd seen the seal ten thousand times. Everyone in Washington, DC, had. Almost everyone in the country recognized the Seal of the President of the United States.

But he'd never seen it on a document with his name before. He'd also never gotten anything in an envelope of such smooth, thick paper.

Instinctively he brought it to his nose and sniffed. No scent. What had he expected? The president's aftershave? He knew President Bergen wore Chrome, and if he closed his eyes, he might pick up the citrusy layers.... No. It didn't smell like anything—fortunately, because the most likely aroma would be from the slightly sweaty mailroom guy who distributed the ever-decreasing number of real paper envelopes delivered to the *District Daily* newspaper office.

Of course the president hadn't personally sent this. But a guy could dream. President Bergen was pretty damn hot for a leader of the free world.

"Waiting for it to open itself?"

Beau spun around in his chair at the sound of Laney Tillman's distinctive voice. She sounded like a bird caught in a car door, except when she laughed. Then she sounded like a donkey caught in a car door. You could hear Laney laughing from a block away.

This morning she stood in Beau's cubicle wearing a mishmash of pinks and pale pastel greens. She looked like she'd been mugged by the Easter Bunny and left for dead. Beau actually closed his eyes and opened them again, hoping he'd only been having a Crayola nightmare.

As the *Daily*'s fashion columnist, hanging out with Laney could seriously damage Beau's street cred. Laney's frilly top and her pants appeared about two sizes too small, probably as result of her gig as the *Daily*'s food writer.

"Jesus, Laney, do not sneak up on a guy like that. I could have spilled my coffee and ruined a perfectly divine pair of new Diesels."

"They look like normal old jeans to me."

"Of course they do. To you." He blew her a kiss and replied in his most soothing voice. As much as he loved Laney, her clothes sense horrified him. "The way foie gras tastes like chopped liver to me." It didn't, but it was fun to push her buttons.

She cringed, then gave him the kind of smile a mother might give her irascible child. "Of course it does. But what's in the envelope already?"

Beau wanted to know too. He eyed it as he took a sip of double-hazelnut, low-fat no-whip. He absolutely missed fat and whip, but the Diesels wouldn't fit if he indulged too often. He set the cup down and slid a careful finger under the flap so as not to damage the beautiful embossed seal.

"Hurry up, I'm graying over here." Laney yanked the envelope out of Beau's hand and ripped it open before he could stop her. The *fffft* of paper tearing deflated his excitement. She slid out a thick card and waved it like her life depended on it.

"Oh. Oh! Beau!" She cleared her throat and started reading in a regal voice:

"'The President and the First Lady request your presence at the Autumn Correspondents' Celebration at the White House. Black Tie...' blah blah blah." Then she stared at him for a moment. "The correspondents' dinner? Really? You?"

"Don't sound so shocked." But Beau *was* shocked. He grabbed the invitation from her and looked to see if it really was addressed to him. Why *had* he been invited?

Laney clearly wondered the same thing. "Have you ever even done a story at the White House?"

"I covered a charity fashion event the first lady sponsored a few months ago. It was to raise money for a girls' school in Africa and—"

"That's it?"

"What do you mean? Angelina Jolie was there too. And you should have seen what the first lady was wearing! The most gorgeous pale pink knee-length—"

"Beau!"

"What? It was beautiful. And her shoes had these little teeny—"

"Focus."

"Would you like me to tell you what they served for lunch?" He frowned when she nodded vehemently. "Look, honey, shoes to me are like caviar to you. Why can't you understand that?"

"Because I don't see how what someone else is wearing is news."

He refrained from suggesting she should start worrying about what *she* was wearing. "But I can understand why food is so exciting for you."

"Everyone has to eat. Not everyone has to wear pink kneepads."

"She wore a knee-length dress. Not kneepads. But she does have lovely knees."

They had this discussion or one like it at least once a week. Despite their inability to see eye to eye on each other's area of expertise, they got along regarding everything else, from politics to films to men, though at the moment, neither had one of those.

"When's this dinner? And what are you going to wear?"

"You really don't care what I'll wear, do you?"

"No. But I can tell you're dying to tell me." She grinned and perched her hefty bottom on the edge of his desk. She reached for the invitation again. "How did you get invited? I doubt many writers from the *Daily* did."

"I wondered the same thing."

The *Daily* was the second paper in town after the *Washington Post*, which attracted the cream of the crop. But downsizing meant the *Post* had to let some good writers go—including Beau—which was how the *Daily* had come about. It focused less on politics and more on everything else and included an expanded Lifestyle section. Food, fashion, and fundraisers were big news in DC, and the *Daily* found an increasing readership of locals who were tired of getting a king-size dose of politics when they also wanted to know which film to see or where to get the best ice cream.

"Maybe we're finally getting some recognition," Laney said.

"Still, I'm not exactly a correspondent." Beau read the fine print on the invitation. "But I get to bring a plus one…. Wo—"

"Yes!"

"How do you know I was going to ask you? Maybe I needed your advice about whom to invite?"

"You mean which of your long list of lovers?"

Beau shrugged. "Right. None of them are really White House material."

"They might have a dark alley around there somewhere…."

"Bitch." He slapped her hand. "I won't invite you after all. I'll Instagram minute-by-minute photos of all the lovely, lovely food they'll be serving, just to torture you. I hear they have a different wine with each course."

Color rose in her face. These were fighting words. "Who's being a bitch now?"

"If you stop making fun of my sorry love life, then I'll bring you along."

"Deal."

BEAU'S THRILL lasted another seventy-three minutes. Then someone kicked the side of his cubicle and erupted in a ball of humanized fury.

"Lemme have my invitation." A six-foot grizzly bear stared down at Beau, who rotated his chair to see what the commotion was about. The bear had a surprisingly neatly trimmed beard and a cream-colored button-down tucked haphazardly into generic worn jeans with tatters at the edges. The pale shirt didn't camouflage the bulge hanging over his waistband. Beau would have suggested a nice olive-colored shirt instead. But now he was face-to-face with that bulge, though he admitted he instinctively checked for another more desirable bulge.

"Sorry, who are you and why are you bellowing at me?"

"I'm not bellowing," bellowed the bear, raising the volume another dozen decibels. He'd only been speaking loudly before, but the guy was definitely bellowing now.

"Can you use your inside voice?" Beau used his campy tone and gave the chubby bear a sweet smile.

This disarmed the bear for a moment. He blinked, then stood up to his full height. "Mike Beaumont. Senior reporter."

Beau stood and held out a hand. "Hi Mike, nice to meet you. Do you think we're related?"

"No. I'm positive we are not related." He paused for a moment, appearing to consider his next words. "I'm here to collect my White House dinner invitation." He pointed at the invitation, which Beau had propped up against his monitor.

Beau grabbed the envelope and glanced at the front. "It's mine. It says 'Matthew.' That's me. You're Mike. Even I can read." He winked at the other Beaumont, who pressed his lips together until they were paper white.

"There was a mistake. For some reason they sent it to you. It should have gone to me."

"What makes you think that?"

"Because they invite me to every White House event for journalists. And I didn't get an invitation this time."

"Maybe you were naughty?" Beau couldn't help using the campy voice again. With considerable effort, he kept himself from batting his eyelashes.

"I was not *naughty*."

The word sounded so ridiculous from this huge man that Beau burst out laughing. By now some of the other writers and staff were looking in his direction, and he fluttered his fingers at his audience.

"I'm sorry." He wasn't, but it wouldn't do to torture the large, angry man any further. "Did you call to see if there was a mistake? Because this one is definitely addressed to me, and I've already got a date lined up. Of course, if someone tells me I'm not supposed to be invited, I'll gladly hand this over." He smiled again, but he hoped like hell there wasn't a mistake. He *really* wanted to go to a big dinner at the White House. He'd give up his seat at a Prada runway show for a chance to attend a White House dinner, if only to be in the same room as the sexiest president in US history.

"I'll be back!" Mike Beaumont said, turned on his heel, and lumbered out of Beau's cube.

"Wait, Mike." Beau stood. He was about the same height as Mike but only half as wide. Beau glanced at the invitation again and put aside the images of him in a tux shaking hands with the president, who would then ask him to dance. He handed the envelope over to its intended recipient.

Mike sneered and ripped it out of Beau's hand with unexpected speed. He turned and lumbered out of the cube again.

"Oh, shit." Laney appeared at the entrance to Beau's cube, frowning. "It probably *was* for him, you know."

Beau nodded. "I know. He was entertaining to tease." He let out a sigh and leaned back in his chair. "Well, it was fun to dream about while it lasted. I guess the ugly stepsister is going and leaving me at home."

"Forget the White House. We'd never find a parking spot. Why don't we get dressed up anyway that night and go somewhere fancy?"

"Deal."

AT LUNCHTIME Beau dragged himself downstairs and around the corner to Subway. He ordered the sandwich with all the Italian cold cuts and cheese, then slid into a booth, but after one unsatisfying bite, he put it down on the table.

"There you are!" Laney frowned as she settled into the booth across from him.

"I never thought I'd see you in a Subway."

"I'll need a Silkwood shower when I leave." She pulled Beau's sandwich toward her, and the frown deepened. "Friends don't let friends eat lunch meat. Unless it's charcuterie, but that's like comparing Korbel to Dom Perignon."

Beau let out a sigh as she trashed his sandwich. But he had no appetite anyway.

"What's the matter, Beau? I'm worried. Subway is slumming it, even for you."

"You're not helping." He continued dining dangerously as he slurped real soda made with high-fructose corn syrup instead of the flavored no-calorie water he usually drank. "It's the whole invitation thing."

"This isn't about the party or Big Mike, is it?"

Beau shook his head. The movement made his teeth ache, and he pushed the soda toward Laney so he wouldn't be tempted to sip more of it. "I actually like my job, but in those situations I feel like a second-class citizen."

"No one at the paper sees you that way."

"Mike Beaumont does. And he's right."

"Forget him. If he was really good, he'd be at the *Post*, right?"

"So would we. The *Daily* is, well, not the *Post*. And compared to hard news like I used to write, only a gig at *Vogue* is going to come anywhere near my old job."

"Don't be so hard on yourself. You are not the only journalist downsized into a features position. How many other options did you have? It's better than being unemployed. Or living someplace like Kansas City." She regularly deprecated her hometown. "Until recently everything was either barbecued or fried."

"Really? I read something recently that said Kansas City was one of the top five cultured cities in the US."

She glared at him. "Come on, you're still much better off than the top reporter in KC."

"Sometimes I'm not so sure. I really loved writing hard news until the *Post* let everyone go unless they were covering the biggest, most controversial stories."

"You're really good at fashion. You always look terrific."

"Why couldn't you be a guy?" Beau cracked a narrow smile. He knew Laney meant well, but he cycled through these doldrums every so often. Today was worse than it had been in quite a while.

"I could if I wanted, but I like who I am right now. Look, get up and we'll go get some of the truffles you like so much. My treat. We can pig out on as many as you want."

"Okay." Beau smiled and got up. Laney was the one who loved those truffles, but he'd go along to humor her so she wouldn't worry about him. But it was going to take more than truffles to blow away the dark cloud that had settled over his mood.

Laney surprised him after the trip to the truffle shop. She wanted to talk about what they would wear when they went out for their alternative correspondents' dinner. She insisted on flipping through the stack of fashion mags in his cube and created some of the scariest color combinations he'd ever seen. But she soon had him smiling and laughing again.

"You know what? Maybe Plan B will be more fun. If all the people there are like Mike Beaumont, I'm not so sure I even want to go," Beau said after work as they sipped Belgian craft beers at a swanky new bar Laney wanted to try.

"Here's to Plan B!" She raised a glass, and they toasted each other.

PLAN B lasted until the following day.

Tom Withers, Features Editor, came into Beau's cube just before lunch. He had the beautiful envelope with the presidential seal in his hand and presented it to Beau.

Beau looked at it, then up at Tom, who was leaning against one wall of the cubicle. "I don't understand."

"Looks like it was a mistake. But the White House won't let Mike Beaumont use this invitation. Apparently it's some security thing. You have to show up with your own invitation because the Secret Service has to do a basic background check on you in advance. They check ID and everything."

"So I get to keep this as a souvenir of the party that almost was?"

"The White House Social Secretary called to apologize after Mike questioned the error." Tom grinned. "'Questioned' is actually a polite word. But she wanted to apologize to you. In fact, she felt so bad about the error, you've been added to the guest list. You've got an official invitation. Follow the directions to RSVP. Mike Beaumont will receive his own invitation."

"Good thing he doesn't have to rely on his charm to get one."

"Agreed. He's not *that* charming," Tom replied in a dry tone.

Having an awesome boss like Tom was one reason Beau had come to love this job so much. "I didn't want to point that out."

"He's a good reporter. Better when he doesn't have to talk to real people. Anyway, the social secretary was impressed with how you handed it over. She thought your gesture *was* charming, and worthy of an invitation."

Beau's spirits brightened further. Maybe he *would* get to dance with the president. "I'll tell Laney the good news."

"But speaking of charm…. Try to watch what you say. Mike Beaumont reported you for sexual harassment because you flirted with him."

Beau recoiled. "It wasn't real flirting—more like a defensive maneuver. Am I in trouble?"

Tom shook his head. "Hell no. His editor was laughing when he mentioned it to me. But you'll have to do an all-day sensitivity training course next week."

"Lesson learned." Beau stopped smiling and nodded. "Thanks."

Tom left and Laney flounced into Beau's cube. "Sexual harassment? What a dickhead!"

"I'm probably prohibited from using the word 'dick' in the office, so you summed up my thoughts."

"How about if I'm your spokesperson when you need to say something with a sexual connotation. At least until someone else complains?"

"Deal."

Chapter 2

"YOU'RE JAKE Woodley, aren't you?" The guy spoke with the slightest hesitation. His eyes danced with excitement, but his fingers trembled around his glass of beer. He rubbed his thumb up and down the glass, the movement catching Jake's eye.

"Yeah, that's me."

"I thought so." The young man smiled and the thumb movement slowed. "You look exactly like on TV."

Jake stared through the guy and nodded to the bartender. "Another one of these." He held up the empty shot glass, then slammed it onto the bar and slid it down the smooth surface toward the sour-faced barman.

Jake had hit that point in the evening when he should slow down, but he didn't want to. *Fuck it, I'm on leave.* He'd purposely passed the row of gay bars along South Beach, seeking a spot like this: more drunks than tourists or temptations.

"I'll buy you a drink." The young guy grinned. He had a nice smile. Nice face. Nice body too, but Jake wasn't in the mood for nice guys. This wasn't a gay bar, and from the guy's demeanor, either he wasn't gay or he was the biggest gay virgin on the planet.

"I can buy my own."

"Oh." Disappointment washed across the guy's face. "I'm Bill." He started to put a hand out to shake, then glanced at it like it belonged to someone else.

Jake didn't say anything.

"My dad flew a Black Hawk during Desert Storm. I can't imagine what that must be like."

"You don't want to."

"Well, I do, actually. I was wondering if…."

"Where's my tequila?" Jake turned to the bartender, who was at the other end of the not particularly long bar. "Didn't you hear me?"

"I heard you," the bartender said and finished drying a glass as if he had all day today and tomorrow to get to his customers. He held the glass up to the light and peered at it, then put it onto the rack and grabbed the bottle of Don Julio Jake had his eye on. He poured more into Jake's glass.

"Don't they have dishwashers around here?"

"They do." The bartender turned his back to Jake and started wiping the bar counter.

"So, Jake, want to—"

"No. I don't. Don't want to talk about flying. Don't want to have a drink with you. If you want to hear what it's like, go ask your fucking dad."

The guy stared at him like a puppy who'd been kicked. Jake wasn't sure how he felt about treating the kid like that. He'd finish this drink and figure it out later. Alone.

"S-sorry." The guy slid off the stool, put some cash on the bar, and slunk away.

"You know how much of a dick you are?" The bartender's voice was ominous.

"Is that a real question?"

The bartender shook his head and went back to wiping down the counter.

"Just give me the rest of the bottle and we won't have to bother each other."

"Bar's closed. Pay up and go."

Jake looked at his watch. "Three hours till closing."

"Bar's closed to you."

"What the fuck's up your ass? Nothin'?" Jake laughed.

"You didn't have to treat Bill like that. He's just...."

"Just what?"

"He's been steeling up his courage to talk to you for two days."

"No pain, no gain."

"He's shy, harmless."

"I don't like talking about combat. And I don't need any hero-worshiping daddy's boys following me around."

"His dad's dead. Got killed back near Mosul. Shot down picking up a Ranger platoon. And he was a buddy of mine from high school."

Jake stared into his glass and felt dizzy, his buzz deflating to a dull drunkenness. There was one good sip left, but he was done. He put the glass onto the bar and pulled out his wallet. "Really?"

"Yeah. I'm sure Bill would love to ask his dad. Too bad he can't. Poor kid's too starstruck to realize what a dick you are. Planning to join up, and he wanted to ask you about Marine Corps pilot training. He hasn't learned it takes more than a big medal and your picture with the president to be a hero."

Jake pulled out enough cash to cover his tab, then another twenty. "I didn't handle that very well."

"No, you fucking didn't."

"I should apologize."

"I don't think he deserves to endure another chat with you." The bartender glowered. He picked up the cash, counted it, and left Jake's tip sitting on the bar when he turned to put the rest of the money into the cash register.

"You don't want a tip?"

"I don't want you thinking you can buy yourself some bad behavior, then go home and feel good about yourself." He slammed the cash register shut and moved to the next customer, grabbed a bottle, and poured. "On the house."

Jake stared, more than a little queasy. He stood, his knees sturdy beneath his weight. He wished he was drunker so he could go back to his room and pass out.

Back in his hotel room, Jake lay staring at the ceiling, watching a spider floating in a cobweb fluttering in the light breeze coming through the window. If he concentrated, he could hear waves crashing against the sand.

Miami, especially South Beach, could be a nice place for a visit, or it could offer any vice a man could want. But at the end of the day, the end of the week, the end of the trip, Jake would still be Jake, and a week of leave wouldn't have smoothed away the bumps in his life.

A chirp from the nightstand caught his attention, and he gave up on the spider as his cell phone flashed to get his attention.

Only two people would be calling him right now. His CO, calling him back to duty for some emergency Jake didn't want to know about, or… the other caller, whom Jake didn't want to speak to in this state. Too drunk to be careful, but not drunk enough to pass out in peace.

When the flashing and noise stopped, he glanced at the phone, noticing the text message contained a photo attachment. He opened the image and smiled at the goofy grin on the face of his twelve-year-old neighbor, Toby, one arm around Daisy, Jake's dog. She was smiling too. Toby took good care of her when Jake was out of town on duty or on leave.

"My pretty lady," Jake mumbled and felt their smiles reaching across the distance to brighten his dark mood.

Missing most of an ear and a foot—a story he'd rather not know—Daisy was the only thing that kept him getting up every day. On late nights and early mornings, Jake wondered whether he'd rescued Daisy or whether it had been the other way around. Some days he worried even Daisy would decide he wasn't worth the effort.

The bartender's words echoed in his head, drowning out the waves crashing outside his window.

"I don't want you thinking you can buy yourself some bad behavior, then go home and feel good about yourself."

He'd never feel good about himself, no matter how much money he left on the bar.

JAKE ARRIVED home from his week of leave in Miami and tossed his duffel onto the couch. His house was stuffy and quiet. Too quiet. No click-clacking of nails across the kitchen floor and into the hallway to greet him. He needed some unconditional love right about now. He hadn't realized how much he'd missed Daisy's complete acceptance. She was still across the street with Toby Miller.

He glanced at his watch. Just past ten. Was it too late to pick Daisy up? Toby was twelve, but his mother would still be awake. What was bedtime for a twelve-year-old? At that age, Jake was still awake, even if his parents thought he should be asleep. He'd bring a flashlight to bed and read under the covers.

He glanced at the door, then back toward the silent kitchen. Did he have beer in there? Maybe he'd go buy a six-pack. Two six-packs. He didn't relish another night alone, even in his own bed.

He had his hand on the doorknob when the cell phone in his jacket buzzed.

"Woodley," he said without looking at the caller ID. He was used to being summoned at a moment's notice.

"Jake, I saw your lights on. Welcome back." Jenna Miller sounded cheerful as usual. She always had a smile in her voice.

"Thanks. I got in about five minutes ago."

"Mom, lemme talk to him!" Toby came through loud and clear. "Jake! How was your trip? Did you do anything fun? I can't wait to hear all about it! Do you want me to bring Daisy over?" Finally Toby paused for air. He'd make a first-class scuba diver someday with that kind of breath control.

Jake chuckled. "Yeah, sounds great, if it's okay with your mom."

"Sure. You can show me your photos!"

Jenna came back on the line. "He'll be over in a minute, but feel free to kick him out after ten minutes. If he's not home in fifteen, I'll come rescue you."

"He's fine, Jenna. Thanks for—" The doorbell rang. "I'll talk to you later or tomorrow."

Jake opened the door, and seventy pounds of retriever flung herself and her one front paw against his chest. When he'd hugged her and got her back on the floor, she circled him, then poked her nose squarely into his balls.

"Hey, girl. I didn't cheat on you with any other dogs." *And only two guys.*

"Hey, Jake." Toby stood in the hall while the dog greetings were taking place. He gave Jake a hug. It wasn't as long as a mom hug, but longer than a guy hug should be. He'd learn.

"Toby, I think you spoiled her. She looks too happy."

"She missed you."

"I missed her too." He knelt down to ruffle Daisy's fur and pull her in for another hug. She wagged her rear half so wildly Jake could barely hold on to her. "Daisy, did you really miss me?"

She butted his chin with her head, and her cold, wet nose went for his crotch again. Nothing like a welcome home from a dog.

"Let me put out her water and food bowls," Jake said, and Toby followed along behind him.

"So, what did you do on your trip?"

"Some diving, fishing, and swimming. A lot of nothing." He wouldn't mention the drinking and the fucking he'd done in between the other activities. Too much of the former meant he hadn't gotten much of the latter. He focused on filling the water bowl and placing it on the floor, purposely avoiding Toby's insightful gaze.

Over the past year and half, their relationship had grown, much to Jake's surprise. Until he'd met Toby, he'd been uncomfortable and incompetent with his sister's two kids. Now, hanging with Toby was a pleasure, and his niece and nephew said he'd become a pretty cool uncle.

"Did you meet any nice guys, Jake?"

"Toby!" Jenna came through from the hallway. "You know better than to ask questions like that!" To Jake: "I'm sorry. You left the front door wide open."

"Thanks. I got distracted."

Jenna gave Toby a loving sneer. "I'm not surprised. Toby, why don't you head home and let Jake get to sleep."

"Okay," Toby said, drawing the word out to seven syllables as if hoping his mother would change her mind before he finished saying it. He put his head down and pushed through the swinging door into the hallway.

"I need to pay him, Jenna." Jake went for the wallet in his back pocket.

"Tomorrow's fine. He can't spend it tonight."

"Internet…."

"True." She grinned and looked at him. "You look good, Jake. Nice and tan." She took a few steps closer and peered at him again. "Well, you might need to catch up on your sleep. Busy week?"

He shrugged and avoided her gaze. "Nothing I'd tell you or Toby about."

"Yeah. I hope not." She chuckled and sat on one of the chairs and scratched Daisy's head.

Jake leaned against the counter. "Don't worry. I'm not in the habit of oversharing. Especially about sex or drinking."

"Tell me about it. You let me know if he gets too nosy. I think he's hitting that age where he wants to talk about those things."

"Do you want me to—" He didn't want to finish the thought. Didn't kids learn enough online that they didn't need the birds-and-bees discussion anymore? Had his father had the talk with him before he was Toby's age? He could barely remember being twenty-two, much less twelve.

She shook her head vehemently. "No. No way."

"Sorry, I guess you don't want him hearing the gay version. I think I can do the straight version. Can't answer too many questions, though."

"No, it's not that at all. He sees you as a role model. I think he wants to be gay, so he'll be more like you."

A role model to a twelve-year-old? Jake was touched but a little worried at the responsibility. "What makes you say that?"

"He asks questions about whether he's supposed to like girls or want to kiss them. Hell, I don't know what to say."

"Didn't read the parenting manual?"

"If only. Let me know if he asks anything too personal. I've tried to answer truthfully, but not if he asks about me or his dad."

"I can do that, if you like."

"Only if you're comfortable." She fell silent, and the lone sounds in the room were the occasional thump of Daisy's tail on the floor and the loud ticking of the clock on the wall. "Well, I better take my own advice and leave you alone to relax and sleep. You due back on Monday?"

"Yeah. I'm looking forward to it. Give me something to do instead of keeping my own company."

"So, no hot guys on the trip who you might see again?" She stood up. "Sorry, that wasn't fair. But I can keep hoping you'll find someone…." She let the thought fade away, but Jake knew she wanted someone to keep him from self-destructing.

"You just want someone else to help with the plumbing and cleaning out the gutters."

She shrugged and walked up to Jake to plant a sisterly kiss on his cheek. "Come for dinner tomorrow. It'll motivate me to do more than microwave or order out."

"Sounds good."

Once she left, Jake settled on the couch with the one bottle of beer he found in the nearly empty fridge. Daisy hopped up and sat next to him as he flipped through three hundred channels of crap. He sucked down the contents of the bottle and wished he'd gone to buy more before he got comfortable. He stood up, and Daisy's gaze followed as he walked over to the high cabinet over the bookshelf on one side of the room. He kept the strong stuff in here. He popped open the door and pulled out a half-empty bottle of tequila. He unscrewed the cap and took a gulp directly from the bottle, enjoying the burn as it slid down his throat. He started toward the couch.

Daisy raised her head and stared at him. She looked disappointed.

"Hey, I'm old enough to make my own decisions."

Daisy put her chin back down on the couch, but her eyes bored into Jake's, and he felt the weight of her disapproval. He couldn't take it. He took another good belt, then put the bottle away in the cabinet. When he turned back toward the couch, Daisy thumped her tail and made a sound he interpreted as approval.

"Fine. You win. This time."

ON SUNDAY he woke at five, grumbling at the alarm clock. He allowed himself one snooze, then a wank before he pulled himself out of bed. How easy it was to get out of practice getting up at the asscrack of dawn. But it was a good thing he did this trial run instead of hoping he could manage on Monday.

Speaking of runs, he needed to get serious with his fitness. He'd missed more days of PT than he'd managed while he was on leave. Contrary to what civilians thought, being on leave did not mean he could sit back and be a lazy slob, no matter how hard he'd tried. He'd be in really sorry shape right now if he hadn't tried to get a run in at least every other day.

This morning October more than made her presence known. He pulled on lightweight running tights and a long-sleeved shirt and wrapped Daisy's leash around his hand. Their breath frosted the air, and the chill prickled the hairs in his nose when he inhaled. Daisy let out a snort but looked more awake than Jake felt. Despite her missing front paw, she had excellent balance and could move surprisingly easily and quickly.

"Yeah, I'd like to crawl back in bed too. But I can see you slacked off while I was away. Yes, that kibble has gone right to your hips."

She wagged her tail, responding to his cheerful tone and not the critical words. He laughed and moved off at a brisk walk to get them both loosened up before he got serious. The high school was two blocks away, and he had the track to himself at this time of day.

They managed four miles without too much grumbling. He missed the firm sands of South Beach. The frozen asphalt wasn't good for his knees, but it beat the concrete sidewalks. He could work out at the base fitness center, but he preferred to have the dark mornings to himself. Usually. Today his head was too full of conflicting thoughts to enjoy the sheer physical exertion of his usual routine. He went easy—for Daisy's sake, he told himself—and didn't do his usual six miles.

Heat steamed off Daisy's coat and Jake's chest as they made a last slow lap to cool down. His throat hurt from sucking in cold air, and the lactic acid made his muscles burn. The familiar pain felt good. How many miles would it take to get all those mojitos out of his system? More than he could manage today.

His mouth watered at the thought of mojitos. Or was it simply the rum that piqued his interest?

Rum, probably. He thought of the bottle of tequila. Six a.m. was probably too early to start doing tequila shots. He hated that he'd qualified it with "probably." Who the hell would know? He glanced down, and the movement made Daisy look up at him, tail wagging.

"Okay. I'll wait at least until noon. Does that meet with your approval?"

"Mornin', Jake." Coach Dobson was directing two skinny, pimply students setting up equipment on the field for early-morning football practice. He'd have the boys finished in time to get to church or he'd never be allowed to work them on the weekend. Members of the team were filing into the locker room. "Been somewhere exciting with the president?"

"Not this time. Went down to Miami for a week."

"Nice work if you can get it." He waved and blew a whistle that must have shattered his eardrums years ago. Jake shouted a good-bye and led Daisy home.

Inside, he pulled warm towels out of the dryer. He used one to dry and warm Daisy, then the other when he got out of the shower. He yanked on a blue-and-green striped rugby shirt, a pair of USMC sweats, and the thickest socks he had.

Settling onto the couch, Jake started on the overweight Sunday *New York Times* as he cradled a mug of strong black coffee. He had the whole day to kill before dinner with Jenna and Toby.

He looked at Daisy and she looked at him. From across the room, the liquor cabinet beckoned.

It was going to be a long day.

DINNER WAS a pleasant interlude, but once Jake was home again, he gave in to the siren call of Don Julio. He knocked back a couple of quick shots, and the noise in his head subsided. The voices he tried to muffle weren't the kind telling him to do crazy things. They were the voices of men he'd never see or speak to again. When he was alone at night, he heard them particularly clearly.

It was a bright, clear night. He could see his breath as he crossed the space between kitchen and garage, but he didn't bother to zip his leather jacket. He needed the cold. He stepped into the garage and pressed the button for the opener and the light. His Harley Sportster gleamed under the dim bulbs. Nice night for a ride.

He glanced at the helmet hanging near the door, then got on the bike without it. He kicked the stand back and started the engine, which was too loud in the enclosed space even with the door open. But she sounded good. He opened the throttle a little and rode down the driveway, remembering to shut the garage door. Then he gunned it and headed for back roads usually deserted this time of night.

His buzz cut did nothing to protect his head or ears from the chill as he sped up once he was away from traffic and bright streetlights. The tequila kicked in, and he felt a little glow. He increased velocity.

He hit seventy, then eighty. He opened the throttle still more, needing the speed, needing the acceleration.

Faster and faster, pushing himself and the machine to their limits, as if he could recreate the moment that changed his life forever. The moment when beautiful metal and glass became a twisted wreck awash in jet fuel and blood. He heard the impact, felt it, smelled the carnage around him as if it were yesterday.

Ninety, one hundred, one oh five. Then he eased the throttle back.

Not because he was afraid to go faster or afraid to look death in the eye. Not because he wasn't ready to end it all. He was.

But he slowed and pulled the motorcycle to a stop because though she had Toby, Jake didn't want to let Daisy down. Didn't want to put her through another round of confusion and loss and abandonment the way her previous owner had.

He pulled his spare helmet out of the equipment box and fastened it under his chin. He headed home close enough to the speed limit. When he turned into the driveway, he spotted Daisy watching him from the living room window, eyes two glowing saucers in the headlights.

Daisy needed him to live, even if he didn't care one way or the other.

For another day, Daisy would be enough.

Chapter 3

ALTHOUGH BEAU was back on the White House guest list for the party, the look on Mike Beaumont's face didn't immediately fade from his memory. He went through the motions writing his columns for a few days, licking his wounds and cursing his situation.

Laney was away for a week covering a gourmet cruise, and Beau found his spirits flagging again. One morning when he ran into Grizzly Beaumont in the *Daily* lobby, the guy looked right though him, and Beau realized he couldn't let the situation fester.

He was as good a reporter as Beaumont, or he had been once upon a time.

Beau actually enjoyed the fashion beat, and he hated how Beaumont had taken the pleasure away.

"I'll show him," Beau muttered to himself as he stood in front of his closet the next morning, trying to choose something to wear. "I'll show him," he repeated, as if that would leave Mike Beaumont quaking in his mucklucks.

The way to show Mike was to write something he would approve of.

And a new project was born: Beau would find a hard-news story to research and write and offer it to Mike's boss, the editor of the news desk. If he could write one, he could write a dozen, and maybe he'd get an offer to move downstairs.

The idea resonated for the thirty minutes it took Beau to get to the office, and then it fizzled out again as he told himself he had too much work to do to go chasing after a story he hadn't been assigned. But by midafternoon Beau had turned in his columns for the week and had plenty of free time and no more excuses.

So he grabbed his laptop and headed around the corner to Café Agatha, his favorite place to write. He got an extra-large latte and settled into a booth, ready to set the newspaper world on fire again.

But it wasn't like riding a bike. He was out of practice brainstorming ideas. He used to write a lot about education policy, so he read up on some of the recent issues in education.

Common core and student loan debt were among the big issues, but education hadn't been sexy a couple of years ago, and it still wasn't sexy. He had to write something that would capture headlines, and education wasn't going to fit the bill—unless he could uncover a scandal.

He didn't have enough connections anymore to find a juicy education topic the local reporters hadn't already done to death.

The best scandals were about sex or money, or both. He didn't have much of either, Beau mused as he finished his second latte. He'd soon be bouncing off the walls, so he switched to herbal tea.

There had to be something good brewing over in the House or Senate.

Beau pulled up the schedule of Senate committee hearings, hoping something would jump out at him.

Closed hearings abounded, mainly in the Armed Services and Intelligence Select committees. Probably plenty of good ideas floating around in those meetings if he had the connections to attend, but it would take serious research to dig up even a tiny gold nugget at one of the open hearings.

For a start, he could spend some time in the Hart Senate Office Building, where the meetings were held, see who some of the personalities on the intelligence committee were, then follow them to see who they met with, try to eavesdrop in the hallway, frequent the bars their staff members liked to visit.

The next afternoon he attended an open committee hearing, then stuck around listening as the staff members collected papers and notes after the senators left. For the next several days, between fashion assignments, Beau enjoyed strolling the halls of power, loitering near the closed hearings and collecting scraps of information.

By the end of the week, his mood had markedly improved.

"DID YOU meet a new guy while I was away?" Laney asked over sushi in the latest addition to Alexandria's restaurant scene. The paint had barely dried, but Laney loved being the first to discover the next hotspot.

"No."

"You're kind of glowing. I haven't seen you in this good a mood for a long time."

Beau shrugged and stuffed a piece of saba into his mouth, eyes watering. He'd overdone the wasabi.

"Well, whatever you did or ate, I want to know the secret."

"Tell me more about the cruise." Beau slurped warm sake.

"Now I know you're hiding something. You hate to hear me go on about food."

"I'm practicing mindfulness."

"By minding *my* business? How is that mindfulness?"

Beau didn't have a clue. It had sounded like a better excuse in his head. He didn't want to let on to Laney what he was doing, in case he failed. She would be supportive no matter what, but he wanted to do this project on his own.

"Then what is mindfulness?" He let Laney lecture him rather than reveal what he was really thinking about.

Chapter 4

MONDAY MORNING Jake arrived at Marine Corps Base Quantico with plenty of time to report to the morning meeting in HMX-1. The Marine helicopter squadron was best known for operating the sleek green-and-white helicopters that landed on the South Lawn of the White House. They whisked the president, the first family, and other world leaders away. While everyone recognized *Marine One*, only the aircraft actually flying the president used that call sign, a fact unknown to the majority of Americans and to the throng of cheering citizens clustered behind the White House waving American flags and presenting an image of support.

Jake greeted fellow pilots and other members of the squadron, some of whom asked about his trip to Miami. He followed them into the long, narrow meeting room where the daily "All Officers Meeting" or AOM was held for the squadron's thirty pilots.

Colonel Lewis, the squadron's commanding officer, strode authoritatively toward the front of the room and commenced the meeting. He assigned a variety of tasks to his squadron, from flying the president—known as POTUS—on a variety of upcoming trips to ferrying other members of the administration around DC and the rest of the country.

Jake was usually included in the POTUS lifts, so when he didn't receive any orders for the next several, he tried to keep his frustration from showing in his expression. After the CO dismissed the squadron, he caught up to Jake in the hallway.

"Welcome back, Captain Woodley. Come and have a word with me after the morning training."

"Yes, sir."

For the next two hours, Jake copiloted on a training flight for another officer. They were flying the CH-53, which was the support helo for the big airlifts. At least one of these went on every POTUS lift, to ferry equipment and the ubiquitous press corps. Flying support aircraft was one of many duties pilots performed while working toward their qualification as presidential pilots. Some would never earn that coveted qualification, but Jake was on the fast track due to his skill and commendations.

Today's training session was uneventful. As they returned to the Cage—the squadron's cavernous hangar, where even the floor was shinier than a new car—Jake spotted another pair of pilots heading out in a Sikorsky White Hawk, a sleek, responsive aircraft that handled like a Ferrari compared to the pickup truck feel of the CH-53.

He longed for more training in the White Hawk, or the stately Sea King, the signature green-and-white aircraft most Americans recognized as *Marine One* from those clips on the nightly news. Jake had recently qualified as a presidential copilot and had flown the president twice. That made it particularly galling that he hadn't been assigned any upcoming POTUS lifts.

Back inside the hangar, Jake headed to the CO's office, saluted, then shut the door as directed by the colonel.

"Have a seat, Jake." The colonel stared at him a moment before continuing, and his use of Jake's first name meant this discussion was more personal than professional. The possibilities caused Jake's stomach to tighten uncomfortably. "I know you were expecting to get put on the next POTUS lift, but I've got another assignment for you."

The colonel had been a constant support and mentor since Jake joined the squadron, and while he wasn't the sort to waste time or breath on small talk, Jake hadn't expected him to cut to the chase so quickly. He was about to ask why, then closed his mouth.

"I hope you got whatever it was out of your system while you were away. You're a top pilot, but your attitude needs serious work before you can move up to the assignments you should be flying." The colonel leaned back in his chair and regarded Jake for a moment before continuing. "After the missions you flew in Afghanistan, the work of this squadron is going to seem tame. But it requires the same full commitment from you, especially if you want to get qualified to pilot the Sea King with the president on board. You deserve that. You've earned that privilege with your skill and your sacrifice in combat, but it takes more to advance here."

None of this was news to Jake. What was news was how well the colonel read his mind. He was bored with the easy missions he'd been assigned. He needed a challenge.

"I've been more… lenient… with you than usual because I understand how difficult the transition has been for you. But I've seen your behavior deteriorate rather than improve. I know you give your all on duty, but this squadron can't afford to be as lax regarding off-duty, uh, indulgences, as combat units. That's all I'll say on the topic. You know how to proceed. If you aren't up to the particular challenges and rewards of HMX-1, there are dozens of pilots waiting to take your spot."

Jake's stomach knotted. The colonel wouldn't say it in so many words, but he was telling Jake to get his drinking under control. In some units, the

CO would probably suggest counseling, but in HMX-1 appearances were critical, leaving much unsaid.

"I understand, sir, and—"

"Don't make empty promises. Just do it."

"Yes, sir." Jake stood up.

"You're not dismissed yet." He opened a drawer and pulled out an envelope, which he handed to Jake.

Jake took the envelope, spotting the presidential seal embossed on the flap. Inside he discovered an invitation to a dinner at the White House the following Friday.

"The president wants to thank you for doing your job so well." The colonel's sneer increased in intensity. "His words, not mine. He likes you."

"I don't think that's the kind of event for me." Jake thrust the envelope back, but the colonel held up a palm.

"That's another order. You will go to the party, and you will represent the USMC and this squadron."

"Yes, sir." Jake nodded and withdrew his hand along with the cream-colored envelope.

"I'll be there too, as will Mrs. Lewis. She's looking forward to seeing you. *Now* you're dismissed. And get a good night's sleep. I've decided to slot you on the veep lift to Florida. Captain Alvarez will be taking another assignment."

"Thank you, sir." Jake stood, saluted, and left, more confused and conflicted than when he stepped off the bird an hour earlier. On the one hand, he would be making more flights, while on the other, the colonel seemed to expect Jake to do things he hadn't anticipated would be part of his duties.

He might be the only person who turned his nose up at an invitation to a party at the White House.

Well, at least he didn't have to agonize over what to wear or how to fix his hair. The Corps made those decisions for him too.

God, he wanted—deserved—a drink, but when he got home, he went for a mind-clearing run with Daisy instead. It didn't stop him from thinking about spending some quality time with his secret boyfriend, Don Julio.

THE FOLLOWING day he copiloted for a formation training exercise with Major Landau piloting. Also taking part in this exercise was a new member of the squadron, Rob Yangley, a captain who had transferred in from the flight school at Pensacola.

"Captain Yangley, you'll work with Woodley in the simulator the rest of the week. We'll schedule additional flight training sessions once you're more familiar with the equipment and the local routes."

"Thank you, Major. Captain Woodley."

"Just Jake."

"Rob."

After they squared away the aircraft, Rob and Jake sat in the pilot's mess sipping coffee. "So, you on the president's flight crew?" Yangley wore the typical awed expression of new pilots for whom the glamor of ferrying the president around seemed almost out of reach.

"Sometimes. I haven't actually piloted him yet, but I've copiloted a few times from the South Lawn to *Air Force One* at Andrews. I usually fly one of the decoy aircraft or the CH-53s carrying press. But I'm training for top qualification in between the other missions. As long as I get to fly, I don't care who I'm carrying." While that was true, Jake still felt slighted when he didn't get the plum missions.

"How long you been in this squadron?"

"Eighteen months."

"And you've never piloted *Marine One*?"

Jake shook his head.

"Do I have to wait for someone to die or something?"

"Something." Jake wasn't in a chatty mood. Yangley should have learned in his initial HMX-1 training that it took two to three years to qualify to fly the president. Jake's extensive experience and aptitude put him about six months ahead of the usual schedule.

"So what have you been doing? You'd think they'd put a big hero like you into the big leagues much sooner."

Jake ignored the editorial. "These Sea Kings and White Hawks are unlike anything you flew in Iraq or Afghanistan. They're really fucking heavy, which throws everything off, and you'll have to start almost from scratch until piloting them is second nature. You'll see once you get in the simulator. Hovering in the Sea King takes more concentration than you'll believe till you try. It's not easy to land on a dime and you do have to land the fucking things. Not like in combat."

"So the president isn't gonna fast rope down onto the South Lawn?"

Jake laughed. "I'd like to see that."

"This one might go for it if you suggested the idea."

President Bergen had been in an airborne unit in the Army and served during Desert Storm. It was one reason he held the respect of most of the military personnel who served under him.

Yangley sipped coffee. "I'm still kind of pinching myself over being selected for this unit. I applied a couple of years ago, and my transfer came through only last month. Beats the fuck out of training newbies on the baby helos."

"Now you know how I feel." Jake threw him a wide smile. Maybe the new guy would be okay.

The afternoon flew by, and one of the other pilots suggested taking Yangley out for beers. Six of them convened at the Alehouse near Woodbridge. They shared some jokes and did some male bonding, but Jake wasn't ready to go when the others started saying their good-nights.

"I'm gonna finish this one." Jake held up a nearly full glass of beer.

"You're not driving, right?" Yangley asked.

"Nope. Gonna cab it. Don't worry." Jake turned to the bartender. "Some Patrón Silver, for a nightcap."

He ended up finishing the bottle.

Jake could barely get the key in the lock when the cab dropped him off. Daisy scratched at the door as he squinted and jabbed the key repeatedly at the surprisingly tiny hole until he made contact. "I'm home, honey."

He had to get onto his knees and slowly put the key in before he managed to connect key to lock. He fell onto the hallway floor. The last thing he remembered was Daisy licking his face.

HE WAS still on the floor when he woke up. It was already light out, which he could see because the front door was still open.

"Fuck," he said when he was conscious enough to realize he'd spent the night facedown in his hallway. He didn't remember leaving the bar. How had he gotten home?

Gradually his brain started filling in the gaps and answering his questions, and he wished it hadn't. He should have left the house thirty minutes ago. He grabbed a quick shower, gargled with industrial-strength mouthwash, and threw on a clean uniform.

He got to work nearly an hour late. Colonel Lewis came out as soon as he arrived. "In my office," he practically growled as he shook his thumb in that direction.

Jake saluted and followed the colonel inside while others in the squadron looked on, then watched him close the door.

"I can see your vacation didn't solve any of the problems we talked about before you took leave. Or after."

"Sir?"

"Jake," the colonel began. He was taking the personal approach again. That wasn't necessarily a good thing. "This can't go on. I have no choice but to ground you until you can get your shit together. I can't send you to fly anyone like this, even the press corps." Normally a jibe at the press corps elicited laughter, but the colonel wasn't in a joking mood, and Jake reined in his amusement.

"Sir, it's not like before. We took Langley out last night."

"Yangley."

"Who?"

"Captain Yangley. Not Langley."

Heat rose on his neck, but he kept his face impassive. "Yes, sir. Yangley. But I was fine on Monday, wasn't I?"

"Jake, if you show up… like this—" He swept a hand toward Jake and exhaled loudly. "—half the time, do you really think that's acceptable? A day here and there where you're at a hundred percent is not how this squadron operates."

"Give me the rest of the week, sir. I'll show you."

"Arriving late already knocked you off the roster for the veep lift. In fact, you're grounded until further notice, and I'm writing you up today. However, in light of your prior record, I won't put the report into your OMPF for the time being." A negative report in his Official Military Personnel File would doom Jake's career. "If you can prove you belong in this squadron, then I'll shred it. Otherwise, it goes in." He looked at Jake the way his father had when he'd found out Jake was gay—disappointment blended with concern, but not animosity. Like Dad's, the colonel's eyes held a glint of hope. "Go home, call it a sick day, then report directly to me first thing tomorrow. I need to figure out what I can have you do to earn your wings back."

"Sir?" The severity of his predicament crashed down like a meteor.

"Home, Captain."

"Yes, sir." Jake stood and saluted, then left. The guys standing in the hallway pretended they hadn't been watching the door and waiting, like vultures. Scuttlebutt would spread this story within the hour. But the CO couldn't be seen allowing Jake to go OFP—on his own fucking program—or risk losing the squadron's respect. Jake flipped the waiting pilots the bird and walked out the way he'd come ten minutes earlier.

It felt like Monday again.

He caught up on sleep until hunger woke him in the middle of the afternoon. Against his better judgment, he washed down takeout from a nearby Mexican place with Don Julio. He finished off the bottle.

"At least it won't be tempting me anymore," he reasoned, but even Daisy didn't believe him. She curled up near the front window instead of at his feet or trying to climb onto the couch.

He'd started drinking early, so by five the next morning, he was sober as a judge. A judge with a hangover he couldn't let the colonel notice, not if he wanted to keep this posting. Did he want to keep this posting? It was a question he asked himself several times a week.

Hell yes. But even if he got booted from HMX-1, Jake would take any aviator slot in any squadron. The thought of losing the privilege of flying terrified him more than anything.

"You dodged a bullet, Jake," Tim Alvarez told him as he poured coffee in the break room before the morning meeting.

He'd run into a brick wall called Colonel Lewis. What could have been worse than that? "Why d'you say that?" Jake stirred in a few packets of sugar. Usually he took it black and unsweetened, but he needed the energy today. He anticipated more impending disaster.

"They did random piss and breath tests on the squadron yesterday. Not two hours after you left. All the pilots and a third of the support staff got tested."

"Seriously?" Jake sipped coffee and thanked his lucky stars. First time he'd felt grateful to get a dressing down. He'd have been suspended, maybe kicked out of the squadron, if he'd been found with BAC over 0.01 on duty. "Anyone get caught?"

"No one failed the Breathalyzer, but a few maintenance guys and one pilot came up positive for recreational substances. They're facing discharges."

"Fuck. Who?"

"That's enough gossip, ladies," Lieutenant Colonel Monroe said. "Get to work." He eyed Jake up and down but didn't say a word. The lieutenant colonel was second-in-command and the bulldog of the squadron. His scowl was permanent. Apparently if you made a face too long it did stick. Jake couldn't recall the man smiling more than twice in the past year. To make matters worse, he had the throaty growl of a drill instructor. More than one officer cringed at the memory of their first weeks in OCS when Monroe was on a tear.

Back in Colonel Lewis's office that afternoon, Jake held his breath as he waited to hear his sentence.

"Jake, I think you've gotten enough of a scare into you to change your behavior while you still can."

"Sir?"

"There's a point where occasional self-medication turns into addiction. Right now you're on the side of that line where you make a conscious decision every time you take a drink. That's why I'm convinced you can avoid what happened yesterday. You know the risks and the consequences. If it happens again, I have no choice but to conclude you've crossed the line and you *will* be transferred out of HMX-1. Your next CO can worry about your future."

The silence suggested it was Jake's turn to speak. "Where do I stand now, sir?"

"I won't be scheduling any simulator time for you in the meantime."

Jake gulped. If he wasn't flying lifts, the simulator was the only way to earn additional qualifications. He saw his future imploding. He didn't trust his voice, so he nodded.

"I'll find other duties for you. We'll see how you perform, and then I'll consider you for more critical lifts, maybe a copilot slot on a POTUS lift if you can prove to me we don't need to discuss this issue again."

"No, sir. Thank you."

"I'm taking a few days' leave while my wife has some treatments. While I'm away, Lieutenant Colonel Monroe will be running the squadron."

"I'm sorry to hear your wife is ill. Please give her my regards." Mrs. Lewis had some rare form of cancer. She'd been a lovely hostess to the officers in the squadron until recently, when her health took a turn for the worse. "And thank you for the opportunity."

"I'll let her know. She'll appreciate the thought." The colonel's frown melted away, but his eyes still held a chilly warning that Jake better not fuck up again.

Later, at home, Jake reflected on the events of the morning. The colonel undoubtedly knew in advance of the previous morning's drug test. But he'd grounded Jake and sent him home, so Jake hadn't been required to give a sample. He definitely *had* dodged a bullet.

He needed to get himself clean again. He didn't want to lose his job. Being in the HMX-1 Squadron was a plum assignment. Guys would kill for his slot. Guys had, during combat deployments. It was supposed to be a reward for service.

But why did the cushy job ferrying government officials, senators, and visiting dignitaries feel like he'd been given a life sentence? Why would he rather face antiaircraft fire and extract a platoon of grunts than fly the president around?

What the hell was wrong with him?

FRIDAY AFTERNOON, while much of the squadron was heading off for a presidential lift to Camp David or the veep lift to Florida, the lieutenant colonel summoned Jake to his office.

"How are you doing, Jake?"

He fidgeted in his seat as the lieutenant colonel's eagle eyes raked him over. "Fine, sir."

"You seem to have taken Colonel Lewis's warning to heart. Or at least you appear to."

"Yes, sir." Jake bit his bottom lip.

"Your behavior should be above reproach on duty or off. Your face is well-known to anyone with a television or the Internet, and you never know when someone might photograph you doing something that could embarrass the squadron, the Marine Corps, or the White House. And it would jeopardize this assignment if anyone in the White House thinks you can't handle the work or might be under the influence while you're flying the president or anyone else around." He paused for a moment and smiled. "Except the press."

Jake laughed along with Monroe.

"Do you have a drinking problem, son, or is it something else?"

Hoping this was a rhetorical question, Jake remained silent.

"I don't doubt for a moment you're one of the best pilots on this squadron. However, you're not remotely the best Marine. I suspect you're aware of both facts. Along with the colonel, I'm willing to help you stay here, so I'll give you a little leeway, but we cannot tolerate a repeat of your behavior earlier this week. I don't care what you do on your own time out of the public eye, but when you come into this building, when you drive onto this base, you have to be one hundred percent ready to do your duty. We never know when we'll be called for any part of our mission. That's no different from Iraq or Afghanistan. We're not flying into combat, but we have to protect our team and our passengers exactly the same way as we would a platoon we set into a combat zone."

"Yes, sir."

"I know from experience a pilot who isn't allowed to fly is bound to get himself into more trouble. No one wants to see that happen to you. I've got a special assignment for you. It's scheduled for this weekend. Tonight, actually. You and Alvarez."

"Tonight?" This was highly unusual. A momentary chill set into Jake's bones, but he brushed it off. He wanted to fly. He was ready to fly. He *needed* to fly.

"Do you have a date, a hair appointment, or something more important than this mission?"

"No, sir."

"Catch a couple of hours of rack time here, then you'll pick up your passengers and take them here." He opened a folder and slid a flight plan and map out of it. The familiar Top Secret watermark slanted across each page, along with a heading at the top: Top Secret Appaloosa.

"Who are we flying?"

The lieutenant colonel pressed his lips together for a moment. "I don't know. It's not important, is it?"

"No, sir."

Monroe handed the folder to Jake. "Familiarize yourself with the details while I get Alvarez, then we'll go over the plans together here."

Jake flipped the folder open as the lieutenant colonel walked out of the office and shut the door behind him.

FOUR HOURS later Jake and Alvarez and an enlisted crew chief settled into their seats in one of the modified Hueys and took off, with Jake piloting. He and Alvarez would swap places on the next leg of the flight. They picked up their passengers, two men who stayed in the shadows so Jake never saw their faces. One of them wore a hat the entire flight. Another had a beard, but that was all Jake could discern. Alvarez sat in the copilot's seat and shrugged when Jake asked a silent question.

Jake put the details out of his mind as he and Alvarez performed the preflight check of the aircraft.

"When are we leaving?" one of the men asked.

"After we finish the checklist," Jake responded. "Sir."

"You've only been here ten minutes."

"Regulations, sir, for your safety." Alvarez responded and threw Jake a commiserating glance.

That shut the guy up.

Once the preflight check was complete, Alvarez told the tower they were taking off. Jake increased the rotor speed and slowly pulled up on the collective, changing the pitch of the blades until the aircraft left the ground. He made tiny adjustments with the pedals to keep the helo straight as they rose with barely a shudder. Once they'd cleared the ground, Jake accelerated their climb and banked left toward their destination.

He loved flying, loved the responsiveness of this machine. He'd flown Hueys and Black Hawks in combat, and maneuvering was second nature, as simple as driving a car. That let him enjoy the flight as they moved low enough to see cars speeding along dark country roads below, with the occasional brightly lit gas station or all-night shop.

The headphones cancelled any cockpit noise beyond the comforting thrum of the rotor blades, including the conversation between their passengers. Helmet mics let Jake and Tim communicate, but by mutual consent, they kept unnecessary conversation to a minimum.

They flew to a small airfield in northern Maryland, dropped the men off, and slept in the bird. In the wee hours of the night, still in pitch darkness, they deposited their passengers at the pickup spot, then returned the Huey to Quantico.

To Jake's surprise, Monroe was there when they landed. He watched them perform the postflight check-in, and Jake couldn't help feeling the grim look on the lieutenant colonel's face was some sort of warning. The lieutenant colonel's all-seeing gaze reminded Jake of the billboard in *The Great Gatsby*. Those wire-rimmed spectacles and intense eyes scared the crap out of him.

As much as Jake wanted to ask Alvarez about this strange middle-of-the-night assignment, he'd wait until they were off the base and out of the lieutenant colonel's presence.

When Jake got home early Saturday afternoon, he downed a few shots of tequila and climbed into bed and fell into exhausted sleep before he had a chance to go over the events of the past twenty-four hours.

He was starving when he awoke, made scrambled eggs, and wolfed them down. Now he was ready to phone Alvarez.

"Tim, you have any idea what the hell we did last night?"

"Nope. And I don't care."

"You ever done one of those before?"

"Twice."

"For Appaloosa?"

"Jake...." Tim's tone held a warning. Naming a classified mission on unencrypted comms was prohibited.

"Same guys, same places?" Jake asked.

"I don't know."

Jake let out a sigh. Something in Tim's tone told Jake it wasn't a good idea to ask questions.

"Is this a regular thing? What about the other pilots?"

"I had the same copilot both times." He didn't say who.

"But it was fucking weird."

"What's weird about it?"

"Hello, secrecy? The way we had to return all the paperwork. The way we had only coordinates and maps with no place names?"

"Did you ask why you flew the missions you were assigned back in Afghanistan?"

"No."

"This is also a mission. If the squadron commander tells us to, we fly. Who, when, where he tells us. That's good enough for me."

"You're right. We just follow the orders." Jake said good-bye and stared at the wall in his kitchen for a while after he hung up. He didn't agree with Tim. For all he knew, he'd just flown Osama bin Laden's little brother around Maryland. He didn't like being in the dark like that.

But he loved flying. He hoped he wouldn't have to choose.

NEAR THE end of the following week, Jake was assigned another last-minute flight for Appaloosa. This time Major Jack Plummer was piloting, with Jake as copilot. They picked up three passengers in Virginia and dropped them off in Maryland before returning to Quantico. Another team would retrieve the passengers the following day. This time Jake recognized one of the men as a Pentagon big shot, Army General Graham.

As with the first secret flight, Lieutenant Colonel Monroe was in the hangar when they arrived and collected their flight plans and paperwork without a word except to dismiss them.

"Do you have a moment, sir?" Jake asked and Monroe led him into the office.

"What's on your mind, Woodley?"

Use of his surname put Jake on guard, but he went ahead anyway. Caution had never been his strong suit. "I'm just wondering who we're flying and why the flights have a code word." Until Appaloosa, Jake hadn't been assigned any noncombat flights with code words. Maybe this was common practice and he simply hadn't been assigned one until now.

Lieutenant Colonel Monroe sat back in his executive armchair and steepled his hands with his fingertips under his chin. "I don't know, Captain. I just pass the assignments to my pilots. I don't ask my CO why we're doing these flights. And I don't recommend you do either."

"But sir—"

"Wait a moment before you go on." Monroe leaned forward and opened a drawer. He pulled out another folder and slid it across the desk to Jake. "Open that."

Inside, Jake found a disciplinary report with his name at the top and a recommendation of losing his commission. A small earthquake erupted in his gut, and the tremors went all the way to his hands. They shook as he closed the folder. He glanced up at Monroe and slid the folder back across the desk.

"I see we have an understanding. I give orders. You follow them. That's how the Marine Corps works. It's how the whole fucking Pentagon works. Men—Marines—who follow orders, who show they can be trusted, get more responsibility and rewards, of which there are many in this squadron. Those who don't follow orders get to make their own rules—as civilians." He leaned back in the chair again. "Any questions?"

"No, sir." Jake blinked and pushed his chair back from the desk.

Chapter 5

TWO WEEKS after Beau received the invitation to the Correspondents' Dinner, he and Laney left the *Daily*'s office in the early afternoon and went directly to his apartment, where they would both get ready for the Big Ball, as Laney insisted on calling it.

"What the devil?" Laney stared at the rack of clothing in the middle of Beau's living room. "It looks like sample sale day at Bloomingdale's."

"You've heard of sample sales? And Bloomingdale's? Where's the real Laney?"

"Shut up." She paused. "Okay, tell me how you got all these gorgeous dresses?"

Her curiosity amused Beau. "I called in some favors and arranged a selection of gowns for you to choose from. And my friend Pierre, who works at the first lady's favorite salon, is coming to do our hair and your makeup."

"I feel like Cinderella."

Thank God Beau had friends in fashionable places. This was just what Laney needed—a fantasy makeover. Otherwise Beau considered going in separate cars.

Three hours later, Laney was ready.

Beau couldn't believe the transformation. Pierre had cut and styled Laney's hair and done some tasteful but dramatic makeup emphasizing her big brown eyes without straying into drag-queen territory. Beau was going to owe Pierre blowjobs for a year to pay him back for this miracle.

"Laney, you look incredible."

"You think so?" She looked in the mirror, staring as if at a total stranger. "Is this really me?"

"Yes, it's really you." Beau squeezed her hand and grabbed a tissue with his other because he saw the hint of a tear glisten at the corner of her eye.

"Wow. Now I see why you get so excited about clothes." She hugged him. "You look fantastic too."

As Beau fiddled with his bow tie, the diamond cuff links at his wrists glinted. It was nice having a friend who worked at a jeweler's. The Tom Ford tux fit him like a glove, and the dark purple paisley silk of the cummerbund added the right splash of color without being *too* flamboyant. He didn't often dress so flamingly as to set his surroundings on fire, but he intended to make a fashion statement tonight. Usually he simply reported what others were wearing, but tonight he would be a participant and not an observer.

Like Laney, he felt a little like Cinderella. He resisted the urge to dance around the living room singing "I Feel Pretty."

Pierre put a few finishing touches on their hair and, more than comfortable in the role of fairy godmother, waved them out the door to the limo the *Daily* had provided to take them to the White House, humming "Bibbity, Bobbity, Boo." Or maybe that was simply Beau's overactive imagination.

SLEEK BLACK limousines lined up along Pennsylvania Avenue, disgorging their passengers at the end of the sidewalk near the security tent protecting them from the elements while they went through the unpleasant but necessary X-ray machines and metal detectors. Those who were deemed harmless were led into the east dining room of the White House. Beau and Laney had a moment to collect themselves before the wall of photographers blinded them.

"Who are they?" more than one person asked as he and Laney strolled past.

"Beau, Laney!" It was Peter Timmons, a *Daily* photographer who covered White House events. He gave them a thumbs-up, then took a series of shots.

Their worst nightmare—being seated with Mike Beaumont at dinner—hadn't come true.

"Oh, I think that's him over there!" Laney stood and pointed. Clearly her family had not taught her manners during her formative years. "Hey, Mikey!" She giggled and waved when he turned around and glared at her.

Beau enjoyed Mike's discomfiture. "He looks a lot better than I expected."

"What? Are you saying you're interested in him or something?"

"Never. Even if he was the last man on earth." Beau sipped his pretty pink cocktail. "Well, *only* if he was the last man on earth." He paused. "But he's wearing a nice tux."

Beau was in heaven as he surveyed the beautiful gowns and jewelry of the other guests, while Laney couldn't get over the food.

She had a lively discussion with the man seated on her other side. When Beau got up to use the bathroom, he spotted a bright flash of color out of the corner of his eye. There, at the opposite end of the dining room, sat a table filled mostly with men. Navy or Marines, based on their uniforms. Beau didn't know much about the military, but he did like a man in uniform, especially just before he took it off. From his angle, he saw few faces full on, mostly men sporting dark jackets, rows of medals, short hair barely covering pale scalps, and a few jewel-toned ladies seated among the men.

Back at their table, Laney barely noticed he had gone.

Beau couldn't wait for the meal and the speeches to finish and for President Bergen to address them. When the last speaker left the dais, Beau glanced at the heavily embossed program that had been left at each place setting.

"The president isn't going to be here?" It came out much more anguished than he'd intended.

"He doesn't attend the autumn dinner, but he'll be at the one in the spring. It'll be worth the wait." The woman to his right patted his arm with a soothing touch.

Beau had to comfort himself with the fact that there would be dancing in the ballroom after dinner, and the lower level of the White House would be open to the guests for mingling in the exact rooms where presidents had entertained distinguished visitors over the centuries.

Once the dinner ended, the guests streamed from the dining room.

"Now what do you want to do?" Laney asked, smoothing her dress as she stood up. She had dripped a little sauce on the bodice, and Beau helped her wipe it up.

"Go finish cleaning your dress up." He took a tiny bottle from his jacket pocket. "Club soda. In the ladies' room." He nodded in that direction.

"You always carry club soda with you?"

"It was in the contract I signed when I borrowed those dresses."

"Oh." Laney's smile faded. "I'm sorry. I should have been more careful." She gave him a kiss on the cheek, grabbed the club soda, then picked up her skirts and raced for the ladies'.

Beau wandered out of the dining room, chatting to the other guests, asking some of the better-dressed people about their clothing and taking notes for the column he'd write about the event. He arranged for Peter Timmons to photograph several of them. Most of the women were thrilled for the chance to be in the *Daily*'s fashion page and were flattered Beau had singled them out.

Being a fashion reporter was a great way to meet people. Beau had the luxury of approaching men as well as women and had made some interesting contacts and connections over the past few years in DC. He'd interviewed and hooked up with several men the rest of the world thought were straight. But the right words and a smile from Beau, and, well, a good time was had by all. So far not a single one of *them* had reported his flirting as sexual harassment.

Quite the opposite.

But a good time was all it could be in many cases, which was why Beau was escorting Laney tonight and not a man of his own.

"All better," Laney said as she approached Beau. The stain was diminished, but her cleavage seemed to have outgrown the bodice. He could hardly fix that in the middle of the hallway with hundreds of guests milling around.

"I think you might want to rearrange things a little...." He motioned toward the relevant part of her anatomy.

"Too trampy?"

"Yeah. This is the White House, not the Moulin Rouge."

She giggled. "Okay. BRB." She ducked back into the ladies' and returned looking a little less bosomy. "Want to dance?"

"Sure, but let's wander around first. I haven't been on a White House tour in years."

"Oh, yes. I want to sit on the fancy couches. You're not allowed when you come in on the regular tour."

They made their way through the traditionally decorated rooms comprising the public area of the White House.

"This isn't where the president lives, is it?" Laney asked as she warmed herself in front of a roaring fire in one room where a huge portrait of President McKinley looked down at them.

"I don't think so. I think the residence is upstairs from here. You saw all those Secret Service guys standing in front of staircases?"

She nodded.

"That's probably where the residence is."

In the library, Beau spotted one of the soldiers on his own. His dark jacket with shiny brass buttons and gunmetal blue pants indicated he was a Marine. Yummy. He had a white hat tucked under one arm, and he was reading the titles on one of the shelves. As if he felt the weight of Beau's gaze on him, the Marine turned his head and looked directly at Beau.

A scorching jolt of energy raced through Beau's chest when their gazes met. The Marine was drop-dead gorgeous. He had bright blue eyes and a distinguished chin as craggy as El Capitan in Yosemite. But his eyes held no warmth, and the zing ebbed away, though Beau couldn't help staring at the beautiful man after he turned his attention back to the books on the shelf, wondering why he seemed so disdainful of the lively party going on around him.

"You know him?" Laney asked.

"Not yet." Beau smiled. "I've never had a Marine."

"Me neither." She grinned. "Go talk to him. And pass him to me if he's straight."

"No. Let's head for the ballroom."

"I can wait for you...."

"Nope." He put his arm through hers and led her from the room. The Marine was nice to look at, but he exuded such negative energy, an invisible force field ready to eliminate anyone who stepped too close. Beau lost interest.

Later as he and Laney danced, Beau couldn't get the Marine's face out of his memory. He looked familiar, though Beau was certain they had never met. Beau knew no Marines. Maybe the uniform and the hairstyle made them all look the same. That was the whole point of the uniform, after all. But the steely blue gaze stuck with Beau the rest of the evening.

JAKE LONGED to leave the White House as soon as respectfully possible. He hadn't wanted to go at all, but Colonel Lewis insisted he attend in order to earn his spot back in the POTUS rotation. With the prospect of flying the high-profile missions as incentive, Jake was happy to attend, but he hadn't realized how fucking boring the dinner would be. But with Lewis there, watching, Jake had only managed two glasses of wine.

Some men from his squadron brought girlfriends or wives, who were thrilled to be at a White House dinner party. Jake couldn't wait to leave, but the colonel seemed insistent on punishing him, so he couldn't leave while his CO was still there. Mrs. Lewis appeared to have recovered some of her vitality and positively glowed. She softened the colonel's sharp edges when they were together, and no one could miss how much the man doted on her.

Once the meal was over, the nightmare portion of the evening began: the guests who insisted on talking to him or asking the same questions about his heroic feats over and over, forcing him to trot out the safest answers he could in order to keep himself from ripping apart inside.

Couldn't the colonel understand how agonizing this was for Jake? He'd rather get shot down and crawl miles over broken glass than tell one more civilian how it felt to be a hero. He hated the word. He was no hero, and every time someone used the word, it felt like another blow coming down on his body, a beating that wouldn't end until he was pounded into a lifeless pulp.

He stopped at each of the three bars set up in different rooms and managed a couple of quick tequila shots at each. The resulting buzz provided a layer of protection, but it didn't make the evening any more bearable.

Almost as bad as the people who asked were those who didn't say anything. Some gazed at him with admiration and unspoken questions. Others stared at him with pity.

One man, however, stared at him in a way he couldn't fathom. He seemed to recognize Jake, but with neither the usual hero worship nor pity in his gaze. Jake had spotted him in the library, then at the edge of the ballroom, and now as Jake moved toward the bar, the guy was there.

And again, their gazes met. The man said something to his female companion, a plump, smiling woman, and now he was heading directly for Jake. He wore a stylish tuxedo, but his purple paisley cummerbund looked like something from the Early Elton John Collection.

Was there time to duck into the men's room or behind the draperies to avoid him? Could he make it to the West Wing door? He knew the Secret Service agent on duty over there tonight, and he'd easily be able to get in to hide from the attention.

"Hey there."

Too late. Purple paisley guy was two feet from Jake now. "Yeah?" Jake gave the word a particularly rough growl to scare him off.

"Uh…." Paisley smiled. He had a nice smile, a knockout smile in fact. He dropped his gaze to the ground in a charmingly shy way, but appealing as that was, whatever he said wouldn't be anything Jake hadn't already heard a thousand times.

"Go on, get it out. Say what you came to say or ask me." Jake tipped his glass for the last mouthful of tequila, then shifted his gaze to the blinding smile right in front of him.

The guy looked him square in the eye. "Would you be interested in a blowjob?"

Jake nearly choked on the last sip. "What?"

"Blowjob?" The guy smiled and melted away the last vestiges of Jake's icy defenses. "If I'm not your type, you can simply pretend for the best ten minutes of your life or—"

"Ten minutes?"

"Fifteen?" Paisley's smile got brighter, elevating the corners of his mouth into a smirk. "Or my friend Laney would be happy to do you. It. Do it to you."

Jake blinked and looked the guy up and down, then back up again. "Don't worry. You're definitely my type."

Jake took his time giving the guy a full once-over.

Nice looking. Good body, almost as tall as Jake, and he had the most sinfully lush lips Jake had seen on anyone who wasn't in porn. When the guy closed the distance between them and crossed into Jake's personal space, the air between them crackled with sexual electricity. The little pilot light of constant low-level arousal at Jake's core ignited to a full flame, and every inch of his skin tingled with anticipation.

"Here?"

"Now," the guy said, the word a delicious promise Jake wanted to cash in.

"Now." It was a statement on Jake's part. A fully formed decision. The guy's smile brightened and his chocolate brown eyes danced, mirroring the way Jake's insides jumbled around with white-hot desire.

The image of his cock sliding between those perfect lips had him hard, and he fought to think clearly enough to decide where to go.

"This way." Jake turned and headed toward the West Wing, away from the guests. A bathroom, a coat closet. Something. Someplace. *Any place.*

The Secret Service agent guarding the door at the end of the hall nodded as they approached. "Evening, Captain." He waved Jake in without requesting his ID or asking about Jake's companion.

The lights were low in the hallway, and Jake opened the first door he came to, not caring what was on the other side.

Paisley went in, then came out again before Jake could take a step inside.

"Occupied." He chuckled. "I think Colonel Sanders was in there. Without his chicken."

Jake tugged on an elbow and opened the next door.

It was a small conference room lit by a couple of lamps. But they were alone.

He'd barely closed the door behind them when his new friend—best not to ask names—was already on his knees with Jake's trousers unzipped.

Then Jake's shorts slid down and a cool breeze caressed his balls. A second later wet heat wrapped around his cock.

"You don't waste time."

"Mmmm-mmm." The guy looked up between the flaps of Jake's jacket from under thick lashes and smiled around Jake's dick.

It looked even better than he'd imagined. He leaned against the wall for support because his knees threatened to give out.

With lips, tongue, fingers, Paisley brought Jake to the edge twice before slowing and beginning the build of heat and ache again. Jake ran the fingers of one hand through the straw-colored silk of Paisley's hair; he needed the other for balance, or he risked falling off the face of the earth.

He closed his eyes and let the pleasure sing through his body, but as he approached the edge for the third or fourth time—he'd lost count—he forced himself to open them. He had to savor the look in those golden eyes as he pumped himself dry down this guy's throat.

Jake groaned as the pressure built to a crescendo.

"Keep going. Don't. Slow. Down." Then it hit like a tidal wave. Though he knew it was coming, it still knocked him for a loop, forcing him to clutch the poor guy's head to keep from crumpling in a wrung-out heap.

And the look on his new friend's face was absolutely beautiful.

As Jake tried to catch himself from falling through the earth, he wondered whether a guy this talented could be a hustler. Would he expect money? If the guy charged him a week's salary, the thrill of doing this in the fucking *White House*, with this guy, would have been worth it.

The guy planted a couple of soft, sweet, unexpected kisses on Jake's cock, then slid his shorts back up. The thin cotton was too much for Jake's sensitive dick, but he didn't have the energy to protest. He could barely remember anything but the way the guy's lips and tongue had felt.

"Thank you," Paisley said as he stood up.

"Why are you thanking me?"

He replied with only a shrug and a shy smile. The guy stepped back one pace, and the room felt like winter had set in. Jake took hold of the guy's hand.

"I'm Jake." It had taken him a moment to remember his own name.

"Hi, Jake. Beau."

Jake wanted to say something, but his brain wasn't ready. His body took over, and he slid a hand behind Beau's neck and pulled him in for a kiss. He started slowly, but the feel of the full, slightly bruised lips against his wasn't enough. He needed to sample, to drink in the sweetness. He explored with lips and tongue, tasting himself in every corner of Beau's mouth. Beau matched Jake's fervor and inquisitiveness. They kissed until they were both out of breath.

"Beau." Jake liked saying the name. "As in Bridges or Schembechler?"

"Bridges."

"Beau," Jake whispered.

"You have no idea how amazing your mouth looks when you say my name," Beau whispered back.

Jake watched the pulse beating beneath the skin of Beau's throat. He pulled open Beau's tie and a couple of shirt buttons before kissing the spot, savoring the saltiness, inhaling Beau's essence.

"Your turn," Jake said as he slid his hands under Beau's shirt and felt smooth, hot skin. Should he risk undressing Beau here?

"Do you want to get out of here, Jake?"

"You read my mind."

"Not particularly difficult. You said it out loud."

"Oh." Heat crept into Jake's face.

"You're beautiful when you blush like that."

"I'm not blushing."

"Fine, warrior. You're not blushing. Much." Beau had a musical laugh. "Let's go."

"I live in Virginia."

"Does she mind?"

It was Jake's turn to laugh, and he almost couldn't stop. It was a terrible joke, but the impish look on Beau's face and his droll delivery made it so much more amusing. He barely recognized the sound. How long since he'd really laughed? Too long.

"As I said, she's not my type."

"I live nearby. We could almost walk."

"Let's not."

Beau grinned and picked up Jake's cover where he'd dropped it, then put it on his head. It was a little crooked, but seeing his hat on Beau's head got Jake pretty worked up again.

"Where do we get a cab?"

They tidied their clothing before making their way back out of the West Wing and toward the north entrance. The wind had picked up and cut through Jake's uniform. Beau must be colder. They linked arms and headed for Pennsylvania Avenue and slid into the first cab they could flag down.

BEAU COULDN'T quite believe his audacity—or his luck—in approaching the silent and stern-looking Marine. He'd only expected a quickie in some dark corner; he never would have expected the guy to introduce himself and then kiss him. It wasn't the way these encounters usually ended. But instead of merely getting off fast—and it would have been fast because Jake was that hot—Beau found himself inviting Jake home.

They could go to a hotel instead of Beau's place. But something about Jake made taking him home the right thing to do. Sure, Marines could be ax murderers too, but odds were Jake wasn't much of a risk. Latex easily prevented most of the other risks.

So Beau gave his address to the cabbie.

"Take the scenic route," Jake said. "Past the Monument."

"That's in the opposite direction," Beau and the cabbie said as if they'd rehearsed it.

"I know." Jake grinned and pulled Beau in for another toe-curling kiss.

"I think I saw this in a movie," Beau said when Jake let him up for air. "But that makes you Kevin Costner, and I end up dead."

"You didn't see *this* in a movie." Jake pulled his white cap off and set it on Beau's head, then slid across the seat so he could get his head into Beau's lap.

When he got Beau's cummerbund off and went for his pants, Beau thought he must be dreaming. "I did see this in a movie. Just not the same movie." He let out a gasp as Jake licked a delicious stripe up the length of his cock. Pleasure radiated through his body, and his nipples tingled. He slid a hand along Jake's head, enjoying the way the short spiky hair tickled his palm and ratcheted him closer to the edge. At this rate he wouldn't last around the block, much less around Northwest.

But Jake knew what he was doing. He varied the intensity, easing back when he sensed Beau was too close. At one point he let Beau's cock slide right out of his mouth, and he sat up to continue the kiss he'd abandoned. He worked his way back down, unbuttoning Beau's shirt and feasting on each nipple until Beau whimpered at the delicious assault.

Whether Jake planned it or not, Beau crested the wave and crashed into unrelenting bliss a few blocks from his place on the return portion of the loop. He took his time coming back to earth, still playing with Jake's spiky hair and trying to catch his breath, though the way Jake kept kissing him made that almost impossible.

"We're here," the driver said, and Beau opened his eyes. "For the third time, guys. We're *here*."

Jake sat up, licking his lips and smiling. "I'll get the fare while you...."

Beau nodded and pulled his pants back on the best he could so he wouldn't be half-naked on the street. He left the shirt flapping open, and the cold night air had his nipples aching again. Jake could warm them up when he and Beau got upstairs.

Beau had trouble with the key to the lobby door with Jake pressed up against him, nibbling at his neck.

"Hey, I can't get this in there with you distracting me."

"Need help putting that in properly?"

"Yes, please." Beau handed the key to Jake, who was more successful. He wasn't trying to keep his pants from sliding down at the same time.

They kissed in the elevator, long, slow, comfortable kisses. Already Beau could tell what Jake liked, and had him squirming and moaning.

They were a few feet into the living room when Beau crashed into something that shouldn't be there. When he flipped the light on, he recalled why he had a rack of women's clothing in the middle of his living room.

"Is there something you neglected to tell me?" Jake asked as he pulled a garnet-colored gown from the rack. "Is there a Mrs. Beau or is it something else?"

"A friend brought them for Laney to choose from." When Jake looked perplexed, Beau went on, "My friend from the dinner. Laney."

"Just a friend?"

"Just a friend. Coworker and friend."

Jake must have been satisfied with the explanation, because he kicked off his shoes and went back to work on Beau's mouth as he slid his palms up Beau's chest, then along his shoulders until he had Beau's shirt and jacket off.

Beau wanted to get Jake's uniform off, but he wasn't sure how to attack the jacket with its ribbons and medals. He reached for the top brass button and worked his way down, for the first time getting a really good look at the medals and commendations on Jake's chest.

"You have a lot of ribbons here."

When Jake didn't reply, Beau didn't press. He wasn't in the mood for small talk right now, but he got the impression that wasn't why Jake hadn't responded.

Jake removed his belt and sword, then carefully draped them over the chair before easing out of his jacket.

"And I thought you were just really glad to meet me."

"I am." Jake grinned, pulled his white T-shirt over his head, then got his pants off. He was nice and hard, based on the way his pale blue shorts didn't fit. "Very glad."

"I've never had a guy with a sword over here before."

"Good."

Beau got a little flutter in his stomach at Jake's evident pleasure in being his first Marine.

Why the hell hadn't Beau had a Marine before? He'd certainly been missing out on a treat if they were all as fit and firm as Jake. But he intended to make up for lost time tonight. And tomorrow morning, because he didn't think he'd be through exploring Jake tonight. The thought got Beau hard again, which seemed to please Jake, who was busy working on getting Beau's pants off.

Beau grabbed the waistband of Jake's shorts and led him toward the bedroom. Had he cleaned it, or was there anything potentially embarrassing in there? He relaxed as he recalled he'd tidied up for Laney and Pierre.

"Wow." Jake was looking around, and Beau noticed his closet was open, disgorging a brightly colored array of achingly fashionable clothing.

"I like clothes...."

"That's not what I was talking about." Jake stared at the bed, a king-size version set on a slightly raised platform positioned under a skylight. "Quite the showplace."

Until this moment Beau had appreciated the arrangement as an interior decorating feature. Now it implied he was the slut of the western world. "It was like that when I moved in."

"Of course it was." But Jake said it with such mirth Beau didn't take it as an insult.

"I don't usually invite people back here, for what that's worth. Not as much showing as you might think."

Jake nodded and kissed Beau. "Now I'm here, what were you planning on doing to me?" Jake stepped back and slid his shorts down his hips. They hung up slightly on his erect cock, but he got them off easily. Beau got his first good look at all of Jake. He had powerfully muscled shoulders that nipped in toward a narrow waist. A few ragged scars twisted along his upper arm and below his collarbone. The sprinkling of hair on his chest turned into a thicker and exceptionally sexy treasure trail below his navel. Beau stepped forward and traced his finger down the line and back up, not touching Jake yet but teasing him a little and getting a good look at that cock. He remembered every inch and contour and vein of it from the blowjob earlier. Cut, not too big, with a pleasing curve.

"What would you like me to do to you?"

"First, let's even things up." Jake hooked a finger in Beau's waistband, and Beau let him tug his fuchsia trunks off.

Jake seemed to approve. He pressed up against Beau so their cocks rubbed together, taking Beau's breath away. Again. He slid his hand down Jake's back and got a nice handful of firm, round ass.

"Come to bed?" Beau backed up and took the first step up the platform. He grabbed Jake's hand and pulled him along, and they tumbled onto the bed in each other's arms, laughing and kissing, hands everywhere.

SUN STREAMED through the skylight and into Jake's eyes, forcing him into morning.

It took a moment for him to remember where he was and whose back he was pressed against.

Beau.

He smiled at the memory of Beau offering him a blowjob at the White House. The smile faded away quickly because Jake's head started yelling at him. Throbbing. Had he had much to drink the night before? Pieces of the dinner and after were missing from his memories.

"Mmm." Beau let out a soft moan and started to roll toward Jake.

Jake prayed he hadn't been really drunk the night before. Then Beau was facing him, warm brown eyes, a sweet, slightly crooked smile, and knockout dimples. How had he forgotten the dimples? In the daylight Beau was even better-looking. First time that had happened. Maybe it had to do with what those lush lips had done to him the night before.

"Morning." Jake wanted to wrap himself around Beau, lose himself in Beau's arms, his mouth, his body, but mornings after hookups were usually awkward. He'd let Beau make a move.

"Who're you?" Beau asked, blinking and looking a little disoriented.

Jake's smile slipped away for good, and he felt an unfamiliar pang in his chest. "I'm... Jake." While *he'd* definitely had this reaction before, it was the first time he'd been on the receiving end of such a question.

Beau pressed his lips together as if thinking. "Right. Jake." Then he slid his arms around Jake and gave him a heated kiss. "You should have seen the look on your face."

"Very funny."

"Okay, maybe it wasn't that funny. I'll apologize. Can you stick around for a while?"

It was an easy out if Jake wanted to leave. He appreciated Beau's no-pressure attitude. Definitely less awkward. "I think I can stay for an apology."

"It comes with breakfast, if you're into that sort of thing."

"I am. I should warn you, I'm a carnivore. So if you're going to offer me fake bacon, I'll save time and leave right now."

"God forbid. Fake bacon has never crossed these lips." Beau licked his lips and Jake's morning wood sprouted a few inches he didn't know he had. "Good thing I'm a carnivore too." Beau slid under the sheets and wrapped his beautiful lips around Jake's cock.

All this and bacon too? Jake couldn't recall being this happy in a long time.

WHEN BEAU was done apologizing and Jake was done thanking him for the apology, they lay together on the bed. Cheerful golden sun streamed through the skylight, illuminating one side of the room. Jake glanced around, taking in the dark furniture and all the color in the place. Lots of plum and fuchsia, with dark accents. If he had to describe the style, it would be Early Bordello. The thought made him grin. He'd never met anyone like Beau.

Certainly no one this gay. It was a nice change from the military guys he'd slept with over the years—most of them so used to pretending in public, Jake had no idea who they really were beneath the uniform, no matter how naked they got together.

"I like a little color," Beau said, as if reading Jake's thoughts.

"I can tell. Was it like this when you moved in?"

"No. It was greige and boring. Now it's... alive."

"That it is." Jake grinned so Beau wouldn't think his comments were criticism. "You mentioned something about bacon?" Way to change the subject. Jake cringed at his lack of tact.

"That I did." Beau leaned down and planted a few kisses on what must be his favorite part of Jake's anatomy, based on how much attention he paid it.

Chapter 6

BEAU WATCHED Jake take a few tentative bites of omelet. He was a pretty good cook—even Laney grudgingly admitted as much—so Jake's hesitation was probably good manners. By now Beau knew what hunger looked like in Jake's eyes, and he was sure he saw it right now.

"I never expected a Marine to be so ladylike at the table."

Steam practically spurted from Jake's ears. "Ladylike?"

Beau shrugged. He'd hit the nail on the head. But he felt a pleasant little tremor as he watched Jake really tuck into breakfast, heaping forkfuls of eggs between those beautiful lips and chomping on crispy bacon. It had been a long time since Beau had someone to cook for.

He finished off another piece of bacon and most of his own omelet and enjoyed the sight of Jake sitting across from him wearing only the pale blue boxer briefs. God, the man had the most perfect chest. He reminded Beau of those superbly sculpted Bowflex models in the ads he used to jerk off to. He wondered how many push-ups Jake could do. It would be a pleasure to watch and count as the muscles in his arms and back rippled.

Then Beau remembered it wasn't polite to drool over his guest. "I've got some fruit salad too. I'm afraid that's vegan."

Jake chuckled. "Sounds good."

Beau got up. As he made his way toward the kitchen, Jake caught him with an arm around Beau's waist. He planted a messy kiss against Beau's abs. "You're a good cook. Thank you."

"Oh, you earned it, soldier."

"Marine."

"Aren't Marines soldiers?"

"No. Soldiers wish they were Marines." Jake grinned.

"You earned it, Marine."

"That's better."

Beau vowed to remember the distinction as he pulled the container of fruit salad out of the refrigerator. He put it on the table and let Jake help himself.

"This is going to sound really out of left field…." Jake gestured with a piece of apple on his fork. "But did you say something about Colonel Sanders last night? Back at the White House?" He furrowed his brow.

Beau replayed that part of the evening and smiled at the memories. "Oh, right. That first door you opened up. I saw a guy who looked like a younger, thinner Colonel Sanders. Same tufty little beard, glasses, one of those Western string ties…." Beau made a tying motion at his throat.

"Was he eating chicken?"

"No. He was talking to a guy with more medals than you have."

"Talking?" Jake gave an incredulous lift of one eyebrow.

"I didn't get a good look, but they both had their clothes on. The other guy was cue-ball bald and wearing dark blue. Navy?"

Jake shrugged. "Possibly. At least you solved that puzzle for me."

A cell phone buzzed from the direction of Jake's pants on the living room chair. Jake didn't rush up to get the phone; instead, he took his time and whispered "sorry" as he put the phone to his ear. "Hey, Toby. I did have fun at the White House. I stayed in DC last night…. Yeah, would you take care of Daisy for me this morning? Thanks." He tossed the phone back onto the chair when he ended the call.

"Daisy?" Beau raised an eyebrow.

"My dog."

"Sure."

Jake reached for the phone and tapped it a few times, then held it up for Beau, who stared at a golden retriever who looked a little battered. "Is she missing an ear?"

Jake nodded. "She's an acquired taste, I guess."

"Looks like she's probably got some stories to tell."

"I'm sure she does. I try not to think of what they might be." Jake's face took on the serious look again. "We usually go running before sunup, so she's probably climbing the walls. Toby's my neighbor's kid."

"Got a picture of him too?" Beau raised an eyebrow.

"Yeah." Jake reached for the phone, then glanced up at Beau and shook his head. "It's not what you think. He takes a lot of selfies with Daisy."

"Sure." But after Jake showed him a few, Beau got a good feeling seeing the close friendship Jake had with his neighbor's kid and his dog. He was probably a pretty decent guy. "If you like, you can borrow sweats or something to wear home. Not sure if you want to put on the sword and the whole getup first thing in the morning."

Jake glanced over at his uniform. "Sweats would be great, actually. Thanks."

"Want me to hang this up? I've got plenty of hangers and garment bags." Beau motioned toward the clothing rack, which he'd pushed against one wall so it was no longer the main attraction in the living room. When Jake nodded Beau got up.

"I can do it. Come back and finish breakfast." Jake held a hand out to Beau.

"I'm done. Just trying to keep from staring at you." Beau liked the shyness that suddenly settled over Jake's face. How could a hunky Marine like Jake with a near-perfect body look so shocked when someone paid him a compliment?

"I have to get used to how forthright you are. I suppose nothing should surprise me after the way you came up and offered me a blowjob last night."

It was Beau's turn to feel embarrassed. "Yeah, I was pretty slutty last night. I didn't think you'd take me up on the offer."

"Didn't you?" Jake cocked an eyebrow. "Do you get turned down a lot?"

"I don't offer a lot, so I'd have to say no. But I actually asked on a dare."

Jake put his fork down. "A dare?"

Beau bit his lip. Why had he said that? "More coffee?"

"Uh-uh. You're not getting out of explaining that easily." Jake smiled, but Beau wouldn't be lulled into safety.

He got up and grabbed a wooden hanger from the rack and slid Jake's sky-blue trousers onto it.

"Come on, Beau."

Beau turned around to face Jake. "Well, you had this annoyed kind of expression on your face every time I saw you. Laney dared me to talk to you."

"And the BJ?"

"Spur-of-the-moment decision. Up close you were a lot hotter than I realized. And you were pretty fucking hot to start with. Still are."

The boyish smile flashed across Jake's face again, making his eyes twinkle. "Well, you got me to smile."

"And then some."

"And then some."

Beau looked down at the uniform on the hanger. It was difficult to meet Jake's eyes despite the fact that they had shared so much of each other. "Your turn. Why *did* you look so annoyed?"

"Maybe because I thought Laney was your date?"

"Bullshit. I don't think you even noticed me."

"Actually I did." He paused in a way that made Beau think he'd left a lot unsaid there. "I get a lot of people coming up to me, asking me questions, telling me what a hero I am. It might sound ungrateful, but I'm tired of it."

"Hero?" Beau wondered if he was supposed to know who Jake was, because he didn't. He looked a little familiar; could he have been on the news? Would he look like an idiot for not knowing? Had he insulted Jake? "What did you do?"

The sour look from the night before settled over Jake's face, smoothing away almost everything that made him attractive. "Nothing. I didn't do anything except my job. I better get going."

"I'll get those sweats." Beau went into the bedroom. He came out with a pair of dark blue sweats and a thick gray sweatshirt. "That should keep you warm, or do you want a jacket?"

"This is fine." Jake stood up and got dressed, then slid on his socks and shiny black shoes. "Well, the shoes don't go with the sweats, but who gives a fuck?"

"Yeah." Beau crossed his arms across his middle and watched Jake slip his wallet and phone into his pockets. He wished he'd kept his big mouth shut, because the temperature in the room had dropped about a thousand degrees after he admitted he didn't know what Jake had done to make him recognizable to the average person. "It's a new look." *Beau the fashion king speaks....*

"Well, uh, thanks." Jake put a hand on the doorknob and Beau nodded.

Fuck this. He walked to the door before Jake walked out, and kissed him. "Bye, Jake."

"I'll return this stuff."

"Okay." Beau shrugged and bit his lip to keep from asking when. "You know where I live."

Jake opened the door, then stopped. He gave Beau another kiss, a simple brush on the lips without a hint of tongue until Beau licked at Jake's lower lip. Beau had thought maybe this good-bye kiss would turn into good-bye blowjobs and maybe end up not being good-bye for a while longer.

But Jake pulled back and walked into the hallway, then flung the garment bag across his shoulder and headed for the elevator. Beau forced himself to close the door loudly enough that Jake wouldn't think he was watching him walk out of Beau's apartment and his life.

He could still ask for Jake's number. Would shouting down from the window be cute in a Julia Roberts way, or more Glenn Close in *Fatal Attraction*?

By the time Beau made up his mind and got to the window, Jake was getting into the back of a taxi.

AS JAKE rode the elevator down, he wished he could rewind the last ten minutes and do them over.

Why had he been such an asshole when Beau had been so kind and giving?

He asked himself the question again as he rode home in the taxi.

Beau hadn't known who he was. It should be a good thing. Jake wanted to live down all that hero bullshit, and Beau offered him the chance. Instead, Jake had practically shoved him away for bringing up the topic. Maybe that last kiss meant he hadn't completely blown it.

You can't have it both ways. Either someone knows who you are, or they don't.

The monuments were dull and gray today, reflecting the sunless sky and Jake's gray mood. Last night they'd seemed particularly bright as Jake and Beau drove through the city and fooled around in the back of another taxi. The memory made Jake glance down at the seat.

What had happened in *this* backseat? He shuddered to think. Not that he and Beau had made any mess. They'd been careful about that. He smiled and warmed at the image of Beau all unbuttoned, leaning back against the seat and looking pleased with Jake's technique.

He daydreamed the rest of the trip and only came back to earth when the taxi stopped.

"This the place?"

"Yeah." Jake grabbed for his wallet and handed the driver the fare plus a nice tip. He grabbed the garment bag and slid out of the car.

Daisy leapt on him as soon as he opened the door. She ran into the front yard and turned in a circle a few times, then leapt on him again, poking her nose into his sensitive spots. She seemed more interested than usual. Could she smell sex on him? Then he remembered he was wearing Beau's clothing. Daisy probably got excited by the scent of another human on her human.

"Need some food?" He shuffled into the kitchen, but her water dish was full and one tiny piece of dry food sat a few inches from her shiny metal bowl. "Looks like you already had breakfast. But you left a crumb!"

Daisy wagged herself over and poked her bowl with her nose, then, discovering that last morsel, slurped it up and went after Jake's crotch again.

"Toby didn't run you enough. I'll take you for another workout soon."

He hung the uniform in the closet and went into the bedroom. He shut the door with Daisy on the other side. She banged with her snout a few times before giving up. She was probably lying with her head on her front paw waiting for him to come out. She could be pretty high maintenance sometimes. When he first adopted her, she'd cry when he went into a different room. Slowly she got used to letting him out of her sight. She still needed regular attention and love.

Just like Jake.

But Daisy attracted the affection she needed, while Jake seemed to repel it.

He started to pull the sweatshirt off, then decided not to. He lay on the bed and sniffed one sleeve. Could he still smell Beau on the shirt? Had Beau worn it, or was it fresh from the wash? It didn't smell like laundry, so Jake tried again to discern Beau's scent on it. He poked his nose into his elbow and sniffed.

Shit, he was turning into his dog!

Beau had smelled nice. He wore a subtle but masculine scent, probably really expensive. Jake thought about Beau's smile when he'd come up and offered that BJ. Then the image of Beau's beautiful and talented mouth flashed through his brain. Predictably, Jake's cock stiffened. He thought about how he looked so sexy, disheveled in the cab, and then again nude in bed.

Jake slid the sweatpants off and wrapped a hand around his erection. God, he was harder than usual, and his nipples throbbed. A fire burned in his core, and he stroked himself as slowly as possible to prolong the pleasure of reliving the night before. He spurted a surprising quantity of jizz on his abs and some got on the shirt. Now he'd have to wash it so Beau wouldn't know he'd worn it when he jacked off.

Though knowing Beau, the information might make him happy.

Knowing Beau.

But Jake didn't really know him. He'd been part of a few hours of Beau's life. Pleasant hours, but not much more. Then Jake remembered the sadness in Beau's eyes when he'd left so abruptly. All the light and warmth had gone out of them.

Maybe Jake hadn't completely fucked this up. He had to return Beau's clothes, didn't he?

Or he could keep them as a memento.

That sounded like a high-school girl or stalker kind of thing to do.

A real man would return them in person and make sure Beau knew how much Jake wanted to see him again.

He rolled over, and his gaze fell on the photo with his crew from Camp Dwyer in Afghanistan.

Sometimes Jake didn't feel like a real man.

BEAU CLEANED the kitchen and the bedroom after Jake left, feeling more alone than he had in a long time.

It had been such a memorable night. His first White House event; his first Marine. First overnight guest here in longer than he cared to remember. First guy who admitted to eating bacon. The occasional hookups Beau spent time with wouldn't even utter the word, instead talking about yoga and chia seeds. Jake was a change from them in so many wonderful ways.

So Beau decided his glass was half-full, rather than half-empty. Forced himself to remember that, but it took a lot of forcing.

He was staring at the morning paper, on his third coffee, reading the headline for possibly the fourth time without taking in any of the words, when his phone buzzed.

Laney's name flashed on the caller ID.

"Hey," he said unenthusiastically when he picked up.

"Ow, you sound like I just shot your dog. I expected deets on you and the scrumptious Marine."

"Jake."

"Oh, he has a name. That's a good start. I hope you did more than introduce yourselves. What happened next?"

Beau shook his head at Laney's inquisition. "Actually we didn't introduce ourselves until after something happened."

"You devil. Tell me more."

Beau filtered through the evening trying to decide what to share. The memories put a smile on his face. "We fooled around at the party—"

"You did? Where?"

"I don't know. Some office or conference room. The surroundings are a little fuzzy."

"What about Jake? Fuzzy?"

Beau shook his head again. "I don't want to talk about this on the phone." It was Washington; you never knew whether someone was listening in. He assumed someone was.

"Fine. I'm downstairs. Can I come up? I have the dress."

He'd forgotten, at least as much as he could with a rack full of women's designer clothes in his living room. He buzzed Laney up, then did a last check in the bedroom and bathroom. Safe enough for Laney.

She burst into the room almost before he got the door open. If he hadn't already been awake, her orange-and-yellow top would have done the trick. Beau wondered where his sunglasses were.

"So, tell me more, tell me more." She sang the line from the song, draped the dress over the nearest piece of furniture, and plopped into one of the kitchen chairs. "Smells like bacon. Nice smoked bacon. Any left?"

"No, but help yourself to coffee." Beau looked at Laney's dress. It lay across the same chair where he'd put Jake's uniform the night before.

"Why are you smiling like that?"

"I'm not."

"Yes, you are." She grabbed the paper, tore through the sections to the last one, and flapped it open. Somehow she managed to scatter paper halfway across the living room. Laney was a walking tornado of mess. "Did you see this?" She thrust a folded-up page at him and tapped a photograph.

It showed the secretary of state wearing a daring strapless gown. "So? I thought you weren't interested in fashion."

"I'm not. Look in the background."

He spotted himself and Jake staring into each other's eyes. Post-BJ, apparently, from the way Jake had his hand on Beau's hip. Beau brought the paper up closer to his face. "Huh. I guess I have photographic proof of something."

"He looks *reallly* happy." She gave a lecherous grin as she stretched the word out. "You need to teach me some tricks."

Beau folded his arms across his chest and looked away dramatically. "I will not. I never blow and tell."

"Ooooh. Please?"

Sometimes they traded morning-after details like this. Neither dated much, so they lived vicariously through the other. "Well...." Beau paused. "He came back here and I made breakfast."

"Come on. You can't leave it there. What happened between leaving the White House and breakfast?"

"We took a memorable taxi ride around town. I don't remember seeing anything out the window."

"Now you're talking. And then?"

"And then he left after breakfast, wearing some of my clothes." Somehow telling Laney more felt different this time. Why did he want to keep his night with Jake private? The whole night felt different from any other hookup he could remember. They'd been comfortable with each other despite the usual awkwardness of a first time with a new lover. And the look on Jake's face when he thought Beau had forgotten not only his name but their night together—well, that told him Jake thought it had been something out of the ordinary.

"So you're going to see him again? At least to return the clothes, right?" She waved toward her dress. "That's a great idea, giving people things they need to return. I'll have to remember that. What happened to his uniform that he had to wear your clothes?" She raised her eyebrows.

Beau shrugged and sipped coffee. Cold. He got up and dumped it into the sink, then poured more. "It seemed a bit formal for the early morning trip home." And it had felt so intimate watching Jake slip on Beau's sweats and shirt. Like they were sharing something beyond their bodies or a cup of coffee over breakfast. "And I don't know if I'll be seeing him. I said something this morning, and he got all weird and left."

"Uh-oh. What did you say?"

"He mentioned something about people always coming up to him and—"

"And offering blowjobs?"

"No. Recognizing him and asking questions. I didn't recognize him, and I think I was supposed to."

"Wait, Jake something, Marine?"

"Yeah. That means something to you?"

"I remember something about a Jake, and your Marine's face looked a little familiar." She started swiping away at her smartphone, muttering to herself. "Oh, here it is. Jake Woodley?"

Beau struggled to remember the name tag on Jake's chest. "I think that's it."

She held out the phone.

Beau grabbed it and saw a photograph of Jake in his full dress uniform—sword and everything—getting a medal from the president for some incredibly brave thing he'd done in Afghanistan. He glossed over the story, but one thing particularly caught his attention.

"Says he's a helicopter pilot," Beau said. "I guess he really is some kind of hero." He wanted to read the story, but he also wanted to be alone with his memories of Jake. They might be the only ones he'd have.

"And he was annoyed you didn't know who he was?"

"He got funny. I'm only guessing why."

"Now I think he's a jerk. If he expected you to know who he was…."

Beau looked at the photograph of Jake receiving the medal again—the Medal of Honor, according to the caption. He didn't look proud or pleased. He looked uncomfortable, with barely the trace of a smile on his face. He looked like he wished he could be anywhere else. The other photos Laney's search brought up showed the same awkward smile. More so in the most recent ones. That wasn't the face of someone who craved recognition and attention.

She glanced at the phone, then shut it off. "Well, he's hot, and the Medal of Honor is the highest award in the military. But is that worth a crappy stuck-up personality?"

Beau recalled the photo Jake had of his dog and the neighbor kid. Anyone who rescued a one-eared dog and liked hanging out with a twelve-year-old couldn't be that much of a dick. "Laney, I don't think he's stuck up. I think he's terrified of everyone knowing who he is."

SUNDAY MORNING Jake woke early and didn't feel the tequila calling him the way he did most mornings. The sun was out, and the weather was beautiful for October. He decided to take Daisy for a hike instead of a run. Toby came along, and they spent a fun morning in nearby Huntley Meadows Park.

It always surprised Jake such an oasis of nature existed a few miles from the congestion of DC and the surrounding communities. Even in October a wide variety of birds called the park home, twittering and chirping a greeting—or more likely a warning of an approaching dog—as the three of them wandered through the meadows and trees. It had been an unseasonably warm and dry fall, so they didn't experience the mud and marsh usually covering the park this time of year.

Jenna packed them generous lunches, but when they got back in midafternoon, he and Toby were ravenous, so he treated Jenna and Toby to dinner at her favorite restaurant. As a single mom, she didn't always have money for splurges, and Jake found these dinners a good way to pay them both back for all the help they gave him and Daisy, given his unpredictable work schedule.

By the time he fell into bed Sunday night, exhausted and happy, he realized he hadn't thought about tequila all day. *Maybe one little nightcap.* But the next thing he knew, his alarm was announcing it was time to get out of bed Monday morning.

On Monday he reported for duty and a trip to Ohio with the vice president. It was a quickie trip, just one night's stay for the aircrews and not much downtime between the veep's arrival flight and his departure.

Whenever he wasn't busy with his duties, Jake found himself thinking of Beau.

He wasn't sure why, besides the obvious.

Jake rarely found himself attracted to guys like Beau. A little too flamboyant and campy. DADT might be history, but Jake was still in his own Marine closet, where he felt some need to be with the manliest guys he could find, like he had something to prove.

But none of them made him feel as alive as he had during those few hours he'd spent with Beau. He loved Beau's laugh, and his smile, and the look in his eyes at breakfast as he watched Jake eat. It stayed with him longer than the look he gave Jake in bed that morning. Not that fooling around with Beau wasn't memorable. It was fun, low pressure, without that usual drive to fuck the other guy's brains out and leave. He'd liked waking up with Beau.

Beau's easy, open smile and flirtatious eyes did something to Jake's insides, something he hadn't felt in a long time.

ON THE way home late Tuesday after the Ohio lift, Jake found himself singing along to the radio. Some old song by Madonna he wouldn't be caught dead singing in front of anyone from the squadron. But he couldn't help belting it out. Then he remembered he and Beau heard it at the White House party before they'd left in a cloud of lust.

God, he wanted to see Beau again, and not only for what would undoubtedly be a stellar fuck.

For a date this time. Because he couldn't get those eyes and that laugh out of his head. Beau's body was memorable, and so were the things he did with it, but that wasn't what Jake kept thinking about. Any *body* could make him feel good, but Beau made Jake feel good inside, made him feel the edges of his soul again. How could he do that in only a few hours?

Beau's chocolate brown eyes, like tiger's eyes, had an indescribable glow that pulled Jake in and wouldn't let him go. Something too warm and bright inside of Beau that had to escape, bathing Jake in its sensuous, captivating light.

Oh boy. He had it bad.

What he didn't have was Beau's phone number. He didn't remember his full name, if he'd ever even asked.

But he knew where Beau lived, and he had to return those sweats, didn't he?

Reluctantly Jake tossed the sweats into the washing machine, along with his gear from the trip to Ohio. Then Wednesday morning he packed the sweats into the saddlebag on his Harley Sportster before heading to the base.

The day went by in a blur of preparations for another trip first thing Monday. He would be flying a cargo helo with reporters. Even that didn't dim his good mood. Grousing about it wouldn't get him put back on POTUS flights. He put his head down and did his job the way he used to during his combat deployments.

He fought the urge to race out the door at quitting time, though the day after they came back from a trip, the CO was pretty relaxed about guys leaving a little early. It was getting dark and was colder than he expected when it was time to leave. He pulled a thick scarf from the underseat storage. He was going against traffic, so the ride into DC was pleasant. The monuments were lit up, glowing in the early evening fog, and he smelled smoke from fires lit in fireplaces of the comfortable-looking houses down the street from where Beau lived at the edge of Georgetown.

The smell reminded him of campfires and cookouts as a kid back in Arizona. He pulled up outside Beau's building, tugged off his helmet, and sat on his bike staring up at Beau's floor for a few minutes.

Is this a good idea? What am I doing here? Maybe he was too fucked up for Beau to be interested in him. Would he want a so-called hero who could barely look himself in the face every morning?

Someone charming and smart and *real* like Beau deserved someone better. He'd spot that Jake was a fake sooner or later.

Then Jake remembered them spilling out of the taxi early Saturday morning, with Beau's shirt—and pants—open. The fire inside roared back to life, but then he felt guilty for thinking about sex. Beau's laughter rang out and Jake knew he wanted to hear it again.

Then he did hear it. For real. Beau and his friend Laney were coming down the steps of Beau's apartment building.

Jake's stomach lurched and he froze, one foot on the ground.

"Jake?" Beau called out.

Too late.

"Hey," Jake said. Brilliant response. Someone skillful with words, like a reporter, wouldn't be too impressed. Jake waved at Laney. "Hi."

"I can call you later, Beau." Laney grinned and started walking away.

"Sorry. I didn't mean to ruin your plans," Jake said, examining his boots. He was afraid to look into Beau's face. He'd be pulled in by those eyes and say something stupid. Stupider. Fuck, that wasn't even a word, was it?

"See you, Laney," Beau said.

Jake pulled the sweats out of the storage compartment. "I brought back your stuff. I would have brought them sooner, but…."

Beau took the clothes. "You look cold. Why don't you come upstairs and warm up?"

Jake slowly looked up to see Beau smiling, light dancing in his tiger's eyes. "No, I'm fine."

Beau took one of Jake's hands and energy rocketed through his entire body at the heat of his touch. "You're freezing. Come on up."

If Jake said no now, Beau would think he wasn't interested. So Jake locked up his bike and followed Beau upstairs.

Again.

BEAU COULDN'T believe he'd found Jake in front of his building. How long had he been there? He looked frozen to the core. But he was damn hot in his leather jacket. Better after he got off the bike. The cut of the jacket emphasized his broad shoulders and slim waist while giving Beau a lovely view of his phenomenally shapely ass.

A Marine helicopter pilot with a motorcycle? Could it get any hotter than that? Beau tried to keep his libido and his body temp under control as they rode the elevator in awkward silence. Last time they'd been in here together, they'd been licking each other's tonsils. He let out a laugh before he could suppress it.

Jake smiled and Beau felt tension ease from his shoulders. Jake had an adorable, slightly crooked smile. Not the smile of a guy who had lived off his good looks his whole life, though he could have easily. Beau knew more than enough of those guys. No. Jake was beyond good-looking, but seemingly oblivious of the devastating effect he had on Beau's sense of balance and propriety.

On Beau's floor they got out, and he fumbled with the keys at his door. Then he dropped them, like an idiot.

But Jake bent and retrieved them, then pressed them into Beau's hand. Their fingers brushed, and Beau couldn't breathe for a moment. He got the door open and practically tripped into his hallway.

"The fashion show is gone." Beau waved in the direction of the living room when he caught his balance and his breath.

"It's a nice living room." Jake looked around, and Beau felt self-conscious about the abundance of purple upholstery. "Colorful."

"That's me. Colorful." He stopped, and Jake bumped into him from behind. Mmmm. Not the way Beau would like, but pleasant. "Want some coffee or… something?" He barely restrained the urge to offer himself.

"No, thanks. I can't."

"I know it's not against your religion because I saw you drink coffee the other day. Unless you converted to a coffee-fearing religion in the meantime?" *Stop babbling!*

Jake shook his head, that adorably imperfect smile expanding to show rather perfect teeth.

Beau tossed the sweats onto the chair, which seemed to have become the receptacle for discarded clothing. Jake unzipped his motorcycle jacket, revealing his uniform, a tan shirt over dark blue pants. The insignia on his lapels glittered in the light.

Jake cleared his throat and stood taller, but he still wouldn't meet Beau's eye. "I, uh. I wondered whether you might want to go out or something sometime." Jake glanced up for a split second, then went back to examining Beau's living room, possibly looking for dirt or something that wasn't purple.

"Yeah. I'd really like that." Beau threw out every rule in the book by saying what he felt instead of playing games. When Jake finally looked up, he rewarded Beau with a diffident smile. Beau's insides liquefied, and he thought he might fall to the floor in a puddle of Marine-induced jellification.

"Really?" The doubt in Jake's voice made him more adorable. Beau wondered why he hadn't yet spontaneously combusted in the presence of Jake's hotness.

"Yes. And if you haven't eaten, I'm actually free right now. And hungry."

"I. Uh. I." Jake gave up.

"Are you really that shy?" Beau stepped up to Jake and kissed him. Jake wrapped his arms around Beau's waist and pulled him in tight while Jake's mouth and tongue reacquainted themselves with Beau's. They kissed for a few deliciously breathless moments. "Cancel that on the shy."

Jake stepped back and seemed to pull himself together. "I can't stay. I need to…. Early morning." He gestured toward the door, then started moving toward it.

"Call me?"

Jake nodded and started opening the door as if he couldn't get out of there fast enough.

"You want my number, or are you clairvoyant?"

Jake stopped in his tracks and turned around, chuckling softly. "That's not one of my skills."

Beau pulled a card from his pocket and wrote his cell number on the back. "Ride safely." Then he watched Jake leave again.

But this time Beau knew he'd be back. He fanned himself to cool off after that kiss. It was probably a good thing Jake left. Otherwise they were heading for a repeat of Friday night and undoubtedly a lot more. Actually the way Jake left before things got hot and heavy made him more of a gentleman in Beau's view. It was sweet and charming that Jake made this surprise visit but hadn't let Beau throw himself at him.

That could wait for date night. Whenever that was.

TWO HOURS later Beau's phone rang.

"You decent?" It was Laney.

"Yes, are you?"

"I didn't have a sexpot Marine ride his motorcycle over to visit me on a school night. Is he still there?"

"No."

"Sorry to hear."

"Don't be. Probably for the best. I nearly attacked him in the hallway."

"Nearly? What stopped you?"

"I don't know. He was so sweet, I kind of felt like I was taking advantage of him."

"Then why did he come by?"

"To ask me out."

Laney's squeal blew out Beau's eardrum. He pulled the phone away from his ear and rubbed it until the ringing stopped.

"Jesus, you could get a job as a car alarm."

"How sweet of you to say. When are you going out?"

"Don't know. He's going to call me to make a plan. I might have scared him away. I don't think he likes purple. But he was tactful about it. I might be more than he can handle in public."

"You let me know if he handles you in public." Laney erupted into uncontrollable laughter.

Beau's call waiting clicked, and he couldn't hang up on Laney fast enough to answer it.

His stomach did a series of flips as Jake announced himself. "I hope it's not too soon to call."

"I'm a little insulted it took you two hours." Beau threw in enough of a self-deprecating laugh that he wouldn't sound desperate or conceited.

"I thought about it for a while. After I got home and defrosted. I should have taken you up on that coffee."

"Why didn't you?" Jake disrupted Beau's usual cool.

"I wasn't sure I could stop at coffee, and I didn't want to rush things with you."

Beau smiled at how Jake didn't consider BJs in the White House rushing things. "You may be too much of a gentleman for me, Jake."

"I wasn't much of gentleman the other night. Though I appreciated that you weren't either."

Beau could hear the smile over the phone, making his heart bounce around in his chest like a rubber ball.

Jake continued, "But now it feels different, Beau. I can't explain."

"I think I understand. It's nice. I'm free on Saturday if you are?"

Chapter 7

AS SOON as Beau hung up, he wished he'd set their date for another night. He had a lot of homework to do before Saturday night.

Thursday morning he went into the paper's office earlier than usual. He'd written his piece for the Sunday paper and gotten started on the feature for the following Wednesday because his editor would be expecting some progress and a finished piece by end of business Monday. But once the column was taken care of, Beau began reading.

He looked up information about Jake in the *Daily*'s system and googled him. Time to read it and bone up on military issues so he could make intelligent conversation with Jake on Saturday. So far Beau hadn't revealed that he was a fashion columnist, and aside from wardrobe and furnishing choices, Jake probably assumed he wrote hard news.

Beau pulled up the stories about Jake's medal and whatever he could find about his deployment to Afghanistan.

Reading the stories put Beau on the edge of his seat, feeling shock and fear he'd never experienced. He was embarrassed to admit he hadn't paid all that much attention to the wars in the Gulf or Afghanistan. He'd never given much thought to the military except that the Marines and Navy had the best uniforms.

Jake had been a helicopter pilot tasked with inserting Marines into combat zones and retrieving them again, dropping them into the fighting, or getting troops out of hot spots. He had flown over a hundred successful missions when disaster struck.

His helicopter was ambushed when he had to put down to collect some wounded men. After a shelling, the aircraft crashed in a remote area with sporadic radio contact, and Jake helped the men get to safety. Most of them anyway. His copilot died in the crash, and his crew chief was wounded by antiaircraft fire and trapped in the fuselage. When a group of insurgents surrounded the aircraft, Jake had to choose between helping the other men and freeing his crew chief. The stories didn't describe details of the ordeal, but Jake had been wounded getting the men to safety and then going back for his injured crew chief.

Jake was awarded the Medal of Honor for his actions, and when he recovered from his injuries, he went right back to his squadron, still stationed at Camp Dwyer. When they finally returned home, he was further honored with an assignment to the squadron responsible for operating *Marine One*, the president's helicopter.

None of the photos was particularly graphic, but Beau wanted to understand what it must have been like for Jake and the other men on the ill-fated mission.

He glanced around the offices as he munched a sandwich at his desk. It was only Thursday, but half the features staff had already left for the weekend after turning in assignments. He didn't much care that he wasn't working on his column. So to further understand what Jake might have gone through, he watched *Black Hawk Down*.

He'd never read the book or seen the film, and it was heartbreaking and powerful. Beau sat back in his chair, head full of images of downed soldiers, blood, and the sound of chaos and gunfire. He had to blink a few times, glancing around in order to center himself in his chair, safe in the *District Daily* office.

His heart pounded, and he clenched his fists so tightly they hurt. And he'd only been watching. What must it be like to live through a crash and attack? Granted, Afghanistan was different from Mogadishu, but the terror must have been similar.

And Jake's attitude to Beau asking him about what he'd done to be called a hero made perfect sense. Along with his inscrutable expression in the photographs at the award ceremonies. Who would want to remember any of that? To anyone else, Jake was a hero, but perhaps he thought himself a failure because he hadn't rescued everyone?

Beau certainly would avoid bringing up the topic, but he felt safe researching some of the other issues facing the Pentagon and the military. To his surprise, many of the relevant stories were written by his namesake and erstwhile nemesis, Mike Beaumont. The guy might be a dick, but he was a talented writer with a sharp, inquisitive mind on an obvious quest for more accountability from the Pentagon. In fact, he'd written a story about the mess at the Veterans Administration long before it became headlines.

Go Mike!

Beaumont the Bear was currently working on a series following the approval, funding, and contract negotiations for a new weapons and communications system. Beau skimmed a few of the stories and then stopped when he spotted a photo of the cue-ball guy he'd noticed talking to Colonel Sanders at the White House. Now Beau's curiosity was piqued, and he scanned a few-dozen other Pentagon stories, trying to catch a photo with Colonel Sanders, to no avail.

He went back to the story about Cue-Ball, who was actually Army General Graham, a member of the Joint Chiefs of Staff. He also happened to be one of the key figures talking to Congress about why the Pentagon needed a new zillion-dollar communications and weapons system with technology that sounded like it had been designed by a video-game company. It concerned aircraft, so Beau forced himself to focus on this aspect of the controversy. Mike Beaumont's stories were a scathing discussion of military waste and how much taxpayer money had been squandered on weapons and aircraft that had never been used.

Probably not good conversation fodder for Beau's date with Jake.

But it did get Beau's mind racing with new inspiration for the story he hoped to write, and not a moment too soon. He hadn't made progress on anything, though he'd enjoyed getting back into research mode.

Instead of attending a Senate Intelligence Committee hearing that afternoon, Beau opted for an open meeting of the Senate Armed Services Committee. Why not kill two birds with one stone? He listened intently, took copious notes, and let his imagination soar, hoping the germ of a story would land on the tip of his nose like the first winter snowflake.

It didn't, but he wasn't discouraged.

ON FRIDAY Beau went into work a little later than usual and got a seat on the Metro with no trouble. The guy sitting across the car from him wore a gorgeous black leather jacket that might have been vintage, but he wasn't close enough to tell. The guy's hair was as black as the jacket, and he wore shiny aviator glasses that completed the look nicely.

With his mind on his upcoming date with Jake, Beau existed in a world of his own as he headed for the *Daily* building. He was opening the lobby door when he realized he'd forgotten to stop at Café Agatha for coffee. He doubled back and around the corner.

He was nearly at the café's door when he spotted the black-leather-jacket guy reflected in the window a step or two behind. He didn't follow Beau in, yet it seemed an odd coincidence since Beau had taken a circuitous route from the Metro to the café. Skinny mocha in hand as he exited, Beau shrugged the incident off.

Later, when he left for lunch with Laney, Beau spotted another dark leather jacket. He felt a little silly, so he didn't mention it to Laney. But the feeling of being shadowed clung to Beau and he glanced over his shoulder every block until he decided his fears were unfounded.

He was a fashion reporter; who would be following him?

BY SATURDAY evening Beau was equipped with enough military and political topics to keep conversation going so he could continue his ruse as a real reporter. Normally he loved his work, but compared to Jake's accomplishments, Beau's felt inadequate. How could a decorated Marine find anything to be impressed about in a fashion columnist?

"Beau, you're being too hard on yourself," Laney had told him at lunch the day before. "If he doesn't like you for you, then you don't need him."

"In theory, I agree. But I kind of want to borrow him for a while. He might not get tired of me right away if I keep him distracted."

"Not everyone is going to be like *him*."

"You don't know that." Beau had forbidden her to mention He Who Must Not Be Named, so he had been particularly piqued she brought him up.

"Beau, honey." She tugged on his collar points playfully. "He was a jerk. And he was a crappy journalist. You went to a better journalism school than he did too. I can't believe the *Post* made him an editor."

Beau's ex hadn't just been an editor, he'd been the one who'd cut Beau's job and forced him to take a job in the Lifestyle section or risk being completely out of work. In the karmic scheme of things, the ex had soon been downsized himself and was teaching part-time at a third-rate J-school in a place where it snowed thirteen months of the year.

Beau shrugged and considered his own career progression. He *had* gone to a respected J-school, but after doing fashion for a couple of years to keep a job, he'd have to prove himself all over again. He'd written himself into a corner—a well-dressed corner, but still one with little career potential. Which was why he had to kick himself into high gear and write something to get him noticed again as a serious journalist. He didn't just want this. He *needed* it.

A loud buzz from the door to the street made Beau jump even though he had been expecting Jake for the past half an hour. He buzzed open the downstairs door and waited for Jake to make his way up, leaving his apartment door open.

"Knock, knock," Jake said, rapping softly on the door and not entering until Beau opened it all the way for him. "Hey, you look great."

Beau couldn't help smiling. He'd spent half a paycheck buying a completely new ensemble to impress Jake. Then he'd opted for something older and more comfortable at the last minute, a mahogany-colored wool Armani jacket over slim dark pants that made his ass look unforgettable.

"You look good too." Good enough to eat, but Beau wasn't going to start that or they'd never make it to dinner.

"Thanks. Did you choose a place for dinner?"

"I had two ideas. You can decide which you like better." Beau had endured two days of Laney offering suggestions, but in the end he chose two places he really liked.

"Okay." Jake came into the living room and sat on the chair where his uniform had spent the night the weekend before.

"There's a great Burmese place near Dupont Circle, or a bistro in Georgetown that's walking distance."

"Let's try the Burmese place."

Beau grinned, pleased that Jake opted for the more adventurous cuisine. "I made reservations at both.... Let me cancel the bistro." He grabbed his phone and tapped at the reservation app, watching Jake out of the corner of his eye. "Okay. All done. Did you come on your bike tonight?"

Jake stood. "No. I drove. It's cold out, so I didn't think you'd enjoy being on the bike. Plus, the helmet would mess up your hair."

Beau slid his hand across the top of Jake's buzz cut, enjoying the spiky ends of the short hair. "I guess *you* don't have to worry about helmet head."

Jake rubbed his hand over his head and graced Beau with the shy smile that made Beau want to rip Jake's clothes off then and there, dinner be damned. But Beau contented himself with ogling Jake's ass as they walked to the elevator.

"Parking is impossible near the restaurant. Let's take a cab?" Beau suggested when they were out on the street.

"Good idea." Jake slid a hand onto Beau's back as they made their way to the next street where they could easily flag a taxi.

Beau slowed his pace so he could enjoy Jake's fingers against the small of his back a little longer. It was a slightly possessive gesture, but he liked it.

After they settled into their chairs at the restaurant, Jake opened his menu and glanced at the offerings. Beau had been to this place a dozen times and had the menu memorized.

"How do you feel about sharing dishes? Or did you want to order your own?" Jake asked.

"I love sharing."

"Good." Jake met Beau's gaze, and Beau got all jellified again. How would he manage to eat without making a fool of himself? "I really like the platha dip and the green tea salad to start. How does that sound?"

Jake's familiarity with the food took Beau by surprise. "Yeah. That's what I usually order. Have you been here before?"

"Not this one. But the owner's sister runs one in Alexandria. I've been there a few times."

Beau nodded. Laney would certainly approve of Jake, if only for his culinary appeal.

Their server returned, and they ordered appetizers and a couple of main dishes to share, along with Burmese beers.

Jake asked the typical getting-to-know-you questions: how long Beau had lived in DC and where he was born. Beau tried to bring up more current events and trotted out some of the military facts and figures he'd researched and memorized. But Jake kept bringing the discussion back to Beau rather than talk about his work or the Marine Corps.

Their main courses had just arrived when Jake slid a hand into his jacket. "Sorry, I have to take this call."

Beau raised an eyebrow. He hadn't heard the phone ring. "Your dog sitter?"

Jake turned slightly away as he answered. "Woodley. ... Yes, sir. ... No problem. Yes, sir," he said again, more enthusiastically than Beau liked. Then Jake replaced the phone in his pocket and turned to Beau. "I'm afraid I have to cut our evening short. One of the other pilots is in the delivery room with his wife, so I have to take his spot in the lift."

"Lift?"

"That's what we call our missions. I have to spend a few days in San Francisco because—" Jake didn't finish his explanation.

"Okay." It was Jake's first mention of his job. Beau felt a tremor of disappointment to receive so little information, but it wouldn't do to ask too many questions so soon. "When do you need to leave?"

"Now. You stay and finish dinner."

"They don't give you much notice, do they?"

"That's the Marine Corps." Jake frowned. "I'm sorry. I promise to make this up when I get back."

"I'll leave with you. You need to get back to your car."

Jake nodded and flagged down their server, had the food wrapped, and paid for the meal.

"Thank you for dinner," Beau said as the cab drove away from the curb.

"Not much of a dinner, but I need to report to duty in two hours."

"So, you have an hour?" Beau slid over to Jake and kissed him. He tasted like curry and beer and something else Beau wanted more of.

Jake slid a hand onto the back of Beau's neck. Warm, strong fingers left a trail of heat as Beau inhaled Jake's scent. "Mmm. That's a nice suggestion, Beau, but I don't want to do that again."

Beau pulled back a little, unsure what Jake meant.

"I *want* to. Really. Badly." Jake breathed against Beau's cheek. "But I'd rather we take our time. No rushing. I wouldn't feel right hopping into bed and leaving half an hour later."

"It would be a nice half an hour…."

"It would." Jake kissed Beau until he believed it.

Then the cab stopped outside Beau's apartment building.

"Keep the meter running," Jake said, though he didn't take his eyes off Beau. He kissed Beau and slipped one hand under Beau's shirt and up his back. "Oh, boy. I'm going to have trouble concentrating on work."

"Oh yeah?" Beau grinned.

"I'll be back Wednesday."

"Should I pencil you into my calendar for Thursday?"

"Nope. Put that in ink."

They made out for a little while longer, and Beau found it all more exciting and romantic than if they had gone upstairs and pulled each other's clothes off.

He was hard and overheated as he watched Jake drive away. On second thought, maybe it would have been better if they'd gone upstairs and had a quick, spectacular fuck.

That was the second time Jake had come and gone before either one of them had actually come.

But when they spent the night together again, Beau suspected it would be earth-shattering.

JAKE'S TRIP to San Francisco involved a lot of activity before, but very little during, the president's actual stay in the area.

While the president flew between cities on *Air Force One*, once he'd landed, it was easier and safer for him to move between the airport and other locations by helicopter. The security and logistics issues for a presidential motorcade made the helos the safest option and spared the area from traffic jams and cordoned-off streets.

For HMX-1, the lift involved getting their aircraft out to the West Coast in advance of the president, and setting up the details of his arrival and flight from the airport to Stanford for a fundraising speech, then back again. After the president departed on *Air Force One*, the squadron would return to Marine Base Quantico and prepare for the next operation. For cross-country lifts, a C-5 Hercules ferried the HMX-1 helos, while the Marine pilots flew their individual aircraft for shorter journeys.

Jake felt shortchanged after leaving Beau, but he had a lot of downtime in California and called Beau each night and they talked for hours, something Jake had never done with anyone before. But Beau was fun to chat with. He had such an oddball sense of humor, though much of it was self-deprecating.

And for some reason, Beau kept wanting to talk about military spending and details of some new weapons and communications system the Pentagon was putting out bids for. Then again, that was Beau's specialty. Jake had done a cursory search after he found out Beau worked for the *District Daily*, and found a long list of hard-hitting articles about the US's role in Afghanistan and whether the Pentagon really needed another aircraft carrier. He seemed fairly critical of the Pentagon, which surprised Jake, but Jake didn't agree with many of the higher-level policy choices either. For now, the topic was best avoided until they got to know each other better.

The squadron got back just past midnight on Wednesday.

Colonel Lewis was still out on leave, and Lieutenant Colonel Monroe called Jake into his office after the aircraft had been squared away in the Cage and left in the capable hands of the specialized crew of mechanics.

"You did a good job on this lift, Woodley. I'm glad to see you're back on track. Take Friday off, and then next week I'm assigning you as my copilot for one of the local POTUS lifts."

"Sir?" Jake didn't want to get too excited, but this was an incredible opportunity.

"We'll see how it goes, and I'm paying close attention to your performance until the end of the year. I'm thinking about putting you into the regular rotation as copilot while you continue to train for pilot."

"Thank you, sir." Jake would be part of a group of six pilots who rotated through that duty. Currently they all outranked him.

"Go home, catch up on your sleep, and we'll talk more about what I expect from you on Monday."

"Thank you, sir. Have a good weekend." Jake saluted and left.

On the way home, he found himself singing along to "Bohemian Rhapsody" on the radio, trying to do all the parts and laughing when he couldn't hit the high notes like Freddie Mercury. He couldn't remember when he'd been this happy. Not since the morning after he'd spent the night with Beau. The thought of their date the following evening put him in an even better mood.

WHEN JAKE arrived at Beau's apartment on Thursday, he found Beau wearing the same outfit he had on Saturday.

"Should I start calling you Miss Havisham?"

Beau laughed. "A Dickens joke. I'm impressed."

Jake's smile flattened out a little. "I have read a few books. I almost majored in comparative lit."

Beau looked contrite. "Really? Well, I haven't been sitting here waiting since you left. But I thought it would be fun to finish what we started the other night."

"Same restaurant?"

"Is that okay with you?" Beau looked pensive.

"Whatever you like." Beau's idea was sweet and romantic, but Jake wouldn't mention how much he wanted that kind of a date with Beau.

So they took a taxi again, but this time they ordered different dishes and Beau asked about Jake's trip.

"After you left so abruptly, I hope you don't mind my curiosity."

Usually Jake didn't mention which squadron he was in, but Beau could easily find out online in under a minute. He hoped Beau wasn't attracted to him because of his high-profile assignment. They'd planned this date long before the issue of Jake's job came up in conversation. "I'm in HMX-1, the squadron that operates *Marine One*. You seem pretty well acquainted with Pentagon and White House issues, but ask away."

Beau looked confused for a moment, then asked, "*Marine One*? That's the president's helicopter, right? Do you actually fly the president?"

"No." Jake waited for disappointment to cloud Beau's face, but it didn't. "Sometimes I fly one of the decoys, but usually I pilot another helo carrying the press, or occasionally I'll fly another senior official. Would you believe it takes about three years of training to get qualified to fly the president?"

"Is the training difficult?"

"Yes and no. I've flown the Sea King—that's the white-top helo most people recognize, and it's a nice aircraft, but it's tough to qualify to fly the president. It's more of a hassle if you ask me."

"Sounds like it's a lot safer than combat missions. But probably not as exciting."

Jake paused for a moment, unsure how to respond. "It's a different kind of challenge. He's the commander in chief... but this assignment doesn't always feel very urgent." He hadn't admitted that to anyone before. He hoped Beau wasn't romancing him to get material for an exposé about how *Marine One* and the HMX-1 Squadron were a waste of taxpayer money. It sounded like some of what he'd written before.

"Is it too cold for a walk tonight?" Beau asked.

Jake silently thanked him for changing the subject. "Let's wander for a while and see."

The air had the kind of chill to it that signaled snow, and the cloud cover seemed heavy. They'd barely gotten onto the sidewalk when Beau shivered and hunched his shoulders against the wind. Jake put an arm around Beau's waist and pulled him in for a kiss. "You're cold."

"You warm me up. Should we go back to my apartment?"

"Don't you want to see a movie, or hear some music at a club?" Jake felt like he owed Beau more of a date than dinner and sex.

"No." Beau looked away. "I mean, yes, I would, but I'd just be thinking about touching you the whole time."

Jake kissed him again. Longer, deeper, hotter. He'd read Jake's mind. "Taxi!"

Chapter 8

THEY MADE it into the apartment before they attacked each other. When Beau began pulling Jake's pants off, they realized they hadn't shut the door. They did, laughing, and went back to undressing each other. They took the edge off by trading blowjobs in the big purple chair, then made their way into the bedroom.

Beau peeled back the thick comforter, and they slid under the cool sheets. Jake pulled the top sheet off and faced Beau, propped up on one elbow. He traced the line of Beau's jaw and caressed his cheek, then played with the soft silky hair as Beau watched, turning his head to kiss Jake's fingers.

Jake lay alongside Beau as they continued touching, exploring each other's bodies, occasionally leaning forward for a kiss. Teasing, playing, pinching, tugging. Beau was slim, in good shape, but not muscular. His skin was smooth, and he had big, sensitive nipples. He made wonderful noises when Jake touched them. And his cock stiffened beautifully when Jake pinched them. If he took one into his mouth, Beau gasped and moaned, making at least as much noise as when Jake had sucked his cock.

"You ready for more?" Jake asked when Beau's cock got thick and swollen again. It hadn't taken much to get him excited, but Jake wanted to prolong this exploration.

Jake was ready, thanks to the way Beau was holding Jake's erection, sliding a thumb through the precome pooling in the slit.

"What did you have in mind?"

"You tell me." Jake put a hand behind Beau's neck so he could get a good deep kiss.

"You're my guest. You tell me. What do you want?" Beau said when the kiss ended.

Jake leaned back and reached behind him for the packets on the night table. He handed a condom to Beau and looked at him, feeling awkward saying what he wanted.

Beau licked his lips and tore open the packet. Then he reached for Jake's cock.

"You wear it," Jake whispered. "If you like to top."

Beau looked into Jake's eyes, surprise evident. "I'm good either way, but yeah, I'd like to." He kissed Jake; then together they rolled the condom onto Beau's erection. Jake turned onto his stomach and spread his legs.

He liked the way Beau used his long fingers to gently spread lube on him, and how carefully he inserted one inside until he had Jake fucking into the bed and groaning. He couldn't wait to have Beau's thick cock inside him.

AFTER THAT successful date, they saw each other as often as Jake's schedule would allow, spending an occasional night at Beau's unless Jake had to report early the next morning. There still weren't enough full nights together for Beau's liking. Jake was oddly reluctant to stay over more than once a week.

One weeknight as Jake buttoned up his shirt after having dinner—and each other—in, Beau decided it was time for a change.

"This is crazy, Jake. You coming here for a few hours, then leaving." Beau tried hard not to sound petulant, but it was difficult. But he couldn't go on like this, no matter how head-over-heels he was for Jake.

"I'd have to get up too early if I stay. You wouldn't get much sleep, and that would get old real fast, no matter what you think. I can get up pretty early because I've been doing it for ten years."

"I can go back to sleep after you leave." Beau let out a groan. This wasn't the first time they had this discussion. But he wasn't going to give in this time. "You've got a house, right? If we stayed there sometimes, you could get up at your regular time. My work hours are flexible, and I don't go to the *Daily*'s office every day."

Jake had his back to Beau as he looked in the mirror and arranged his insignia, so Beau couldn't see his reaction. "I don't know...."

"Jake, I don't want to push here because things with us are good. At least I think they're good."

Jake turned around and sat at the edge of the bed, hand on Beau's shoulder, smoothing it, caressing it. "Yeah, they're good." He smiled. He'd lost the initial charming shyness, and when Beau looked in his eyes, he thought he saw genuine affection glowing in the bright blue depths. "*We're* good." Jake leaned down for a convincing kiss that made his trousers stand at attention.

Beau gave a flirty blink and rubbed Jake's nice, firm bulge. He planted a kiss on it, then sat up. "Jake, if you're living with someone, or married, please let me know right now. If you've got a wife, I can handle that. I just need to know what I'm up against so I know what to do. Because I don't like this arrangement."

Jake's eyes widened and he stopped stroking Beau's arm. "Wow. I didn't realize you felt that way."

"Which part? About your place, or about the wife?"

"My place. There is no wife or girlfriend or boyfriend."

"Why not? I've only mentioned it three or four times now. Do I need to write it on my dick for you to notice something?"

"It couldn't hurt." Jake chuckled, then stopped when he realized Beau wasn't making a joke. At least he realized.

"What's the deal? Why haven't you invited me over?"

Jake got all shifty and frowned. The light dimmed in his gaze. "Your place is nicer. And I do live with someone. Daisy."

"I'm starting to think she's the wife you've got locked up in the attic and that your name is Rochester, not Woodley."

"A *Jane Eyre* joke? Cute."

Beau was mad at himself because Jake suddenly got even sexier because he recognized the joke. "Well?"

"My place smells like dog, and it's simple bachelor quarters. Not comfortable like your apartment."

"Do you have a bed?"

"Sure."

"Then it's perfect."

"You're pretty easy to please."

Beau did the flirty eyelash thing again. "You've got the right moves." Then he got serious again. "I want to meet Daisy. Or is it something else? Afraid your neighbors can't handle it? Or maybe I'll be a bad influence on Daisy, or you don't want Toby to see another man sleep over? Fuck what the neighbors think. And if that's more important than me, then fuck you too. And not in the fun way." Beau got up and pulled on a pair of sweats and a shirt. He wanted to cover up all his skin because he knew if Jake touched him again or looked at him, he might back down.

"It's not any of that. Toby knows I'm gay though I haven't had any overnight guests since he's been hanging out with me and Daisy. But he can handle the truth. And the neighbors can fuck themselves if they *can't* handle the truth."

"A Marine joke. Cute."

Jake shrugged. "I like that you realized it was a Marine reference."

Beau crossed his arms over his chest and started tapping one foot before he realized he was doing it. "Then what's the problem?"

"I didn't think you'd like coming over. Your place is spotless. You've got a lint brush in every room, and you always look like you just stepped out of a magazine photo shoot—except for right now."

Beau looked down at his relatively sloppy outfit. In his defense, they were designer sweats.

"And face it, you have a lot of personal grooming stuff."

"It would be a night here and there, not a dogsled expedition to Antarctica." Beau prayed the joke would defuse the situation before Jake felt cornered.

Jake's eyes crinkled as shook his head, but he was smiling. "Okay, you've convinced me. Why don't you come over on Friday, stay the night, the weekend if you want. Then we can reassess the situation."

"It sounds like you're planning a military exercise."

Jake shrugged, which kind of offended Beau, but he decided not to mention it. Best to quit while he was ahead.

"Do we have a cease-fire?" Jake raised an eyebrow hopefully.

"Yes." Beau wrapped himself around Jake and kissed him ferociously until they ended up undressed again. Consequently, Jake left much later than he intended, but he had a huge smile on his face and an urgent need for dry cleaning.

WEDNESDAY AND Thursday after work, Jake scoured the kitchen and bathrooms. He put clean sheets on the bed, and he moved Daisy's doggie bed into a downstairs room so she'd be less likely to interrupt them in the bedroom. He shopped for groceries and let Toby and Jenna know Beau was coming for the weekend. It felt like he was bringing a guy home to meet his parents.

"That's cool, Jake," Toby said. "I want to meet him. Do you want Daisy to stay with us? Mom, we should let Daisy stay here so Jake and Beau can have private time."

Jake tried not to gape at Toby's forthright comment. "Thanks for the offer, but Daisy and Beau need to get to know each other."

"Toby, why don't you get started on your homework?"

"*Mom*." Toby groaned and dragged his heels as he left the room.

"He's too old not to know what you're doing when you make him leave," Jake said as Jenna shook her head.

"I know. He's a little too old for his age. I'm sorry if he gets personal with you. And I will keep him out of your hair while Beau is around."

"I'll arrange for you two to come by for a meal, so he and Beau can meet."

"It might be better for me to arrange a visit to his grandmother's for the weekend if you like."

"Don't change your plans. He'll be really mad at you, and I don't want to be responsible for that." Jake grinned.

"You're so good with him. I don't know whether you want kids of your own, but you'd be a great dad."

Jake managed a weak smile, then went back across the street, trying to decide how he felt about her compliment. He liked Toby, and he enjoyed spending time with his sister's children, but the idea of his own kid had never dawned on him.

As he finished vacuuming on Friday afternoon, he couldn't help thinking about Beau with a kid. Not that they were anywhere near even making jokes about their future or kids. Jake chuckled at the image of perfectly dressed Beau changing a diaper, or a kid spitting up all over Beau's spotless shoulder. The guy would probably put on a hazmat suit before he touched a child.

Which reminded Jake that it was time to get Beau from the train station in Alexandria.

Rush hour traffic was miserable, and he was twenty minutes late to the last station on the Yellow Line. It was a commuter stop, mostly parking lot and traffic. Beau stood on the curb with a plum-colored suitcase and a matching overnight bag. He wore a pristine camel-colored coat. At least he'd planned ahead by wearing something Daisy-colored.

Jake pulled up to the curb, and Beau smiled and waved when he spotted the car. His cheeks were rosy and his eyes were watering. He'd probably been standing out there awhile, but he didn't say a word.

"Sorry. Traffic." Jake hoisted the suitcase into the trunk. It wasn't as heavy as he'd expected, and it went flying against the trunk lid because he'd used so much force.

"No problem." Beau kissed him as Jake tried to put the trunk lid down.

Jake glanced around out of the corner of his eye, but no one walking past seemed to notice, or if they did, didn't care. He'd never kissed anyone out here, but Alexandria was pretty gay-friendly.

In the car, Jake gave Beau a more enthusiastic welcome kiss.

"Now that's more like it."

"You looked so cold." Jake hoped Beau couldn't tell he was lying.

"You need to learn how to warm me up better." Although Beau's tone was playful, Jake detected a slight edge to the words.

"Are you hungry?" Jake changed the subject with so little grace, he expected Beau to comment.

"A little. What did you plan for dinner?"

"I got groceries for a few meals, so we can cook, or go out. You decide."

"Let's stay in and cook. We go out all the time in DC, so it will be nice to have a cozy dinner at home. In front of the fireplace. You have a fireplace?"

Jake nodded and breathed a sigh of relief he'd brought in wood and cleaned out the flue. Everything was ready to light as soon as they got back. The Corps had taught him to plan and prepare well. "Sounds good. But my kitchen isn't as nice as yours."

They turned onto Jake's street, and his gut tightened as he pulled into the driveway. The curtains fluttered as Daisy poked her head through them, smearing her nose on the inside of the window. Even though he'd cleaned, he couldn't shake the dread that Beau would be judging him and his house. Memories of a thousand inspections bubbled up inside him, memories of drill instructors' insults and shouts and orders to do this or that over and over again. Having a CO throw his gear across the room, having to repack someone else's shit because one of their group had done something wrong.

"Oh, this place is cute." Beau got out of the car and swept his gaze across the front of the house. He sounded surprised.

"It's not as cute inside." Jake unlocked the door and prayed Daisy wouldn't knock Beau down or destroy his coat or nibble at his expensive luggage. Daisy came out like she'd been shot from a cannon. She wagged her whole body at Jake and then moved to inspect Beau.

Beau leaned over and scratched her head. "Hey there, Daisy! At least I know you're not the insane wife." He grinned at Jake, then walked inside.

Jake fought off the urge to glance around to see if the neighbors were watching.

He got Beau settled on the couch and started the fire.

"I'll open some wine, or do you want a cocktail?"

"Wine's fine. White or sparkling if you have it."

Jake brought glasses and a bottle of sauvignon blanc into the living room. "Nothing's fancy here. And the couch has seen better days."

Beau pulled the bottle out of Jake's hand and placed it on the table with a thunk. He grabbed the glasses and put them down beside the wine, then made Jake sit.

"Jake, I don't want to hear you say that one more time."

"Warn you about the couch?"

"No. Stop telling me how your house isn't nice or my kitchen is bigger. I didn't come here for your kitchen or your couch. I don't even care if you have a bunk bed or we end up sleeping in the car. I came here to spend time with you. So we can have more time together without you running yourself ragged driving back and forth to see me all the time. I don't care about furniture or things or dog hair. I care about you."

Jake looked at the huge glob of fur already stuck to Beau's thigh and Daisy's nose poking Beau in the balls and he started laughing. Then Beau joined in, and they finally shared a proper happy-to-see-you kiss.

"Now that's out of the way, maybe you could show me your bunk bed before dinner."

But Beau couldn't seem to wait to get upstairs. He pulled Jake's shirt off and had Jake's pants around his hips before Jake could get a word out.

"Never mind the bed. Just fuck me on the couch. I like the fire." Beau bent over as Jake put on a condom.

When Jake slid inside, he closed his eyes and let his body and senses take over, changing his motion based on Beau's sounds and movements. When he opened his eyes again, Daisy was watching him, head cocked. At least she was lying across the room and hadn't tried to join what must appear to be a game.

They both finished quickly. Plenty of time for more later. Jake spooned up behind Beau on the couch and kissed his shoulder.

"I love your couch. I don't know why you were complaining."

"I love my couch too. It's much more fun when you're here."

"I'm glad you think so." Beau pulled Jake's head down and craned his own neck for a wet kiss. He pulled away with a gasp. "Your dog just licked my balls!"

"Should I be jealous?"

DAISY BEHAVED herself for the most part. What Jake was really dreading was dinner with Jenna and Toby. Maybe dreading wasn't the right word. He wasn't sure how Beau would handle Toby.

He needn't have worried. Everyone got along fine. Jenna brought over side dishes of roasted potatoes and brussels sprouts and helped Beau set the table. Jake grilled steaks in the backyard under Daisy's watchful eye, rewarding her with a tiny bit of rare meat. Inside, Jenna and Beau chatted while Toby flitted back and forth so he could hang out with everyone.

Jenna's concern with Toby's budding curiosity about sex meant dinner conversation zigzagged between various topics and strange segues. Beau seemed as confused as Toby, because Jake hadn't warned him in advance. But Toby seemed to like Beau, and Beau was undaunted by a kid's presence. He talked to Toby like any other adult, gaining his immediate favor.

When Beau and Jenna insisted on doing the dishes, Toby played an auto-racing video game with Jake on the couch.

"I like Beau a lot. He's funny and really handsome."

"He is. I like him a lot too." Jake concentrated on the game, not wanting to go down the slippery slope of Beau's attractiveness. He swerved out of Toby's way in the game, hooting with victory after passing him; then crashed his car into the stands. He might be able to fly a helicopter out of danger, but he pretty much sucked at this car-racing stuff.

"You need to get a helicopter flying game." Toby seemed to sense Jake's thoughts.

"Do they make them?"

"I'll find one. I've got lots of dog-sitting money saved up."

"Don't you have a birthday soon?" Jake asked as they started another round of car racing.

"I want to buy my own things. I need to learn responsibility."

Jake nodded as he glanced over at Toby. "That's good to hear."

"You should too, Jake."

Toby's voice was serious, and Jake looked over at him. He sounded a little like the colonel, which alarmed Jake.

Toby put the game controller down. "I have something for you." He stood up and stuffed a hand into his pants pocket. When he pulled it out, he was clutching a handful of condoms.

Jake stared at them.

"Take them." Toby put them in Jake's hand, then sat down.

"Where did you get those?"

"At school. In health class. We learned about safe sex. Please be safe, Jake. I'd hate for something to happen to you if you aren't. Okay?"

Jake nodded. "Thanks, Toby. Beau and I will be safe." He wasn't sure whether he should be proud of Toby or horrified that a seventh grader had shown more concern for his health than his own dad did when Jake began experimenting with sex around the same age. A knot the size of Alaska formed in his throat, and he couldn't get any words out.

When Jake heard Jenna and Beau coming into the living room, he jammed the condoms into his pocket.

"Who's winning?" Jenna asked, ruffling Toby's hair until he swatted her hand away.

Jake had crashed his car on the first lap.

"I'm winning, Mom. But I think we should go so Jake and Beau can have some privacy."

Jenna stared at her son as if she'd just met an alien.

Toby winked at Jake as he put on his jacket, then waved to Beau.

"He's a pretty cool kid. I can see why you like him," Beau said after Toby and Jenna left.

"He's certainly full of surprises." Jake put the condoms in Beau's hand. "He gave me those and told us to be safe."

"Let's not disappoint the kid." Beau shifted so he could straddle Jake's lap and ground himself against Jake. "I guess I can't go home until we use them up."

"You want to use all four?"

Beau already had Jake's shirt half unbuttoned. "Are you up for the challenge?"

It only took a little more pressure from Beau before Jake was hard and pushing his hips against Beau's ass. "Does that meet with your approval?"

"It'll have to do."

SUNDAY MORNING they woke tangled up in Jake's bed. The door was shut, and Daisy was on the other side of it.

"Good morning," Beau said with a sexy catch in his throat. His morning voice always did wicked things to Jake's libido.

"Better than good." Jake nibbled at Beau's neck and slid a hand down his torso. "You sleep well?"

"You tired me out plenty."

"We can spend the day in bed if you like."

Beau sat up. "I'll be even more exhausted."

"What's wrong with that?"

"It's nice and sunny. Can we take a ride after breakfast?"

"Sure. What about going to the park with Daisy?" Jake flicked his tongue across Beau's nipple.

"I meant on your motorcycle."

Jake pulled away and the smile melted off his face. "Why?"

"Why not? It'll be fun. Exciting. A little dangerous. Just like you." Beau rubbed Jake's head.

"I don't think that's a great idea right now."

"Please?" Beau cocked his head in a way that Jake usually found charming. But not today.

"No, Beau. Just leave it there." Jake tried to keep the emotion—anger, fear? He wasn't sure—out of his voice.

"Is there something wrong with the bike?" Beau didn't seem to get it.

"No. Why isn't that enough?" Jake sat up and slammed his fist against the headboard, making it shudder and bang against the wall. Daisy howled from the other side of the door.

Beau leapt back like he'd been slapped.

It was then Jake realized he'd lashed out and snapped at Beau. A shadow of something flickered in Beau's eyes, something dark where before there had been light and joy.

"Never mind." Beau pulled the sheets up, a barrier between his body and Jake's, as if sensing a sudden chill in the room.

Beau's tone made Jake shiver a little.

"I'm sorry, Beau. I didn't mean to—"

"It's okay. I should probably get going…." Beau's eyes were wide like a spooked horse's.

Jake's gut roiled. He'd scared Beau away already, literally. He put a hand on Beau's arm as he started to get out of bed. They planned for Beau to stay until the afternoon, maybe another night, but mentioning that would only make things worse. But he couldn't let Beau leave like this. Not yet.

"Please stay for breakfast. I got stuff for pancakes. Berries and…." He held his breath as he watched Beau turning over the options.

Beau narrowed his eyes and shook his head.

"Then we can take a ride on the bike after breakfast." Jake hoped Beau didn't hear his voice waver.

Beau didn't reply, just walked into the bathroom and shut the door.

Jake slammed himself back against the pillows. He couldn't explain why he didn't want to take Beau on the bike. He hadn't ridden it for a few weeks. The bike scared Jake a little. Or he scared himself when he rode it. He felt its power and danger pulling him to a place he longed to go. Now he was terrified Beau would see that inside him, feel that, see through Jake's disguise of being a normal guy, boyfriend material.

Beau looked at Jake with the kind of light that could see into Jake's dark places, and Jake didn't want that. He wanted to feel Beau's light, not bring Beau into Jake's cold, dark, dangerous world.

Beau came out of the bathroom, pulled clean clothes from his suitcase, and got dressed.

"Please, don't go like this." He watched Beau struggle to roll the suitcase across the carpet's thick nap. "Look, why don't you leave your stuff here. You can have space in the closet. I have uniforms and not much else in there, so there's lots of space."

"No, thanks. I need to go home. I'll get myself to the station. Don't trouble yourself." Beau walked out the front door while Jake stood at the bottom of the stairs with a sheet around his waist. He hesitated a moment too long, and when he lunged for the door, Beau had already shut it.

He would run after Beau even if he was naked. But the look in Beau's eyes kept Jake from following.

"I DON'T know why that upset you so much." Laney shoved half a pancake into her mouth. She'd dragged Beau to Matchbox, her favorite breakfast place, to cheer him up after she insisted on retrieving him from the Metro station in Chinatown. The pancakes seemed to cheer Laney far more than Beau.

Beau shredded another of the pancakes on his plate until it disintegrated into crumbs.

"Look, if you're not gonna eat it, don't waste it."

Laney never wasted food.

"I haven't told you the whole story, Lane. But his voice was like ice. Like someone poured ice water on me when he said no. It was scary. He frightened me with a kind of hidden violence in that one word, and then he hit the headboard. I felt like I'd been physically hit."

She put her fork down and reached for Beau's hand. "You're scaring me. Do you think he'd hurt you? Hit *you*?"

Beau hadn't asked himself that. Yet. He'd tried to sound calm as he left, but his pulse was pounding, and he didn't want to run. He knew if you ran from a dog, it would chase you. If you walked away, it ignored you. Only food tried to escape. Beau didn't want Jake to chase him.

"I don't think so." Beau paused. "No. He was really good with Daisy and the kid, Toby. If Jake was violent, I don't think Jenna would let her kid hang around. But there's something dark in there. Like a cave. The deeper you go, the darker it gets."

"Or a black hole. Sucking you in and you can't escape." Laney's voice got low and dramatic.

"Maybe not that dark."

"Beau, Jake's been through a lot of bad stuff. I can understand how he might have some dark spots. Some places where he can't see out and you can't see in. Do you think he could have PTSD?"

"I don't know that much about it, but he doesn't have nightmares or get frightened by loud noises. I don't think he'd be allowed to fly the president around if he had any symptoms. Still, there's something dark in him."

Laney pushed her plate away, breakfast half-eaten. Beau knew he'd worried her when she lost her appetite. "Beau, honey. Did you ever think that maybe what Jake needs is some of your light?"

Chapter 9

OVER THE next few days, Beau thought over everything Laney had said. Maybe he had been too harsh on Jake. Something about the motorcycle spooked him, and Beau should have asked instead of stomping off. For a writer, he really sucked at communicating. Why was it so much easier to ask total strangers questions than the man he was falling in love with?

Because he cared so much more about Jake's answers. And he didn't want to scare Jake off either. He still hadn't owned up to being the fashion Beaumont and not the politics Beaumont. First things first.

Jake was scheduled to be out of town for a veep lift until Thursday, so Thursday afternoon Beau took the Yellow Line to the last station and a taxi from there to Jake's house. He had no idea whether Jake would be home yet, but maybe Jenna and Toby would invite him in for coffee if he had to wait.

It was so much colder out in Virginia than in the city. All the open spaces gave the wind momentum. Beau pulled his favorite royal blue coat closer around his throat as he walked up Jake's driveway. The living room curtains fluttered. Daisy was home. Either Jake was here, or he was coming back soon.

Here goes nothing.

Beau rang the doorbell. He heard Daisy fling herself against the front door and whimper excitedly.

"Beau?" Jake shouted from the other side of the door. "Give me a minute."

For whatever reason, he left Beau on the doorstep, literally cooling his heels. A few minutes later, he opened the door, and Daisy rushed Beau before he made it inside.

Jake was shirtless, wearing sweats with USMC in faded red silkscreen down one leg. The pants hung low on his waist and his hair was messy. Either just-woke-up or just-got-fucked messy. Beau looked around for evidence of the latter. Jake smelled minty, covering up something like a recent blowjob.

"Daisy, calm down. Heel." The words had no effect, so Jake gently tugged her collar. "What are you doing here?" He closed the door behind Beau. He stood and looked at Beau with bloodshot eyes.

"I hear this is the place to get some killer pancakes."

"Yeah, but…." Jake stretched and the sweats slid low enough for Beau to stare at the dark line of hair heading into Jake's pants. "We usually only serve those at breakfast." He looked Beau in the eye, as if waiting for Beau to declare his purpose.

"I happen to be free for breakfast. Are you?" Beau bit his bottom lip and stopped breathing. He had no right to expect anything from Jake right now, but if Jake sent him away, Beau thought he might crumble to the floor or maybe start crying. That wouldn't be particularly attractive.

"Yeah. I am." Jake paused. "Beau, I'm sorry."

"Jake, you really scared me the other day. I'm not sure why you got so upset, but I want to talk about it."

"Come here." Jake tugged on Beau's arm and pulled him in for a tentative kiss.

Beau wrapped himself around Jake and kissed back because he couldn't say what he wanted to any better with words.

"You want some pancakes now?"

"Not yet." Beau slid a hand down the back of Jake's sweats and enjoyed the warm bare flesh. "I need to work up a good appetite first."

"I can help with that."

They went upstairs and fell into bed, kissing, undressing each other. Beau lay back and reached over to the nightstand where Jake kept the condoms. He slid the drawer open and Jake leapt up.

"I'll get the stuff." Jake plunged a hand into the drawer.

His action was so furtive, it caught Beau's attention. But by then Jake had a slippery hand between Beau's thighs, and he got distracted.

They made love. It started out slowly, then got more intense, as if they had to somehow prove how much each wanted the other, needed the other. After, when Jake went into the bathroom to clean up, Beau rolled over toward the edge of the bed and slid the drawer open.

A tequila bottle lay on its side between a fresh vial of lube and a box of condoms. The bottle was empty. He slid the drawer shut before Jake came back to bed.

"Hungry yet?" Jake asked.

Beau nodded. "I could eat something. Like food, even."

Jake ruffled Beau's hair playfully, maybe with a bit of undisguised jealousy for the long locks. "Wait here." He pulled a pair of camo-patterned boxers out of the dresser and slid them on.

Once Beau heard Jake clattering around the kitchen, he sat up and looked in the other drawers. He saw two bottles, one empty, the other half-full. He shut the drawer, wondering what to do with this knowledge.

On one hand, they were still on shaky ground after the miscommunication over the weekend. But if Jake was drinking, and hiding this many bottles, it scared Beau. He hadn't seen Jake drink excessively, and he didn't smell like booze when he arrived at Beau's. Maybe he hid his drinking until he was alone. It explained why he'd put off having Beau here for so long and didn't stay at Beau's as often as he could. It also explained the minty freshness after Jake left Beau on the doorstep for a few minutes.

Jake's footsteps on the stairway put Beau's internal debate on hold. They dined in bed on warm, fluffy omelets bursting with cheese and tiny dice of smoky ham. Jake even made fruit salad.

"Oh God, I'm stuffed." Beau put his tray on the dresser and took Jake's, since his plates were empty.

"Want anything else?"

"I'm staying until you make me pancakes." Beau slid under the covers and pressed himself to Jake's warm naked flesh.

"What if I don't make them till Sunday?"

"Then I'll stay till Sunday."

"You didn't bring a suitcase."

"Am I going to need to get dressed between now and Sunday?" Beau nibbled at Jake's ear, then kissed his way to a nipple and took another playful bite.

"Not if I can help it."

They made love again, slowly, gently, and sweetly enough to clear away any concerns Beau had.

HE WOKE up to pitch darkness punctuated only by the dim blue numerals on the digital clock.

2:41

The bed beside Beau was empty, the sheets cool. The bathroom door was open, the room dark. Beau found his shorts on the floor and pulled them on, then walked into the hallway. He saw a glow coming from the living room. He slowly made his way there.

Jake sat on the couch, silhouetted by the embers of the dying flames. He held out one arm over the arm of the sofa, clutching a bottle. The fire illuminated amber liquid.

Beau was only a few feet away when Jake noticed him. Shiny wet trails on his cheeks. He took the bottle out of Jake's hand and held it to his mouth, taking a long pull of the spicy tequila. His lips stung when he pulled the bottle away and stood in front of Jake.

"You want to talk?"

Jake shook his head.

Beau nodded. He sat next to Jake on the couch and put the bottle on the table out of Jake's reach. He could hear Jake's breathing, heavy and labored, like he'd been running or making love. Then Jake crumpled and lay with his head on Beau's lap. He shook with a few silent sobs, then raised his head.

"You shouldn't have come back, Beau. I'm not good for you."

Beau stroked Jake's head and neck and shoulder. "Yes, you are. We're good together."

Jake shook his head. "Go back upstairs. Leave me alone in the dark. My darkness."

The words brought back Laney's comment.

"You're not alone. And it's not dark if we're here together." He leaned down and kissed Jake's shoulder, which was covered with goose bumps. "Come upstairs with me. It's nice and warm up there."

Jake shook his head.

"Are you drunk?"

"No. Not nearly enough." When Jake sat up, his eyes were wet. "Go on back to bed without me. I'll be up in a while."

"Jake, I don't understand why you'd rather be here than with me."

"I don't deserve you, Beau. Don't deserve...." He turned and looked Beau in the eyes. "Promise me you'll leave in the morning and not come back."

Beau's gut knotted with fear and helplessness. This was no time for joking about pancakes, but he couldn't stand aside while Jake fell into such a dark place.

"Tell me why. If you can explain everything and convince me, then I'll leave. But not until you give me a good reason."

For a moment Jake glared at Beau with narrowed eyes. Then, as if he saw something in there, he nodded and leaned back against the sofa. "I can't do this anymore. I can't lie with you, enjoy being with you, not when my men will never...."

"Your men? Is this about the crash?" Beau had avoided the topic until now, but maybe that had been a mistake. Maybe Jake hadn't gotten over his experiences in Afghanistan. Beau needed to know whether Jake ever would, whether Jake could ever accept what had happened.

"Yes," Jake whispered. "They're dead. I don't deserve to be happy knowing it's my fault. How can I?"

"I don't understand how it's your fault. Will you explain it?"

"You know what happened. You read about it, didn't you?"

"Not the details."

"We crashed, antiaircraft missiles. I couldn't get everyone out of the bird. Tried to treat the ones who could walk, get them to safety, then I went back."

Beau nodded, not wanting to interrupt. Jake's voice was a raspy whisper, and he stared straight ahead, as if talking to someone who wasn't in the room.

"Got most of them freed, except for my crew chief. Copilot was… gone."

Beau finally heard the details of this life-altering incident, directly from Jake. He'd instructed the survivors to move away from the downed aircraft, and then when the insurgents made their way to the crash zone, Jake had run in the opposite direction, drawing fire away from the injured men. He went down and was captured. He gave up some false information before faking unconsciousness. Thinking he had more valuable intelligence, they left him alone to get medical help, long enough for him to escape. He tried to get back to the helicopter but was disoriented. After another day and night evading the insurgents, he was finally able to radio for rescue. Everyone he'd gotten out of the helicopter had been lifted out and survived. His copilot and crew chief had been lost. The tail gunner kept shooting at insurgents until he'd bled out, but he'd given Jake cover to get the survivors away in the other direction.

"Jake, you saved all those men. How do you see that as failure?"

"I lost my crew. I had to talk to their wives, see their kids." He shook his head. "I should have done it differently."

"What? Crashed better? Could you have crashed in a better place?"

Jake shook his head. "The tail rotor was shot to hell. Couldn't maneuver."

"If you died, would it have saved your crew?" Beau asked, but he suspected logic had nothing to do with Jake's pain. If only he could understand what Jake needed. Was there a magical phrase to put Jake at ease? Release him from this crippling guilt?

Jake shook his head again, but he looked at Beau and squeezed his hand. "I've relived it a thousand times. I don't think I could have done better."

"Then what is it?" Beau had a big decision to make sometime soon. Nothing he could say would pull Jake out of this, and he wasn't sure whether he could stay with Jake otherwise. He couldn't watch this pain pull Jake down. At some point Jake would give up trying to resist it.

"I'm not a hero, Beau. I can't stand the word, but it's the one everyone likes to use." He reached for the tequila and took a swig, then he held on to the bottle as if letting go would cause him to float away.

The newspapers, the television reports, the medal. Everything referred to Jake as a hero. He'd done some incredible things. Beau couldn't imagine getting out of the helicopter, much less pulling anyone else out and then decoying the enemy away. And that wasn't the most incredible part of Jake's story.

"You're right. You failed at part of what you think you should have achieved."

"Yes. That's it. Exactly."

"But the rest of it was successful. To the men you saved, you are a hero. And the men in your crew could have died in much worse circumstances if they'd been captured. And the crew chief was a hero. You two worked as a team until the wounded men were out of the most immediate danger. I'm sure knowing that helped his wife cope with her loss."

"I suppose. We did work together on that."

Beau was talked out, exhausted. Living in Jake's pain for only an hour had sapped his energy. "You get up every day and keep doing your duty. I don't know how you do that. It's incredible."

"It's my job." Jake scratched behind his ear.

"You're the strongest person I've ever met. I'm the one who doesn't deserve you." Beau kissed Jake's cheek, then got up. "I'm going back to bed." He could barely walk to the stairs. He'd cycled through so many emotions tonight. Best to wait until daylight to consider what kind of future he and Jake might have.

"Wait, I'm coming too." Jake stood and put the bottle on the table, then followed Beau without glancing back.

WHEN BEAU woke the next morning, it was still dark. The bed was empty and cool next to him. He closed his eyes, let his head fall back to the pillow with a groan, and tried to calm his pounding heart. He couldn't go through this every night and morning, wondering what Jake was doing. It would kill him.

Sounds from downstairs caught his attention. Jake's voice and Daisy's collar jingling. Footsteps on the stairs. He pretended to be asleep. The bed sank slightly as Jake sat at the edge.

"Beau?" Jake touched Beau's cheek, soft as a whisper, and Beau opened his eyes. Jake sat next to him, wearing his uniform. "I didn't want to wake you earlier. Want some breakfast or do you want to go back to sleep?"

Beau raised himself onto his elbows and glanced at the clock: seven thirty. "I'm awake. Just some coffee, I guess."

"Come down when you're ready." Jake planted a soft kiss on Beau's cheek and went back downstairs.

Beau stopped in the bathroom, then pulled on his jeans and a clean T-shirt from a drawer. Coffee aromas tickled his nose when he was halfway down the stairs, and when he hit the kitchen, he couldn't stop smiling. The table was set and Jake was at the stove making pancakes.

"There's coffee and juice on the table. Let me get the first batch for you." Jake pulled a plate out of the oven and set it in front of Beau. It held a stack of beautifully browned pancakes, crispy around the edges and all perfectly shaped. Beau slathered them with butter and maple syrup as Jake joined him at the table.

"I have to be at roll call by nine, but I don't want to rush you. There's money for a taxi to the Metro if you want. I'm sorry I don't have time to drive you."

Beau nodded as he chewed and examined Jake's face while Jake was focused on his own plate. A ridge had formed between his brows, an indication of worry. He put on a bright smile, but Beau knew Jake wasn't pretending their midnight discussion hadn't happened. This wasn't the right time to bring it up, but they needed to talk about it again. Beau needed answers to questions he'd been unwilling to ask the night before. And he hoped Jake would open up to him voluntarily.

"Thanks." Beau stuffed more pancake in his mouth and savored the perfect texture and taste. "These are great. Better than advertised."

"I wish I didn't have to rush breakfast, but I can't take the day off." Jake stood and put the frying pan and mixing bowls in the sink and ran water over them.

"I wouldn't expect you to."

Jake turned off the water, dried his hands, and sat back down. "I wanted to. I…." He looked away nervously. "I need to talk to you about last night."

Beau nodded. He didn't trust his voice. Or his heart. His chest ached because their next discussion might be the last one, and Jake recognized that too.

"Take your time." Jake put a key ring with two keys on the table. "Lock up if you leave. Toby will take care of Daisy when he gets back from school." Jake stood, then reached down for Beau's hand and planted a kiss on the fingers before letting it go gently. "We'll talk tonight when I get home." He grabbed his hat from a hook near the kitchen door and gave Beau a sad smile before he left.

Daisy ran to the front of the house to watch Jake leave, and Beau had to fight off the urge to do the same. He shared the rest of the pancakes with Daisy, then cleaned up the kitchen and washed the pans.

The mundane task freed his mind, and he replayed the events of the night before. After Jake's overreaction concerning the motorcycle the previous weekend and his drinking, Jake's mood swings and unpredictability troubled and saddened Beau. He felt for Jake and the monstrosities he endured in combat, but what if things got worse?

Should he leave before he got too hooked on Jake?

Too late.

Beau finished tidying up the kitchen, and with an unsteady hand and a pained heart, he left Jake a note.

I went back to DC. I need a little time to think.

It shouldn't have taken an experienced journalist half an hour to write twelve words, but Beau knew he was doing the right thing—for both of them.

He called a cab, and when it arrived, Beau petted Daisy before leaving. As he locked the door, he noticed the keys were shiny, brand-new. Had Jake made them for him? No way to know now. Beau pressed his lips together as he slipped the keys into the newspaper slot and let them fall with a metallic clang to the floor inside.

JAKE HATED leaving Beau that morning. Worse, he hated himself for fucking everything up again.

After upsetting Beau on Sunday, the last thing Jake expected was to find Beau on his doorstep. Beau had been the brave one, because he'd come to Jake instead of waiting for the apology Jake owed him.

And then Jake snatched defeat out of the jaws of victory.

Falling asleep in Beau's arms was just about perfect. And Jake couldn't handle perfect. Jake didn't deserve perfect. Perfect scared him, and he wouldn't let himself accept anything wonderful without first trying to fight it off.

Now Beau had seen Jake not quite at his worst, but perhaps at his most honest.

But Beau hadn't run away. He'd tried to understand Jake, tried to put the pieces back together.

He wouldn't stick around for long if that happened again. It was only fair to let Beau know it was likely to happen.

Beau was the first man who made Jake understand what it felt like to be in love. And because Beau deserved better, Jake knew he had to let him go. Beau was a wonderful, warm, compassionate man, and he belonged with someone who wouldn't put out his light.

JAKE REPORTED to the AOM a few minutes early, earning surprised glances from his colleagues and a tight nod from the CO. Because he'd taken a sick day earlier that week, he'd lost his spot on the presidential lift the following week. He accepted the consequences, knowing he'd only get worse if he and Beau split up.

"One last point before we get to work, men," Lieutenant Colonel Monroe said after he'd given out assignments for the next two weeks. "A reminder that the White House Christmas Party is almost upon us again. For some of you, it's a highlight of squadron privileges. For others, not so much." A handful of people chuckled and glanced at each other. "If you don't plan to attend, you'll free up a spot for someone else in the squadron. If you haven't done so, make sure to RSVP and get your guests' names to Corporal Kay by COB tomorrow so the Secret Service can process clearances in plenty of time. Since POTUS will be present and no lifts are scheduled until after the party, the whole squadron will be in town for the event. That's it. Woodley, I need to see you in my office. Otherwise, dismissed."

Almost in unison, thirty pilots started to file out of the room. A few poked jokes at Jake for his sick day—no one believed he was sick—and for being called to Monroe's office. He felt like the squadron's equivalent of Ferris Bueller.

Jake let the comments roll off his back and grinned good-naturedly. Over the past two months, he'd been on his best behavior without any effort. Beau had put him in such a good mood, it was easy to come to work and do 110 percent every day. Now, he knew he was in danger of losing everything he'd accomplished. He should have been fully qualified as a presidential copilot by now, and he was still months away.

The lieutenant colonel wasn't in the office when he arrived, so Jake went inside and waited. He sat down, and as soon as he heard Monroe at the door, he sprang to attention.

"At ease, Captain. Have a seat."

"Yes, sir."

"Woodley, glad to see you're feeling better. You don't look so good, though. You should be able to catch up on your sleep this weekend since you'll be in town."

"Yes, sir. I'm disappointed to miss the lift."

"Me too. You really earned the spot, but you know the rules. I can't make exceptions for you, though you are my best pilot. I wish you didn't keep sabotaging yourself."

"Sir."

"But that's not why I called you. Not the only reason." The lieutenant colonel stared at Jake. It was a common tactic to see what people would say. Most couldn't endure silence without feeling the need to speak. When Jake didn't reply, Monroe continued. "Your guest for the party, Matthew Beaumont, has been denied approval."

"What?" Jake couldn't keep the surprise from his response. "Sorry, sir. I don't understand."

"The Pentagon disallowed his attendance."

"Because we're gay?" Jake tried to keep emotion out of the question.

"I'm sorry you feel the need to ask, but I wondered about that too. I questioned the decision. It seems he's said or done something that put him on a watch list."

"You mean like a terrorist? Because he's been to White House events before. I *met* him at a White House event. He passed their security check."

The lieutenant colonel frowned. "They said it's a national security thing, and I didn't question it. He's a journalist, right? Has he written anything that might expose any sort of classified information?"

Jake appreciated that Monroe didn't ask whether he had given Beau any information. "No, sir. There are two Beaumonts at the *District Daily*." Jake only recently discovered this when searching for more of Beau's stories, though Beau hadn't yet cleared up Jake's original assumption he was the political reporter. "*Matthew* Beaumont writes the fashion column. Not politics."

Monroe's gaze bored into Jake, and Jake held his ground. "I see. The White House has the final say here, so if they've approved him before…." The lieutenant colonel didn't finish the sentence, but Jake understood. He could bring Beau, but if the White House turned him away at the event, he'd been warned.

"Yes, sir." Jake started to stand.

"Not so fast." Monroe smiled. "Since you're not going on the lift as originally scheduled, I've arranged for you to have time in the simulator with Major Landau while we're away." Landau's wife had recently given birth, and he'd asked not to be put on overnight lifts for a few months.

"Really, sir? Thank you."

"Now you're dismissed."

Jake left the office almost walking on air. Being assigned simulator time meant he was back on track for getting full qualification as a presidential pilot. He couldn't wait to tell Beau.

And then Jake remembered: he'd left a mess between himself and Beau. The issue of the White House holiday party was moot if they weren't still together in two weeks.

Chapter 10

"I THINK you should have kept the keys." Laney slurped the last of a frozen cocktail through a straw and rubbed her temples as she leaned against the counter in Beau's kitchen. "I mean, he did make you pancakes." Her opinion of what constituted a good relationship clearly bore no resemblance to Beau's.

He sipped his drink as Laney refilled her glass. "Where did you get these?" He hadn't realized you could buy frozen drinks by the gallon anywhere but New Orleans.

"New Georgetown bar called Rue Bourbon. According to the PR, they 'bring Bourbon Street to Main Street.' Good drinks. Strong." She tottered on high heels as she poured. They looked great on her, though out of place with the rest of her thrown-together outfit. *Baby steps*, Beau reminded himself.

"I'm not sure that's a good thing."

"The drinks or the keys? Or the pancakes? I forgot the question." Laney covered her mouth as she let out a surprisingly ladylike hiccup.

Beau laughed and moved the Styrofoam container of drinks out of her reach. "All of the above. I definitely don't think Main Street is ready for Bourbon Street. And the pancakes were good. Better than I can make."

"Well, the last pancakes you made me tasted like school paste." Laney made air kisses across the table as she insulted Beau's occasional culinary ineptness.

Beau shrugged. He wouldn't mention that Laney couldn't even make paste. At least it kept her from asking more questions about his night with Jake. He was torn between getting advice and revealing too much.

The doorbell rang, allowing him to avoid the decision for a little while longer. "That'll be the delivery guy. Buzz him in?"

Laney tottered over to the door, buzzed the downstairs door open, and then hovered in the doorway as the guy presumably rode the elevator to Beau's apartment.

"I don't remember ordering *that*." Laney giggled and backed into the apartment.

Beau looked up from his drink to see what had gone wrong with their order. Jake strolled in holding two bags of food.

"I ran into the delivery guy downstairs, so I saved him a trip."

Laney licked her lips and pushed some money into his waistband with a shrug. "That was the delivery guy's tip."

"I hesitate to ask where you ordered from," Jake said. He poked his nose in one of the bags as he put them on the counter. "Smells like Indian. Do they have stripper delivery guys?"

"At Sitar? No." Beau couldn't help smiling. "At least to my knowledge. I'll mention it to the owner, though."

Laney grinned and held on to Jake's arm. "That was a big tip, Jake. At least take your shirt off."

"Laney, let's start eating." Beau wanted to get some food into her before Bourbon Street ended up all over his kitchen floor. He reached for a bag, and his hands bumped Jake's. They looked at each other, and Beau felt that same thrill, the same butterflies as the first time he'd talked to Jake. Suddenly the previous terrible night didn't seem so bad.

Together they prepared a plate of food for Laney, piling on rice and fragrant cardamom-spiced chicken in yogurt sauce along with some vegetables. Jake settled Laney on the couch while Beau made up another plate and put it on a tray for himself and Jake. He stowed the container from Rue Bourbon in the refrigerator and poured them sparkling water with lemon slices.

"Laney, we need to talk in the other room, okay?" Beau said.

Laney nodded, chewing happily. "Hey, if you guys are gonna have sex, turn on some music, okay?"

Beau shook his head and headed for the bedroom. He sat on the chair near the bed, while Jake sat at the edge of the bed with the platter on his lap.

"Beau, we need to…. I need to talk to you about last night."

It was true, but Beau wanted to prolong the inevitable as long as possible. "Let's eat first? It's nice and hot."

Jake nodded. They attacked the platter of food. The world seemed normal again as they stabbed at chunks of chicken and scooped up the aromatic sauce with pieces of thick naan.

Beau was such a coward, because he didn't want to bring up the night before. He made another excuse to postpone the discussion.

"Let me check on Laney. You want a drink?" he asked, his host instincts kicking in. A drink wasn't the solution. It had been the problem in the first place.

"No, I'm good," Jake said.

"I'm sorry. I wasn't thinking." Beau stood up, suddenly unsure what to do with his hands.

"I'm driving. You go ahead."

"Be right back." He found Laney asleep on the couch. She'd put her empty plate on the table before lying down, and Beau let out a sigh of relief. He'd pictured cardamom-scented upholstery, but Laney had been either very careful or very hungry. He didn't want to say which he thought more likely.

He refilled their glasses of Perrier and fresh lemon slices, then took a deep breath before going back into the bedroom.

Jake was still sitting at the edge of the bed. He looked handsome and strong in his everyday uniform. He looked like he'd keep Beau and everyone else safe from terrorists, even if he couldn't keep Beau safe from his own heart.

"I'm sorry for showing up without any notice. I should have called, but I… I was afraid you'd either say no or you'd be out, and then I thought I might be a little jealous." Jake gave Beau the shy grin. "I'm always a little jealous of Laney."

"She says the same thing," Beau said. He looked at the chair, then decided to sit on the bed near Jake. It was dangerous, but the Rue Bourbon concoction made him feel like taking risks. Or maybe it made him remember all the things he loved about Jake. "I wonder what Daisy says about me?"

"Only good things." Jake frowned a little, then glanced at Beau. "It's not always like last night. *I'm* not always like that. I'm sorry you saw that."

"I'm not." Beau hadn't realized it until that moment, but he wasn't sorry at all. "I need to know what I'm getting into. Tell me about the drinking."

Jake nodded. "It's not every night. In fact, it hasn't been like that for a long time. Not since I met you. I know you might not believe that."

"Then what happened?"

"After last weekend, I hit a bad patch. After you left, I… well, I missed reporting for this week's lift and lost my spot on the next one too."

"*Don't* put that on me." Beau hadn't meant the words to be so harsh, but he needed to say it.

"I wasn't. It's my problem. And it's not the right way to deal with a problem."

"Then why?"

Jake scooted away from the edge of the bed and leaned back on his hands. He didn't look at Beau. "It won't make sense, but let me try to explain. Before you make any decisions."

"Okay."

"I don't usually have trouble sleeping. That still makes me feel guilty. Part of me thinks I should be up at night, thinking about the crash, about my crew, about what happened. If I drink, then somehow it's not my fault I *can* sleep." He glanced at Beau, but without meeting his gaze. "I know a lot of guys with PTSD *can't* sleep. They relive things, can't stop thinking about it. I think I should be more fucked up." He let out a soft, ironic laugh that held no mirth. "And that's fucked up too. The tequila eases the guilt."

He was silent for so long Beau figured Jake was done. "Just tequila?"

"Occasionally bourbon. But no drugs. I promise." Jake took a deep breath. "When I met you, I felt really good. Because you wouldn't like me if I wasn't okay, so your liking me convinced me I was okay. Then last weekend I lost it again. I figured you had realized I wasn't good for you, and when you came back, it was too good. It brought back the guilt."

"So you feel guilty with me *and* without me? But for different reasons?"

"Hell, I don't know anymore." Jake hung his head. He dragged a hand from his forehead down over his eyes and held it there. His body shook the way it had the night before.

Beau put his arms around Jake and pulled him into his lap. He stroked Jake's cheek and forehead. He didn't understand what Jake was going through or what he needed. But Jake had told him the truth, and it felt good to have his trust. That he cared enough to share his pain and confusion with Beau. Beau leaned down and kissed Jake's head, the short hair spiky against his lips. Jake took one of Beau's hands, and they stayed there like that for a long time.

Then Jake sat up. "Beau, you're… you're a wonderful man and you deserve someone who *isn't* such a mess. I better go…." He stood and Beau grabbed his hand.

"Are you saying good-bye and that's it?"

Jake looked away and nodded, then pulled out of Beau's grasp and got halfway to the door.

"I'm not ready to say good-bye to you, Jake. So don't leave, or I will be." Beau's tone was forceful, authoritative, otherwise he suspected his own tears would win out. He couldn't breathe from the weight that settled onto his chest when he thought Jake might leave. He was scared, both for himself and for Jake.

Jake stopped and turned around, eyes dark, as if he was afraid to hope. "What?"

"Jake, I love you. I know you're not perfect and neither am I. But I think we're both better together than we are apart. If you can accept my issues, then I can accept yours. And I hope you'll let me know how I can help you."

"Really?"

"Of course. I'm here for you. I am really worried about the drinking. I won't lie and say otherwise. But if you're honestly trying to work on that, then I'm willing to help." Beau had been here before, more than once, and he was terrified of being here again, with Jake. Lies and broken promises had nearly killed him before, so Jake's honesty and ability to accept his problems meant he had a fighting chance.

"I threw all the bottles away. Got rid of all of them."

"I know."

"You looked?"

"Yes." Beau had felt terrible snooping before he'd left that morning, but he'd needed to know. Sure, Jake could buy more, but taking the small step of pouring them out was a step in the right direction.

Beau held his arms out and Jake stepped into them, pressing Beau's head against his chest and holding him tight. Then Beau pulled Jake down to sit next to him at the edge of the bed and drew him close for a kiss.

The door burst open and Laney stood in the doorway, staring at them. "You were supposed to put the music on!"

ON THE way home Saturday morning, Jake felt like he'd won the lottery. Beau loved him and was willing to give him another chance. Along with knowing he'd earned time in the simulator, he was getting his life back on track—or less likely to derail—thanks to Beau. When he pulled into the garage, he glanced at the motorcycle half-hidden under the protective tarp.

A hole opened in the pit of his stomach and filled with memories of his reckless late-night rides. But when he thought of Beau, the abyss closed, putting Jake back on solid ground.

He *should* take Beau out on the bike. He was coming later, for dinner, then to spend the night. Jake tried not to be upset that Beau wanted some time to himself on Saturday, but he understood and accepted his culpability.

He vowed to show Beau just how much he meant to Jake.

JAKE PICKED Beau up from the station and actually got out and opened the car door for him. Beau was torn between being flattered by the gesture and being a little annoyed. He didn't say a word as Jake slid back behind the wheel.

"I thought we could go into Old Town, unless you have something else you'd rather do." Jake pulled out of the station, turning in the opposite direction of his house.

Beau loved Old Town Alexandria but didn't think Jake would enjoy the charming colonial atmosphere. Boy, was he trying hard to get back in Beau's good graces.

"Sure, that sounds great. Good thing I'm dressed for it." Beau wrapped his pink-and-gray cashmere-wool scarf more tightly around his neck.

"Is it too cold? Okay, we'll go with Plan B."

"No, that's fine. Should cut down on the crowds." Beau squeezed Jake's knee and got a tentative smile in return.

They spent a couple of pleasant hours strolling along the cobblestone streets flanked by Georgian row houses of historical interest, and along the murky Potomac, which was lined with trees wearing the last of their autumn colors.

Beau stooped to pick up a crisp orange oak leaf. "Too bad the street sweepers are so diligent here. I wouldn't mind a few piles of leaves. It really makes the season. It's all too dirty in DC."

"Sorry I've only got pine trees at my house. We could plant an oak or maple, but you'd have to wait at least till next year for a pile of leaves."

Beau looked up from the leaf and directly at Jake. Where had that comment come from? The idea of Jake talking about the future, a future longer than a year... wow. He really didn't want to lose Beau, and it made Beau's heart melt a little. He reached for Jake's hand and tugged him along the path because he didn't know how to respond to what Jake had just said.

Jake squeezed back, then slid his arm around Beau's waist.

They stopped in front of a window at an art gallery on King Street.

"That has to be the ugliest thing I've ever seen." Jake shook his head at the green, yellow, and pink modern painting featured in the window.

"It might not be the ugliest, but it comes pretty close. I think Laney has an outfit by that artist."

Jake let out a sharp peal of laughter. "I expected you to give me some discourse on modern art."

"Let's go inside and see how ugly the rest of the stuff is." Beau was a little miffed by Jake's comment. Once inside he asked, "Do I do that? Give discourses?"

"No. I mean you know a lot about art and food. I learn something every time we're together."

"Is that just you being polite?"

"No. I like hearing about things I don't have much experience with. And I don't think Laney's clothes are all that bad."

"Only thanks to years of coaching. You should have—" Beau stopped. Crap, had he just outed himself as the fashion reporter? And the day had been going so well.

"You probably are the best-dressed journalist. Usually reporters are more casual, even scruffy. At least in movies." Jake grinned.

"Well... thanks." Best not to let on that Beau was about to have a meltdown and confess. "Oh, look at that!"

For twenty minutes they discussed what they thought the artist was trying to convey, making up ridiculously pompous interpretations of the pieces, peppered with arty-sounding jargon about conceptualizations and chiaroscuro, nonobjective art, and the use of tertiary colors.

"You seem to know a lot about art." A middle-aged couple had walked up, and the man asked Beau, "We're thinking of buying something that would be a good investment. Something to leave to our kids. Which painting would you suggest?"

Beau glanced at Jake, who was barely suppressing a grin, his eyes dancing with mirth. To keep from laughing, Beau looked away. "Honestly?" He risked another look at Jake. "None of them. Unless you particularly like them. I think they're hideous."

"Thank you," the woman said and tugged her husband away. "I told you these are crap. Just because you can't figure out what it means doesn't mean it's important art."

Jake grabbed Beau's elbow, propelling him out the door, and they both lost it on the sidewalk. Beau laughed so hard his sides ached, and Jake was gasping for air.

When they composed themselves again, Beau said, "Ironically all that horrible art really works up an appetite."

"Good timing. Sevilla Oeste is around the corner. Do you like tapas?"

"Hell yes. But on a Saturday, we'll have to wait until breakfast time, and we still might not get a table." The Spanish restaurant was at the top of all the local "best" lists.

"Unless someone made a reservation."

"You got a reservation? Who do you know?"

"Laney." Jake raised an eyebrow and threw Beau a look that made him want to jump Jake's bones right there. "I hope that was okay."

Beau pulled Jake in for a kiss that would have melted paint off the historically accurate walls.

"I guess that's a yes?" Jake asked when they came up for air. "I'm kind of warmed up now. Let's just go home."

"Uh-uh. We can fool around any time, but a reservation at Sevilla Oeste…." Beau put an arm through Jake's and they headed for the restaurant.

SUNDAY MORNING Jake watched Beau sleeping for several minutes, not believing how lucky he was to have Beau. To still have him. He hadn't completely fucked things up between them. Funny, sweet, sexy, beautiful Beau. Jake could go on.

"Thank you, Beau," he whispered.

Beau's eyes fluttered and he smiled in his sleep. Had he heard Jake, or was he dreaming of something else? Beau's smile made Jake want to give him whatever he wanted. He gently shook Beau awake.

"Sleeping Beauty, I brought you some coffee."

Beau sat up and blinked a few times. "What time is it?"

"About ten."

"How'd I sleep this late?" He paused, then nodded. "I remember. I guess the real question is why aren't you this exhausted?"

"I am. But Daisy woke me up. I'm on her schedule, remember?"

Beau sipped coffee, then kissed Jake. "Mmm."

"Me or the coffee?"

Beau sighed again. "Both."

"I think someone needs a shower."

"Do I smell that bad?" Beau sniffed in the direction of one armpit.

"No, I just want to get you into the shower."

"Oh, a dirty shower, not a clean shower?"

Beau's gravelly morning voice worked its magic on Jake and his cock swelled.

"Dirty it is." Beau looked down at Jake's tented boxers and wrapped a hand around his erection. "And getting dirtier." With a couple of strokes, he had Jake fully hard. "Now, Marine, get out of those shorts!" Beau mimicked a drill instructor, and Jake hopped up and followed orders.

They played in the shower until the hot water began to run out. Then they toweled each other off and Jake slipped into a pair of comfortably worn jeans and a thin honey-colored sweater nearly the shade of Beau's hair.

"How on earth do you manage to get dressed while I've barely wrapped the towel around myself?" Water droplets fell onto Beau's shoulders as he dried himself.

"Many mornings of not-so-sexy drill instructors timing me. Now it's second nature."

"Such a shame." Beau traced a finger down Jake's chest, then around a nipple. "I do like to watch you get dressed sometimes."

Jake grabbed Beau's hand and kissed the fingers. "Later I can take my clothes off and put them back on as many times as you want. Meet you downstairs. Take your time."

He hadn't meant it quite so literally, but by the time Beau came into the kitchen—impeccably dressed in ass-hugging chinos and a pale green sweater that looked soft even from across the room—Jake had breakfast ready.

"Bacon, poached eggs, and fruit."

"Poached eggs?" Beau asked as he sat down.

"Makes me feel less guilty about the bacon." Jake pulled out the plates he'd left warming in the oven and put them on the table.

Beau picked up a piece of bacon and looked it at lovingly. "I don't think I can eat again, not after last night."

"You are talking about dinner, right?" Jake put a bowl of sliced pears and melon on the table.

Beau let out a soft snort. "Yes. The other thing I've always got an appetite for." He pulled Jake close and rubbed his face against Jake's crotch.

Jake ruffled Beau's hair and settled into his chair.

Despite Beau's comments, he managed to consume several pieces of bacon and an egg.

"You still want to play in a pile of autumn leaves?" Jake asked as he started his second cup of coffee.

Beau looked up from the paper and his eyes sparkled. "What? I forgot I even said that. What did you have in mind?"

"A trip to a park where they don't rake up the leaves."

"Okay. Can we bring Daisy?"

Daisy thumped her tail and swiveled her good ear when she heard her name.

"I thought we might…." He paused, still debating, still considering taking the easy way out. "Might take the bike." There, he'd said it. Made the offer, taken the plunge. His heart thumped like it might break free, and he waited.

"Oh." Beau put the paper down and stared at Jake. "Oh. Yeah. I'd like that. If you're sure."

He'd given Jake an out, but Jake didn't take it. "I'm sure. Let's find you a jacket and we can go whenever you're ready."

One of Jake's old leather jackets almost fit Beau. It was a little loose on him but otherwise suited him well. There was an extra helmet in the garage, and Jake adjusted it for the proper fit. Then he pulled the tarp off the motorcycle and looked at it, wondering whether this was a good idea. When he rode, it had power over him, rather than the other way around. He rode it when he felt like letting go.

"Jake?"

Beau's voice startled Jake. The damn bike still controlled him. "Hmm?"

"You okay?"

Jake gazed at Beau, then at the bike, and back to Beau. The last thing Jake wanted was to hurt Beau. Taking him on the bike would keep Jake from doing anything stupid. Prove to Jake that he was in charge, not the darkness. With Beau, Jake wouldn't be tempted to cross that line. He got on the bike and had Beau climb on behind him. Then he started it. The engine thrummed with power.

"Oh yeah. I'm great."

RIDING THE Metro home Sunday night, Beau replayed their morning. He'd been unsure when Jake suggested they take the bike out, given that it had been such a sore point the previous weekend. In the garage, at first Jake kept his distance from the machine, as if it frightened him, but once they started out, Jake seemed to enjoy himself.

Beau certainly had. He loved the way the bike tilted around corners and the feel of Jake's hard body when Beau held on tight. He understood the excitement of speeding down the street, the bike's power humming through his body. With the visor open, he felt the wind on his face, accentuating the speed.

When they parked at Fort Foote, Jake no longer seemed wary of the bike. Beau had never been to this park, a former Civil War fort complete with two huge cannons still standing. They kicked their way through piles of leaves, sat on the cannons, took a bunch of photos, and fooled around in the woods. They tired themselves out and had a nap when they got back to Jake's.

"Daisy's looking at me like she knows I'm the one who didn't want to take her," Beau said as he and Jake relaxed on the couch. Daisy would have loved running at that park, and other people had dogs with them. He felt selfish for choosing his own desire for a ride that excluded her from the fun.

"She's perfected that guilt-trip look, so don't take it personally."

"We should definitely take her next time."

Daisy thwacked her tail against the wall as if she understood.

"Next time we will."

The way Jake said that sent the butterflies scampering in Beau's stomach. It sounded so natural, so possible: *next time we will*.

Even now, as Beau unlocked the door to his apartment, the words had the power to thrill him. There would be bumps along the way, but maybe this thing with Jake would really work.

Beau dropped his keys in the glass bowl on a stand near his door, and instead of clinking, they clunked as they hit the surface of the table. He stopped and looked at the bowl. It usually sat at one end of the table, and now it was centered. The other end of the table usually held his mail, but he'd tossed all the junk and left the surface clear before he left for Jake's.

What the hell? Was someone in here while he was away, or was he imagining things again?

Chapter 11

THE FOLLOWING weekend, Beau went to Jake's again. They were going to a party at the house of one of the officers who wasn't on the weekend lift, and Beau would stay until Monday morning.

Saturday afternoon Jake found Beau in front of the mirror in the hallway.

"Does this look okay?" Beau asked, turning for Jake to see his outfit. Jeans and a gray-and-black sweater.

"You look fine." Jake realized that wasn't the answer Beau wanted to hear. "You look great," he amended.

"Am I okay for your coworkers? What are they going to be wearing? Should I—"

"They're going to wear jeans and sweaters or long-sleeved shirts. They've been wearing uniforms for at least ten years, and on days off, most of them don't care much about clothes. It's more trouble to decide. Unless their wives or girlfriends pick something out. You're not there to impress anyone, just to have fun."

Beau stared at him for a moment, then nodded. "I don't know what they're expecting."

"They're expecting you to be nice, and if you don't like them, to not show it."

"I wouldn't be rude."

"Then you'll be fine." Jake liked that Beau cared to make a good impression, but he hadn't realized how out of his element Beau would be with a bunch of Marines.

When they arrived at Tim Alvarez's house, Beau was the center of attention with the pilots and their partners. But as the party settled in, Jake noticed for the first time how the men and the women gravitated to different parts of the house. At first Beau hung with the guys but didn't talk much as the conversation turned to work.

Then Beau wandered toward the kitchen for a drink, and Jake suspected he'd feel equally out of place with the women. He felt useless, not knowing how to help.

When Beau came back into the room, the discussion had turned to sports.

"Beau, who's your pick for the Super Bowl?" Alvarez asked.

Jake held his breath, knowing Beau wasn't into football.

"My team's already out of the running. 49ers. Not sure why they can't win more with that coaching staff."

"You from California?" a pilot named Alec Lowell asked.

"I went to grad school near San Francisco. I'm from Seattle originally."

"I'm from Washington. Went to U-Dub," another guy chimed in.

"Me too," Beau replied.

Jake relaxed.

Tim left to check on the food. For some crazy reason, he'd decided to grill burgers and steaks, even though it was December. He bundled up in a parka to monitor the cooking. By the time the food was piled high on platters, Beau had charmed the Marines and their partners.

"So, Styx, where have you been hiding Beau?" Alvarez asked.

"Sticks, like chopsticks? That's your nickname?" Beau raised an eyebrow at Jake.

Jake couldn't decide which question was more dangerous to answer. Thinking back to the night they met at the White House, he made a quick decision.

"Call sign. Not nickname. It's serious business for pilots and air crew." Jake tried not to smile, because most call signs were rude, ridiculous, or plain embarrassing. Lowball—Lowell's call sign—was one of the worst. But Jake had suffered through all three indignities at one point or another until he got a name that stuck. "And it's Styx, with a *y*."

"Like the river?"

"Not exactly," Jake hedged.

Paul Ryder let out a hoot. "You tell it right now, Styx, or we'll set you straight. Ah... well, you know what I mean." He went beet red to the top of his scalp, which was visible under his short blond buzz cut.

Jake groaned. "During training I had the unfortunate call sign of Woody."

"And not because of his name!" Ryder added.

"Thankfully, when I got my first tour, another guy was already Woody. Since I was pretty tall, and not as buff and manly as now"—the comment drew laughter—"they called me Sticks—S-T-I-C-K-S." He paused. It had to come out. "Then one night a bunch of guys were at some bar with a jukebox, and I'm told I started singing along to some Styx song... so they changed the spelling." Jake sped through the last part of the explanation as quickly as possible.

Beau laughed along with the rest of the guys. "Which one?"

"Which what?" Jake asked, knowing the rest was unavoidable.

"Which song?"

As if they had rehearsed it, Jake's buddies replied in unison, "Mr. Roboto." They practically pissed themselves laughing.

"He was so wasted, he was still singing in his rack at two a.m. Someone had to put a sock in his mouth." Ryder, now a major, had been in the same squadron as Jake back then, a few years ahead of him.

"Ryder's call sign is Bunion, like the thing on your foot. It's so much more embarrassing than Bunyan, like the lumberjack," Tim Alvarez added.

Jake nodded along as they finally got their laughter under control and wiped tears from their eyes. "Nugget," he said to Alvarez, "I wouldn't laugh too hard or I'll explain *your* call sign." To Beau he added, "Even Tim's wife doesn't know the real story." That deflected the laughter away from Jake.

"I guess it explains why the radio in your car is tuned to the eighties station. You just can't get enough, can you?" Beau asked with a wink.

A LITTLE while later, when Beau was going to the kitchen for a Coke, Jake asked, "Can you bring me another beer?"

Beau's smile faded. "Why don't you come with me?"

A few of the guys teased Jake that they weren't actually going to the kitchen, and Jake's ears heated up. In the kitchen he opened the ice chest and started to pop the top off a bottle when he spotted Beau's frown.

"What?"

"Are you going to drink that?"

"Yeah."

"I thought we talked about this."

"It's just beer." Jake put the bottle on the counter. "I have it under control. I told you I was better."

"I thought you meant you weren't going to drink. I didn't say anything about the first beer. Or the second, but…."

"At all?" Jake didn't remember saying that. "I don't have a problem most of the time."

"How do you know today isn't a problem day?"

"I don't know. Maybe because you're here."

"Last time I was here you had a problem."

"I'm okay now."

"Jake, I'd rather you didn't drink any more today."

"I can stop. Or don't you believe me?"

"I believe you. So, would you please stop?"

"I can stop. I don't want to. When I want to, I can. A couple more."

Beau took a deep breath. "Okay. I can let you drink more beer. And I *can* give you another chance. But maybe I just don't *want* to. Can you accept that?" Then Beau put his can of Coke down and moved toward the room where they'd dumped their coats.

Jake grabbed his beer, followed him in, and shut the door, ignoring a few catcalls from guys in the living room. "What are you doing, Beau?"

"Getting my stuff. I'll get a cab to the Metro unless someone is leaving soon who'll give me a ride."

"That's it?"

"Yes."

Jake started to bring the bottle to his lips and stopped. He didn't have a problem. He simply wanted a beer. What was wrong with that? It was just a beer.

Then he remembered the last squadron cookout. Someone had driven him home. That hadn't been the first time. But he'd been drinking only beer at those parties too. He looked at the bottle, then at Beau.

Would he really have to choose one or the other? That seemed unnecessarily harsh. What gave Beau the right?

"Who do you think you are to make that decision for me?" Jake's tone turned harsh.

Beau's features seemed to melt a little, and his eyes got dark and sad. "If you can't stop for your own good, Jake, and you can't stop for me, I'm afraid for you. Only you can make the decision. I want to support you, but I can't accept this becoming a regular occurrence. And please don't say it's just one party. There will always be another party, another excuse. I won't listen to excuses and apologies."

Jake started to raise the bottle unconsciously, again. He *wasn't* in control. Something else drove him. It could be force of habit, but it wasn't Jake's choice the way he had believed. He put the bottle down on the dresser and stepped away as if were a rattlesnake.

"That was harder than I thought," Jake admitted.

Beau reached for his hand. "I thought it might be. But I'm here. Be honest with yourself, and with me, and we can do this."

"What will the guys think?"

"Jake, not all the guys are drinking. Some of them are having soft drinks, or sparkling water."

"Really?" Why had he never noticed before? Drinking at Corps parties had been second nature.

"Do you want to go home now? Together?"

Jake nodded. He squeezed Beau's hand and stepped forward to give him a kiss.

The bedroom door opened and someone said, "Oh, sorry."

"We're getting our stuff," Jake said.

Beau thanked the hosts, said good-bye to the other people he'd met, and received warm farewells from everyone.

In the car Jake turned up the heat. He still had mixed feelings about Beau butting in like that, but as he pulled out of the driveway, he realized he had a clear head leaving a squadron party for the first time he could remember. It was a good feeling.

THE NEXT morning Jake asked Beau to help him get rid of all the alcohol in the house. The beer in the fridge. Some hard cider. Then the booze. It was embarrassing to realize he had quite a few bottles hidden around the house. But Beau helped him pour everything down the drain without any commentary or judgment.

"There's some pretty decent wine there," Jake said, staring at the wine rack in the dining room. "Should we pour that out too?"

"Was it expensive?"

"Some of it is. Maybe we can put it in a cabinet and lock it. I'll give you the key. Okay?"

"Sure. That's a good idea."

Jake found a lock and let Beau change the combination.

Then he looked up AA meetings nearby. "There's one on base," Jake said, scrolling through the list on his laptop.

"Do you want to go to that one?"

"What do you mean?"

Beau lifted a shoulder. "Everyone on base knows you by sight. You may not feel comfortable talking there. Then you may find excuses not to go."

Jake nodded, grateful Beau was there helping him through this. "I'll try a different one. But maybe it would be a good thing for other guys to see they're not the only ones going through this."

"I love how you want to help other Marines, Jake. It's admirable, and it's one of the things that makes me not want to give up on you. But first you need to think of yourself and getting better. Then you can offer something useful to someone else."

"You sound like you've been through this before. Did you have a problem?"

Beau shook his head and got a faraway look Jake hadn't seen since that night Beau had found him by the fire. "No. My mom does. She lied to herself even more than she lied to us kids and my dad. She had to nearly lose everything and everyone before she admitted needing help. Now she's a sponsor, and she's helped a lot of others. I don't want to see you go through what she did, or what she put us through. I can't watch that happen to anyone else."

"I wish you'd told me about that before." A huge lump formed in Jake's throat at the pain in Beau's voice, in his eyes. How much of it had he caused?

"It wouldn't have meant anything to you if I had. You weren't ready to hear it." He took Jake's hand. "As long as you're honest about the problem, and about the challenges, I will support you. As soon as you start lying or making excuses…." He shook his head. "I know you can do this. If you can survive all the other difficulties you've faced, you *can* do this."

That night, as he lay next to Beau in bed, Jake decided being with this amazing man was so much more satisfying than another drink. He hoped he could keep his promise to himself—and to Beau.

A FEW nights later, Jake surprised Beau with an impromptu visit, and Beau had to stuff a bunch of new samples he'd brought home from a spring preview show he'd attended that afternoon into the closet. He never expected he'd be back in a closet of sorts, but he still hadn't figured out how to come clean about his job. After all, Beau had expected honesty from Jake. It was a matter of time until reciprocity would rear its ugly head and Beau would have to face his own wildly colored music.

Thankfully they had dinner and some extraordinarily satisfying sex before the worst happened and the situation got stickier, and not in the good way.

Jake lay with his head on the pillow, smiling at Beau. And he should be smiling, after what Beau had just done to him. "So I was checking out some of your old stories."

"You were?" Beau's stomach clenched, so he asked in his sassiest voice, hoping to distract Jake. Either he still thought Beau was the other Beaumont, or he was going to call him on the fashion stuff.

"You never mentioned you were embedded with an Army platoon in Iraq."

Beau stopped breathing so his brain wouldn't be distracted from getting him out of this sticky situation. "I w—I mean, no, I didn't."

Jake didn't say anything, but Beau knew Jake's bright blue eyes were lasers capable of reading everything Beau was thinking on his face and in his brain. He gulped.

"You might have gotten me mixed up with another reporter at the *Daily* called Beaumont. Mike Beaumont."

"You weren't in Iraq?"

Beau shook his head, then studied his toes. "I'm on the features desk. I cover fashion." He mumbled the last word so even he couldn't tell what he was saying.

"Fast what?"

This had to stop, if only so Beau could get his heart rate back into the red zone, because right now it was in whatever was higher than red. The dead zone.

"Fashion. I'm the fashion reporter."

He waited. Watched Jake look around the room again. "Well, that certainly explains—" He paused and gestured to the room in general. "—this. It was fashion or home decor. I mean, a purple couch…. And that." He pointed toward the satin brocade-covered chaise longue Beau had recently acquired for the bedroom.

Ouch. That was a gorgeous couch, but Beau had bigger issues to contend with. "I didn't mean to lie to you. In a way I kind of thought you'd figure it out because of… this and me." He waved a hand toward the designer clothes he'd draped across the chaise longue.

"You never said you wrote news, so you didn't lie."

Beau hung his head. "It's fashion news. But I feel like I misled you. I didn't think you'd… think I was good enough for…." He gave up while he was behind.

Jake scooted closer and wrapped his arms around Beau's shoulders. He put his forehead against Beau's. "I don't care what you do. I love you, not your job." He kissed Beau softly, but Beau pulled away.

"You do? You love me?" Beau's heart rate shot up into the dead zone again. He hoped it wouldn't explode before they experienced some in-love lovemaking. Then he could die happy. Happy and in love.

Jake made a second attempt at the kiss, this one successful. "I'm not so good with words. That's your business. I'm about actions. I kind of thought you'd figure out how I feel about you, because…." He grinned the crooked smile and made Beau's heart melt before kissing him like he couldn't live without Beau.

This was going much better than Beau could have predicted, though maybe Jake's admission of love was a result of what Beau had done to him earlier.

"You want to help me break in the chaise longue?"

Jake scrunched his eyebrows up so they looked like they were connected. "Oh, you mean that super-gay little couch?"

The description wasn't far off. "Yeah."

"Your wish is my command." Jake stood and, to Beau's surprise and delight, pulled the top sheet from the bed and draped it over the chaise. "Now what would you like me to do?"

Jake sat and pulled Beau onto his lap and they kissed for a while. Beau rolled a condom onto Jake, applied plenty of lube, before straddling Jake's lap again. They discovered the little couch lent itself to a wide variety of positions, and exhausted themselves before exhausting its possibilities.

Jake lay along the length of the chaise and pulled Beau tight against him. "You really are full of surprises."

"Sorry." Beau played with one of Jake's perfect nipples in the hope of distracting him.

"You know I'm addicted to excitement. Don't ever stop surprising me."

As Beau finally relaxed, he was so glad he'd taken Laney's advice to give Jake another chance, and so glad Jake hadn't been upset at finding out about Beau's deception. Gazing into Jake's Caribbean blue eyes, Beau saw the light inside of Jake glow even more brightly.

JAKE LOOKED forward to Beau staying over that weekend. He'd had a rough week. He was still on slightly shaky ground in the squadron, and the Appaloosa missions were starting up again. He'd missed his Friday AA meeting because he couldn't leave the base in time, but he knew if he told Beau, he'd get an earful, even if he wasn't drinking again. Maybe he deserved it.

In the middle of the night on Saturday, Jake stared at the ceiling while Beau slept soundly next to him. Something about that annoyed Jake. How could Beau be so relaxed? Everything was easy for him. He didn't have to juggle real problems the way Jake did. He'd never understand why Jake wanted a few drinks now and then.

Jake got out of bed and went downstairs. He settled onto the couch, and Daisy hopped up next to him and set her head in his lap. Usually this was the time he'd crack open the tequila. Would Beau notice if he went to the store? Maybe he could get away with it. Jake glanced toward the stairs, heart heavy in his chest.

He was better than that. He hated these thoughts racing through his head. He didn't want to lie to Beau, but this restlessness was unbearable.

"Jake?"

Beau's voice startled him, and he turned toward the staircase. "What?" The word came out like gunfire.

"Are you okay?"

"Are you checking up on me?"

"No. I was just worried."

"Don't you have anything else to worry about? What else *could* you have to worry about?" Jake couldn't stop the anger from overflowing.

Beau came up beside the couch, looking hurt. "What's wrong? I thought you were doing better."

"What do you think? That a few meetings is going to make all the problems go away? That I'll suddenly feel guilt-free and happy? It doesn't work like that. And you should know that by now."

"What are you talking about?"

"You googled me, didn't you? After we met." What journalist worth his salt wouldn't google someone before they'd spent much time together?

"Yeah, I did."

"Then you read the stories about my medal, long before I told you. But you didn't ask me about what happened. We never talked about it until that night. You knew who and what I am." He needed to understand why he hadn't frightened Beau away yet. His emotions were like a roller coaster, but Beau remained steady through everything, even Jake's harsh words and insults.

Beau sat at the other end of the couch, with Daisy between them. A buffer zone he knew Jake would never cross. "I knew you would have a lot of bad memories. But I also know that's not all you are. You are much more than the sum of your bad experiences. I'm not ignoring them, but you don't give yourself credit beyond them. That's what has to change. Your perception of yourself and not my perception of you."

Beau's words left Jake speechless. He'd pushed Beau away in several different ways, yet Beau didn't give up. He always seemed to do the opposite of what Jake expected. Now Jake longed to understand more about this man who had burst into his life and brightened up the darkest corners of it. "I don't understand you, Beau."

Beau looked directly into the intensity of Jake's gaze, unafraid. "You told me you didn't like to talk about it, and you hated strangers coming up and asking you about one of the most personal experiences in your life. Why would I?"

"Even that first morning, you were hardly a stranger." Jake attempted a grin, but he couldn't summon much levity.

"But you weren't ready to talk to me about it. You got uncomfortable when I first asked, because I didn't know who you were when we met." Beau tilted his head and peered into Jake's eyes. "You don't remember that, do you?"

"I'm sorry if I jumped down your throat."

"You weren't sorry about jumping down my throat the night we met. And neither was I." Jake basked in the warmth of Beau's smile, even though he didn't deserve it.

Tension eased out of his body as he realized he hadn't fucked up everything good in his life.

Beau continued, "Of course I looked you up right away. If I'd known about the medals beforehand, I might not have walked up to you the way I did."

"I'm glad you did, though. And it means a lot to me that you never pushed me to tell you. I wish I'd trusted you sooner, but I was afraid to frighten you off." Jake chewed on his lip and looked at Beau. "I looked you up too. A couple of days later." He felt his neck heating up. He hadn't exactly played it cool, calling Beau so soon to set up a date, and now admitting he'd checked him out online too.

"Really?" It was Beau's turn to look cagey.

"I knew you wrote the fashion column, and I was waiting to see when you'd tell me."

"So you knew back on our first date, when I was trying to talk about military stuff?"

Jake nodded. Warmth curled through his belly at the embarrassment on Beau's face. Jake reached for Beau's hand and squeezed. "I liked how you tried to impress me. You *did*."

"I did?"

"Sure. That's why I called again and visited you...." Jake squeezed Beau's hand again. "I read the pieces you wrote in journalism school and when you worked at the *Post*, on health policy. They were really good."

"You're wondering how I ended up writing about the first lady's shoes instead of whether calling ketchup a vegetable has led to the decline in children's health and nutrition levels and a rise in childhood illness."

"Something like that. But I realized you wouldn't talk about it until you were ready."

Beau smiled. "Downsizing led me to be a journalistic whore. My next stop will be the tabloids. 'When Will Angelina Find Out Brad's Been Shagging Jennifer Again?'" Beau looked down at Daisy and stroked her fur. "The *Post* cut their staff, combined a lot of specialties, and I made a decision that I wanted to write for the *Post* more than I wanted to write something substantial. I transferred to fashion, but a year later they still cut my position. I'm hanging on by a spaghetti strap at this point." He smiled, and Jake was glad to see he was trying to make light of the situation.

"It's not that dire?"

"Not really. At the moment I'm not too worried. My boss likes me, but...."

"Everyone seems to like you. You have a nice way with people." Jake envied how easily Beau could talk to total strangers and make even the grouchiest of them break out in a smile—or at least stop frowning. It worked on Jake when he was determined to be an asshole, like a few minutes earlier.

"All I do is make sure to smile, and to make people feel good about themselves."

"It's more than that." It was that light shining out and warming everyone around Beau. At first Jake thought it was reserved for him and felt an uncomfortable jealousy at the way Beau lit up around others, but then he realized Beau did save something special for him, a warmer, deeper glow, one that set Jake's blood and body on fire with a single smoldering gaze. It was so powerful it could take Jake's breath away, make him dizzy. Even thinking about it had a powerful effect on his body and his mood.

"I don't know what it is, but I'm glad it worked on you." Beau pulled Jake's hand to his mouth and kissed the backs of the fingers, then turned it over and kissed the palm.

Jake loved the intimate gesture, and immediately felt guilty that their discussion had started out with his angry words.

If Beau didn't believe in him so much... well, Jake knew where he'd been heading before. He was so much better with Beau in his life.

Chapter 12

ON SUNDAY they took a scenic drive for lunch at a quiet country inn. It wasn't Jake's ideal Sunday morning, but Beau really wanted to eat there.

"Laney's been raving about this place for ages." Beau punched their destination into Jake's GPS, then reached out to squeeze Jake's knee. "She insists we need to get out of the city and unwind. The place is romantic and in the middle of nowhere, but they have incredible food."

Romantic and the middle of nowhere made Jake hate the place already, but the promise of a good meal and the way Beau's face lit up as he spoke made the trip worth it.

Despite GPS and his phone, Beau still got them lost on the way to the place, all the way out near Manassas. But the drive was nice—if you were into Civil War battlefields. It seemed every mile held another historical landmark sign, and Beau looked like he wanted to stop at a few, so Jake sped up. He'd stopped at more than his fair share as a teen on uncomfortable family holidays in a borrowed motor home, fighting incessantly with his sister as they bounced along highways winding through Arizona, Colorado, and Wyoming. Besides navigation he and Beau didn't talk much, which worried Jake. Beau usually had plenty to say, but it might take a little while for the awkwardness to evaporate as Jake worked through his drinking problems.

The restaurant was in a charming inn. The whole place smelled like the holidays—pine and cinnamon and delicious baked goods—and as soon as they walked inside, a hostess offered mugs of fragrant mulled wine or sweet cider. Beau tensed as, without thinking, Jake reached for a glass of wine, and when he opted for cider, he earned a room-brightening smile.

The lobby was festooned with pine boughs and smelled like the forest. Jake understood why Laney recommended the place. It was incredibly romantic, and to Jake's surprise, the ambiance grew on him. Maybe at some point in the future, he should bring Beau here for a weekend.

The atmosphere seemed to melt some of Beau's latent apprehension, because he put his hand in Jake's and squeezed as they walked across the lobby to the small, intimate restaurant. The dining room held ten or twelve tables, all of them full, but since Laney had used her reviewer's clout to make their reservation, the hostess seated them at the first open table.

"It's nice to know someone," Jake said. "I've never been given such great service."

"We've only just sat down," Beau said as he opened his menu. He sipped mulled sweet cider as he read. "I don't know how I can possibly choose one thing."

"Have everything if you want."

"And then when I gain six hundred pounds, you won't want me anymore."

"Yes I will. As long as you can still give good blowjobs." Jake winked and hoped the people at the next table, a couple in their late fifties or sixties, hadn't heard.

"Do you think that skill would deteriorate?"

"I hope not." Jake concentrated on his menu for a few minutes. He couldn't choose either. "Maybe I'll close my eyes, point, and see what I hit."

"Are you talking about choosing lunch or something else?" Beau asked in a sassy voice that Jake had thought he might never hear again.

"You've never complained about my aim before."

The server arrived to describe the specials, keeping their discussion from straying into more dangerous territory.

After a difficult decision, they ordered and snacked on fresh-from-the-oven cinnamon-dusted scones while they waited for their food.

"Beau, the White House holiday party is next week." Jake paused, watching Beau's face before continuing.

"I remember."

"Would you still like to go with me?" Jake wouldn't assume anything about their original plans.

"But I've got nothing to wear."

"I'm sure you can charm some bluebirds into making you just the right thing."

Beau burst into laughter, then put a hand over his mouth. Tears streamed from his eyes. Jake realized people were watching them.

"A big, strong Marine who can also make Disney princess jokes." Beau grinned. "I think I love you."

"Is that a yes?"

"Yes."

Jake reached for Beau's hand, turned it over, and kissed the palm. "I know I love you."

"That's a relief. Because I'm pregnant."

A plate crashed to the floor a few feet from their table, and Beau put his hands to his face again. Jake tried to avoid the gaze of the shocked server who'd dropped it, but he couldn't help laughing too.

Thankfully it wasn't their food, and their server brought heaping plates of omelet, hash browns, and eggs Benedict a few minutes later, after they had both composed themselves enough to eat.

Beau popped another bite of eggs Benedict into his mouth and closed his eyes in obvious ecstasy.

"I should tell you one more thing about the White House party." Jake took a sip of the delicious spicy cider, hardly missing alcohol. "My CO told me the Pentagon has you on some no-party list."

"I don't get it. Should I be flattered or offended?" Beau glanced at Jake with an easy grin.

"The Pentagon wouldn't approve you as my guest for the party. But as long as the White House security staff has vetted you, I don't see how the Pentagon can keep you away."

"You mean they might not let me in?" Beau's posture stiffened, and he put his fork down on his plate.

Jake shrugged. "I think we should go and see what happens. If they don't let you in, then we'll go somewhere else. Okay with you?"

Beau took a few bites of hash browns, then nodded. "I wonder if they got me mixed up with the other Beaumont. He's been extremely critical of the Pentagon plans to upgrade several satellites and install a newer than state-of-the-art communications system in the Pentagon building. It's a sensitive issue, and the Senate hearings are coming up."

"I didn't realize you kept up with that stuff."

Beau gave a charmingly guilty smile. "Remember how before I got up the courage to admit I was the fashion columnist, I read up on a number of military issues and Pentagon news so I'd have conversation topics for our dates?"

"Which is why you kept talking about military spending at the Burmese place."

Beau shrugged and Jake's heart melted. He'd never considered Pentagon wrangles over new digital communications romantic, but the fact Beau had tried to impress him made Jake love him more. And it cemented Jake's vow to get his act together, deal with his demons, and not give Beau any reason to leave him.

"Oh, look!" Beau leaned low across the table and nodded his head toward the hostess's stand. "But don't look."

Jake glanced over as subtly as possible and saw who had gotten Beau's attention: Young Colonel Sanders had arrived, and was led to a table in the far corner. He sat at a table that was already occupied.

"Looks like he's having a secret rendezvous with the cue ball," Beau said.

"Maybe they were doing more than talking in the White House too." Jake grinned. He didn't mention he knew the cue ball was General Graham and had flown the man around several times. The Appaloosa missions were not for public discussion, even with Beau.

Beau tried to look over, but he would have had to crane his neck in a particularly obvious way. "What are they doing?"

"Drinking coffee. They don't look particularly happy with each other. Probably not a romantic tryst after all."

"I'm dying to find out who Colonel Sanders really is!" Beau wiped his mouth with the fancy cloth napkin, then got up. He approached the empty hostess stand and casually leaned over so he could read the reservation book. The hostess came back, and Beau chatted with her for a few minutes, during which she smiled and blushed. Jake couldn't wait to hear what Beau was saying.

"Have you ever heard of Victor Mann?" Beau asked sotto voce when he returned. "The reservation is in his name. Interesting ménage…."

Jake shook his head, but he was already pulling out his phone and googling. "He's the head of Green Dynamics. I suppose that—"

"And look who else just arrived. Senator Bingham. He's the head of the Senate Armed Services Committee. He's also the grayest man I've ever seen. Gray hair, gray skin, gray suit. If ever a man was made for black-and-white photography, he's your guy."

Jake was impressed Beau recognized Bingham. Despite Beau's not-colorful description, Jake wondered about how this information fit with Beau's fashion-writing job. But the fleeting doubt was swept away a moment later when a fourth member of the group sat down.

"Look at that Astrakhan-collar coat. God, I hope it's fake and not made of adorable little lambs. Still, it probably cost a week's pay. That must be Mann, and he doesn't look like the kind to opt for faux fur. I think I hate him already, on principle." Beau glowered for a few moments until he pulled himself back together.

"So much for your ménage theory," Jake said, hoping not to have to discuss coats or satellites for the rest of the meal. "But that's an interesting group."

"It definitely is." Beau's eyes twinkled again, but he hardly touched the rest of his meal.

THE WHITE House Christmas party was the following Saturday. On Friday Beau headed for Jake's. He had to stand for most of the journey, pressed between a pastrami-scented man and a martini-scented one who looked to be a congressional staffer, based on the price of his suit and the brand of his shoes. Beau wished he could ignore details like that, but he found it impossible. At least he was free to make fashion-related comments around Jake. It was such a relief after hiding the truth.

They pretended to watch an artsy French film after dinner, but they soon gave up on trying to focus on the subtitles and gave in to focusing on each other until they exhausted themselves and fell asleep on the couch. During the night they got into bed and slept gloriously late. Daisy spent the night with Toby.

In the morning light, Beau noticed Jake's dress blues—hanging in the garment bag he'd lent him—on the back of the door. A dry cleaner's tag hung from the bag's zipper.

"I can't wait to see you in your stunningly irresistible uniform again. Can I play with your sword?"

"You already are."

Beau realized he did have his hand on Jake's dick at that moment. It made Beau awfully happy, so it was difficult not to touch it.

"And I feel suitably patriotic about it too." Beau gave it a squeeze, and Jake started humming the "Marines' Hymn." "But I'm talking about the other sword. When I saw you in that uniform, I thought about those recruiting commercials."

Jake frowned. "Those are pretty powerful."

"Is that why you joined the Marines?" Beau pulled his hand off Jake as the conversation grew serious.

"I'd be lying if I said I wasn't influenced. But not by the uniforms, and definitely not by the haircuts. I loved the idea of being part of a small, elite military unit. If I was going to join the military, it had to be the toughest branch." Jake had a faraway look in his eyes, as if thinking about a place he hadn't visited in a long time.

"Why did you want to join the military?"

Jake shook his head. "Maybe to prove something to myself. Maybe to prove it to other guys. I wanted to belong in a way I hadn't since I realized I was different and that meant I had a secret. I didn't want to look any different from other guys, but if someone was going to hassle me for being gay, I'd be able to pound him into the ground."

That surprised Beau. He hadn't sensed that kind of violence or fear in Jake except that one time weeks ago.

Jake picked up on Beau's thoughts. "I wouldn't actually pound anyone. But no one with a functioning brain is going to risk calling a Marine a faggot."

"Except maybe another Marine."

"You're not far wrong there."

"Jake, I have a hard time understanding how you can do what you do, fly under incredible circumstances." He thought back to the squadron party and how even though Jake's colleagues accepted and joked with him, Jake was still at some inexplicable distance from the others in the squadron. "Aside from knowing you'd be deployed to Iraq or Afghanistan, how did you manage during DADT? Why on earth did you want to get yourself into that situation?" Beau tried to laugh. "Or was it because you knew you'd be around a lot of really hot, fit guys?"

"That was part of my biggest fear. Too many hot guys to be attracted to, especially in boot camp, when you're in a lot of group showers."

"Sounds nice." Beau gave a campy grin, then got serious again. "I suppose at the time you were afraid you'd be found out?"

"Every single day. But it takes a lot of determination and self-discipline to get through boot camp, OCS, or TBS."

"TBS?"

"The Basic School. Sort of like graduate school after we get commissioned. But that was simply another layer of it. Even for officers. Maybe worse for officers."

Beau laid his head on the bed and stared at Jake, inches away. So close he could feel Jake's heat, his breath breezing over one ear. The demons inside would have to be fierce to bend a man like Jake Woodley. Beau was a little worried this discussion might awaken them, but he was here for Jake, in case.

"Then why join the Corps?"

"I wanted to fly. Sure, I could do that in the Air Force or Navy, but the Marines—they're the pinnacle of manliness. Maybe deep down I still felt I had to prove I was a man." Jake shrugged, but Beau saw a familiar pain and doubt in his eyes.

Beau had struggled with those same fears and needs. He'd found a different solution. He didn't respond, let Jake keep talking.

"I thought I wanted to fly fixed-wing—airplanes, fighters—until I saw my first helicopter during training. We did some exercises where they transported us in helos, and I got interested. Got yelled at for paying more attention to the pilot than to the drill instructor." Jake had a distant look as he clearly relived the moments.

Beau loved hearing Jake talk about this and seeing a look of satisfaction rather than pain or distress. He reached for Jake's hand and kissed his fingers.

Jake returned the soft kisses, then went on. "Once I got sent to flight training, it got easier to interact with the other pilots. We all had the same goals, the same desire to fly. We talked about little more than helicopters and flying, and that shared passion bonded us. Once we got deployed, it was all about doing a job and keeping guys from getting killed. I guess I proved myself well enough so that later when some guys found out I was gay, they didn't say anything. They already trusted me completely. If I'd been found out sooner, back in basic, there wouldn't have been that loyalty."

"There's really a bond between Marines? That strong?"

"It's hard to explain to anyone else. If the Marine Corps does one thing well, it's creating loyalty. To the Corps, to your fellow Marines, above any duty to country. No matter how different we all are when we join, there's a huge part of every Marine that's the same after we've been through training, and especially after a combat deployment. You have to know the next guy so well, not only to trust him with your life, but so you won't let anything happen to him."

Beau nodded. He'd watched documentaries about Marine training, seen how they broke down the recruits, then built them back up into fighting men. He wouldn't mention those or his other research, but hearing Jake explain it made everything come to life.

"Can you tell me a little more about your job now? Beyond the sound bites and headlines." He'd made a special effort not to ask more than Jake chose to share with him, knowing that despite being high-profile, the job involved a lot of sensitive information.

Jake raised his eyebrows for a split second. "You don't want to hear about my combat missions?"

"No. Not now. Unless you really want to talk about that."

Jake shook his head. "The squadron's called HMX-1. The *X* used to be for experimental because they did a lot of testing of new aircraft. Not so much in my unit. We don't do much more than fly the president, his staff, other dignitaries around." Jake's voice went flat and the light disappeared from his eyes.

"Why don't you like it?"

"I know it sounds ungrateful, but this job feels too safe, too easy. After being in Afghanistan, knowing I was supporting hundreds of guys on the ground, saving lives, killing bad guys. It's *too* much of a change. I'd rather fly the new aircraft they're developing."

Beau noticed with relief Jake mentioned saving lives, rather than obsessing over the two he hadn't. "So your job now is completely safe? Nothing can go wrong?"

"With a craft as complex as a helicopter, a million things could go wrong. We still have to make sure each flight is safe, and there's always the risk of a problem with equipment, or, in the worst-case scenario, being attacked, especially if we're flying the president."

"And you could respond to that?"

"Sure. After all the training, and the combat experience we have, anyone who attacks a lift would get blown away, whether it's an air or ground attack." Jake stopped and shook his head, then leaned over and planted a soft kiss on Beau's cheek. "I see what you're doing. And thanks." He lay down and pulled Beau in for a much more aggressive kiss. "Damn you, Beau, I really do love you."

"Prove it."

"Again?"

"Aren't you up for the challenge?" Beau reached out for Jake's cock and felt it. Then Jake gripped Beau's hand, and together they pumped until he was fully hard.

"What do you think now?"

"I don't know…," Beau teased.

Jake growled and rolled Beau onto his back, pinning his wrists above his head and rubbing his erection along Beau's abs. It was good and hard, and the friction from Jake's belly got Beau equally aroused. Jake leaned down for a rough kiss, still thrusting along Beau's hip and abs.

"Good. Feels. Good." Beau panted between the words. He loved Jake's weight on him, the heat and power behind the kiss. Every nerve ending was alive and singing. His nipples were tight, sensitive, transmitting every movement of Jake's body as it slid against Beau's.

Jake stopped moving and let go of one wrist as he reached for a condom.

"Keep moving," Beau whispered. "I'm close." He wasn't, but he would be if Jake kept doing what he was doing.

"Really?"

Beau nodded and Jake grabbed Beau's wrist and started moving again. Jake let out a surprised little sound, then moaned. "Oh, this is good."

He attacked Beau's mouth as he picked up speed and power and fucked Beau's torso.

The pressure and friction against his cock and nipples and the ferocity of Jake's thrusts had Beau coming much sooner than he wanted. But damn, it was fantastic. He pressed up against Jake as he spurted between their sweaty bodies, and he saw the glimmer of surprise in Jake's darkened eyes.

Jake shifted so he slid through Beau's slippery puddle, and soon he was writhing and grunting and gasping as he came against Beau's belly. The hot splashes felt good, and Beau let out a sigh until Jake swallowed the sound. But Jake lifted his head when he needed air and panted against Beau's cheek.

"My hands?" Beau said, and when Jake let him loose, he slid his palms along Jake's shoulders and back until they were on Jake's ass. He massaged the firm globes, pressing Jake harder against Beau's abs, cementing them together more firmly.

They kissed some more; then Jake rolled off Beau and turned toward him.

"I've never done that with my clothes off." He traced a finger through their combined semen. "Makes a hell of a mess."

"Hell of a mess." Beau grinned as Jake smeared the puddle all the way up to Beau's nipples, then licked his fingers clean. "Mmm, that reminds me. When's breakfast around here?"

Chapter 13

"I HOPE we don't have any trouble with the security check," Jake said as he and Beau stood in line the following evening to get into the White House for the holiday party. The cold air froze the inside of his nostrils when he forgot to inhale through his mouth.

"I don't care. If I can't get in, you should go without me, at least for a little while."

Jake turned to see whether Beau was joking, but the warm smile and his familiar smoldering brown eyes told him Beau was completely serious. And the smile warmed Jake up a little too much. "I can't. I wouldn't."

"The whole place is decorated. I saw some photos from a shoot we're running tomorrow. It's lovely."

"Then I can't see it without you."

Beau took Jake's hand in his and kissed it, then let go. "I'm sorry. I forgot the rules."

"I'm sure that one kiss won't get me in trouble." Jake had reminded Beau of the Marine Corps' ban on public displays of affection, and he glanced around to make sure neither Colonel Lewis nor Lieutenant Colonel Monroe were nearby.

The woman behind them had a huge smile on her face, and considering her escort was talking to someone else in line, Jake suspected it was because she could see how head-over-heels in love with Beau he was. He hadn't realized the extent of his feelings until that moment. It was more than the new relationship phase. Sweet, considerate Beau wanted to make sure Jake didn't miss out on a once-in-a-lifetime party.

"The food's supposed to be really good. You should have heard Laney going on about it."

"Is she here?"

"She was trying to get in, but her friend in the White House Mess might not have as much pull as she hopes."

"We should take some leftovers for her."

"We can put them in your lid."

"Cover. It's called a cover. Not lid." Jake couldn't suppress his laughter.

"Whatever it is, you look so handsome I kind of want to do something inappropriate while we're standing on line." Beau stepped a few inches closer but didn't touch Jake. "Or we can reenact our first meeting…."

"You know what you're doing to me right now?" Jake whispered.

"I have a pretty good idea."

The line moved forward. They had progressed to the space heaters, where a group of teenage carolers wearing thick scarves and almost obscenely fuzzy mittens serenaded—distracted—the freezing guests. Jake's ears were so cold he was ready to yank a woolen cap off the nearest kid. Sure, it was easy to have a big smile on your face when you were wearing mittens and a thick coat. He decided to grow his hair as long as he could get away with until spring.

When they got to the security checkpoint, Jake handed his invitation to the Secret Service agent and went through the metal detector after being reminded to remove his sword. Of course, the brass on his jacket set the alarm off. Someone else told him he couldn't bring a sword into the White House, but it would be held for him until he left the party. Another agent let him through the barrier where he started to unclip the scabbard from the sling attached to his belt.

"No one said he couldn't wear the sword last time we were here," Beau chimed in. "He flies the president's helicopter. I'm sure he's safe enough even with a sword."

"The president wasn't at the last event," Jake said. He glanced around to see other people in line watching with interest. From their expressions, they were with Beau on this.

"Let me ask." The agent mumbled into his wrist.

"It's fine. I'll leave it here." Jake really didn't want to let the sword out of his sight, but he didn't want this to keep Beau from attending the party. "Or go in without me while I deal with this."

Beau reached for Jake's hands and pressed them back toward his belt. "No, it's not okay. It shouldn't be okay. You served your country and went through a hell of a lot to earn that sword and come back here to wear it."

People in line expressed their dismay at this situation.

"Okay, you can wear the sword in. Sorry, Captain." The agent waved Jake and Beau through to the entrance door.

A few people cheered, and Jake felt a familiar unpleasant weight on his chest at being the center of attention. But he loved how adamant Beau was about the issue.

Once inside, Jake stepped out of the flow of people to reclip the sword scabbard to the sling hanging from his belt. "I guess you passed the security check, too? I wasn't paying attention after the metal detector."

"They didn't even ask for ID. I guess you distracted them enough." Beau grinned.

"What? That's not good either. I wonder who else got in who shouldn't."

"Are you saying I shouldn't be able to get in?" Beau narrowed his eyes.

"No, but they should have screened you." Jake glanced around to see who else was coming through the door.

"I'm teasing. They looked me up and let me through. But that sword trick might help us crash other parties around town." Beau passed a table with mulled wine and started to reach for two cups, then moved on.

"Beau, go ahead and have some. It'll warm you up."

"We'll find something else warm." At another table farther along, they found a server with a tray of Mexican-style hot cocoa. Beau grabbed two cups.

Jake reached for one, and Beau moved that hand out of his reach. "These are mine, buddy. Grab your own."

"Grab my own what?" Jake asked. "But I'm the one with frozen ears, after serving my country with a shaven head…. So gimme a cup."

"You're right. You deserve this." He handed the second cup to Jake. "Besides, you look so hot in that dress uniform, I barely need this to warm up."

Beau's jokes still caught him by surprise. Jake liked that. He'd never met anyone like Beau, and certainly never dated someone as fun and kind and so damn good for Jake. Except for a few days, he'd been on cloud nine—and not drinking dangerously—almost since the day they met.

Still, the idea of drinking cocoa at a holiday party made him feel like a teenager. But after he took a sip of the rich chocolate blended with cinnamon and spicy chili, he reevaluated the situation.

Once they got inside the main party, the heat made Jake pull at the collar of his dress blues jacket. A crowd bunched up to drop coats off at the cloakroom. Too bad Jake couldn't leave his uniform jacket there. Beau hadn't worn a coat over his tux, so they bypassed the human traffic jam and made their way to the first room.

One of the smaller ballrooms had been set up with half a dozen buffet tables, including a carving station with juicy prime rib, sweet glazed ham, and more turkeys than Ben Franklin could have imagined. The pilgrims would be in a food coma with this much delicious fare in front of them. The other tables had a variety of finger foods. Jake and Beau made their way around the room to see what was on offer.

"You want to eat first or wander some more?" Jake asked.

"I'd like a little snack, then I want to gawk at the holiday decorations." Beau gave Jake a tentative smile. "Is that okay?"

Though Jake had less than zero interest in decorations, he wouldn't dream of keeping Beau from enjoying that aspect of the White House at the holidays. This was Jake's second holiday party, so he wasn't as overwhelmed as he'd been the year before.

Watching Beau's face light up like a kid on Christmas morning every time he spotted something special was sheer pleasure. They spent what felt like ages in the Blue Room as Beau examined the ornaments on the official White House Christmas tree.

"There's one thing you need to sample before we leave the buffet area," Jake suggested. "The eggnog here is to die for."

"You sound like Laney." Beau grinned and his eyes shone with pleasure. "But if it's got alcohol, I don't want any."

"I think they have two versions. And you don't have to abstain because I am. You're making me feel guilty."

"Then let's try some."

They zigzagged around the other guests as Jake steered Beau toward the drinks table. Half a dozen servers in crisp white shirts and black pants poured wine or ladled eggnog. Soft drinks were also available, but not many people seemed to choose them.

Jake stepped forward to take one small crystal cup each of spiked and virgin eggnog and returned to Beau.

"Cute cups," Beau said with a frown.

"This stuff is strong, so a little goes a long way. Pace yourself." Jake held up his cup. "This one is booze-free."

Beau shook his head.

"It's a White House holiday tradition, so treat yourself this one time. You know Laney would murder for a chance to drink this."

"In that case." Beau beamed and clinked his cup against Jake's, and they sipped.

"Whew, it goes down nice and smooth, then it leaves a trail of fire down your throat." Beau fanned himself.

"Exactly. The Navy runs the White House Mess, and you can be sure they know their way around a bottle of rum." Jake grinned. "Do you think I've earned a sip? A little one?"

Beau looked directly into Jake's eyes so intently he could tell probably what Jake had been thinking three years ago.

"Sure. Have a sip."

Jake took the little cup from Beau and sipped. It was stronger than he remembered. It tasted great, so smooth and creamy, with the kick the virgin nog didn't have. He could drink ten cups of this. He felt Beau's stare and took a deep breath, waiting to see how difficult it would be hand the cup over.

Maybe this was Beau testing him. Jake smiled and gave the cup back. Beau set it down, unfinished, on one of the silver trays held by a staff member.

Had he passed? Or had he failed by simply asking? Beau gave no indication of what he was thinking, but he slipped his arm through Jake's and led him back through to the Green Room and the Red Room. The decor in each area represented a different period style of holiday decorations, in keeping with the first lady who had furnished the room.

"I can take photos?" Beau asked.

"I guess." Jake looked around and noticed other guests snapping shots, with none of the ubiquitous hulking Secret Service agents blinking an eye.

Beau pulled a tiny camera from his inner breast pocket and started taking photos. He had Jake pose in front of a beautifully decorated Christmas tree in the Red Room, and someone else offered to take photos of the two of them. Beau was enjoying himself so obviously, Jake was glad he hadn't been turned away at Security. It wouldn't have been any fun coming here without him.

After viewing all the decorations, they filled small plates with delectable foods from around the world and sat to enjoy them.

"It's not anywhere near as crowded as the last party," Beau said.

"This one is limited to White House and Executive Office staff. Apparently there are several different holiday parties for different levels of staff, and the president doesn't attend all of them."

"He's coming to this one?"

"So I've been told. They usually don't say when he'll show up, but you'll know once the crowd starts shifting. There will be a receiving line if you want to meet him."

"Really?"

"Do you want to?" Jake didn't have to ask, but he liked the flicker of exasperation that traveled across Beau's face.

"Of course I do."

BEAU WAS having the time of his life, though he still hadn't processed how he felt about Jake wanting some eggnog. He'd save that for later, but he had made Jake spend more time around the fancy decorations as a fairly harmless punishment.

But the night was definitely improving. They had barely finished their food when word went around the room that the president and first lady were at the party, receiving guests outside the large State Ballroom in the East Wing. The line moved fairly quickly, but as they got closer, Beau noticed the president made a point to say something to each of the guests as he shook their hands. Butterflies battled with prime rib in Beau's stomach, and he wished he hadn't eaten anything.

When they were right in front of the president, Beau realized he was even handsomer up close, though he also looked older and more tired than he did on television. All this chatting and handshaking was probably no fun. The man had to do this almost every day, on top of keeping the free world free.

"Nice to see you here, Captain Woodley." The president held his hand out to shake Jake's, and Beau couldn't help being impressed that the president knew Jake by sight. "I hear you're on your way to becoming my official pilot."

"Yes, sir. I'm working hard on that. This is my guest, Beau Beaumont."

"Nice to meet you, Beau. You write for the *Daily*, don't you?"

"Y-yes, sir. N-nice to meet you." Beau's hand shook as he stuttered his way through the most inane thing he'd ever said.

"I think Beau's the only one who liked the red dress I wore to the dinner for the president of Spain last month. Thank you, Beau." The first lady shook his hand and gave him a lovely smile.

"I thank you too, Beau." Then the president added more quietly, "Red usually isn't her color."

Beau's heart was still going like a jackhammer as he moved away in a daze.

"You made quite an impression," Jake said, giving Beau's hand a quick squeeze.

"I sounded like an idiot."

"Everyone does the first time. I could barely reply the first time he said good morning to me."

Beau frowned. "I didn't realize you'd met him more than once. But I was hoping you'd say I didn't sound as dumb as I thought I did. He seems to like you."

Now Jake looked uncertain. "It does seem that way. I'm as surprised as you are."

From the other room, the music floated through the door, audible over the guests' voices.

"Want to dance?" Beau asked.

"If you do."

They made their way to the large ballroom, where a small orchestra played a stately waltz. Or maybe it was a foxtrot. Beau hadn't done much ballroom dancing, and everything sounded the same to him.

"I can't dance to this." Beau started to leave, but Jake held on to his elbow.

"Sure you can. We'll start out slowly."

Jake put an arm around Beau's waist and held the other up for Beau to clasp, before moving them to the edge of the dance floor. "Follow my lead. I'll count for you. Start with the left foot.... Left, two, three, four." Jake counted and directed Beau, not reacting when Beau trod on his foot like an elephant. Marines really were tough.

Beau concentrated so hard he was afraid to say anything, but after a few minutes, he started to get into the rhythm and feel more comfortable as Jake moved them carefully around a safe little patch near one corner. He liked having Jake's arm around him and loved how confident Jake was. Beau's previous attempts at dancing with another man had felt like a battle for control. With Jake, it felt almost effortless and very enjoyable to let him set the pace and direction.

When the first song was over, Beau was actually disappointed.

"This one is a foxtrot," Jake said and talked Beau through the steps and count before they started moving again.

Jake stepped away from Beau as the foxtrot ended. "Let's take a break."

"What's next?"

"I need a little cool air and some water."

"That was fun," Beau said as they sipped water and watched the couples whirling around the room. They formed a mosaic of color interspersed with elegant black and white and the occasional flash of a military uniform.

"Glad you think so. Next time, try not to grip my hand so hard." Jake held up his left hand to show Beau the red marks his fingers had made. "And try to relax and enjoy yourself. It's okay to mess up."

Beau looked away.

They took to the floor again for a very slow version of the waltz "Shall We Dance" from *The King and I*. Beau hummed along against Jake's ear and imagined them whirling around the ballroom like Deborah Kerr and Yul Brenner. It was one of his favorite songs from the film. He used to whirl around the room singing whenever his family watched the film.

Soon the orchestra took a break and a DJ took over, playing more modern dance music.

They got back on the dance floor when a Madonna song started. Jake looked like he was thrilled to be revisiting the eighties.

"I wonder if they take requests." Beau grinned. "How about 'Mr. Roboto'?"

"Very funny. Go ahead. I'm not sure you can dance to that one."

Beau felt much more comfortable, and he and Jake were having a great time, when a low murmur went around the room behind them. Before Beau realized it, the president and first lady were on the dance floor. Since Beau and Jake were near the outside, the president had moved up near them.

"Mind if we join you?" the president asked and started dancing along to "Like a Virgin." It was surreal. While the four of them formed a square, the president made eye contact with Beau and Jake as well as his wife.

OMG, I really am dancing with the president! Beau nearly had to pinch himself as he shimmied and shook his booty along with the leader of the free world.

When the song ended, the first couple moved on and joined in with some other couples, but Beau still understood it had been a special moment. He didn't know of any other president who had danced with two men in public.

Once the orchestra came back, the president and first lady stayed on the dance floor for a few songs. Later, when they headed out of the ballroom, the president approached Beau and Jake and moved close to Jake to whisper in his ear. Then he saluted and left the room.

Jake winked at Beau and refused to tell him what the president had said, no matter how much Beau glared at him.

"You do realize you just lost your chance to relive the night we met." Beau tried sexual blackmail, to no avail.

"That's okay. I'm still happy to relive the cab ride." Jake's sexy glance had Beau's resistance falling as parts of his anatomy did the opposite.

And as Jake kept his promise on the ride home, Beau felt only the tiniest twinge of guilt over the blackmail. Then again, he was distracted from thinking of much but Jake's hands and mouth.

Later, as they crawled under the covers in Beau's apartment, he was too on edge to sleep. "It wasn't a slow dance, but still I got to dance with the president. It was one of my fantasies, you know?" Then Beau began singing "I Could Have Danced All Night."

"The ball is over, Eliza Doolittle. Come here and warm me up."

"I'll keep singing until you tell me what the president whispered in your ear," Beau threatened.

"Fine." Jake let out a loud sigh. "I'll tell you. But please stop the torture."

"I have a nice voice."

"During the day you have a decent voice. At two a.m., it's not quite as nice."

Beau rolled with his back to Jake and pressed his toes against Jake's warm skin until he roared.

"My God, you've got ice cubes instead of toes!" Jake kissed Beau's shoulder. "That's got to be worse than waterboarding. I'll inform the UN."

"You got waterboarded?" Now Beau felt like a total idiot for not understanding what Jake had been through in Iraq and Afghanistan. He couldn't keep his voice from wavering with fear for Jake, even now. He craned his head to look over at Jake.

"Close enough, during resistance training. All pilots have to take it, in case we get captured." Jake paused, clearly guessing what Beau was thinking. "I never got waterboarded in real life, though."

"Oh. Good." Beau reapplied the toes.

"Fine. You win. You win."

With a satisfied grin, Beau rolled over. "What did he say?"

"He said you've got a cute ass." Jake reached across Beau's hip and gave said ass a squeeze.

Beau smacked the hand away. "Well, he can tell me to my face—or to my ass, in person. And till then, I'm saving it for him."

Then he treated Jake to another chorus.

Chapter 14

JAKE MANEUVERED the helicopter, following the curve of the Potomac, glancing over at Major Landau in the copilot seat to his left. He concentrated on keeping his breathing steady and not gripping the cyclic too tightly. The controls were so responsive, even a whisper of pressure could send the aircraft too far left or right. Up ahead, the pale column of the Washington Monument thrust toward the clouds like an albino giant's penis. The thought brought a smile to his face, and he used too much brainpower pushing the irreverent idea from his thoughts.

The helo tilted by millimeters, enough to throw everything off. When Jake corrected course, he overshot slightly and lost altitude. He pulled up on the collective to ascend, making simultaneous adjustments with the pedals to stabilize the craft. At one hundred feet off the ground, he was less than halfway up the monument's full height, and he saw the detail of the white blocks far too close to his window.

The next thing he knew, the aircraft was flying at high speed directly at the midpoint of the column. He couldn't correct quickly enough, and the side of the Sea King scraped against the monument, breaking the rotor blades and sending the aircraft spiraling as the ground rushed toward him in a sickeningly familiar scene.

Everything went black.

"Jake, you have to concentrate."

Jake fought to catch his breath as the major shook his head. The simulator was so realistic, he'd felt like they'd hit a brick wall, though they hadn't experienced the actual crash to the paved plaza at the base of the Monument.

"I am. I was." Jake's body shook from terror, though they'd been safe in the simulator in the hangar at Quantico. Then, to his horror, he burst out laughing. He couldn't control that any better than he had the Sea King. He'd logged so many hours in helos, it felt as normal as driving a car, yet his muscle memory deserted him when he needed it most.

"Let's take a break. Decaf only for the rest of the day. Stop trying so hard."

They headed to the break room for a much-needed timeout.

"I don't know what happened." Well, he did, but he couldn't tell the major he'd imagined flying past an albino phallus, could he? "How many tries do I get?"

"It's not a video game. You have as many as you need to get it right," Major Landau said.

Jake sipped peppermint tea and tried not to picture losing his posting to HMX-1 and being asked to resign his commission. "I need to pass this test."

"No. You need to focus on the flying. You've done this enough times it should feel like breathing. Second nature. Let your instincts take over the controls. In combat, you didn't think first, did you?"

"Hell no. If I did, I would have had a breakdown. The key is not thinking. But I'm not flying to save anyone's ass here. The pressure is off. Well, it's a different kind of pressure."

"Then imagine the monument is an enemy aircraft."

"Better than a big dick," Jake muttered under his breath.

The major laughed. "You definitely need to get over BDS." Big dick syndrome, the pilots called it.

It sent Jake into another fit of laughter. "Sorry, but it might be impossible for *me*."

The major's neck turned a shade that would make a lobster jealous. "Let me rephrase that."

Jake got back into the simulator and purposely flew right into the monument, to get it out of his system. Then he performed two perfect landings on the South Lawn before steering the Sea King to Camp David, where he landed perfectly in daylight and at night.

"Good work, Styx. We'll do another practice run in the morning, and then I'll have you run the simulator exam sequence. I think you've done enough for the day."

"Thank you, sir." Jake pulled his headset off and hung it up in the simulator. He went back to the break room for the required half an hour. He hadn't suffered a bout of simulator sickness for a long time, but protocol still required the pilots to take a break before driving. Newer pilots occasionally experienced dizziness, fatigue, headaches, or nausea. Jake had been flying so long, and under such extreme conditions, he barely reacted, but today the symptoms returned with a vengeance.

ON THE way home, a strange sense of peace settled over Jake. His career was moving back on track. He hadn't fucked anything up lately, unless hitting the monument in the simulator counted. He'd smoothed everything over with his CO, he was back on rotation as copilot for the president, and he was making good progress toward qualifying as pilot.

And his relationship with Beau had never been better.

To Jake's surprise, that last point had become more important than the others. He'd always been so career driven and never let a relationship get in the way. Sex was easy to get when he wanted it. But since he'd met Beau, the idea of having the stability of a boyfriend proved more and more enticing, and more important.

In the past Jake avoided giving anyone too much attention, and now he was the one who felt slighted if Beau was working late or hanging out with his friends instead of with Jake. The past few weeks, Beau had spent more nights at his own place in DC. Jake still wasn't sure if it was left over from their previous difficulties, or because Beau preferred to spend more time with Laney.

Not that Jake would ever tell Beau how to spend his time, but he'd gotten so used to a good-night phone call when they spent nights apart that he missed the routine when Beau wasn't available.

As Tim Alvarez would say, Jake was growing up. He'd be an adult any day now.

Jake turned into the driveway, spotting Daisy's nose smashed against the front window as he pulled slowly into the garage.

It was cold and dark, but he took her for a walk to work out the day's tension. Then he had an enjoyable evening at Jenna's house for dinner. Toby asked a million questions about the holiday party and insisted Jake show him photos.

"You and Beau got to dance with the *president*?" Toby was practically vibrating with excitement over Jake's stories. "Is he as tall as he looks on TV? Is he a good dancer? What did you eat?"

The questions came nonstop, and Jake struggled to get more than a few bites of food until Jenna halted the interrogation until after dinner. For dessert, they had warm apple pie with rich vanilla ice cream and hot chocolate. Jake forced himself to waddle across the street, and he vowed to set the alarm an hour earlier than usual for a few weeks so he could get in an extra mile or two to burn off dinner and the rich food he'd indulged in at the holiday party.

THE FOLLOWING morning, after a satisfying run that left him loose-limbed and relaxed, Jake made his way to Quantico earlier than usual, so he was calm and ready when he approached the simulator for his exam. He spotted Lieutenant Colonel Monroe talking to Major Landau, and Jake's shoulders knotted instantly.

Was Monroe going to do his check ride in the simulator? All Jake's confidence ebbed away and his head spun. He gave Monroe and Landau a stiff salute and held his breath.

"Good luck, Jake." Monroe nodded, scowl-free for once, and walked away.

"Ready?" Landau nodded toward the simulator door.

Jake pressed his lips together and rotated his shoulders to loosen the muscles. "Yes, sir." He took a deep breath and entered the simulator.

The major settled into the copilot seat and had Jake do a few easy maneuvers before having Jake do the full preflight checklist, starting the run from Quantico to the White House and then to Camp David and back again. Jake had to fly the route twice during the day, twice during simulated night, then twice during inclement weather—a windy thunderstorm that tested every ounce of his skill maneuvering the huge helo, then a relatively calm but blinding snowstorm.

Despite his smooth performance, when Jake set the Sea King down again at Quantico, he was practically drenched in sweat, though outside the "helicopter," snow still raged around the aircraft.

"Excellent, Jake," Major Landau said.

Jake knew by the major's use of his name that he probably hadn't done too badly. When he fucked up, Major Landau and Lieutenant Colonel Monroe called him Woodley or by his rank. The major jotted notes on his clipboard as he'd done during the exam.

"You passed. Congratulations."

"Thank you, sir."

"Let's take a few minutes to go over the video of your flights."

It was Jake's turn to take notes as the major gave him tips to avoid the minor problems he'd had on the South Lawn and then again during one night approach to Camp David. Jake asked a few questions; then, over lunch, they discussed the next steps in Jake's training. The major dismissed him for the day a few hours early, and Jake was surprised to leave the building and walk out under a clear gray sky rather than a raging snowstorm. Sometimes the simulator felt so realistic he forgot it wasn't.

As soon as he got home, Jake walked Daisy. Later, with his feet up in front of the fire, he called Beau.

"Got some news," Jake said. "Do you have a few minutes?" Usually he didn't call Beau during work hours, though Jake doubted any real-life fashion emergencies would keep Beau from answering the phone, but sometimes he was difficult to reach during working hours.

"Sure. You okay?"

"Fantastic."

"I like the way that sounds. Tell me." Beau's voice came across the miles, warm and liquid, as if he were sitting next to Jake, and the sound of it got Jake a little more aroused than he would ever admit to Beau.

"You busy this weekend?"

"I have a fashion show to attend Friday afternoon, then I'm done for the week. Why?"

"I kind of lied to you the other night." Jake held his breath and hoped Beau's sense of humor was in place today.

"About what?"

"About what the president said to me."

"You mean about my ass?"

"Yeah."

"That's not really news." Beau chuckled, and Jake felt the tension drain out of his shoulders. Not so much a little bit lower. He shifted in his seat.

"He told me it would be okay to have a guest when I do my training at Camp David."

"*Camp David?*" Beau was probably bouncing up and down. "You're going to Camp David?"

"For a few days of training. We practice landing and taking off about a thousand times, day and night."

"And you're staying over?"

"Yeah. There's a lot of night practice. As long as I pass the simulator exam."

"When's the exam?"

"Today."

"And if you pass, then you'll be going? That's fantastic. I'm kind of jealous, and I'll miss you."

"Not just me. *We'll* be going."

"The squadron?"

"No. You and I."

"We? Really?" Now Beau's voice telegraphed his excitement.

"We *are* going. I passed."

Loud whoops of delight erupted through the phone, and Jake held it a few inches from his ear. Even Daisy's head shot up at the noise, and she scrambled behind the easy chair.

"I take it that's a yes to the invitation?"

"Hell yes! What should I wear? Is the president going to be there? Did he actually say *anything* about my ass?"

Jake's mood soared even higher with Beau's excitement. "Sorry. He did not. I'd have to defend your honor if he did."

"Then why did he whisper to you?"

"I guess it was in case you weren't the guest I might want to invite."

"What do you mean?" Beau paused, and Jake could tell he was upset at the thought. "I thought we're…. I'm not seeing anyone else, and I didn't think you were."

"I'm not." Jake wished he could reach out and stroke Beau's cheek until he relaxed. "Shhh. Don't worry about that. And I've never brought anyone to any of these events. You're the first guy I've taken home to meet my president."

Beau burst out laughing. "Really?"

"Really. So, do you want to stay over at Camp David for a night or two?"

"Try and stop me." Then Beau's laughter stopped. "Are we allowed to have sex there?"

Jake grinned and imagined himself and Beau in one of the officer cabins. "Try and stop *me*."

Chapter 15

LATE FRIDAY afternoon, Beau shivered at the entrance to Huntington Station. He had gotten a brand-new coat, a russet-colored wool blend Ralph Lauren that looked fantastic, but he left it at home in favor of a long china-blue peacoat. He had paused in the hallway before he left his apartment, gazing longingly at the Ralph Lauren, but decided not to make any russet-colored waves this first weekend with Jake's senior officers.

The wind whipped around his ears, and he pulled the cashmere scarf—in out-and-proud dark mauve—closer to his throat as he waited for his ride out to Camp David. Since he couldn't exactly hitch a ride in the president's helicopter, he would be riding along with Sharon, the wife or girlfriend of a guy called Lowball. Beau had met Lowball at one of the squadron parties Jake had taken him to, but he couldn't remember anything about Sharon. Over the two-hour ride, he suspected he would learn far more than he cared to know, but if he envisioned any future with Jake, it would be a good idea to make friends with the rest of the pilots' partners.

The contents of two more trains poured out of the station and into the parking lot, to retrieve vehicles or be picked up, leaving Beau icy and wishing he had Sharon's phone number to check where she was. A sweet little silver Mercedes Roadster approached and he wondered whether he should consider buying a car. He wouldn't mind hitting the open road with Jake in a sexy two-seater like that. Then again, a model with a backseat had its advantages.

The Roadster pulled up to the sidewalk and the driver rolled down the window.

"Are you Beau?" asked a handsome man in his thirties with the prettiest blue eyes Beau had seen since Jake's.

"Yeah."

"I'm Rick, Sharon's… friend."

This intrigued Beau. Sharon had two guys? "Where's Sharon?"

"She flew up with the squadron. I'm your chariot. Get in."

Beau wondered whether this was a dream or some kind of test. If he got in the car with a hot stranger, would Jake jump out of a surveillance van and break up with him?

"Okay, thanks." Beau started to open the door.

"You must be positively arctic! Toss your bag in the trunk."

Beau was, so he hopped in after putting his weekend bag away. He'd barely closed the door before the powerful heater melted away a layer of ice he imagined had formed on any exposed skin. He relaxed into the contoured leather seats. The car smelled of new leather, but the delicious scent of Rick wafted over.

"I thought Sharon was driving me."

Rick glanced over and treated Beau to a lovely smile. Maybe he was a dentist, or dating one. "I think you got her mixed up with someone else. Sharon's one of the pilots who flies with Jake. She's doing copilot training this weekend, and I'm along for the ride, same as you."

"Have you been to Camp David before?"

"First time. And there's a slight change of plans. The forecast calls for heavy snow, so we get to go by air."

"Air?"

"In one of the cargo helos that usually take journalists. All the guests are getting the not-quite-VIP treatment. We're not allowed to fly in the president's helos. National security, they say. Like we'd tell the Chinese how comfortable the seats are." Rick grinned as he drove. He was skillful behind the wheel, zipping between cars and changing lanes as effortlessly as breathing. Beau sat back and enjoyed the ride and the way Rick smoothly shifted gears on the powerful car.

Rick took an exit for Quantico and drove up to the guard post at the Marine base. He gave the guard on duty their names and had to hand over their identification before they were allowed to drive on. A second guard post protected the HMX-1 hangars. Beau hadn't been here before, but Rick knew his way around.

After they parked and grabbed their gear, they went inside and Rick introduced Beau. He'd met a few of the other pilots at Alvarez's house and at the White House holiday party, and he a remembered a couple of girlfriends and wives. There were several female Marines on the flight crews, and Beau had to rely on clothing to determine who the civilians were.

"Good to meet you, Beau. I'm Lieutenant Colonel Monroe. Hope you have a nice weekend. If Styx passes the next exam, he'll be included on more lifts, including a few international trips on the president's schedule. So enjoy seeing him now."

"Thank you, Lieutenant Colonel."

"Call me Ben. You're a journalist, aren't you? *Post*?"

"No. *District Daily*." Beau made sure to say the name like it was better than the *Post*.

"You should get yourself on the press list for an upcoming trip." The lieutenant colonel smiled and was halfway down the hall before Beau could gather his wits. At least he didn't have to explain he was the fashion columnist. Probably not much chance he'd qualify for any presidential trips unless the president was heading for Fashion Week in Milan. The idea made Beau laugh.

After a short wait, everyone filed outside, where a dark green helicopter waited, its rotors moving slowly and almost silently. A Marine in uniform stowed the luggage in the aircraft, then rolled out a low staircase so everyone could climb inside. Beau had to crouch to keep from hitting his head on the fuselage and he entered. The roof wasn't much higher. He had no idea it would be so cramped.

Inside the helo wasn't plush, but the seats were comfortable enough, and the helicopter easily held the six passengers along with the crew.

"I've never been in a helicopter," Beau admitted to Rick, who was seated next to him.

"Jake hasn't taken you up before?"

Beau shook his head, trying not to feel slighted that Sharon had clearly brought Rick flying.

"Well, you're in for a treat. Unless you get airsick. A helo's nothing like a plane. First off, no one serves cocktails. And it's a lot shakier."

The rotors picked up speed after the door was closed, and it became difficult to hear each other. Should Beau be offended that Jake hadn't given him a ride in a helicopter yet? It wasn't like Jake had his own helicopter, and Beau didn't think flying civilians around in Marine helicopters on the weekends was standard practice. He'd assumed this weekend at Camp David was a special occasion during the holidays, while the president was out of Washington.

"Maybe you'll get a chance for him to fly you over the weekend." Rick leaned close to Beau to shout into his ear.

He smelled really good, and Beau tried not to inhale his intoxicating scent. He wanted to ask what it was but didn't want to sound like he was coming on to Rick. As it was, Rick was awfully friendly and gave Beau a certain smile. Even if Sharon's boyfriend was bi, he shouldn't be hitting on Beau.

Maybe if things didn't work out with Jake, Rick would be available, Beau joked, mostly to keep his mind off his sudden trepidation about flying in the kind of machine that had killed Jake's crew and nearly killed him. Other recent reports about military helicopter crashes sprang into his brain.

The rotors' noise increased and the aircraft lifted with a mighty tremble, then lurched to one side as the pilot banked away from the building where Jake's squadron was housed. The sensation of moving through the air in a helicopter beat a plane, hands down, Beau realized. He had the sensation of moving through space vertically as well as horizontally, the acceleration completely different from a plane's takeoff. Even after they took off, Beau felt the aircraft moving, turning, ascending.

The Marine seated to Beau's left turned to him. "First time?"

Beau nodded.

"This is a modified Huey," he shouted in Beau's direction. "One of the models our guys fly in combat. Those don't have any seats though, and can hold a dozen guys in full combat gear. They usually keep the doors open so they can shoot at the bad guys before the bad guys shoot you down. You hook yourself onto a bar so no one falls out."

Was this the same model helicopter Jake was flying when he'd crashed? Knowing this helicopter was similar made Beau feel closer to Jake. He paid special attention to how the pilot controlled the aircraft by using the stick and foot pedals and a lever that looked like a parking brake. The pilot and copilot chatted, giving Beau a good idea of the camaraderie between pilots. He liked learning about this part of Jake's life, one that meant so much to him.

The ride took a little more than an hour. It was nearly dark when they made a fairly sudden descent. Snow flurried around the front windows as the pilots worked to set the helicopter down. Wind buffeted them, definitely not something you could feel in a commercial plane, and he gripped the side of his seat until his fingers ached.

"These pilots aren't trainees, are they?" he asked the Marine sitting next to him.

"These pilots?" The Marine paused; then a smile played around the corners of his mouth. "No. We save the trainee pilots for the journalists."

Beau wasn't sure whether to relax or hit the guy. He considered doing both, but by then the helicopter had set down and the Marine hopped up to open the door. Wind and snow swirled inside, and Beau wound the mauve scarf one more turn around his neck.

"Good job for your virgin flight." Rick put his hand over Beau's and gave it a far-too-friendly squeeze that kind of took his breath away. "Next time it'll be a lot easier and you'll enjoy it more."

"Not the first time I've heard that." Beau grinned and Rick flashed a knowing smile back.

"Was it true the other time?"

"Well, yeah."

Rick didn't reply as he stood and preceded Beau down the stairs. Before Beau made it to the doorway, the freezing wind had his eyes watering. He gripped the railing carefully and stepped down, his knees giving way slightly as he adjusted to solid ground.

He'd barely set a foot on the tarmac before Jake was there, tugging him to one side, wrapping him in a tight, warm embrace, and kissing him, ignoring all the rules about PDA.

Beau enjoyed the welcome, more so because Jake's fellow pilots and their guests were around. He kissed back enthusiastically.

"I'm so glad you're here."

"Me too." Beau found himself shouting even though the rotors had been shut down.

"Which bag is yours?" Jake asked.

Beau cocked an eyebrow, then glanced at the half-dozen bags set on the light dusting of snow. Only one was plum-colored.

"Right, I recognize it." Jake bent to retrieve the bag, then slid an arm around Beau's waist. "We'll get a ride in the jeep to our cabin. If the snow piles up, we'll break out the snowmobiles." Jake grinned like any man with big noisy toys with big noisy engines. Beau figured a helicopter pilot wouldn't need more vehicles to make him happy. He already had a motorcycle.

Once they were in the jeep and the enlisted driver shut the door, Beau turned to Jake. "Why are there so many military jeeps here?"

"Camp David isn't a civilian operation. It's run by the Navy and the Marine Corps. There are enlisted barracks and officers' quarters. We'll be in one of the private cabins."

"Where does the president stay?"

"At the main lodge. There are other guest cabins nearby for VIPs. We'll be in another area of the camp, but tomorrow you can check out the rest of the camp, including the lodge. We just can't stay there."

"Are you working all day?"

"Morning and then after dark. I'll have the middle of the day free to spend with you. I report back to duty after dinner, so you'll have to entertain yourself for a few hours. Or talk with the other guests in one of the common areas."

"Thanks for bringing me here."

"I'm following orders from the president." Jake gave Beau a salute that made him look suddenly much more like a Marine officer. Beau felt so proud of him again.

The officers' cabins were sprinkled in a nice wooded area with enough distance between them for privacy. Their cabin had a bedroom and a living room, with a small refrigerator along one wall. Meals would be taken at the mess hall with the others. The furnishings were as comfortable as a modest hotel.

"And there's a double bed," Beau commented as he surveyed the quarters.

"I see you've got your priorities right." Jake put Beau's suitcase on the low dresser. "How was your first helo flight?"

"I loved it. A plane's kind of like floating, but the helicopter makes you feel like you're moving. I can't explain it. Kind of like a motorcycle. A flying motorcycle." The words tumbled out in Beau's exhilaration, and he felt like a kid.

"You don't have to explain it to me. I know what you mean. I'm glad you enjoyed the flight."

"I wish you'd been flying us." Beau realized Jake had unpacked his suitcase and expertly put everything away in the space of three minutes. "I had a few questions though. About helicopters."

"Go ahead."

"It was so damn loud. The president must have some heavy-duty earplugs."

"The *Marine One* models are soundproofed. The rotors barely whisper if you're in the passenger area. I'd show you but then I'd have to kill you." Jake winked.

"Why?"

"There's a lot of communication equipment and other special features that are classified. It's part of why those aircraft are guarded or kept behind extra barriers, even on base."

Beau asked another dozen questions, noting how animated Jake got when he talked about flying. He looked and sounded so confident, so unlike the man Beau had found drinking on his couch in the middle of the night. The memory shook Beau, but the joy of how far they'd come brightened his mood.

Beau moved to the bed and pulled Jake down next to him and proceeded to unbutton his shirt. "How long until dinner?"

"Does it matter?" Jake asked, letting Beau do as he pleased.

"Nope."

Once Beau got Jake out of his uniform, he wished he hadn't been so hasty. He loved how Jake looked in it. Then again, Jake looked pretty fucking spectacular *out* of uniform too. Especially the way he sat, legs spread, cock jutting toward the ceiling and nipples hard nubs in the chilly room. All of Beau's senses were on high alert, and he started on his own shirt. Once over his initial trepidation on the helicopter, he'd been thinking about getting naked with Jake.

"Let me do that." Jake tugged Beau by his belt so he stood between Jake's knees. Jake pulled Beau's shirt free and slid warm palms up Beau's torso. "Your skin's so hot." He kissed Beau's belly and rubbed his erection through his jeans. He leaned forward and scraped his teeth along the ridge of Beau's cock. Despite the layer of the denim, it sent electric currents to Beau's core.

"Hurry up."

Jake undid Beau's pants and slid his silky fuchsia boxers down enough to pull the head of his cock into his mouth. He moaned around Beau, and Beau slid his palms across Jake's short hair. Jake glanced up from under long lashes and looked so damn sexy, lips wrapped around Beau's cock, that Beau lost control and came almost instantly. Pearly drops trickled down Jake's chin and throat, so Beau licked it away, then pushed Jake down onto the bed and reciprocated very slowly until Jake begged for Beau to finish him off.

After, they lay together, skin to skin.

"Good thing I got your uniform off after all."

"After all?"

"You look so hot in it, I had considered having you fuck me while you're wearing it. But then I would have made a huge mess all over it."

"I have other shirts."

Beau's heart swelled because Jake didn't seem to mind even if Beau came all over his uniform. It was a small point, but for some reason it meant a lot to Beau at that moment. "I love you, Jake."

"I'll keep my uniform on later if you like."

"I fucking want to have your babies, Jake."

"Yeah." Jake flashed a cocky smile, and Beau rubbed Jake's head in mock exasperation.

Then they kissed and caressed each other until Jake decided they should get to the mess hall.

DINNER FELT like a family picnic: plenty of hearty food and good-natured ribbing between the officers. Beau was starting to get to know the guys and their guests. Sharon, who was Captain Sharon Phillips, sat across the table from Beau, with Rick at her side. Rick got along with the others and joined in the conversation, but Beau held back.

"Why're you so quiet?" Jake asked softly.

"Just trying to get my bearings here, with the others. It's still a brand new world to me."

"Everyone likes you."

Beau shrugged. A few people he hadn't spent time with before asked about his job, and he said he wrote for the *Daily*. He didn't elaborate, and no one asked for details. One of the wives asked how Beau and Jake met, and Beau shared a PG version of the night at the White House.

After dinner, Beau watched Jake practice takeoffs and landings until he was bored senseless and colder than a snowman's ass. Wind gusted and snow swirled, preventing each maneuver from being absolutely perfect. And still Jake kept going, time after time. Pride for Jake bloomed in Beau's chest. So few pilots were trusted to fly the president of the United States. It only reinforced how skillful Jake was and how respected by his peers and superiors. Though he had told Beau about his job, Jake somehow managed to make it sound about as important and exciting as shoveling shit.

But now Beau had a new understanding of Jake and how seriously he took his duties.

Back in their cabin, they made love, slowly at first and then with more intensity, as if Jake had come back from a year of combat deployment. He held on to Beau so tightly, but not simply with passion. Each breath, each kiss, each thrust told Beau how much Jake loved him.

As Beau caught his breath, Jake took one of his hands and softly kissed each fingertip, then traced lazy shapes along Beau's chest and belly.

IT WAS still dark out, and Beau was disoriented when he woke with Jake wrapped around him. Then he remembered they were at Camp David. *Camp David!* Beau wished he could write about this, but he had been advised not to report about anything except the decorations, and even that article would be vetted by the Pentagon and White House. He was probably still on the Pentagon shit list, even if the White House seemed to like him.

Jake shifted on the bed next to him and rolled over to press his lips against Beau's. He leaned on an elbow, and reached out for Beau's cock. The touch was soft, too gentle to arouse him, more of an appreciation. A beautiful smile curled the corners of Jake's mouth. He looked more relaxed than Beau had ever seen. It made Beau want to jump his bones, but when Jake made love, he got a serious look on his face until it was over.

But contented Jake was incredible, even just to look at. Scratch the part about looking. Now Beau was on the verge of getting irrevocably aroused. He pulled Jake's hand off his cock.

"Do we have time?"

"Time?" Jake sounded like he was still half-asleep. "Of course."

He didn't seem even remotely asleep when he leaned over and gave Beau an incredibly competent blowjob. He made it last. Beau was so transported he didn't realize Jake had gotten himself off before Beau had a chance to participate.

"We don't have much more time." Jake grinned. "I want to cuddle some more. It's a little surreal having you around while I'm working. But you're a lovely distraction, at least for the moment."

Beau enjoyed being wrapped in Jake's strong arms. How had he gotten so lucky? One slutty comment and look where they'd ended up. A little bit of a gay fairy tale.

"I don't want to be too much distraction. What if you crash?" As soon as the final word was out of his mouth, Beau cringed. The last thing he wanted was to remind Jake of his one life-defining crash.

"I won't. I'm an excellent pilot when no one's shooting at me, and most of the time when they are. You'll see."

Chapter 16

BREAKFAST WAS lively. It was too early in the morning for much cheer, though Christmas was only a week or so away. The squadron was mostly business now. Jake loved having Beau here with him. It was an incredible privilege, and he was still a little awestruck the president had personally suggested Jake bring a guest. Jake didn't know the president had any clue about HMX-1 pilot training, unless it involved transporting him.

Beau seemed to get along well with everyone here—Marines and civilians. He could really charm anyone. It was that smile. It had won over Jake almost from the moment they met, and he figured it must stand Beau in good stead at work. It still surprised Jake that Beau hadn't been able to build himself a more fulfilling journalistic career.

"Styx, report to the pad in fifteen." Lieutenant Colonel Monroe put a hand on the back of Jake's chair. "Morning, Beau."

"Morning, Ben." Beau looked a little more comfortable than the night before.

Monroe nodded to them and walked out the door.

After breakfast, Jake and Major Landau went to the hangar to retrieve the Sea King. The maintenance crew had been up before the crack of dawn, polishing and tuning and inspecting. Jake and the major did their preflight walk-around; then the ground crew towed the aircraft to the landing pad and they got inside and lifted off for the first set of practice runs.

They spent two hours with Jake practicing landings, takeoffs, hovering, and flying around the rest of the camp. He found it easier to maneuver the monster helo each time he sat at the controls. Though he'd flown this model dozens of times in the simulator, nothing compared to the way the genuine article felt under his command, the thrust and acceleration, the freedom of almost unlimited flight. And the safety of not having Taliban RPGs aimed at him and his men.

"Excellent job," Major Landau said as Jake touched down outside the hangar. "It's almost lunchtime. Take the rest of the afternoon off and then report at 1600 hours for dusk and night practice."

"Yes, sir."

"The wind's died down. Good weather for the snowmobile. You should take Beau for a spin. Ask Gunny Jenkins to set you up."

Jake nodded. It took him a moment to remember Beau was here with him. Flying took so much concentration he put everything else out of his brain when he worked. He was grateful for the ability to compartmentalize. He hadn't been sure he could do it, and he would never tell Beau that when he was in the air, Beau and their life together ceased to exist. Such intense focus was vital.

Beau was waiting in the living room of the main lodge with some of the wives and girlfriends when Jake finally tracked him down.

"Before you ask, we're cleared to be in here," Beau said as Jake entered the room and pulled his cover off.

"I know. Besides, I trust you." Jake inhaled the scents of cinnamon and pine along with the comforting smell of a wood fire. Flames snapped and crackled inside a lovely flagstone fireplace with an enormous hearth.

"I'm doing a story on the Camp David holiday decorations. My editor cleared it with the White House protocol officer."

"What the hell is a protocol officer?"

Beau shrugged.

Pam Alvarez approached with a tray. Beau opened his mouth as she handed Jake a mug of cocoa. It smelled heavenly, and the heat warmed his hands perfectly. He took a sip and nearly fell over.

"Yeah, Maricruz brought some rum," Pam said. "If you're still working, don't swallow." She gave a loud giggle and looked at Beau.

The rum tasted good and warmed him up, but Jake put it down on the table and settled next to Beau on the couch. Now he understood the flash of emotion in Beau's face when Pam served him cocoa.

"I'm not even going to respond to that," Jake replied softly to Beau.

"Have some of mine." Beau handed Jake his mug, clearly the kids' version, but Jake didn't mind. He expected they'd have another discussion back in the cabin.

"Jake, come on over and enjoy the fire," Maricruz Salazar said. Her husband, Carlos, was a crew chief, one of the enlisted Marines who wore dress blues and saluted the president as he entered or left *Marine One*. He and his counterparts were the most-photographed Marines in the world. They rotated working POTUS lifts or they would never get to see their families.

Jake stayed with Beau, and the ladies who usually fussed over Jake like six extra mothers gave them some space. Now Beau was here, perhaps they'd decided Jake was already well taken care of.

"How does a spin on the snowmobile sound, Beau?"

"Sounds cold, but fun."

"When you're ready, get bundled up, and we'll go out for a while. I'm going back to the cabin to change out of uniform."

"I'll go with you." Beau waved to the ladies, and they all gave him hugs and kisses as he prepared to leave.

Outside, Jake had to ask. "How'd you amass such a fan club?"

"I know what women want."

Jake responded with a skeptical frown, but he picked up the pace. His soft garrison cap left his head and ears so exposed he was afraid an ear might snap off. "I shudder to ask."

"Samples. Of clothes. I collected some scarves and gloves at a show I covered the other day, so I handed them out as early Christmas presents. And I had tickets to a few upcoming fashion events inside the Beltway."

"That seems awfully underhanded."

"In Washington it's business as usual. Quid pro quo." Beau grinned as he unlocked their cabin and let Jake enter first.

Jake couldn't smile. The reality of Beau's comment was all too depressing. Jake had managed to stay out of the exchange of favors that masqueraded as politics, unless he counted the Appaloosa flights. But he'd seen plenty of it in his military career. If you weren't at the top of your game, you figured out your competitive advantage and horse-traded your way to the best postings, promotions, and perks. Had some of the men in HMX-1 gone that route rather than earning their posts the old-fashioned way?

Hell, maybe that *was* the old-fashioned way.

As long as he could keep flying, Jake hoped to avoid that moral morass. The day he needed to resort to underhanded tactics would be the day he'd quit and find another way to feed his passion for flying.

Beau pulled a thick sweater out of the drawer. "You're awfully quiet, babe."

Beau glanced up, and Jake wondered if he should have kept his mouth shut. "It's much colder than I expected." He didn't want to tell Beau how the Appaloosa missions concerned him.

"Let me warm you up a little."

Jake nodded and reached for Beau. They lay down on the bed, Jake spooning Beau. "I saw your face when Pam handed me the drink."

Beau let out a sigh. "I didn't want to say anything in front of anyone else."

"I put it down right away."

Beau rolled over to face Jake. "How did that feel?"

"Okay, I guess. I didn't have trouble putting it down."

"Did you want to drink more? I wondered that about the sip of eggnog at the White House party too."

"Not really. I know I'm flying later, so I wouldn't have had any alcohol today. But at the party, I didn't exactly want to drink more." He *had* wanted more, but he'd stopped at one sip. Partly for Beau, and partly to prove to himself that he could.

"What do you mean?"

"It tasted good. I could have enjoyed a small cup of eggnog, but I think I could stop at one. I wasn't trying to get drunk. I didn't want to be drunk."

"When do you want to be drunk?"

It was a good question, and Jake had to think about it for a moment. "I haven't wanted to for quite a while. The dark places aren't so dark with you around."

Beau gave him a warm smile and brushed his fingers against the short hair above Jake's ear. "I'm glad to hear that."

"Work's been great, too. And you've made me look at the crash in a different way, so I'm not blaming myself. You've had such a great effect on me."

"What about if I'm not around?"

The words made Jake gasp. "Don't say that." He looked into Beau's eyes, wondering if he was losing Beau.

"Your drinking shouldn't be dependent on me, or your job, or what other people think of you, Jake. It has to be how you feel about yourself."

Jake nodded. Beau was right, and Jake couldn't lean on him forever. There would come a point when to keep Beau, Jake would have to be able to stand alone. His belly tightened in fear at the thought of that, of losing Beau.

Beau kissed Jake's cheek and rolled away, then stood up. "We're going on the snowmobile, right?" He stripped down to his candy-cane-striped boxer briefs and matching socks before pulling a pair of snow pants out of the drawer.

Jake sat at the edge of the bed watching. He wouldn't mind a little lick right now. The room was chilly, and through his shirt, Beau's nipples were tempting plump buds. Before Jake could reach out for Beau, he'd pulled on a long-sleeved sweater. But the look on Beau's face told Jake he'd perfectly understood. He peeled the sweater and shirt off and Jake closed the distance and took a nipple between his lips and sucked.

"Mmm." Beau made pretty little moans, getting Jake rock hard. He went for the other nipple and plunged a hand into Beau's shorts and grabbed a handful of ass.

But when Jake tried to get the shorts down, Beau pushed his hands away and dropped to his knees in front of Jake.

"My turn, Captain." He rubbed Jake's erection through his pants. "Keep your uniform on for me?"

Jake nodded. Beau knelt and unbuckled Jake's shiny belt buckle and went for the zipper. Then he unbuttoned the shirt of Jake's service uniform and reciprocated the attention to his nipples. Jake leaned back and arched into Beau's skillful mouth. He closed his eyes.

When Beau closed his lips around his cock, Jake threaded his fingers in Beau's silky locks. He was jealous of the soft hair that never let itself be tamed. Jake couldn't get enough of touching it, though he tried to restrain himself. Sometimes when Beau was asleep, Jake would twist a lock around a finger.

Now, he gave himself up to Beau's incredible mouth, hot, wet, and able to drive Jake wild. Sounds and vibrations from Beau's moans intensified the pleasure, and Jake was torn between letting go and fucking Beau's mouth or enjoying the treatment for as long as possible. In the end, he did both, pinching Beau's nipples as much for his own enjoyment as for Beau's.

When he'd finished, he made Beau stand, and slid the candy-cane boxers down and licked to his heart's delight.

"DON'T THINK that gets you out of the snowmobile ride you promised."

"Oh, you thought the ride was on the snowmobile?" Jake chuckled as he cleaned them up with a warm cloth.

"I'd like some sort of ride today, because what I just got from you wasn't a ride at all. You up for one right here, right now?" Beau cocked an eyebrow. Truth was he was a little saddle sore from the night before. And he could tell from Jake's expression he wasn't up for more yet. Luckily they both found oral sex satisfying. Jake was a fun lover, taking as much pleasure from giving as receiving orgasms. Well, maybe not precisely the same amount, but he sure didn't hold back in pleasuring Beau on a regular basis.

"Tell you what, first we'll go on the snowmobile, then we'll see about a different ride later on. Just remember I have to report back to duty at 1600."

"At the White House? Today?"

"Not 1600 as in Pennsylvania Ave. Sixteen hundred hours as in four o'clock."

Beau grinned. He loved the slightly exasperated look on Jake's face. He could be so damn serious. But he'd loosened up a lot since they'd met. Beau was willing to take all the credit for that.

They slid into long underwear, waterproof snow pants, and parkas Jake had borrowed. Beau's china blue peacoat wasn't going to cut it for a snowmobile ride.

"Take the wool hat and an extra scarf and the warmest gloves." Jake shook his head. "Not the purple ones. They're pretty, but not warm enough."

"Yes, sir, Captain, sir." Beau swaddled and swathed himself to the point he was sweating inside the cabin.

Jake came up and wrapped the scarf so it covered Beau's mouth.

"You trying to tell me something?" Beau asked, though his words were muffled.

Jake shook his head, a smirk threatening to take control of his face.

Well, Beau could repay him by keeping his mouth shut later, when Jake *didn't* want him to.

They walked to the shed housing the snowmobiles, and Jake slid one out on its skids into fresh snow. Beau was surprised to see the snowmobile moved on a spiky tread reminiscent of a tank. Yikes, if that went over your foot. He backed away a few paces.

"You ever been on one of these before?"

Beau shook his head. Now they were outside, he was grateful for that second scarf.

"Hold on to me, just like on the motorcycle. It's going to be loud, so if you need to say anything, get your mouth by my ear, though with the helmets on it will be hard to hear you. Hand or touch signals work best. If you want me to stop, just tug at my left elbow. Okay?"

Beau nodded.

Jake straddled the snowmobile, but as Beau was about to climb on behind him, Jake stopped him.

"Let me get it started first. It needs to warm up for a few minutes before we get going. This one's cold since no one's used it today. You can wait in the shed, out of the wind."

Beau nodded, but he waited and watched as Jake pushed a couple of buttons and the monster roared to life. Jake twisted one of the handlebars and then got off. He went back into the shed and motioned for Beau to follow.

"Helmets. Just as important as a good coat. Snow looks soft, but you have no idea what's underneath. I don't want anything to happen to you." He smiled and reached out to pull the scarf off Beau's mouth for a quick kiss, then replaced it. He helped Beau put the helmet on before donning his own.

"Lelow," Jake said.

It took Beau a moment to realize he'd said "Let's go." No wonder he'd suggested a hand signal. He climbed on the machine behind Jake and circled his arm around Jake's waist.

Jake said something that might have been "Ready?"

"Yes." Beau nodded in case Jake couldn't translate. His helmet smacked sharply against Jake's and smooshed his nose. This was much more complicated than he'd expected. It better be fun.

Jake started off slowly, for which Beau was grateful. After a few gentle turns, he acclimated to the motion. At first they kept to the side of the footpaths, which had been trodden by others; then Jake headed off on pristine snow and opened the throttle.

They accelerated smoothly, and Beau found it almost intoxicating, especially around curves and bends. Wind whistled through his helmet, but the warm clothing and toasty boots and gloves protected him surprisingly well. Jake whooshed through a pine forest and then up a gradual slope to a spot where they could see much of the rest of the camp below them. Then they took off again and roared through the wilderness.

Except for the incredible noise and the gasoline smell, the ride was wonderful. Snowmobiles were clearly not all that good for the environment or the wildlife in the park, but for a little while, Beau could shut off the Sierra Club-indoctrinated portion of his brain and enjoy the sheer pleasure of gliding along at dangerous speed, plastered against Jake's back. When they slowed again, Beau felt hugely disappointed. He wasn't ready for the ride to end.

Jake stopped the snowmobile, pulled off his helmet, and twisted around. "Doing okay?"

Beau tried to pull his own helmet off and forgot the chinstrap. Jake helped him. So much for looking badass. "Hell yeah. I'm having a great time."

"Want to drive?"

"What?" The idea frightened and excited Beau. Jake never offered to let him drive the motorcycle. "Really?"

"Slowly. Stay in this clearing, okay? And listen to my instructions. Okay?"

"Deal."

When Beau took over the controls, after a lesson in using them and locating the emergency kill switch, he opened the throttle infinitesimally. The machine barely inched forward, so he opened it some more. It lurched ahead and Jake's helmet smacked into Beau's. There was a sweet spot between inching and surging, and with practice he might find it. He dialed it back and moved along fairly smoothly.

Shit, I'm actually driving this thing! He tried a turn, then another, and soon he had the hang of it. He tried to go a little faster, and the acceleration made his stomach rumble in a good way. Soon he understood the thrill and lure of fast cars, motorcycles, and maybe even helicopters. He kept pushing the speed until Jake yanked on his arm, and reluctantly he closed the throttle down. Now he felt like a grandmother walking around the park. Jake gave the hand signal to stop, and Beau did.

He climbed off the snowmobile and pulled off his helmet. He needed a little fresh air. He heard voices nearby and strained to listen, expecting to see someone else from the HMX-1 group. Then two men emerged at the far edge of the clearing where Jake and Beau had stopped. Neither of them were from HMX-1, but Beau immediately recognized one from his posture and the

Astrakhan collar on his coat. There was something furtive in their body language, and Astrakhan's companion appeared tense, his posture stiff. Two straight men here for some private time away from prying Washington eyes?

"Ready to go back?" Jake asked, his voice carrying over the virgin snow around them. One of the figures at the edge of the clearing looked up, and Beau squeezed Jake's arm, but it was too late. The two men went back under the cover of woods before Beau could hear what they were saying.

"Wha—"

Beau put a finger to his lips and cut Jake's question off. He pulled his helmet on, and when Jake got onto the snowmobile, Beau climbed on behind him. They rode leisurely back to the shed, where Jake put the snowmobile away and stowed the gear they'd borrowed.

"I take it you enjoyed the ride?"

"Incredible doesn't begin to describe it," Beau replied when he'd unwrapped his face enough to communicate properly. "Can we go again later?"

Jake grinned. "We'll see. Are you saying you'd rather do that than indoor sports?"

Beau had to think about that for a few moments. He decided not to answer.

Jake put his arm through Beau's. "It's okay. We can do the other at home. I'm glad you're enjoying yourself here."

"Me too."

They risked a walking kiss and nearly ran into Lieutenant Colonel Monroe.

"Sorry, sir," Jake said, nodding respectfully.

"You're off duty for the moment, Jake. Relax."

"Yes, sir. Uh, Ben."

After Jake changed back into a clean uniform, they spent the rest of the afternoon in the main lodge in front of the roaring fireplace as the pilots exchanged increasingly improbable stories of their exploits, until they had to report for duty.

"See you at dinner." Jake squeezed Beau's hand, then got up.

"You gonna watch?" Nancy-something asked.

"No. I think I'll spend a little time working on my article. I've got plenty of ideas now."

Beau retrieved his laptop from the cabin, then, back in the lodge, curled up on a couch still within the circle of the fire's warmth. As the women chatted and gossiped, he tapped away at the keys.

Though it wasn't his department, Beau felt like contributing some gossip of his own about Young Colonel Sanders. He was starting to think the guy was following him.

But what he was really writing had less to do with gossip or fashion than it did with Victor Mann and Green Dynamics.

DINNER THE second night at Camp David was much more relaxed.

"How was your session today, Styx?" Sharon asked.

Beau was grinning and started humming "Mr. Roboto," but he reached over and held Jake's hand. "At least they didn't start calling you Roboto."

"Small mercies." Jake turned to Sharon. "Let's just say it's getting better."

"Mine was a disaster. I'll probably be restricted to the simulator for the foreseeable future."

Several other pilots joined in the discussion, commiserating and offering advice. Their jargon left Beau feeling like he'd landed on an alien planet, but he loved seeing Jake in his element, respected by his peers.

On Sunday, while Jake was training, Beau sat in the main lodge to work on both the Camp David story and his military spending story. Around twelve he figured Jake was done and it was nearly time for lunch, so he packed up his laptop and headed outside. The temperature had risen, and the sun spread its warmth. He spotted Jake playing basketball on a court near the mess hall.

His opponent was Rick. The two men were evenly matched in height and skill. They smacked into each other with grunts as they blocked and fought for the ball.

"Have a seat." Sharon waved to Beau, and he joined her. "They're so intense. I don't know why guys have to be so competitive."

Beau didn't play team sports like basketball—swimming and cycling were more his style—and he felt a little offended by Sharon's comment, so he aimed for chitchat. "How long have you and Rick been dating?" He was curious what she would say about Rick.

"We're not dating. Rick's—" She stopped and glanced over at Jake and Rick.

Beau assumed Rick was bi or gay, but he didn't expect the look on Sharon's face. It told him far more than he wanted to know. His stomach clenched.

"Are you saying Rick and Jake…?" He practically choked on the words. They burned in his throat, and he thought he might be sick. Not because Rick and Jake had apparently been something to each other before Beau. It wasn't even that Jake hadn't told Beau. But Jake had let Beau and Rick spend time together. Now Beau felt like an ass, like the next guy in Jake's bed, who might be here today hanging with the squadron and tomorrow be just another name they forgot when Jake brought a new man along to a picnic or poker game.

As if sensing the eruption building steam inside of Beau, Sharon got up and went inside.

Alone, Beau watched Jake and Rick shooting hoops, blocking each other fiercely, shoulders and hips and torsos crashing into each other. He saw the game not as some harmless fun, but something else, some violent sports foreplay. Was Jake enjoying the chance to touch Rick, or was it the other way around? Did either of them know Beau was watching?

Every smile, every smack and grunt, every touch took on monumental significance until Beau had to get away. He went back to their cabin and locked the door before lying facedown on the bed, feeling betrayed.

Knocking on the door startled him. He decided to ignore it, and it turned to pounding.

"Beau? Open up."

Beau let Jake pound a few more times before getting up and letting him in.

"You okay?" Jake looked Beau up and down. "You look kind of pale."

He felt kind of pale, but he lied. "I'm fine. How was your basketball?" He hoped the word didn't come out as violently as it felt on his lips.

"Uh, okay, I guess. I lost." Jake chuckled as he pulled his sweaty shirt over his head. "Rick beat the pants off me."

"I hope he used a condom."

Jake threw his shirt against the wall so hard it almost stuck there. "What's gotten into you?"

Beau let that go without the obvious reply. He shrugged and sat on the bed with his laptop.

Jake kicked the nearest chair. "Fucking Sharon and her big fucking mouth."

"Is it true?"

"It depends what she said."

"Nothing much. Just that you and Rick… were *you and Rick*."

Jake stepped out of his sweats. Beau tried not to look because he loved watching Jake undress. Now he smelled good, the scent of clean sweat, his body radiating more heat than usual.

"That's a bit of an overstatement. Did you think I was a virgin when I met you?" Jake pulled his underwear off. "Remember you're the one who propositioned me before you even said hello."

"Are you saying I'm slutty?"

"You were that night."

"So were you."

"I'm not disputing that." Jake flung his shorts into a bag in the corner with the rest of his dirty clothes. "What are you mad about?"

"I'm not mad. I'm hurt. I don't want to be another in a line of guys you bring to cookouts and Camp David, and then feel like a fool because the other pilots know I'm only temporary. So you two alpha males can just have each other and—"

Jake's features morphed into a scowl, but then the hard edges of anger softened and melted away. He sat on the bed next to Beau, who forced himself to shy away from Jake's strong, naked embrace.

"You're not any of those things, Beau. I didn't mention Rick because he wasn't important enough to mention. He and I fooled around a few times. He's good in bed, I won't lie. But after we fucked, we didn't have anything to say to each other. He didn't call. I didn't call. I could easily get what he offered from someone who wasn't a fellow pilot's friend. And he never came to any squadron things with *me*. No one but Sharon knew."

Beau let Jake hold him. Maybe because he was naked and smelled extra manly. Maybe for entirely different reasons, but the naked manliness didn't hurt. "Really?"

"I've never had anyone at my house, or introduced them to Daisy and Toby, or made them pancakes or told them I love them. Those things are special to me. You're special to me."

"I am?" Beau asked just to hear Jake say it. He admitted it felt good to hear these affirmations.

"I couldn't stop thinking about you after we met. I still can't."

"You can't?"

"Beau, sometimes you're a real idiot."

"What if someone else walked up and offered you sex?"

"Like who?"

"Does it matter?" Beau glared at him.

"Sure. If it's anyone but you, I'd say no. I don't cheat. If I'd been in a relationship when I met you, I'd have turned you down, no matter how sexy you were."

"I'm sorry. This is a whole new world for me. I'm still learning my way around it."

"Today was your one free jealous freak-out. And now you know I wouldn't touch another man while we're together."

"Okay." Beau felt more relieved than embarrassed after his overreaction. He let himself enjoy Jake's naked manliness a little more. "Don't you feel jealous about me?"

"Only with Laney. You spend more time with her than with me. So far I've been operating on the principle we were in an exclusive relationship."

"You're jealous of Laney?"

Jake gave a charming shrug.

"How much time do we have before lunch?" Beau asked and stole a salty kiss below Jake's ear.

"Enough time for my shower. Then we should pack. We're heading out after lunch so we can be back to Quantico before it gets dark."

Beau nodded. He didn't want their mostly magical weekend to be over. He'd learned a lot about Jake's world this weekend, and he was more certain than before that he wanted to be part of Jake's life for a long time to come.

Chapter 17

AFTER THE Camp David weekend, Jake landed more choice squadron assignments, and Beau made the round of inside-the-Beltway holiday parties, including the inevitable charity fashion shows, auctions, and other unavoidable fashion and feature events. Laney brought him to far too many holiday dinners, and he had to start working out to keep from putting on weight.

Not that Jake would notice. He was barely around two nights in a row, and on the occasions when he and Beau stayed together, Jake fell asleep, exhausted, sometimes before they'd gotten past foreplay.

"Where's Jake this week?" Laney asked near the end of January as they sampled the fare in a brand-new Italian restaurant she was reviewing.

"He's actually going to be here for almost a whole week. We're going to celebrate late New Year's Eve together and stay in that romantic little inn near Manassas."

"New Year's Eve? How sweet that he wants to make up to you because he had to be away then." Laney beamed whenever Beau told her how sorry Jake was he traveled so much. He'd been gone at Christmas too, but with Beau at his parents' place near Seattle, it hadn't mattered as much as New Year's.

"He's down in Georgia right now."

"With the president?"

Beau shrugged. "He didn't say, but that's what I assume."

"Because the president is in town. So is the veep and all the other big shots. State of the Union is in a few days. No one travels then. Anyone who isn't in DC gets their ass back here right about now."

Beau should have known that. Suddenly his gnocchi alla romana tasted like sand and glue. He put his fork down with a clang and pushed the dish away. "God, I'm stuffed." He pasted on a smile and made an excuse to leave while Laney was only halfway through the desserts.

Laney got up when he did, insisting she had enough notes for her review. "I think you're coming down with something," she said as they stepped out onto the sidewalk.

The wind picked up, and Laney wrapped her scarf around her neck, then bumped into Beau because she wasn't watching where she was going.

She fell, and Beau turned toward her to stop her decline. He spotted a dark flash behind him. When he turned he realized it was probably their reflection in a shop window. As they crossed the street, the feeling of someone behind him intensified, but when he turned, he only saw a man in a baseball cap, head down as he walked into the biting wind.

"We should have taken a cab," Beau said when they got back to the newspaper office. They'd both been roped into writing extra articles for a Valentine's Day supplement, which meant extra work and later nights. He'd been at the office late for most of the past week. Laney was able to escape using the excuse of attending imaginary evening food events or writing reviews, like the Italian restaurant they'd been able to enjoy at leisure for at least a little while.

Until tonight Beau had appreciated the work to take his mind off missing Jake. Now the sour taste bubbled in his gut as he stared at his monitor, trying to concentrate on work. Where the hell was Jake? Had he lied? Where had he been all those other nights?

No way could he concentrate on penning "Sweet Gifts for your Sweetie" right now. No amount of red-and-white underwear, edible garter belts, and fuck-me pumps got his mind off the possibility Jake hadn't been honest with him.

He called Jenna to confirm Jake was out of town. He'd already dialed before he realized he needed a cover story.

"Yeah, I-uh was thinking of going over and making him a surprise... uh, dinner. I wanted to get the date right."

"Tomorrow night," Jenna said. "You're spoiling him, you know. But he deserves it."

"Yes, he does. He sure deserves something *special*," Beau agreed through gritted teeth.

Next he called Sharon, fighting off the urge to ask for Rick's number. She wasn't home, so he left a message.

If Jake was out of town on a lift but it wasn't the president or veep, it could be someone on the cabinet. Beau dug around the *Daily*'s intranet of Washington events and VIP schedules, but he couldn't find anyone who admitted to being in Georgia this week.

It was almost midnight, so Beau went home with nothing to show for the night's work but the beginnings of an ulcer.

BEAU GOT up early and went into the office prepared to expand his mission. If he could find any VIP who was in Georgia, he'd stop questioning Jake's honesty. He wanted to believe Jake, but now that Beau thought about it, he recalled a number of trips when Jake had almost pointedly *not* mentioned the destinations.

He'd give Jake the benefit of the doubt, but he still wanted to find an explanation before asking directly.

When he—literally—bumped into Mike Beaumont outside the Starbucks across the street from the paper, a light bulb went off. Right after he knocked a coffee cup and paper bag out of Beaumont Bear's hands.

"Hey Mike, can you help me with some research that's giving me trouble?"

"Only if you buy me another coffee and two donuts to replace those. I stood on line for a fucking hour to get those!"

"I'm so sorry!" Beau turned his smile up a few notches and promised to bring them to his desk. Beau smiled his way to the front of the line in Starbucks, explaining he'd knocked over someone's drink, and could he please, please, *please* get a replacement? He walked out with two venti-sized specialty drinks, a box full of pastries, and two warm breakfast sandwiches. The cashier wouldn't let him pay for any of it. He was practically thanking Beau by the time he left.

His hands were full, so he was grateful when a tall man in a dark wool coat held the door to the *Daily* lobby open for him. Beau turned to thank him, but he was gone already.

In the bear's office, Mike Beaumont made him sit and watch as he scarfed down most of the baked loot. "Okay, what did you need?"

"I'm trying to figure out who's been in Georgia the past few days?"

"Most of the residents of Georgia, I'd expect. Oh, was that USA or former Russian republic Georgia? It doesn't matter. It's the same answer."

Beau smiled and laughed at the rapier wit. "I meant government officials. I—"

"Internet? Intranet?"

"I already checked. Almost everyone is here for the State of the Union. Or at least their schedules say they are in town."

Mike slurped coffee, then let out an award-winning belch. If his mother was in a three-state radius, she was probably embarrassed at the volume and duration. "Okay, lemme check my sources." He leaned forward and tapped so fiercely at his keyboard he could have powered the entire building by keystrokes.

"None of the cabinet. A congressman from Georgia—again, no surprise. A Pentagon guy... nope, that's next week." He attacked his mouse and then shook his head. "I can't see anything else that's newsworthy here."

"It might not be newsworthy. See, my boyfr—"

"Stop right there. Please don't tell me I just wasted sixteen minutes looking for your boyfriend. Get *out*."

"Thanks, Mike!" Beau smiled, standing. "I really appreciate your help. I knew you'd know where to look."

"Out!"

"Sorry." Beau headed for the door. "He flies *Marine One*, so if POTUS isn't in Georgia...."

"Out!" But this time Mike's heart clearly wasn't in it, and he waved Beau out as if shooing a fly from a warm breakfast sandwich.

BEAU WAS at his desk before he realized he'd forgotten to get the congressman's name and the name of the database Mike had used. Then next time he wouldn't need to ask Mike Beaumont for anything. Beau was finishing a chocolate croissant when Laney came into his cube.

"You ate a Starbucks croissant? I don't even know you anymore." She covered her eyes with the back of her hand in a dramatic fashion reminiscent of silent-film heroines.

"It was delicious too." He laughed as she made the sign of the cross and backed out of his cube. "Now you know how I feel when you wear velour!" He was on a roll today. Or a croissant.

Mike didn't answer his phone. Or he was just ignoring Beau. But Beau knew where Mike ate lunch at least four days a week, so he staked out a table at the Dumpling Emporium a few blocks away from the *Daily*'s office. As Beau contemplated a doughy pot sticker, the pieces fell into place. Mike was almost exactly dumpling-shaped. Apparently you were what you ate. He rethought all those blowjobs he'd given Jake.

Maybe he shouldn't swallow.

Mike strolled in a few moments later, and Beau waved to him. He peered across the tables full of happy, doughy diners and shook his head, but he almost smiled for a moment. When he'd placed his order, he sat down next to Beau.

"I've never seen you here before."

"I had no idea what I've been missing." Beau grinned and pushed some kind of Eastern European dough pocket in his mouth, unaware how long it would take to chew and swallow. "Yummy." It was, actually, especially with the accompanying dipping sauce.

Mike's order came and they chewed for a few minutes like a couple of cows. It wasn't in silence, since pot stickers involved far more slurping than Beau realized.

"So why have I seen you twice today after not running into you at work practically since the—"

"The Great Invitation Fiasco of 2014?"

"Yeah." Mike eyed Beau warily as he wiped dipping sauce from his beard. "I'm not into guys."

"Your loss. Sorry, I probably shouldn't say that, or so they told me in the sensitivity training I was sentenced to."

"Yeah…." Mike gave a shrug Beau chose to interpret as an apology.

"But that's not why I'm here, Mike. I wanted to get the name of that congressman."

"Right." Mike downed another pale lump. "Did I say congressman? It was Senator Bingham."

"He's from Georgia?"

"Yeah."

"And he's on the Senate Armed Services Committee, right?"

"Yes." Mike actually broke into a full-on half-smile here—practically a miracle for the guy. "You're not as ignorant of politics as you look."

"I'll take that as a compliment." Beau paused. "Would it be strange for him to be having brunch with General Graham, the Pentagon guy, and the guy who runs Green Dynamics—Victor Mann?"

Mike swallowed his pot sticker whole, and Beau slapped his back a few times as Mike's face cycled through a dozen shades of red. Beau didn't think he could get his arms around the barrel chest in the event the Heimlich was required. That would probably result in another round of sensitivity training, if not an assault charge. He handed Mike a glass of water. Nice and safe, if not as effective.

"You saw those guys having *brunch*?"

"You make brunch sound like it requires penicillin."

"For straight guys, maybe. Where?"

"The Inn at Manassas."

"No shit."

"They have eggs Benedict to die for."

"I'll keep it in mind." Then Mike rolled his eyes, so Beau decided to get up and go while he was ahead.

He felt a little guilty for not telling Mike he'd seen Mann at Camp David too. For the moment, he'd keep that nugget of information to himself. But now Beau had enough information to start forming a theory.

That Georgia connection, tying Bingham to Victor Mann and Green Dynamics, was no longer a coincidence. And he still hadn't identified Colonel Sanders, but he wasn't going to give up.

Back at his desk, Beau checked the photos of every senator and representative from Georgia and soon discovered Colonel Sanders was in fact Representative Theodore Redfern.

Beau was so excited at the discovery that he nearly raised his arms in the "touchdown" gesture used by football refs.

Now it was time to learn about Green Dynamics and Victor Mann.

Between fashion assignments, Beau threw himself into research, regularly working late into the evening. He still didn't want to discuss his theories with anyone else, so occasionally when Laney wanted to make evening plans, Beau used Jake as an excuse. And sometimes he fabricated plans with Laney when Jake asked how he spent the nights they spent apart.

He'd also stopped glancing over his shoulder regularly to see if he was being followed.

Chapter 18

IT WAS dark, and cold winter rain pulsed against the windows when Jake finally let himself into his house for the first time in nearly a week.

He dumped the contents of his flight bag into the washing machine, then stripped down to his skin and got the first load started. Once he was upstairs, he cursed himself. There would be no hot water until the wash cycle finished.

He was naked and had fifteen minutes to kill. He was lying down on the bed wondering how he'd spend the other thirteen minutes when the phone rang.

"Jake? Are you running late? I'm at the station."

Crap. He was supposed to pick Beau up at Huntington Station. At least he wouldn't need to jerk off now. He threw on sweats and headed out. The car had just about warmed up by the time he spotted Beau waving at the curb.

Beau opened the door and got inside and immediately wrapped himself around whatever parts of Jake he could reach. God, he smelled good, and he was warm and a little bristly with stubble.

"Razor broke?"

"I'm trying something new. You like?"

"It'll take some getting used to." Jake rubbed the backs of his fingers against Beau's cheek. "Yeah, I like it." He imagined how it would feel on the insides of his thighs.

"I'm glad to see you missed me." Beau had an eagle eye for a hard-on.

Beau wrapped a hand around Jake's upper thigh and kissed him hard enough for Jake to wonder whether there was a hotel between here and home. God, he needed some self-control, at least for the next ten minutes. He put the car in gear, but Beau kept his hand on Jake's thigh for the rest of the ride home, humming the "Marines' Hymn." Well, Jake was already at attention and drove as quickly as he could considering the weather.

Once home, they'd barely made it into the kitchen when Beau's impatience surged past Jake's. It was nice to be the less aggressive one for a change. Then again, Beau seemed to take the lead quite naturally. He had Jake up against the kitchen door and had pulled his sweatshirt up, nuzzling below Jake's navel with his delicious new stubble when Jake heard it.

Somewhere downstairs a tank rolled over a refrigerator. Since he had no tank and the fridge was fine, it had to be the washing machine emitting the kind of noise you never wanted to hear from anything—especially if you were riding in it. Jake chose to focus on Beau instead.

The crunching stopped. If Beau noticed anything, he never let on. He was on his knees and Jake's sweats were halfway down his thighs when the racket started again. "Ignore it," he said to Beau.

Beau let go of Jake's cock and sat back on his heels. "I'm sorry. Even I can't ignore that. Do you have a car crusher down there, or are you printing money?"

Jake would have chuckled, but his hard-on was more off than on at the moment, and Beau frowned at the unfortunate downturn of events. "Fine. I'll go see what happened." He pulled the sweats up with one hand and went down the half flight of steps to the laundry room.

He flipped the lights on and spotted a couple of inches of sudsy water on the floor and more gushing out of the washer. He'd taken one step inside when the sweats slid down and tripped him, and he went sliding bare-assed across the room. This was also when he realized the water was ice cold. Leaping up in surprise, he grabbed for purchase and knocked over a box that landed with a crash like it was full of bottles. Which it was—a remnant of the time when he was pretending he wasn't drinking much.

"Jake? You okay?"

"Fine." Jake was back on his feet, leaning across the washing machine to stop the cycle, when something—Beau, as it turned out—smacked right into the backs of his knees. "What the hell?" He turned to see Beau lying on his back in the slippery, soapy mess.

Then Beau let out a chuckle. As he tried to stand, he went down again, pulling Jake with him.

"Which way did the Road Runner go?" Jake asked, trying to catch his breath between bouts of laughter.

"Thataway." Beau jabbed a thumb toward the door. "But the Three Stooges should be here any minute."

"Why isn't it draining?" Jake was on his knees, feeling around for the drain in the middle of the laundry room floor. He discovered the obstruction and yanked it up. "I was looking for this sock."

"You may just have solved the mystery of the universe. You found one of the disappeared socks!"

"If it's the answer to the universe, there must be forty-one more socks around here."

Beau grabbed Jake and kissed him. "I really do love you. You're always surprising me."

Jake shook his head. "I actually had this whole thing planned."

"I love the idea of a bubble bath, but next time can we do it in the bathtub—with *hot* water?"

FIFTEEN MINUTES later Jake had made Beau's wish come true. They were upstairs in a tub full of warm, sudsy water. They moved the production to the bed, still dripping wet, steam rising off their bodies. Jake slid inside Beau and stopped, holding him and enjoying the feel of their bodies together. They kissed for a while, and Jake twisted his fingers in Beau's hair.

"I missed you so much, Beau. And not just this."

"And the doorbell should ring right about now. Wait for it…." Beau glanced toward the door. "No doorbell. Maybe our luck has changed."

Jake started moving. Though Beau was bottoming, he was fully in charge, wanting to try four different positions. Jake held back so long he thought he might have had a reverse orgasm and nothing would ever come out again.

"Close?" Beau asked in a throaty whisper.

"I was close an hour ago." Jake was hovering over Beau, and a drop of sweat fell a few inches below Beau's collarbone.

"We were in the laundry room an hour ago."

"I know."

"Why didn't you say anything?"

Jake didn't reply.

"Were you waiting for me?" Beau licked his bottom lip. "'Cause I was waiting for you."

Jake started laughing and lost control, coming when he wasn't quite ready for it. He grabbed Beau's cock and stroked, but it took a while to get Beau off, and Jake was so tired he almost gave up.

Beau leaned back and shook his head. "That was awful."

"Yeah, it was." Jake slid out and lay back on the bed next to Beau, both of them staring at the ceiling. "I think it was the worst sex we've had—together, that is."

Nodding, Beau said, "Definitely. But it still wasn't bad." Then he shook his head. "Yeah, it *was* bad. Sorry." A burst of laughter overwhelmed him.

WARM LIPS and smooth, warm skin woke Jake the next morning. Then Beau leaned back and propped himself up on an elbow.

"Morning, Captain."

"Morning." Jake pushed the sheet down Beau's hip, disappointed to discover he was at ease and not at attention. Jake realized he wasn't particularly hard this morning either. He hoped their crappy sex hadn't done any damage, then laughed at his ridiculous fear.

"You still look tired." Beau pulled the sheet up to his waist.

"Gee, thanks."

Beau scooted forward and caressed Jake's temple. "You okay?"

"Not really."

"Is it work? You've been gone so much, and I've missed you, but I know that's the job."

"I still can't get over how lucky I am to have you, Beau. A lot of pilots' wives or girlfriends make a fuss when they travel so much, but you don't."

"Maybe because I don't have to worry you'll sleep with some other woman while you're away." Beau grinned.

Jake let Beau's smile warm him. It was still his favorite thing about Beau. His smile and his melty-chocolate-brown eyes. The way the smile curled up and made Beau's eyes glow more fiercely, till the heat spilled out. But this morning something was a little off there, the light a bit dimmer than usual. It came to Jake that he'd seen it the night before but had chalked it up to his imagination.

"Good point."

"So how was the trip? You were in Georgia?"

"Yeah. Another boring trip."

"Not Atlanta, then?"

"Nope. Some dinky-ass town with about 402 residents."

"You counted?" The glimmer faded a bit more.

Jake shook his head. "Spotted the city limits sign when the lieutenant colonel and I drove to the one café in town, located by the one stoplight."

"What were you doing in a place like that? I guess you weren't flying POTUS?"

A rumble started in Jake's gut because Beau never asked about his flights. "No."

Beau's gaze was so sharp it practically pierced Jake's skull. Was Beau fishing for information or simply making conversation? Jake hated to make the distinction. Hated that he couldn't explain.

"Come on, it can't be a big dark secret who your passengers were?" Beau chuckled, but it sounded hollow as it bounced off the walls.

"It's complicated." Jake had promised himself never to lie or to use bullshit phrases like that with Beau. Their relationship was too important. But these flights were classified, and Beau shouldn't be pumping him for information. He was the fucking fashion columnist, so why had he suddenly taken such a huge interest in Jake's missions?

The reality hit, opening a hole the size of Antarctica in Jake's belly. He'd met Beau *after* he started flying these men. Beau had approached *him*.

Was this all a ruse? Had Beau started their relationship to find out about this project?

No, it couldn't be true. But the possibility made him sick to his stomach.

Beau was staring at him, mouth a thin white line that spelled trouble. "Complicated? Jake, you're scaring me." And he sounded so fucking convincing Jake wanted to trust him.

"I promise to explain everything later. Tonight. Tomorrow. *Soon.* I need to sort something out first."

"Is there a problem at work? Can I help?"

"I'm afraid not. I could really use some of your advice, but I can't discuss squadron business. I'm trying to figure out who I *can* talk to."

"I get it. What about Colonel Lewis? You've always said he supports you, cares about your career."

Jake nodded. It was a great idea. "I'll let you know tonight what happens."

"Sure, tonight." But his voice sounded weak and faraway.

"Come here?" Jake reached out, but Beau leapt up.

"Crap, is that the time? I gotta get going." He raced for the bathroom and came out dressed.

"Where's the fashion fire?"

"I have a meeting this morning, and I can't be late."

"Let me take you to the station. Gimme a minute to get dressed." Jake climbed out of bed.

A horn sounded from the street. "That's my cab. I booked it last night, thinking it would be easier and you'd get more sleep."

Jake sat at the edge of the bed and wondered if his whole world had just come crashing down on him. Then Beau stopped in the doorway and gave him a real smile. He came back to the bed and planted a real good-bye kiss on Jake. Then he raced down the stairs like Cinderella at midnight.

Jake savored the taste of Beau's lips as he prayed his overactive imagination was just that.

AFTER BEAU left, Jake's mood sank even lower. He didn't have time to get Daisy from across the street before he had to report for duty, so he'd see her later. It would be nice to have a good run and work out some of his frustration. The PT he managed during the time away served to keep his body in tune, but it did nothing for his mind or his soul. Those could only be repaired by quality time with Beau, Daisy, and the rest of the people who mattered to him.

He drove to the base on autopilot, hoping to find a solution for the multiple loyalties pulling him to shreds. If he discovered Beau was just another reporter intent on a story and willing to go to these lengths to get it…. Jake could barely contemplate how deeply devastated he'd be. He found himself wondering if he had any booze left in the house or whether he should pick some up on the way home.

No. I won't go down that black hole again.

Ironic that it had been Beau who'd originally pulled him back out, into the light.

Beau couldn't be faking his interest, his support through Jake's challenges with alcohol, their whole relationship. Not with so many wonderful memories, special moments, and so much genuine tenderness. Or had Jake imagined most of that? He'd had friends who'd gotten hooked on strippers or hookers, who actually thought those women were in love with them. Beau wasn't in that category, but hustlers had ways to make a man believe impossible things when he wanted to believe.

And Jake wanted to be loved by Beau. He'd been an easy target.

"Captain? The gate's up, sir."

"What?" Jake found himself at the Quantico gatehouse, with the guard on duty looking worried. A loud, long honk behind him blew away the last remnants of cloud in his memory. He made sure to drive more carefully. He entered the second security perimeter and parked near the Cage. He was in plenty of time for the AOM and stopped for a cup of coffee in the break room before making his way to the meeting.

The lieutenant colonel gave out assignments for the next two weeks. Jake was relieved to hear he had been assigned as copilot for a two-night POTUS lift to Maine right after the State of the Union. Maybe those clandestine missions had earned him the kind of reward he really wanted.

He worked with Major Landau and the rest of the crew assigned to Maine on the flight plans and details. The advance team was already on location with the Secret Service, and the major allowed Jake more responsibility in designing the flight plan. It was a satisfying morning.

By the time his lunch break was over, he started to feel almost normal again. But once he'd arrived back at the Cage, Lieutenant Colonel Monroe called him into the office. The familiar burning in his gut started up.

"I've got another assignment for you. Copiloting for me."

Jake's heart stopped. "Instead of Maine?"

"Don't give yourself a coronary. No. Once you're back. I'll take care of the flight plans, and we'll leave that evening. Two nights."

"Yes, sir."

"Take the rest of the day off. You've been putting in a lot of extra hours, and I want you to be well rested for the POTUS lift."

"There's still work to do on that."

"Major Landau can manage the maintenance requests. You can handle the rest tomorrow. Half a day off won't make a big difference."

"Thank you, sir."

Jake drove home in a great mood, and after he and Daisy went for a long run through the park, he felt almost back to normal. He called Beau, and when he couldn't get through, he left a voice mail suggesting they meet for dinner.

He'd made a big decision during the run. The cold fresh air circling his brain had clarified his priorities.

It was a risk, but he was ready to bet everything on his relationship with Beau being real. He would like to come clean about the Appaloosa flights and hush-hush nights away. He wouldn't divulge classified information, only that the nature of the assignments worried him. He needed to get this off his chest, needed another opinion about whether he was overreacting. Talking to Alvarez or Plummer or even Landau was out of the question. Neither had questioned the orders, and Jake couldn't risk being reported for insubordination—or worse.

The whole situation made him uneasy, even with friends and colleagues. When had he stopped trusting the other guys in the squadron? When these flights resumed in January? Now they were almost weekly. They were isolating him from his peers and driving a wedge between himself and Beau.

If he went down in flames—figuratively this time—it would be his fault, and he alone would suffer the consequences. He refused to take anyone down with him.

Back home, Jake sat on the couch and scratched Daisy's ears for a while, gathering his courage. Then he grabbed the phone and dialed the one person who could really put his mind at ease.

"Hello?"

"Colonel Lewis, this is Jake Woodley." The colonel was still out on leave to help his wife. When Jake arrived at HMX-1, Lewis had helped him survive the enormous transition from a combat posting. He'd helped Jake avoid the drug testing when he'd been at his worst. Colonel Lewis was the only senior officer Jake trusted right now.

"Hello, Jake, how are you?"

"How is your wife, sir?"

"She's been doing much better. Thank you for asking. What's on your mind, son?"

"Sir, I'm worried about a few things going on in the squadron."

"This isn't a secure line, so if you're going to discuss anything classified...."

"No, sir, but I need some advice, and it does involved classified information."

"The phone isn't the best way for that."

"Can we meet?" Jake's stomach unknotted slightly when the colonel didn't immediately tell him to talk to someone else.

"Today's not good. How about tomorrow? I'll go on base to see you. Come to my office at ten hundred hours."

Before Jake could ask to meet off base, the colonel hung up. Well, it was better than nothing, and he'd taken the first step.

With the rest of the afternoon free, he could get to DC early and maybe convince Beau to skip out on work. With that early morning meeting he'd run off to, Beau deserved an early dismissal too.

With a weight already off his mind, Jake took the Metro to the *District Daily*'s offices. He'd wait at Café Agatha, around the corner from the newspaper office, where Beau liked to write when he wanted a change of surroundings. Jake looked forward to surprising him by being early for a change.

He had his hand on the café door when he spotted Beau sitting at his favorite table, a pale lavender scarf loosely wrapped around his neck. With his back to the door, he wouldn't notice Jake. Then a burly bearded man wearing a green sweater Beau would call seafoam or pale sage made his way to the table with two coffees, set them down, and settled into the chair next to Beau. Heads together chatting, they seemed comfortable, almost intimate.

Jake ducked out of sight, went to the other side of the café, and dialed Beau's cell phone as he stared at a framed cover of Agatha Christie's *Elephants Can Remember*, featuring a garish orange version of the eponymous pachyderm.

"Beaumont," Beau said. His caller ID would have flashed Jake's name. Why had he answered so formally?

"Hey, Beau, did you get my message?" Jake took a breath as he willed his heart to stop pounding.

"About tonight? I'm not sure yet what time I'll be finished. I'm swamped at work."

Except Jake knew he was in Café Agatha and didn't have his laptop.

"I have something important to tell you." Jake paused. He ignored his churning stomach and pressed on with the original plan. All his tactical training told him to fall back and regroup, but he charged ahead anyway. "About Georgia. I told you I'd explain it."

"Really?"

Jake wished he could see Beau's face or body language. Was the other man listening? Was he holding Beau's hand? Touching Beau's leg under the table? Was Beau playing that guy against Jake for some reason?

"Yes. I need your advice actually." Jake glanced at an unsmiling portrait of Agatha Christie, mirroring her black-and-white melancholy. The formal tone of the conversation with Beau sapped his strength and his confidence more than he cared to admit. Where was his flirty, sexy, exasperatingly outrageous Beau? "How about meeting me around six at Tartare?"

"Okay, sounds great. Gotta run now, I'm kind of in a meeting. But I'll see you later."

"Love you," Jake told the little beeps that meant Beau had already hung up. He checked his watch. Barely four. It would be a bad idea to go to the bar right now.

Bad idea. Bad idea. Bad idea. His new mantra.

"THIS SEAT free?"

Jake swiveled on his barstool toward the tall man wearing a pin-striped suit who stood at the open spot at the bar with a questioning smile.

"Yeah, sure."

The man sat down gracefully on the stool, which in Jake's experience was a difficult feat to accomplish. He ordered a beer and pulled a phone out of his pocket, like nearly everyone else in the place.

It was a little after six, and Beau hadn't arrived yet. Jake was halfway through a nonalcoholic beer, a European brand that tasted ten times better than the American ones. If Beau hadn't arrived by the time he finished, he'd call.

He watched the bartender wipe down the marble-topped bar between pouring drinks and pulling drafts from brass-tipped keg handles. This was one of Beau's favorite places, a brasserie-style bar with bistro food, the French equivalent of comfort food. Tartare served only European beers, and the food had unpronounceable French names for things with perfectly acceptable English descriptions. Beau preferred steak *frites* over steak with french fries, but Jake liked the food here no matter the name.

"I'll be back," Jake told the bartender and made a quick trip to the men's room.

When he returned his half-full (he was trying to be optimistic) glass was now completely full. He glanced around and caught the bartender's eye. The guy nodded toward the well-dressed man next to Jake, still swiping away at his phone.

"Thanks for the refill."

The man looked up. "My pleasure." His open, friendly smile reminded Jake a little too much of Beau. Jake waited for the guy to start up a conversation, but he didn't.

Just as well. As he took another sip, Jake almost wished he'd ordered a bourbon or scotch, something to calm his nerves. Seeing Beau at the café had rattled him, and he hated to begin questioning everything about their relationship. It was all in his head. Everything was fine between them. Nothing had changed except Jake's sudden and inexplicable paranoia.

His phone buzzed—Beau calling.

"I'm just finishing up, so I'll be there in about fifteen. I can't wait—crap, I have to take this call. See you soon. Love you." Beau made kissy noises, then hung up before Jake could get in a single word. That felt reassuringly normal, and Jake relaxed. He took a long swig of beer. It tasted so much better after the call. He'd been imagining everything.

"Got stood up?" The stranger put his phone away and rotated his stool toward Jake.

"No. Just running a little late." Jake got a good look at the guy's face for the first time. He was model good-looking.

"His loss, my gain. I'm happy to keep you occupied until he arrives."

Jake blinked a few times, first at the sudden friendliness, and second at the guy seeming to know something about him.

"Sorry, I could hear it was a man's voice." He shrugged and held up his glass to toast Jake's.

Jake took another sip. "Have we met?"

"Maybe. At FBs?"

Fast Balls was a gay sports bar in Alexandria. Only regulars called it FBs. But that wasn't it. Jake shook his head.

"Well, I'm Brett."

"Jake." They shook hands and discussed the Redskins' continuing abysmal performance.

Jake felt a tap on his shoulder and turned around to see Laney.

"Hi Jake, you okay?" She had a sour-lemon twist to her mouth.

"Sure. Just fine."

"Beau'll be here in a few minutes. Stopped to powder his nose or something."

Jake turned back to Brett and reached for his glass. It was empty. He didn't remember finishing it.

BEAU YANKED open the door of Tartare and the aroma of hoppy beer, good wine, and roasting meat tickled his nostrils. He hadn't been there in a while, and he was surprised Jake chose it. Not at all Jake's kind of place, based on their visit a month earlier, so he took it as a good sign for whatever Jake would tell him, and not a breakup.

"*Bonsoir, mon beau* Beau!" Henri, the maître d', almost shouted the warm greeting that always made Beau smile.

"Hello, Henri. I'm meeting a friend. Maybe he's in the bar?"

"Monsieur Jake? He arrived a little while ago. And Mademoiselle Laney is here too."

"Merci." Beau made his way toward the bar, but a quick glance didn't find Jake anywhere. Laney was at a table with two other features writers from the *Daily*.

"Beau!"

He waved, but the look on Laney's face sent Beau's stomach hurtling as though he were on the downslope of the world's steepest roller coaster. "What?"

"Come here." She stood up and grabbed his sleeve, then practically dragged him toward the quiet area near the restrooms.

"You're scaring me, Lane." Beau sucked on his lower lip and glanced around again. He looked toward the men's room door, willing Jake to come through it.

"Jake left. He was acting weird and then he… left."

Beau scrunched his forehead and pulled his phone out. "Maybe he's not feeling well."

"I'll say." Laney scowled, but she didn't elaborate.

Beau called Jake, but he didn't pick up, so Beau left a message. Then he texted, "I'm at Tartare." He turned back to Laney. "I'm sure he'll get right back to me."

Laney stared at her shoes. "He left with a guy, Beau."

Her tone made Beau's stomach flip-flop, and he put a hand against the wall to steady himself. "Something must have come up. Work or something. Was it a Marine? Secret Service?"

"He was wearing a really nice suit, like a lobbyist. Expensive. And he had really nice hair." She made a wavy motion above her shoulder.

No military guy or Secret Service agent had nice hair. "I'm sure it was something important."

"When I said you were on your way, he told me to mind my own fucking business, or words to that effect." Laney grabbed for Beau's arm and squeezed.

That didn't sound like a national security issue, and it didn't sound like Jake. He was always polite to Laney—to everyone, in Beau's experience.

Beau nodded as the implications sank in. Jake was usually really good at communicating, leaving texts or voice mails. He'd promised to tell Beau where he'd been when he said he'd been away on a lift earlier that week. But things had been weird between them, and maybe Beau had missed the signs. Could Jake have been away with the guy of the perfect hair and expensive suit? Something about the description reminded Beau of Rick, supposedly not even an ex. Was that what Jake was going to explain tonight?

Knowing it wasn't a good solution to his unease, Beau couldn't help asking, "Lane, where do we get those cocktails by the gallon?"

Chapter 19

EVEN BEFORE Jake opened his eyes, sunlight sent bright daggers deep into his brain. He squeezed his eyes tight, and that tiny movement alone made his head throb like a bass drum.

He stretched, eliciting more pain. He felt weak and achy.

He sat up slowly so his head wouldn't explode, then opened his eyes to help get his balance.

The first things he noticed were dingy beige walls with unidentifiable stains. He looked around the best he could without actually turning his head. Even swiveling his eyeballs hurt.

"Where the fuck…?"

What had he and Beau drunk, and why had they thought going to a sleazy motel was a good idea? He remembered considering it the evening before—no, two evenings earlier—after he'd picked Beau up at Huntington.

"Beau? What were we thinking?"

No answer.

"Beau?" Jake's gut twisted. He managed to stand up, though he was half-bent over as he made his way to the bathroom, arriving just in time before he puked. He lay on the filthy floor, trying not to think about what might be on there as he emptied his stomach and quite possibly heaved up a lung and kidney.

Sour bile and another taste he couldn't place lingered in his mouth, even after he washed it out with water as dingy as the walls.

He spent what felt like an hour trying to get back to the bed.

Then Jake realized he was naked. This just got worse and worse.

He found his clothes scattered on the floor. His nice new jacket was rumpled but thankfully not torn. The shirt was missing a few buttons. He felt sick again and decided not to dress until he was done vomiting.

He looked at himself in the bathroom mirror after this bout of heaving was over. White flakes peeling away from his chin and throat sent him back to the toilet.

What had he done? Who had he been with? It couldn't have been Beau because he couldn't imagine Beau abandoning him here, no matter how badly their discussion had gone. Shards of the night before came into focus.

He'd waited for Beau at the bar. He'd limited himself to one NA beer. None of the real stuff. He remembered Laney's face. That was it.

He should call Beau. Apologize. He wasn't sure what to apologize for, but he had a feeling an apology was necessary. He found his pants, socks, shoes. His wallet was in his pants; money, ID, everything was still intact. The only thing missing was his cell phone.

And his underwear.

Maybe the guys in the squadron had gotten him drunk and were playing a joke on him. This was the kind of thing they'd do, especially since he hadn't told them he was off the booze. He hoped that's all it was. He put on the clothes he could find and searched for the phone. It hurt like hell, but he bent to look under the bed. He wouldn't have been surprised to find a dead hooker under there, but mercifully he only spotted dust bunnies and a spider that easily deserved a spot in the *Guinness Book of World Records*.

If the guys in the squadron had done this, one of them would have his phone. Fuck, what time was it?

Seven forty-five, according to the clock on the nightstand. He could call in sick and figure out the rest later, when his head stopped fighting back. But he was supposed to talk to Colonel Lewis today. He couldn't reschedule, and it wouldn't look good to show up for that meeting, then go home. He had to get to the base.

He always kept a clean uniform in his locker there. He washed up as best he could in the disgusting bathroom, making himself presentable enough to get on base, then went to the motel office to have them call him a taxi.

"Oh, I didn't expect you or your sick-fuck friend to show your faces this morning."

Jake stared at the man behind the desk. The guy scratched at his grizzled beard and frowned. "If you two left that room a mess, you'll be getting a bill from me. Don't you think you can worm your way out of it."

"Can you call a cab for me? How far's the nearest Metro station?"

The man shrugged and scratched his belly, probably trying to keep his pudgy stomach from escaping the tight, grungy T-shirt stretched across it. No way would Jake ever visit "Stubbie's—the Best Crabs You Ever Caught." They should pay this man *not* to wear a shirt advertising their establishment.

Jake pulled himself to full height, squared his shoulders, and gave the motel clerk the sneer he learned from the drill instructors in OCS. It could put fear into just about anyone. It served Jake's purposes when the guy frowned, picked up the handset of an ancient phone, and started stabbing buttons.

Wanting to get out of the fetid lobby as quickly as possible, Jake waited for the cab outside, though he didn't turn his back on the proprietor. He pictured the guy pulling a 32 gauge out from under the counter and showing

Jake what he thought of him and his "sick-fuck friend." Dizziness washed over him again, leaving him shivering and nauseated.

What friend?

Twenty minutes later Jake climbed behind the wheel of his car and drove unsteadily out of the Huntington Metro parking lot. His dizziness hadn't abated, so he kept to the right-hand lane and safely under the speed limit. He couldn't risk getting pulled over because he would probably fail a Breathalyzer. He should have taken the cab all the way to the base, but he hadn't been thinking clearly.

He waved to the guards and thanked his guardian angels for getting him to the base in one piece without getting pulled over.

He raced to the locker room, took a shower, and started to dress in uniform.

Major Landau came in and started to dial the combination on his locker. "Hey, Jake, you missed the AOM." He glanced up and his eyes widened as he took in Jake's appearance. "You okay?"

"Maybe coming down with a—" Jake's knees gave out again. As the major was helping him up, someone else came into the room. Jake's brain had gone blank, and he didn't understand a word the major was saying to him.

Then Lieutenant Colonel Monroe came in, and Jake's brain started working again.

"Captain, I hate to do this, but it's for your own good, as well as the squadron." Monroe handed Jake a cup of the type used for piss tests. "I need a sample right now."

"I'm not drunk." Jake didn't feel *drunk*. He couldn't describe what he did feel, but it wasn't drunk or hungover.

"Then you can prove it, right now. Get yourself to the head." He nodded in that direction.

Jake couldn't avoid this unless he knocked the man out. So he filled the cup, with Monroe watching, put it in a bag, and handed it to the lieutenant colonel.

"Now get yourself presentable and wait in my office. I want you to stay there while the lab processes this."

"What about the AOM?"

"Forget it. You're grounded until this test comes back clean."

He should have called in sick. Fear of what the test might reveal made him vomit again. After, he rinsed his mouth and washed his face. In the unflattering light, his eyes took on the hollow cast he'd seen on guys huddling in doorways.

When Jake walked out of the head, he realized Lieutenant Colonel Monroe was still in the locker room. His gaze bored holes into Jake's body.

"Is Colonel Lewis here yet?" Jake hoped he sounded better than he felt.

"The colonel's not coming in today."

"I have a meeting scheduled with him." That was the one ray of hope in what appeared to be a massively fucked-up day. He wanted to explain what he thought had happened the night before. This wasn't drunk. He'd never blacked out like this from booze. He'd certainly tried hard enough over the past two years.

"The colonel called and asked me to handle that. Now pull yourself together. You're a disgrace to the uniform, but I don't have the authority to kick you out of the Corps or I would right now. Wait in my office." He walked out of the bathroom.

Jake couldn't imagine his day getting any worse. He put on his uniform. He loved the uniform and everything it represented. He'd earned this uniform. He'd earned his wings and ribbons and medals. He'd even earned the Medal of Honor he tried to forget for so long. Beau had convinced him of that. He could call Beau from Monroe's office while he waited to hear his fate. He wanted to talk to Beau so badly right now.

When transferring his wallet from his civvies, he dropped it and the contents spilled out onto the floor of his locker. He shoved money and cards back inside, and when he bent down, he spotted a clear little packet. He reached for it, discovering too late it contained white powder, and now his fingerprints. It sure as hell was not his. How had it gotten into his wallet? But he knew how. Just not *why*.

His day had officially hit rock bottom. This wouldn't just get him fast-tracked to involuntary separation. This would get him time in prison.

"Woodley? Jake?" It was the major. He sounded concerned.

Jake froze. He had to get rid of the powder. He raced toward the back exit from the locker room, racking his brain for a good place to drop it. No time to flush it. If he got outside, he could throw it into one of the puddles left by salted snow. The chemicals might destroy his fingerprints. Why hadn't he taken more chemistry?

The fire exit door was just three feet away.

Before he reached it, an MP stepped to block his path.

He'd been so close.

Chapter 20

BEAU STARED at his laptop, but he couldn't see a thing. He couldn't think, couldn't focus. He could barely breathe since Laney told him Jake had left with another man the night before. A man he'd been looking awfully chummy with, laughing and smiling—right after he told Laney to fuck off.

But Jake didn't normally talk like that. Unless Jake was drinking again, but even so…. And why?

"Beaumont, get your shit together."

"Sorry, Mike. What were you saying?"

"Georgia towns with population around four hundred. What did you come up with?"

"Uh…. Right." *Focus*. But Beau didn't care anymore. He didn't want to know where Jake had been. Mike's face got progressively redder and puffier, so he pulled up the notes he'd made. "Centralhatchee. Tiger. Moreland. Green Springs." He looked up and paused as Mike searched through one of his databases.

"Nothing. Nothing. Nothing. Noth—wait. Bingo." Mike thumped a huge paw on the desk. "Green Springs. Hometown of a United States Representative."

"We knew that, didn't we? Redfern."

"Actually, no. Haven't I taught you to be patient, Grasshopper?"

Beau wasn't in a laughing mood, but he waited.

"Senator Bingham was born there, but now he lives in and represents Pennsylvania."

"What does that tell us?" Beau asked.

"But wait, there's more! Green Springs is also the nearest town to Green Dynamics, which has received Pentagon contracts for… I can't add that all up, but it's a lot of millions. And they're vying for another zillion or so more on the new communications project and a portion of the tech for a new weapons system down the road. That's a good reason for all those guys to hang out so much, outside the Beltway."

"How is Jake connected?" Beau doodled on his pad.

"That squadron doesn't just fly White House and Cabinet officials. They'd definitely ferry General Graham, and anyone he wanted to bring along. But trips like that would be classified. The Pentagon doesn't usually advertise where the Joint Chiefs are."

"Classified? No wonder Jake didn't tell me where he was going or why. Or mention that he knew Graham and Mann...."

"This isn't about Jake anymore, Beau. It's about why those guys are hanging out and the pies they have their fingers in."

"So, Senator Bingham is what, channeling contracts to Green Dynamics to help out some childhood buddy? Is that news?" Beau's head was swimming with facts, and he hadn't yet found the right thread to pull. Mike had his own set of data, and together they'd figure this out.

But Beau's heart wasn't in it anymore.

Mike was firing on all cylinders now. "Not news yet. Let me pull up more about Green Dynamics. It sounds kind of nice. Environmentally aware."

"Well, it's not. They're on a list of top polluters in their district." Beau was glad to show he'd done his homework. He'd found Victor Mann's dirty laundry already. He hated the guy even more since he had.

Mike let out a low whistle and graced Beau with a look of admiration. "So the senator is pushing dirty technology? Still doesn't sound like something to make these guys skulk around over brunch."

"Well it might be a big deal if they got contracts that should go to more environmentally sound companies." Beau's brain started connecting facts. "Isn't there some law about that? DoD, other agencies, expecting government contractors to meet minimum environmental standards? Unless they are the sole supplier of the technology."

"It's less of an issue for Pentagon contracts. National security trumps environmental security." Mike stared at his screen and nodded. "Right. I think we're onto something now."

"I'm still not sure, Mike. If we add up how much Green Dynamics will profit on the contracts associated with Bingham and Redfern, compared to the annual profits of Green Dynamics, it's not as significant as I would have expected. Assuming the contracts will keep getting funneled through for years, the numbers still don't merit the risk."

Mike nodded. "Then money isn't the only explanation, at least not for Mann. He must be getting something else out of it."

"We need to dig into his financials and contacts. The same for everyone on the board. What else?"

"We should find out everything we can about Green Dynamics and who else they do business with." Mike's pen scratched as he furiously scribbled notes on a pad.

"I've done some of that already."

Mike stared at him. "You have?"

"I told you seeing Mann made me curious. It's why I know that money is barely more than pocket change. I don't know much about technology, which is where I'm drawing a blank. Because if it's not the money on those contracts—"

"It could be where else the technology is going?"

"Right." Beau felt that pleasant tension of knowing he and Mike were onto something potentially huge. It had been years since he'd experienced this high, but he kept dropping back to earth. As Mike jotted notes, Beau leaned back in his chair and checked his phone for the millionth time, hoping to see a text or voice mail from Jake. Nothing. Nothing until one e-mail from "Brett," with a subject line of "Jake."

Beau's heart was pounding as he opened the e-mail. It said, "Wish you were here?" Then he opened the attachments and his world ripped apart.

Mike clapped his hands. "You listening, Beau? Hey, are you okay?"

But Beau didn't think he'd be okay for a long time. He raced out of Mike's office and around the corner to Café Agatha, where he sat in his favorite booth in the corner and made a call.

"I DON'T have swear words strong enough for this, sweetie." Laney rubbed Beau's hand, then slid an arm around his shoulders. "You have to breathe. Please? I'd be lost if something happened to you. Please don't do that to me."

Beau blinked, thinking maybe Oedipus had the right idea when he blinded himself. But he'd never be able to unsee what he'd seen. Jake with Nice-hair Guy. Photos of them undressing. A couple of selfies of them kissing. Several of them giving each other blowjobs, with Jake looking like he'd won the lottery as he had his lips wrapped around the other guy's huge dick. He never smiled that much around Beau's dick.

"Beau, he looks really out of it."

"No. He looks really *into* it." He grabbed the phone away from her. "Stop looking." He shouldn't have told her, and he definitely shouldn't have shown her the photos. Couldn't bear for her to see his shame, because he'd gone on and on about what a wonderful guy Jake was, how everything felt real with him. Had Jake found someone else down in Georgia? No, maybe Georgetown. At least Jake hadn't lied about flying to Georgia for work.

Laney grabbed the phone back and tapped it. She opened her laptop and stared at the screen. Beau reached out and yanked it around to see she was looking at the photos—blown up almost larger than life. "Laney! You e-mailed them to yourself? I can't believe you've betrayed me too."

"Beau, calm down. I'm trying to figure out where they are. Nothing identifiable in the room, except how filthy it is." She kept looking. "I don't think this is what you think."

"Can you tell if someone's altered the image?"

She leaned toward the screen and squinted, then pressed her lips into a pained twist. "I don't think so."

"Then it's what I think."

"No. Look at his eyes. He's wasted, Beau."

"Not too wasted to fuck around." For once Beau wished Jake had drunk more.

"There are no pictures of them fucking."

"Maybe I'll get those tomorrow." The mere idea would have made Beau sick, if he had been able to eat.

"But why would Brett e-mail these to you? Who is he anyway?"

"I don't know anyone named Brett, and I don't recognize him." Beau couldn't bear to look more closely.

"Did he ask for money?"

"Money? Laney, why would he ask *me* for money? He might ask Jake. Fucking bastard. Maybe I should forward these to his CO. Do you think they'd kick him out of the Marines for this?"

"I don't know, but I'm sure they'd kick him out of his job, because the president is not going to want photos of his pilot fucking another guy's face, no matter how nice his hair is."

"Laney!"

"Sorry. I lost track of the message there. Really, sorry." She put her arms around Beau again and cried against his shoulder. "Let's go. You want to come home with me?"

"My day is already bad enough." But he managed a tiny smile. Her place was always a mess. But it didn't hold any memories of Jake the way Beau's apartment did. "Yeah, let's go to your place."

Maybe Laney understood, because she collected their stuff, left a big tip, then steered Beau through the door.

BEAU WOKE up in Laney's bedroom. She was sitting in a chair still gazing into her laptop.

He rubbed his eyes. "What time is it?"

"Almost seven. Are you hungry? I can order takeout for dinner."

"I don't feel like eating. Ever. And don't tell me food can fix anything. It can't fix this."

"Come here. I have more good news."

Beau pulled the sheets over his head.

"Seriously, Beau. I'm positive he's drugged. His pupils are dilated and—"

Beau exhaled violently against the sheets. "Just forget it. Gay men take drugs sometimes when they hook up."

"Do you and Jake do that?"

"No. He's too straitlaced for that." He paused. "Me too. I gave up that shit back in college." Mostly, except for a few instances he wouldn't tell Laney, but those too had been years ago.

"Will you look at this one? Tell me what this white stuff on his face looks like."

Beau groaned. He didn't want to see white stuff on Jake's face. He'd already seen white stuff on him in one of the photos, and it had been enough.

"It's powder. Look." Laney sat on the bed and pulled the sheets off Beau's face. "Look."

He nodded and sat up to see what she was talking about. It could be white powder. What did it matter now? If Jake had snorted something, that didn't make the situation any better.

"Beau, why don't you call him? Give him a chance to explain."

"No."

"Can I call him? Because I'll give him a piece of my mind if he doesn't have a good explanation." She grabbed Beau's phone off the night table. "You have a lot of missed calls." She swiped a few more times. "None of the numbers are in your contacts list. Quantico, Virginia, according to the phone." She glanced at Beau. "The calls are either *from* Jake or *about* him. Your ringer's off."

Almost as soon as she corrected it, the phone rang. She held it toward Beau, but he shook his head. Laney answered.

"Beau's phone. He's sleeping. ... Laney, a friend. ... Oh, no. Is he...? ... Uh-huh. ... Uh-huh. ... Yes. Hold on a minute." She stared at Beau.

"What?"

"It's Tim Alvarez. Jake's in the hospital."

"Hospital?" Beau took the phone. "Tim? What happened?"

"Beau, I've tried a few times to call."

Now Beau's chest hurt like he'd gone a few rounds with Floyd Mayweather. "Jake's in the hospital?" He let concern overrule the anger and hurt.

"He crashed his car driving home, but it's not bad, nothing broken. He's going to be fine. He's had a really bad day."

Well, he wasn't the only one. Beau waited for the rest of the story.

"He got detained by the MPs this morn—"

"Detained! For what?"

Laney grabbed Beau's arm, but he turned away until he knew what was going on.

"Suspicion of possessing a controlled substance." Tim Alvarez paused.

Drugs? That didn't sound like Jake at all, though Beau hadn't seen as much of him recently. Not as much as Brett had. Concern and anger battled in Beau's gut.

Tim continued, "Then they released him, and when he tried to drive home, he went off the road. He's bruised, nothing broken, and they're releasing him now. I can bring him home with me, unless you want to come out to his place...."

"I'm heading out now. I'll get a ride out there. Thanks for letting me know." He hung up.

Laney stared at him, wide-eyed.

"Can you drive me to Jake's? One of the other pilots is bringing him home."

"What do you mean, bringing him home?"

Beau shook his head, wishing he knew what to say.

"Does that mean you're not mad about the photos?"

"Hell yes, I'm mad. But I'll give him a chance to explain. Depending on what he says, his day may be about to get a whole lot worse."

WHEN LANEY and Beau pulled up to Jake's house all the lights inside blazed and a blue SUV stood in the driveway.

"You want me to go inside with you?"

Beau glanced over at her, debating whether this had been a good idea after all. On the ride from DC, his brain concocted a dozen scenarios for Jake's behavior, arrest, and car crash. Beau wanted an explanation, but as the iconic phrase went, he wasn't sure he could handle the truth. Having Laney there could be more embarrassing than helpful.

"Beau, honey, I'm here for you. Whatever happens, I've got your back." She rubbed a hand up and down his arm and put on a brave face.

"Thanks. Yeah, come in." It took all Beau's strength to open the car door and force himself to walk to the house.

Jenna and Toby were in the entryway, and Tim Alvarez was coming down the stairs. It was like a class reunion, and Beau couldn't stand everyone being there while he talked to Jake.

Tim shook Beau's hand and nodded politely to Laney. "Beau, glad you could make it so quickly. Jake's been asking for you."

"But he's okay?" Toby asked, moving toward the stairs.

"Toby, stay down here." Jenna reached for his shoulder. "Take Daisy into the living room."

"But I want to see Jake!"

"He's asking for you, Beau. And for Daisy." Tim moved closer to Beau. "He's in some trouble with the squadron, but I don't know what."

"You said he got arrested?" Beau kept his voice low.

Laney stared at her shoes. Jenna told Toby they needed to get home and left discreetly after handing Daisy's leash to Laney.

"I saw it happen, but neither the lieutenant colonel nor the major elaborated on the situation. I guess he was released and on his way home when he went off the road. He's banged up a little, but nothing's broken. He's not supposed to drive or drink. They have to wait for a tox screen before they can prescribe anything, so he can only have over-the-counter stuff unless they call in a prescription for anything stronger."

"Okay. Thanks for getting him from the hospital and for letting me know."

Tim clapped a hand on Beau's shoulder. "Sure. Give me a call later with an update."

Beau nodded and moved toward the stairs. His stomach might have been trying to force its way out through his skin, it hurt so much. But he had to know.

"Wait," Laney called and handed over Daisy's leash.

The dog practically dragged Beau up the stairs. Otherwise he might not have made it all the way to the second floor. Throat tight and heart pounding like it was trying to make an *Alien*-style escape along with his stomach, he pushed the door open to see Jake lying in bed.

The sight stopped Beau in the doorway.

If he hadn't been so fucking mad at Jake, he would have been in tears. Jake had a bandage on one cheek, and he had a black eye. His lower lip was swollen and caked with blood. He looked more like he'd been rolled by a biker gang than in a supposedly minor auto accident.

"Beau." Jake tried to smile but grimaced in obvious pain. "It's probably not as bad as it looks. But I'm told it looks bad."

Beau nodded, not sure what to say. On any other day, he'd race to Jake's side the way Daisy had. Jake dangled a hand off the edge of the bed to stroke Daisy's head, and she sat down obediently as if knowing she shouldn't leap onto the bed.

"Tell me what happened, Jake. And start with last night."

JAKE SWALLOWED, his throat so dry he expected it to crack. But every ache in his body faded away as he watched the look on Beau's face. It wasn't concern; it was anger, maybe even animosity. It frightened him more than anything he'd already been through that day. Waking up naked in the disgusting motel, finding a packet of what he thought was cocaine in his wallet, getting detained by MPs, crashing his car.

It had been one fucking mess of a day, but the narrowed eyes and set of Beau's chin as he glared down at him was the worst.

"I was at Tartare, having a nonalcoholic beer at the bar and talking to the guy sitting next to me—"

"Brett?"

Jake blinked. "Yeah, I think that was his name." How did Beau know that? "I remember seeing Laney. Then I don't remember anything until I woke up this morning."

"NA beer?" Beau scoffed as he folded his arms across his chest and leaned against the door jamb.

"Half an NA beer. I went to the bathroom, and the guy—"

"Brett." Beau's tone was openly hostile as he uttered that one syllable.

"Right. He'd ordered me another round. It's kind of hazy... but I don't remember drinking that beer. And no, I didn't touch any tequila. I swear...." He looked around. "I swear on Daisy's life." Daisy bobbed her head at hearing her name and laid her muzzle down on the bed, loving gaze planted on Jake. He stroked her head for confidence.

"Go on."

Jake closed his eyes for a moment, trying to pull the events out of the haze. "I woke up at some sleazebag motel about ten miles from here. I couldn't remember anything after the brasserie. I was dizzy and couldn't see clearly. And I was naked." Jake stopped and waited for his stomach to settle down. "I have no clue what happened. I know that's probably hard to believe."

"I believe it." Beau's tone wasn't reassuring.

"You do?"

"I believe you don't remember what happened." Beau's hot glare could set the room on fire.

But Jake had to keep going. "Beau, something happened last night, and I don't know what. I could barely drive to the base, and Monroe noticed and forced me to take a drug test. Then I found a packet of white powder in my wallet while I was waiting for the results."

This seemed to get Beau's attention. He stopped sneering, but he didn't say anything.

"Someone had called the MPs, reported me behaving erratically. When they searched me they found the packet and detained me. They questioned me, held me for a while, then later told me it was baby powder. None of it makes any sense. I don't know why someone wanted me to think I'd taken coke." Why wasn't Beau reacting to any of this? "I know I've had some issues with drinking, but you know I've been handling it pretty well since the party at Tim's. I would never in a million years take drugs. I won't take prescription pain meds because I don't want to risk becoming dependent and jeopardizing my commission or my pilot slot."

Beau blinked, which was the most emotion he'd shown. Jake felt like he was in the MP station again, where they didn't believe a word he'd said.

"Why don't you believe me?"

"I believe you about the cocaine. I know how much the Corps means to you."

"And the rest? I'm sorry about last night. Shit, Beau, I'm really scared. I think I might—"

Jake stopped himself short of saying what he thought he might have done in the motel, but the possibilities made his stomach churn. He had absolutely no memory of that portion of the evening, and he was grateful.

"Have you told me everything?"

"As much as I remember."

Beau handed his phone to Jake. He glanced at it and threw up into the garbage can Tim had had the foresight to leave by the bed.

"Is that Brett?" Beau asked when the heaving stopped.

Jake nodded. He closed his eyes, but he couldn't unsee the photo of him with Brett's cock down his throat. When he opened his eyes, Beau was gone.

"Beau!" Jake rushed to stand up and the room tilted sickeningly again. How could he still be drugged? They'd said his blood-alcohol content had been normal both on the base and at the hospital, but his body felt drunk. He made it to the landing and sat on the first step, looking down at Beau, who stood at the foot of the stairs. Worse than being detained by MPs, being in a crash, or even of seeing the photo was the fear that Beau wouldn't believe him—and that he might lose Beau over something he couldn't imagine doing.

"Beau, I couldn't have done that. Not willingly. I wouldn't.... I went into the District early planning to surprise you at Café Agatha, but you were there with someone when you told me you were in a meeting. I was so hurt you'd lied. I wasn't spying on you, but.... But I... I wouldn't have slept with anyone else, even if you told me to get lost." Jake leaned on the railing and made his shaky way down the stairs.

Beau looked up at Jake. "What did you say?"

"Which part?"

"The café?"

Jake repeated it. Laney clamped a hand over her mouth. Beau rubbed his forehead. Everything moved in slow motion. Jake's knees buckled and he tripped down the last two steps.

BEAU FELL to his knees at Jake's side, gently pushing Daisy and Laney out of the way.

"Jake?"

Jake rubbed the back of his head as he sat on the floor, eyes dark and stormy. "I get why you don't believe me. *I* wouldn't believe me. No matter what I say, you have a photo." He paused. "It's not fake, is it?" He grabbed the banister and pulled himself up, then shuffled toward the kitchen, one hand splayed against the wall as if to help him keep his balance.

Beau left Laney in the hall and followed Jake into the kitchen.

"I do believe you, Jake." Beau softened his tone.

Jake stopped and stared at Beau without speaking, but the tension seemed to ebb from his face.

"I believe you. We'll figure this out."

The incredulity and relief in Jake's eyes told Beau he'd made the right decision. He had to take a leap of faith. If he landed on his head, it couldn't possibly hurt more than his heart already did.

"You do?"

"The hospital called Tim, right before he left here, and said they had lab results to explain what caused the memory loss, dizziness, nausea. They wouldn't tell him what—privacy issues—but I think you might have been roofied."

"What?" Jake clutched for a chair and lowered himself into it carefully.

Beau rushed to help him. He hated himself for doubting Jake when he'd been the victim of the drugging and sexual assault too. "Call the hospital and get the results."

"I lost my phone."

"Laney, did Tim give you the hospital number?"

Laney came into the kitchen and handed Beau a piece of paper. He called and handed the phone to Jake, who recoiled at it. He was clearly still shaken by the photo. Beau wished he hadn't shown it to him now. If he'd waited five minutes longer, he would have known Jake had been assaulted and not willingly unfaithful. Laney squeezed Beau's hand as Jake talked to the hospital, and Beau reached over to hold Jake's.

"You're right," Jake said when he'd concluded the call. "They found Rohypnol in my blood, but they also found cocaine. I'm screwed as far as the Corps is concerned."

"But if you weren't responsible for your actions when it happened, how can you get in trouble for that?" Laney looked like she might cry, mirroring Beau's feelings and fears.

"I'm in a zero-tolerance job. I have to be prepared for the worst, once the full tox screen results come back from the tests Monroe ordered. They won't let me stay in the squadron with a positive drug test. I might not be able to find a nonaviation position in the Corps." What would he do if he couldn't fly? The mere possibility made him want to grab a bottle. No time for that self-destructive behavior now.

"But why did Brett do that?"

Jake stared at her. "That, Laney, is the billion-dollar question."

Chapter 21

LANEY LEFT a little while later. Beau ordered delivery from an Italian restaurant they both liked, but neither had much appetite.

"Beau, you should have gone with Laney."

Beau's stomach lurched. "Don't you want me here?"

Jake didn't reply.

"The hospital said someone should stay with you tonight to look out for a head injury." It was the least of Beau's reasons for staying. He didn't know whether Jake was putting on a bold front under the bruises or needed his space. "If you want to be alone, I can stay downstairs, or sleep in the chair by the dresser." Maybe Jake didn't want to be touched after what Brett had done.

"I can't ask you to stay after what I did."

"Jake, *you* didn't do it. It was done to you." Beau had to remind himself of that whenever he thought about the photos. Laney wouldn't let him delete the e-mail because it was evidence, but it made Beau want to throw the whole contaminated phone away. "I'm sorry I didn't believe you." Beau looked away, unable to meet Jake's gaze.

When Jake put his hand on Beau's and squeezed, Beau thought maybe things would be okay again between them.

"Jake, we need to find out why."

"Spoken like a true reporter." Jake managed a crooked smile, then stopped and touched his bruised lip.

"There has to be a reason. What does anyone have to gain from this situation?"

"I don't know."

"Let's think this through. What are the ramifications, for you and for me?" Beau stood up and grabbed a pad and pen out of a drawer. It felt good to concentrate on something other than what Jake had been through. "Okay, go. First, what happens to you as a result?"

"I could lose my commission. Lose my job—"

"What does that mean, precisely?"

"Isn't it obvious?"

"Not to me. What will that prevent you from doing?" Jake looked blank, so Beau rephrased it. "Let's turn that around. What does your job allow or require you to do?"

"I'm still not thinking too clearly, but I'll try." Jake nodded. "Fly the president, fly other officials, visit the White House...."

Beau scribbled as Jake listed specifics. "Could it be someone trying to get your job, get your assignments?"

"No. Everyone in the squadron follows the same path of increasing responsibility. How fast you go is based on skill. Getting rid of me won't guarantee anything for anyone else. They still have to earn it."

"What have you been doing lately? Who wants to get you off those assignments?"

Jake sat up straighter. "It's the opposite. I've been trying to stop flying certain assignments." He glanced up at Beau. "It's what I wanted your advice about last night."

This news reassured Beau as much as anything else. Jake wanted his advice. "Tell me."

"I've been making a series of flights, mainly to Georgia, but to some other destinations, and I don't want to. The orders are classified, but there's something fishy about it. I was supposed to talk to Colonel Lewis about it today and—"

"Slow down." They were making progress. "Someone could have tried to keep you from talking to the colonel. You were in Green Springs?"

"How did you know?"

"I did some homework. You told me the population, and I couldn't help looking it up."

"You were checking up on me?" Jake furrowed his brow.

Beau shrugged. "Sorry. Reporter instinct, not stalker boyfriend." A white lie.

"And you figured out where I'd gone from one throwaway comment I made? I'm impressed."

This was no time to gloat, but Beau was becoming more confident things might be okay between him and Jake and that something was decidedly fishy about his missions. He liked having Jake compliment him for a change.

"Did you know Senator Bingham on the Armed Services Committee is originally from Green Springs?" Beau watched Jake's face.

"No. Why is that important?"

"Because Green Dynamics is vying for some extremely lucrative defense contracts. And remember we saw Bingham and the head of GD with the cue-ball guy from the Pentagon having brunch? I also saw the Green Dynamics guy with Cue-Ball at Camp David. The day we went on the snowmobile. They went into the woods when they saw us."

"How on earth did you recognize them? Everyone was bundled up."

"I recognized Mann's coat. And Graham's posture."

"A coat? Really? That's your proof?"

"We're in my wheelhouse on this, Jake. Trust me. It's a very distinctive coat. I've never seen one like it before."

"Why didn't you say anything then? Still, I don't see how it all connects. What's wrong with them meeting? I don't know anything about Pentagon contracts or Senate committees."

"That's what I was doing at the café. You saw me with Mike Beaumont. He covers exactly these kinds of issues for the *Daily*, and we're trying to put our heads together to figure out precisely how all the pieces add up with those trips. Now, back to the list. How you fit into the picture and why would someone want to discredit you or to break us up."

"Maybe it's a threat. Showing me you're a target too." Jake's lips were a narrow white line. "I can't let them harm you because of something to do with me."

"I'm fine. Now that you are." He clasped his hand around Jake's. "Are you okay? Besides the bruises? After Brett...." Beau couldn't say the words.

"I'm more worried right now about losing my commission and you. I haven't had time to think about much else."

"I love you, Jake."

Jake smiled for the first time since Beau arrived. "I needed to hear that. And I need for you to stay with me tonight."

DURING THE night Jake stared at the ceiling, unable to sleep. He'd dozed a little, but now he was wide awake while Beau slept next to him.

He still didn't recall much of the night before and he wasn't certain he wanted to. Seeing the photo of him with Brett almost felt like it was another person—not him. What hurt so much was knowing how upset Beau had been over it.

Jake had been through plenty during combat, and he'd trained for much more. What happened with Brett—what Brett did to him—paled in comparison. At least for now. If Jake's life got back to normal, if he kept his commission and his HMX-1 posting, it might fade away completely, or come back to haunt him. For the moment he put this incident away in a compartment the way he'd learned during SERE training.

By the next morning, aside from his bruises, Jake felt almost normal again, physically. But emotionally he was a disaster, with concern for Beau. Was he Brett's next target, or did whoever was behind this have something worse in store for him?

"Beau, I'd like you to stay here today." Jake sipped coffee Beau brought him in bed.

"Do you need me?" Worry creased Beau's features even more.

Jake shook his head. "I want to make sure you're safe."

"Safe?" Alarm flashed across Beau's face.

Jake wished he'd phrased it differently. "Just in case."

"I have to get into the office. Mike texted me that's he found proof of something, and…."

Beau looked so eager, Jake put his worries aside. "Maybe you'll figure out who's behind the other night, too."

"I'll try." Beau leaned down to kiss Jake and grabbed his things.

Jake went downstairs and watched him get into a cab, his breath a white plume in the winter morning chill.

Upstairs again, he examined his face and body in the bathroom mirror under the unforgiving lights. He looked worse than yesterday. The bruises had ripened to blackish green. He appreciated Beau not mentioning just how awful he looked.

Fed up with being idle but too sore for a run, he took Daisy for a walk. For a change he chose not to push himself, and the slower pace let him mull over the situation with more attention.

He was drinking his third cup of coffee when there was a knock at his door, startling him and causing Daisy to bark. He hesitated before answering it, because it couldn't possibly be good.

"Jake? It's Toby!"

"Coming!" Jake opened the door and Toby raced in and gave him a hug, causing Jake to wince slightly.

"Oh my God, your face! Are you okay? I was so scared when Mom said you had a car accident and then made me go home." He talked as if he had to get all the words out in the shortest possible time.

His concerned tone and worried eyes showed an unconditional love Jake really needed. "I've just got some bruises. I'll be back to normal by dinner time."

"You should come over for dinner."

"I've got a lot of leftover Italian food. You guys should come here and help me eat it. Tell your mom."

"Okay. I gotta get to school now."

"See you later." Jake endured another hug, then watched Toby race down the icy driveway, hoping he wouldn't slip and break his neck.

With the whole day stretching ahead of him, Jake was at a loss. He had so few days off and spent most of them with Beau. But this involuntary idleness had him climbing the walls. He could get serious and contact a lawyer, or he could start considering his employment options if he got drummed out of the Corps.

He was staring at a legal pad on which he'd managed to write the numbers one to five and nothing more. He scratched his head and was considering brewing another pot of coffee when the landline rang.

The sound startled him and sent his heart racing. He ignored it, but the phone kept ringing, and Daisy raced to the table and barked at the phone, then stared at Jake. He could picture her thoughts: "Timmy's down the well, you have to help!"

Too many *Lassie* reruns when he was in his formative years.

Finally he got up and answered.

"Jake, Lieutenant Colonel Monroe here."

Cold fingers gripped Jake's heart and squeezed till it stopped beating. "Yes, sir?"

"Can you come into my office now?"

"I was under the impression I'm suspended."

"That's what I'd like to discuss with you."

"Yes, sir. My car's—actually I have no idea where it is, so I'll—"

"Your car?"

"I was in an accident yesterday when I left the base. I guess it's been towed. I'll phone a taxi. Would you please send word to the guard shack to let it on base?"

"I had no idea about the accident. Are you okay?" For a change, Monroe sounded human. It made Jake suspicious.

"I've got a headache and a bruise or two."

"Good to hear it's not more serious. Come directly to my office when you arrive." He hung up.

Forty-five minutes later Jake was in uniform and walking through the hallway to the lieutenant colonel's office. A few other officers and an enlisted man passed him, giving him curt nods—and a half-assed salute from the enlisted man. He already felt like he was on the way out. It was an embarrassing and depressing end to a career during which he'd worked hard to achieve and to be an asset to the Corps. He'd only recently come to terms with accepting the honors he'd been awarded—thanks to Beau—and now he faced being stripped of everything that defined who he was.

Certainly not America's hero anymore. At least not if America saw the photos Beau had received. Jake's gut turned over.

The lieutenant colonel's office door was open, but the office was empty, so Jake sat in one of the guest chairs and waited.

Ten minutes later Lieutenant Colonel Monroe entered. Jake stood at attention.

"Have a seat, Jake."

He hoped the use of his first name was a good omen rather than an indication he'd been stripped of his rank.

"I got the preliminary drug test back, along with the blood tests that the MPs ordered while you were in custody." He opened a drawer and withdrew a manila folder.

"Yes, sir."

"Good news and bad news. Which do you want first?"

"It doesn't matter."

"The good news is you're clean of all banned substances. Except one."

Here it comes.

"They found Rohypnol in your system. The symptoms are similar to intoxication, but your BAC was insignificant. I had to order these tests. You understand."

Jake blinked. What about the cocaine? "Rohypnol?"

"Someone slipped something into your drink. It's the date-rape drug, so I hope, uh, there's nothing else to report."

There was, but Jake certainly wouldn't report it to Monroe. "And my posting here?"

"Except for trying to leave the building, you've broken no laws or regulations. And there's no intent to pursue that charge. Your lapse of judgment is understandable given the Rohypnol. So you're cleared of any possible charges. I'd like you to return to duty, as soon as you're physically able to. You can start with desk duty until you're cleared to fly." He glanced at the papers in the folder again, then closed it and placed it on the desk halfway between himself and Jake.

"Yes, sir. Thank you, sir."

"What happened with this car accident?" Monroe tilted his head and peered at Jake. Something in his gaze triggered a reaction deep within Jake's brain, sounding a warning his conscious mind couldn't interpret.

"That's all a little hazy. I made a police report at the hospital, and Tim Alvarez made sure I got home okay."

"Have the base docs give you a thorough exam, then let me know when you're up to coming back to work. Can you stop at the base clinic this afternoon?"

"Yes, sir."

"Fine. Then give me a call when you find out how long it might be before you're cleared."

Jake stood. "There was one other thing…."

"Right. There is." Monroe gave Jake that pointed look again. "I know you had an appointment with Colonel Lewis. But given the situation with

Mrs. Lewis and this current setback, I should handle whatever it was you wanted to talk to him about. I prefer to wait on that for a day or two, until you're back to full power." He thrummed his fingers on the file folder. *Tap-tap-tap-tap. Tap-tap-tap-tap.* Jake watched the fingers go down and then back up in succession. The sound filled the office. Jake felt like he was the next victim in a Hitchcock film.

"That sounds best, sir." He saluted and left.

It was lunchtime, so he went over to the officers' mess in search of Tim. Jake found him with Sharon and Lowball.

"Good to see you back, Styx," Sharon said. "But I'd hate to see the other guy."

"He got off lightly," Jake said, cringing at the inescapable irony.

Tim leaned forward as he glanced around, probably looking for other officers from their unit. "You back to duty okay?"

"Piloting a desk till I get cleared by the doc."

"Hey, how's Beau doing? You've been away so much lately, I don't think I've seen you two at any of the parties since Camp David," Sharon asked as she worked her way through a grilled chicken salad.

Jake couldn't remember the last time he'd eaten, and suddenly he was famished. "I'm gonna grab some chow, then I'll be back." He got on the shortest line and ordered a grilled chicken platter before rejoining Tim and Sharon. He felt dozens of eyes following him back to the table. Clearly scuttlebutt traveled fast here, even when there wasn't anything to it. He should have known.

"Hey, Jakey," Sharon started. "I'm sorry if I got too personal asking about Beau. If things aren't okay, then forget I asked."

Tim chuckled behind his napkin as he wiped his mouth. "Nothing to worry about, Share Bear. I saw Beau yesterday." Then Tim turned to Jake. "He came right away after I called, but he didn't look too happy. Maybe I'm the one who put my foot in it."

Jake stopped shoveling food into his mouth and swallowed. "He's been under pressure at work." He hoped they couldn't tell he was lying.

"Good." Sharon stood and clapped a hand on Jake's back, making him realize his shoulder and ribs still ached. "Let's make a plan with you guys. You can meet Pete." She stood up, grabbed her tray, then walked off.

Jake looked at Tim and raised an eyebrow.

"Pete's her new man. He's an instructor at The Basic School. Major Stick Up his Ass is what I like to call him."

With his mouth full again, Jake couldn't reply, so he nodded.

"Look, buddy, did you talk to Monroe about those overnights? Because I don't have any problem with them. I'm not sure why you do."

"I didn't say anything." Jake chose not to address the issue of his problems or to mention what he'd told Beau.

"Good. Get your flight clearance sorted out soon. Since you're grounded, Monroe is piloting the next one himself, and he's an absolute bastard to fly with."

"Heading over there after lunch."

Jake managed to see one of the docs after a short wait. It was almost embarrassing to get priority because of his unit, but he walked out with clearance for desk duty and a follow-up in two days to assess his flight readiness.

He rented a car on base and drove home, expecting to spend the rest of the day tracking down where his car had been towed and replacing his cell phone. Had the weather been warmer, he'd have ridden the bike, but after the crash, he wasn't interested in pushing his luck on icy roads, and he preferred not to freeze his ass off.

Back home with a replacement phone, he endured nearly two hours on the phone with the insurance company and the police, and he'd arranged for a claims inspection. Two minutes hadn't gone by after he put the receiver down when the phone rang again.

"Jake, I've been trying to call you for an hour." Beau sounded as distressed as Jake had ever heard him, which was saying a lot after the horrible events of yesterday.

"I don't have call waiting. Sorry. What's wrong?"

"Someone was in my apartment."

The skin on the back of his neck prickled. "Are you sure?"

"Of course I'm sure. I wouldn't be upset if I wasn't sure. The kitchen table chairs are broken. And it sure as hell wasn't Goldilocks."

Jake couldn't suppress a half smile at Beau still having a sense of humor; he didn't like those chairs. "Probably not Goldilocks."

The silence grew so cold he started to shiver. "Beau?"

"I asked the super and he checked the security cameras. Someone was here this morning. They wore black ski masks. Not Goldilocks or even Little Red Riding Hood. Not by a long shot." His voice quavered, and the prickling on the back of Jake's neck increased. "If I hadn't gone directly to work from your place, I would have walked in on them."

Jake didn't scare easily, but now he was frightened. He wouldn't take chances, not when it came to Beau. "Are you home?"

"No. I'm at Laney's. But I'm going to meet Mike back at the office later. We're making progress."

"Stay at Laney's. Don't go home and don't go out. I'm coming over and I'll go with you to the office."

"You don't have to. But I have to meet up with Mike."

Jake paused for a moment, weighing options, fitting pieces together. "Have him go to Laney's. I'll be there as quickly as I can."

"Now you're scaring me, Jake. What's going on?"

"I'll tell you when I see you. Don't leave that apartment—for anything or anyone but me." He put the phone down and sensed rather than heard a car going past his house. It was moving too slowly, which was why the strange sound pattern had twigged his attention. He went to the window and spotted a dark sedan with tinted windows near the bottom of his driveway. It sped up and away down the street.

Someone was after him or after Beau, and they'd left subtle in the dust a day back. Jake just didn't know *why*.

Without wasting time to get out of his uniform, he headed for the rental car. Someone had stuck something under the wiper blade, probably one of those ads. He crumpled it up and jammed it into his coat pocket, then slid behind the wheel.

He was on the Arlington Memorial Bridge when he remembered he'd told Toby they could all have dinner together. That would have to wait.

Once he entered the District traffic, he hit nearly every red light. A dark car with tinted windows came up behind him once. Then, several blocks later, it was in the next lane. He'd probably seen a million of those inside the Beltway, the kind that drove lobbyists or congressmen around. It couldn't be the same one he'd seen on his street.

But something strange *was* going on. Too many things happening at once. The roofies, the photos, the accident, the break-in at Beau's, the dark car moving like a shark past his house. If he scratched the last one off the list, it still added up to something significant. Nothing much had happened until the other day, then *bam*, he suddenly had the worst luck.

What had started this? He tried to recall his movements and conversations, but he couldn't concentrate on the traffic at the same time, and the dark car—or one identical to it—nearly rear-ended him when he slammed on his brakes at a red light he noticed at the last minute.

He went around the block twice, then deliberately went through the next red light. No other car followed him through the intersection. He'd lost the tail, if he'd actually had one. He felt more relaxed as he drove to Laney's. Her high-rise condo not far from the Watergate had underground parking for residents and guests, but Jake's parking karma kicked in and he found a spot right in front. He buzzed Laney's number at the lobby door and jammed his hands into his pockets as the wind picked up. He found the ad from the windshield, and he absent-mindedly smoothed it out as Laney's voice came over the speaker.

"Heya, Jake. Beau's gone down to the garage to meet Mike B."

The door buzzed, but Jake was rooted to the spot, staring down at the paper in his hand.

> *You and your friend should stop poking around where*
> *your peckers don't belong, or it won't just be his furniture that*
> *gets broken.*

Where was Beau?

Squealing tires and a car alarm sounded from the direction of the underground parking garage.

Jake ignored the buzzing door and raced through the pedestrian gate into the garage. A dark sedan speeding up the ramp nearly sideswiped him, but he leapt between two cars as it whizzed past. At that speed the driver misjudged the distance, and the iron gate scraped along the passenger door with the sound of tearing metal.

"Beau!"

"Help! Get help!" someone shouted from one level below.

Jake raced down and found the bearded guy he'd seen with Beau—Mike Beaumont, he now knew—leaning over a crumpled form that looked horrifyingly familiar. "Beau! Beau! Call 911!" he shouted to the guy.

"My cell's not working under here." The guy sped toward the exit faster than Jake thought his chunky body could move.

"Beau!" Jake fell to his knees. Beau was on his side, where he'd fallen near the bumper of an SUV. Jake thought he might have been smashed up against it. Beau wasn't moving, and blood streamed from his mouth and nose.

Time stood still for a few panicked seconds until his medic training kicked in. Jake checked for a pulse—he found it—and searched for other injuries, smoothing his hands along Beau's extremities for broken bones. He suspected a lower leg fracture, and the way Beau was breathing shallowly made Jake suspect at least one broken rib.

Thank God he's breathing at all. Jake realize he'd been holding his breath and gasped for air, furious with himself for letting Beau leave alone that morning.

Mike Beaumont jogged back down, out of breath and face beet red. Jake had to appreciate he was still moving quickly, despite the obvious strain to his unfit body.

"Ambu—" He panted. "—lance is. On the. Way." Then he knelt down on the cold cement floor. "Is he okay? Beau?"

"I think he's got a broken leg, maybe ribs."

Sirens grew more distinct, then stopped in midwail, but familiar flashing lights glowed and reflected off the cars as the ambulance made its way toward them.

The EMTs worked on Beau. They were transferring him on a spinal board to a gurney when Laney came hurtling toward them from the elevators.

"Oh my God, Jake. Mike. What the hell happened?"

"I'm not sure." Jake kept his gaze on Beau as the EMTs wheeled him to the ambulance.

"You left me up there buzzing and buzzing, and you never showed up. Now I see why." Laney was crying, and mascara dripped down her cheeks. When she tried to wipe it away, it smeared worse.

"I'd like to ride with him," Jake said to one of the EMTs. Then, to Mike and Laney, "Can you two meet us at the hospital? GWU?" he asked, and the EMT nodded.

"Yes." Mike put a comforting arm around Laney as he handed her a handkerchief to wipe her face. Jake was worried as hell about Beau, but he liked knowing Beau had other friends who were more than coworkers and cared this much about him.

Jake tried to stay out of the EMT's way as the driver closed the back doors. The siren went back on as they reached the street, and then the vehicle slowly picked up speed.

"I did some training with Navy corpsmen. Can I help at all?"

"Can you take his pressure?"

Jake nodded, glad for the simple task. It kept his mind from focusing on the fact that Beau hadn't opened his eyes yet. Jake called out the low reading, then held Beau's hand.

"Beau! Can you hear me? Squeeze if you can."

Beau's faint response cheered Jake while he was helpless to do more. Jake braced himself as the ambulance took the curves of New Hampshire Avenue, but by the time they reached George Washington University Hospital less than a mile away, Beau wasn't squeezing anymore.

Chapter 22

AT THE hospital, the EMTs opened the ambulance doors, retrieved Beau's gurney, and unfolded the wheels as Jake hopped out. He followed behind as a triage nurse took over, then pushed him aside when Beau was wheeled into an exam room.

"I want to—"

"I'm sorry, Captain, you'll need to stay outside. Can you tell me what happened?" A nurse wearing a scrub cap gave him a sympathetic smile, and he told her what he knew. She closed the door, leaving Jake watching through the window as Beau moved out of his line of sight. When another gurney nearly mowed him down, Jake retreated to the waiting area. He didn't want to be in anyone else's way.

The buzz of patients waiting and the drone of CNN on the television in the far corner further jangled his nerves. Thankfully it was only ten minutes before Mike and Laney arrived, both with knitted brows and long faces.

"Did you hear anything yet?" Mike asked.

Jake shook his head and kept pacing.

Laney reached a hand to Jake's arm, stopping him. "You've got blood on your uniform." Laney squeezed her eyes shut and pulled at Jake to sit next to her.

When Jake glanced down, he saw the blood, drops and smears on his shirt and pants. Suddenly the hospital faded away. He was back in Afghanistan, crawling out of a pile of twisted metal and broken glass. He saw his flight suit was splattered with blood—his and that of his passengers and crew. Noise swirled around him, shouting, gunfire. He swerved out of someone's grasp. *I need to check for survivors.*

More gunfire sounded. Metal hitting metal so loudly he thought his head would explode.

"Jake? Jake, come sit down with me."

Then he was back in the hospital waiting room, where an orderly was picking up items from a cart right in front of Jake. He must have knocked the cart over. Jake let Laney lead him back to the seats. His head hurt, and so did his arm where Laney was gripping it.

"I'm fine. Let go." He jerked his arm from her grasp and scowled at Mike, but he sat down.

"How about some decaf, or tea?" Mike stood up and nodded in the direction of a hot drinks machine.

"No, thanks."

Mike went to the machine and Laney stared at the television in the corner.

Jake rubbed his forehead. He'd never had that kind of flashback before. He recalled the crash in far more detail than he would like, but he'd never gone *back there* before. It scared the fucking *crap* out of him. This kind of thing meant PTSD, and then he'd never be permitted to stay in HMX-1, might not even be allowed to fly again.

Steeling himself for the worst, he gripped the sides of his chair and looked down at the blood on his shirt again. Nothing. Still in the hospital waiting room. And Beau still in the exam or operating room. He touched the bloodstains and prayed that wouldn't be the last memory he would have of Beau.

A moment later Mike returned with coffee and handed it to Jake, who took it without comment. It tasted like crap, but that, along with the heat, was welcome and familiar.

Mike wandered off toward the doors, pulling his cell phone out of his pocket, and Laney remained next to Jake, sipping her own cup of coffee, rocking silently in her seat, dealing with her own fears. She'd been friends with Beau far longer than Jake had known him, and it dawned on Jake how much what had happened today upset her too.

"Laney, are you doing okay?" He kept his voice low, not trusting it.

His words startled her out of her own reverie, and she turned to Jake. "It doesn't feel real yet. I'm not sure when it will kick in." Her lower lip quivered, but she put on a remarkably brave face. She clutched a handkerchief she must have used to clean away the mascara. A man's handkerchief, probably Mike's.

"You want me to get something from the cafeteria for you?" Jake wanted to do something for Laney, as well as take his mind off the interminable wait for news of Beau's condition.

"I'm not sure I'm *that* upset." She forced a chuckle. "Usually food makes me feel better. When I'm upset, Beau writes me a prescription for pistachio ice cream or salted caramel truffles or something." She made a noise between a laugh and a sob, which summed up Jake's state of mind at the moment too.

"Mac and cheese. That's what I go to when I'm stressed." Talking about it made him feel a little less frantic.

"Really?" Laney turned to stare at Jake.

"My mom used to make it from scratch. I'd always feel better then. After I grew up, she admitted her secret was that it took a while to make, so the problem was usually forgotten by the time it was ready." The memories gave Jake a warm feeling, and he vowed to call his mother once he knew how Beau was doing. He'd make plans for Beau to meet his family. If.... No, *when*—

"I'd love her recipe."

"I'll ask her." He took Laney's hand in his and glanced toward the double doors, willing them to open.

"Jake, why do you think this happened? Who would hit him and keep going? Is it the same people who were in his apartment?"

The sound of throat clearing made them both look up. Mike stood a few feet away. "Jake, can I talk to you a minute?"

"You okay?" he asked Laney as he stood up.

"Sure. I'll wait here in case there's any news."

Jake followed Mike to the far corner of the room.

"I have a pretty good idea who did this—and why."

"Mike, what the hell? You need to talk to the cops."

"It's the story we're working on, Beau and I." Mike glanced around the waiting room. He'd positioned himself with his back toward the wall. It was a position Jake recognized immediately. Mike was scared, and he needed to keep an eye on his surroundings.

"Tell me, right this instant. What have you gotten him into?" He fought off the instinct to reach for Mike's neck. The danger wasn't coming in the door, the danger was Jake.

"Not here."

"I'm not leaving Laney, and I want to stay close in case there's an update. Spill."

Then Mike pulled his laptop out of his messenger bag and handed it to Jake.

Jake had only read four paragraphs before the truth sank in.

It wasn't Mike who had put Beau at risk. It was Jake himself. "Who else has seen this?" Jake needed to know who to blame for hurting Beau.

"No one. My boss knows part of it, but he hasn't read this yet. I just got the last pieces of proof this evening by text. That's why I left you and Laney for a few minutes."

"But someone found out or suspected what you two came up with. Someone who—" More of the pieces clicked home. The roofies and the photos. The accident. They had come after Jake first, and then when he didn't go down, when Beau kept working on this story, starring Jake's Appaloosa passengers, someone went for Beau.

Silencing Beau would remind Jake to keep his mouth shut too. Only he hadn't told Beau anything about Appaloosa.

"For money? This is just about money? Beau's life is worth—"

"Millions. Tens of millions. I don't have good estimates yet. But, no." Mike paused and looked Jake in the eye before continuing. "It's about a lot more than money."

He took a deep breath and kept reading. Half of what he read he knew already, but Mike and Beau had strung the pieces together into something coherent, a totality Jake hadn't considered.

Now he felt sick. It was all his fault. A few careless words, a coincidence that might not have been so random. Jake's comments about Beau's writing credentials. Beau spotting people who shouldn't be together. A beard. A coat. It all added up to a story Beau somehow stumbled upon. The irony was this story was incredible journalism, but it might kill Beau.

"How much of this is Beau's idea?"

"Most of it. I helped him with some research and how to find proof of enough of his suspicions for us to put all the pieces together."

"You have proof?"

"Yes. Enough to at least get an official investigation started, I believe. There are some deadlines coming up for Congressional approval, and the scrutiny would put the projects on hold long enough to bring everything to light. What happened to you, to Beau, it's proof we're onto information someone wants hushed up. We've only scratched the surface, so it could be much bigger."

"I agree. Promise me you won't do anything with this story yet."

"You want to bury this?" Mike scowled.

"Hell no. I need a few days, maybe a week, to make some arrangements first."

Mike shook his head. "I can't wait a week. My ed—"

"A couple of days, then. I'll keep you and Beau in the loop."

"Okay."

First, Jake had to protect Beau. Then he could make these men pay.

ONCE JAKE had confirmation that Beau was out of danger and had seen proof with his own eyes, Jake and Mike went to a café near the hospital. He would rather sit beside Beau's bed, but he needed the rest of the story as soon as possible, to protect Beau. They left Laney in Beau's room with orders to call as soon as he was awake.

Jake was extra careful not to give Mike any classified information, but if Mike suggested something Jake knew not to be true, he felt comfortable denying details.

After going through everything, especially the events of the past few days, Mike suspected someone was listening in at his house or office. That's how they knew where Beau was. Or they were listening to Beau's phone. Probably both.

Jake called up one of his buddies from The Basic School who worked IT in the Pentagon Communications Office, Hank Zane—Zany to pretty much everyone. Zany confirmed General Graham had authorized listening in on his house, Beau's place, and both men's phones, ostensibly to determine whether Jake had shared classified information with a foreign government.

Putting aside the horror of strangers listening to him sharing intimate moments with Beau, Jake focused on how to get proof of who was involved.

"The first strange thing I noticed was the Pentagon not wanting him to attend the White House party. I thought they'd mixed him up with you. I said he was the fashion columnist and harmless."

"I'm not sure he'd appreciate being described as harmless." Mike quirked one corner of his mouth.

"You know what I mean."

"Beau wasn't harmless. Not after he saw those guys at Camp David, and they saw him."

"Cue-Ball and Fur Coat?" Why hadn't Beau said anything at the time? Jake might have questioned the Appaloosa orders far sooner.

Mike nodded, breaking into a smile at Beau's crazy descriptions. Jake had thought them humorous until he'd discovered what the men were capable of.

Jake concentrated on remembering exactly what had happened. "He saw Colonel Sanders with Cue-Ball—Graham—at the White House when we met. I didn't pay any attention until he mentioned the same men at brunch."

"If they saw him with you at the White House, at brunch, and again at Camp David, no wonder they thought *you* might have given Beau enough information to figure out what they're up to. They probably still think he's covering Pentagon issues, especially after he started dating you."

Jake felt a twinge of guilt. "I had a few doubts myself. Beau approached me, and later I wondered whether he'd done that just to find out about the classified missions."

"Beau's not disingenuous enough for that kind of subterfuge. He's an open book."

"That's for sure." Jake sat back and thought over the months they'd been together. Beau's candor and happy-go-lucky attitude had first attracted him. How had he ever believed Beau had been putting on an act?

Jake was pretty sure he was the one "they" were after. Beau was collateral damage.

He and Mike came up with a slightly crazy and potentially very dangerous plan.

But it was better than the alternative.

JAKE PUT General Graham's spurious suspicions to good use. Zany used his admin access to schedule Jake, under a fake name, directly into Graham's calendar for a meeting the following day.

When Jake arrived the general's secretary buzzed him into the inner office. Graham's eyebrows shot up toward the smooth dome of his head once he moved far enough into the enormous, richly appointed office for Graham to recognize him.

"What are you doing here, Captain Woodley? You're not on my schedule."

Jake smiled as he sat down in front of Graham's desk. Clearly the guy never expected his pilot to show up like this in his office. "I'm turning myself in. I'm guilty. I leaked classified information. About your late-night flights."

Graham's cue-ball head began to glisten with perspiration. Jake liked the reaction he got. "What?"

"I know I've been suspected of that."

The general took a deep breath, then stared at him askance. "Go on. What did you tell and to whom?"

"You know, it's the craziest thing. I've been dating this guy. A journo. He doesn't cover politics or the Pentagon. He covers fashion, for fuck's sake. So I figured who would care if I mentioned some trips I was taking, flying you and Bingham and Mann around. How would I know he'd twist the whole thing into some convoluted conspiracy theory that might embarrass the Pentagon? Or that he'd start writing a story for his newspaper?"

"What story? There's no story there. It's simply Pentagon business, classified information you know better than to discuss with anyone. But there's no story."

"Why would a meeting be classified? Why would you be meeting the head of Green Dynamics in the middle of the night? You know something else interesting? Until I began flying you, I was barely treading water in my squadron. Suddenly, my bad behavior was overlooked. But the minute I questioned orders, I was removed from other missions and denied access to training. Maybe there's a story there?"

"You told this to your boyfriend and he's writing a story about how you started fucking up when you came back from combat? Nothing sinister about being assigned less important duties. No newspaper—even in DC—would run a story as thin as that. It happens to servicemen every day. Some of them even take their own lives. A tragic end to a glorious career no one would even question." Graham stood up, his imposing bulk an undisguised threat.

But Jake wasn't scared, and he wouldn't back down.

"But it's not only about me, it's what else I told Beau. It's what he's seen too. At the White House and Camp David. But you already know what he's working on. So you tried to scare me, and then Beau? Well, all that's in his story too now. The break-in, the trumped-up reason for the wiretaps, my drugging and assault. How nice that your operative took photos. Readers love proof like that. Congress might too. And I'm not talking about Bingham's committee. You know what I'm talking about."

Graham's face turned various shades of red, and he opened his mouth and closed it again before finding his words. "What drugging and assault?"

"Stop the innocent act." But Jake wondered why Graham didn't question the other incidents and accusations. Maybe Graham had nothing to do with sending "Brett" after Jake. "Is someone else calling the plays now and leaving you on the sidelines?"

Now Graham looked like he might keel over from heart failure.

"As soon as Beau gets out of the hospital, he's going to turn in the story of the century."

Graham showed no surprise about Beau being in the hospital. "Why would anyone believe you or what you've told him?"

"Because we both know this isn't about secret meetings to discuss government contracts. I've seen proof of what Bingham and Mann are *really* up to."

"Bingham and…. What do you mean 'really'?"

"But I can convince Beau to kill the story, as long as you quietly slow down the defense communications project and don't award any contracts to Green Dynamics."

"If such an article is published, you'll only tighten the noose around your own neck for leaking classified information. No matter how irrelevant you deem that information to be, there are consequences. Right now the whole country still sees you as a hero. Your future in the military—the Pentagon if you want it—is unlimited. Once you learn the rules and play by them."

"I'm willing to take that risk."

"For him?"

"No. Just on principle. To do the right thing for the right reason, regardless of what happens to me."

"Aren't you a little sanctimonious?"

Jake exhaled, disgust rising. "No, s—" Jake had lost all respect for Graham and couldn't muster the discipline to call him sir. "These are the values I believe in. The values this country was built on, and the values we fight for every day all over the globe. The values you took an oath to uphold."

"You're willing to give up your career over this?"

"If I have to. So, do we have a deal? You slow down the project and award the contracts strictly on merit. As long as you and your friends leave me and Beau alone, he won't write the story."

Graham sat down in his chair and waited a moment before replying. "A deal? Who would believe Beaumont or you? Your alcohol problems would wash any credibility away."

Graham knew Beau's last name, even though Jake hadn't mentioned it. "Maybe no one, at least at first. But his story would encourage at least a look into the allegations, following the money trail the Treasury would be able to confirm. That's enough to slow the process down, and that's all it will take to discredit the Georgia boys and you. People have lost top Pentagon positions for a hell of a lot less."

The general leaned back in his chair as if he had all the time in the world. He did, which was why Jake had to find a way to crack his facade. A bead of sweat dripped down Graham's temple, and Jake thought he might have panicked the general more than he was trying to let on.

"Give me a moment to make a call, Woodley. Wait outside."

Jake got up and went to sit in the outer office, where the general's secretary stared at him as if he were an errant pupil outside the principal's office. She glanced at her monitor a few times, then back at Jake. Several minutes later her phone buzzed.

"Yes, General? GWU Hospital? Right away, sir." She tapped at her keyboard. "The call is going through now."

Vibrations in Jake's pocket announced the arrival of a text message from his buddy in the Communications Office:

Right on schedule—Zany

About five minutes later, the phone buzzed again, and the secretary sent Jake back into the general's office.

"I thought about your proposal." He made the word sound obscene. "Frankly, you haven't got a pot to piss in on this one. No leverage, Woodley."

"I'm not so sure. You said Americans see me as a hero. That's worth something. I've flown the president's helicopter. He'll listen to me. I can't believe he would be involved in this scheme, not when it jeopardizes our national security so severely."

"Slowing or stopping the comms project is what will jeopardize national security." Graham shifted uncomfortably in his chair, then looked Jake squarely in the eye. "And according to my sources at GWU, Matthew Beaumont died forty minutes ago. Any story that was in his head is... gone."

He said the final word with such delight, Jake nearly hurled himself across the wide expanse of desk to strangle the general.

Jake tried to steady himself, but his knees threatened to give way. "What?" His breath came in short gasps, and he held on to the back of a chair.

Then the door opened and a handful of MPs entered.

They cuffed Jake and escorted him from the room.

JAKE WAS taken to the Pentagon Police Department offices on the ground floor. Along the way people in the halls turned to see who had been detained. Fellow Marines looked away, a few others glared at him, strangers looked mad enough to spit on him. Disappointed expressions reminded him he still had a recognizable face.

That was good.

Someone put him into a detention room, cuffed him to a table, and left. They probably needed time to decide what to charge him with. Graham might come up with a whole laundry list of things Jake hadn't done, a frame-up he might not be able to fight. He could end up in custody until his court-martial.

He may have miscalculated his risk with this plan. At least his talk with Graham had confirmed that the general knew about what happened to Beau, but not about the assault on Jake. The downside was someone else was making decisions. Higher in the Pentagon?

Jake decided even if he got in trouble, it was worth it. Beau was worth it.

He thought about how Beau looked lying on the floor of the parking garage, bleeding. How pale he looked in the hospital bed. But Jake pushed all of those images out of his brain and focused on how Beau looked asleep on the pillow with the morning sun turning his hair into a bronze halo. The way his smile could warm Jake's heart and soul. He remembered how handsome Beau looked at the White House holiday party, beaming as they mingled with the president and the first lady on the dance floor, the DJ blasting "Dancing Queen" and "Like a Virgin."

But the most prominent image was how Beau had looked the night they met as he came up to speak to Jake. If Jake ended up in a military prison, that was the version of Beau he'd dream about every night.

A knock sounded and the door swung open. It could have been an hour or three hours since Jake had been stashed here. He hadn't bothered counting to keep track of time the way he'd learned in survival school. If he got sent to Guantanamo, then he'd start worrying.

Colonel Lewis entered. "Jake."

Jake started to rise, but his wrists were shackled to the table.

"You can forgo standing at attention on this particular occasion."

Lewis was the last person he'd expected to see. He was in more trouble than he thought. "Sir, what are you doing here?"

"As your CO I was informed of your arrest. I came as quickly as I could. What's going on here?"

"What did they tell you?"

"A security leak. You've been accused of sharing intelligence with a foreign power."

That sent Jake coughing. He had miscalculated, badly.

"What have you done, Jake?" The colonel sat down across from Jake, worry creasing his brow.

"Would you believe me if I said I hadn't?"

"Of course I would. You have more integrity than most of the officers I've met in my career. It's why I've been so concerned about you, even while I was on leave."

It was Jake's turn to blink. Something didn't add up. If Colonel Lewis was worried about him, why had he canceled their meeting?

"Then, sir, may I ask why you assigned me the Appaloosa flights? At first I thought it was because you trusted me, but then once I realized who I was flying, I didn't know whom to trust."

"Appaloosa?"

"Lieutenant Colonel Monroe said you selected me and Alvarez."

This looked like news to the colonel, who pressed his lips together and frowned. "Start from the beginning."

WHEN HE'D finished, Jake felt like he'd shed the weight of the world from his shoulders.

"Now what *exactly* did you say to Beau about these flights?"

"Only that I'd been to a little town in Georgia with 400 people in it."

"And he managed to string the rest together from that?"

With more pride than fear this time, Jake nodded. "Later I told him I was uncomfortable with some assignments, and he suggested I ask your advice. That's when I phoned you at home."

"After we spoke, I called Lieutenant Colonel Monroe. He said he didn't want to trouble me and would handle the situation. I wanted to speak with you, but Monroe insisted I didn't need to come in."

To Jake, that was all the proof he needed, but it wouldn't convince anyone else.

The colonel spotted Jake's reaction. "What?"

"After we made the appointment, that's the night someone drugged me at the bar in DC. I woke up in some motel near Fort Belvoir." He took a calming breath. "They took photos… and sent them to Beau. And I got drug tested the next morning and detained by MPs on base until they said my BAC was fine. On the way home, I crashed."

Lewis's gaze sharpened, and he appeared increasingly shaken as Jake detailed the events of the past few days. "Whoever is behind this is certainly willing to take drastic measures."

"Sir, Lieutenant Colonel Monroe told me something different about the results of the blood and urine tests than the ones I got from the hospital, where they found something else." Jake wasn't sure he should mention the cocaine, but the lieutenant colonel's omission of it was significant.

"And you think he's hiding this information? Why?"

"As a threat?" Jake remembered the way the lieutenant colonel had thrummed his fingertips on the folder with the report. Jake's imagination or something more sinister? At the moment, *everything* had taken on sinister overtones. He wished he could talk this over with Beau.

Lewis frowned. "Well, he can't threaten me. I'd like to see the proof Beau and this other reporter have. If it's conclusive, I'll take my concerns as far up the food chain as I can."

"I don't know who else is involved…."

"Do you suspect it goes as high as the White House? The president?"

Jake shook his head.

"Then I'll bring it to him if necessary." He gave Jake a reassuring smile. "I'll also work on getting you released into my custody, though with a national security issue, I might not pull much weight. Now, tell me where I can get the proof I need to help you."

"Let me write it down for you." He took the pen and scrap of paper the colonel handed over and wrote the address as well as a warning: *Don't go directly there. You may be followed.*

Lewis looked at the paper, then got up and left without taking it. It might have been overkill, but Jake swallowed the paper.

He closed his eyes and tried to calm the thundering in his chest.

Shortly after the colonel's departure, Lieutenant Colonel Monroe entered, his familiar scowl intensifying Jake's sense of panic and betrayal.

"Woodley, what the hell have you gone and done now?"

"What are they saying I've done?"

"Threatened a senior Pentagon official and revealed classified information to a *reporter*." The last word came out as if it might explode.

"Sounds about right."

The scowl deepened, but the lieutenant colonel ignored Jake's familiarity. "I just ran into Colonel Lewis and he's very concerned about you.

I am too. You're one of our best pilots, and it would be a damn shame if you sabotage your career like this."

"I told you I wasn't comfortable about the Appaloosa flights. I just didn't realize who else was involved."

"I should have paid more attention to those concerns. But when I brought this up with the colonel, he said you'd been having some problems and the flights would be a good distraction."

Jake's head was spinning. They each cast suspicion on the other.

Had he put his trust in the right man?

"I'll do what I can to help you through this. I understand it's even more devastating now...." Monroe paused as if unable to find the right words.

Jake waited.

"... now after Beau... I was so sorry to hear he didn't make it."

Jake's pulse skyrocketed again. "How did you hear that?"

"Right before I came in here, Colonel Lewis said it was a result of injuries from a car accident.... I'm sorry. I hadn't heard he'd been injured. Was he in the car with you the other day?"

Jake stared at Monroe and shook his head.

"Well, the few times I met him, I liked him a lot." This was the first time Jake had seen a shred of genuine emotion in the man.

"Thank you. In that case, sir, he and I are going to need your help."

"What?"

"He's not dead, but he is in a lot of danger. I've made a very big mistake."

Chapter 23

BEAU SAT with Mike in a Denny's a mile away from the Pentagon, waiting. His cracked ribs hurt when he breathed, and his head ached when all he did was think about something. But he wasn't going to stay one more day in the hospital while Jake was putting his perilous plan into action.

Zany called to report the plan was unfolding as expected. Jake had gone to see General Graham, who called the hospital. Zany intercepted the call via the internal communications system and, pretending to be a nurse, told Graham Beau was dead.

That had been enough to make Graham feel safe, and he ordered the Pentagon Police Department to arrest Jake.

"What do you think they'll do to him?" Beau asked Mike. "Is he in any danger there?"

"I think he'll be fine if they detained him at the PPD. It's when they hide you in the secret basement or send you off to another country that you have to worry."

Beau's throat tightened. "Secret basement? Another country?"

"Where there's no rules against 'enhanced interrogation techniques.'"

Beau stared at Mike.

"Torture. Didn't you see *Zero Dark Thirty*?"

"No. And I'm not sure I want to." Beau's gut seized. Could Jake be facing something like that? What had they gotten him into? This was such a fucking insane plan. He wrapped his hands around the coffee mug and peered into the dark liquid as if it held the answer to all their concerns.

This was all Beau's fault. If he hadn't tried to write hard news again, if he hadn't looked up Georgia towns or asked Mike about young Colonel Sanders, none of this would have happened. A few bruised ribs and a concussion were nothing compared to what Jake had been through with Brett. It turned Beau's stomach again as he replayed the events of the past few days, especially Jake getting drugged and narrowly escaping being found with cocaine.

Mike ordered more coffee and turned to Beau. "We just have to wait and see who Jake sends here. See who he trusts."

They had taken a booth near the back so they could see who was at the door before anyone arriving would notice them. They'd located the rear exit beyond the bathrooms. Jake had instructed them to go to another restaurant if Denny's didn't have an easily accessible secondary exit.

Beau was standing up to stretch his legs, moving slowly to avoid hurting his aching ribs, when he spotted a familiar face coming through the door.

Jake's commanding officer entered, then glanced around the restaurant, stopping to speak to the hostess who wanted to seat him. The colonel's eyes betrayed his concern, and he looked so much older than he had a few months ago when Beau first met him.

"It's Colonel Lewis," Beau told Mike.

"Stay here. I'll talk to him. Wait for my signal." Mike got up and waved toward the colonel, who peered at him warily. He and Lewis exchanged a few words, then sat down at a table in the middle of the dining room. Mike was supposed to ascertain that Jake had sent him before Beau came out and they explained what they needed.

Mike scratched the back of his neck with his left hand—the all-safe signal—and Beau approached the table.

The colonel's head shot up and his eyes went wide, as if he'd seen a ghost. He stared at Beau for a moment before he collected himself.

"B-Beau, I thought you were... are you okay?" His hands trembled and his gaze practically bored a hole between Beau's eyes.

"Close enough, but they didn't want to let me out of the hospital."

"Probably safer now, eh?" The colonel composed himself again. "Tell me everything so I'll know how to help."

"What did Jake tell you?"

"That someone's after all of you because you have information about a conspiracy or cover-up regarding Pentagon contracts."

"It's much more than that," Mike said. "And it's not just about money."

"What?" The colonel seemed even more surprised. He glanced between Beau and Mike a few times. "Beaumont... you two aren't...."

Mike chuckled. "We're not related, no."

In fact, they looked more like the before and after photos for an incredibly effective weight loss and plastic surgery clinic.

"Let's get back on track here," Beau said. "The sooner we get real proof, the sooner we can get Jake out of custody. I'm worried about him."

"Right." Mike took a breath. "So, we've got direct links between Green Dynamics and General Graham, as well as Senator Bingham and Representative Redfern. Beau and Jake are eyewitnesses that they've all been meeting in a variety of locations. Jake may have seen money change hands. Cash. It's too easy to trace bank deposits nowadays, and most offshore banking centers are complying with US requests to track down money, thanks to the rewards."

"Rewards?"

"The Treasury and Homeland Security are working to track terrorist money and reward informants. And because this has national security implications, they'd be able to follow the money even if it's gone offshore. I think that's why these guys have gone to cash."

"How is national security involved?" the colonel asked, voice wavering.

"I should start at the beginning," Mike said.

He and Beau went over the details they'd dug up about the senator and Redfern channeling contracts to Green Dynamics when it shouldn't have received any. But the projects had been broken down into a lot of small contracts that fell below the threshold where certain safeguards and bidding requirements kicked in.

"So we need your help, sir, to get access to phone records and banking information of anyone connected to Graham. We're sure he's paying off others in the military. Lieutenant Colonel Monroe, for one, since he's been giving Jake these classified missions. But you'll be able to help us convince the oversight committees and DHS to investigate."

"Beau, I'm sorry about what's happened to you—and to Jake—but I suspect this isn't what it appears to be. I don't have any authority in this area, except to connect you to the proper channels to report your suspicions. You still haven't tied this to national security."

"We've discovered it's not just kickbacks," Mike said.

"Colonel," Beau added with emphasis, "there's at least one man on the Green Dynamics board who has financial connections to a joint technology venture with the Chinese. And not a private-sector project. The Chinese military controls the majority of the project through their Academy of Space Technology, basically an offshoot of a Chinese government agency."

"What?" Lewis looked like he'd just discovered a dirty bomb under his chair. "How did you find this out?"

"We poked around in the civilian's finances and connections the best we could. But we know there are members of our government involved in facilitating this technology transfer. We have someone digging through Graham's contacts, but it's not exactly kosher," Mike said. "We need official help to get any traction."

"Beau, could I have a private word with you?" Colonel Lewis stood and glanced toward the back hallway where the bathrooms were situated.

"Sure." Beau got up and followed the colonel on shaky legs.

"Your buddy Mike is already in trouble with the Pentagon, did you know that, Beau?"

Beau remembered Jake telling him about the Pentagon warning before the White House holiday party, so he suspected as much. "Does that matter?"

"Well, Pentagon and administration officials aren't likely to listen to him. Are you absolutely certain about what you've discovered? I'd hate to have this reflect badly on your career and Jake's if you get mixed up with Mike Beaumont." The colonel peered at Beau, but his expression wasn't one of concern. "You understand how serious Jake's situation is over this? No matter what you think you've discovered, he'll be punished for discussing classified information. What proof do you really have?"

"I've seen everything Mike found, and it's not simply a story cooked up by a reporter with an antimilitary agenda."

"I'd need to see proof before I agree to help. I would be risking my own reputation by simply accusing men like General Graham and the congressmen."

"Sure. It's all on a flash drive." Beau touched the pocket of his shirt. A cold, hard mass expanded in his gut as the expression on Lewis's face morphed. "You're involved too, aren't you?"

The colonel pushed Beau against the wall and reached for the pocket, which was empty. Beau had simply been rubbing an itch where his bandages chafed the skin, but the colonel grabbed his shirt in a fist and Beau decided it was time to get out of there. He pushed Lewis off him and ran out through the back door.

He came out of the building into a small parking lot and raced to the right, with the colonel far too close behind. Then Beau swerved around the corner and came face-to-face with a brick wall and a row of rusty metal trash cans.

No way out.

He spun around, but the colonel blocked his escape. Beau panted. His ribs didn't ache as much as they were slicing through his side from the inside out. Could he get past the old man? Lewis might be older, but he was in much better shape than Beau, and he probably hadn't been hit by a car in the past two days.

"What do you want from me, Colonel?"

"You don't have enough proof, but I can't allow you to print your story. I didn't take that much money, but... you'll ruin me."

"Okay, I won't." Beau didn't know what else to say.

"I don't believe you. Your word won't cut it with me." He reached behind his back and pulled out a small handgun.

Beau's heart thundered as if it might be able to fly him to safety. So far he was still on the ground. He leaned forward, hands on his knees, ignoring the pain shooting through his chest. If anything he'd be a smaller target, but he'd try to make a run for it. In his peripheral vision, he eyed the trash cans.

"Colonel, don't!" Jake's voice rang out from behind the colonel, and Lewis turned his head, giving Beau enough time to grab a trash can lid and wield it like a shield. But the colonel didn't listen and steadied his aim on Beau.

"Go away, Jake. I don't want to have to hurt you too."

"Let Beau go. This is between you and me now."

Lewis didn't take his eyes off Beau, but he backed up a few paces and rotated toward Jake's voice. Beau realized now he probably had a clear shot at Jake too. Was Jake armed?

"Beau, are you okay?" Jake's voice was strong, confident. It gave Beau courage.

"Yeah. Mostly. Are you?"

"I'm fine."

"Jake, don't come closer or I'll shoot Beau. Neither of you can reach me before I shoot the other."

Beau wished he knew what Jake was doing. The colonel changed position as Jake must be moving closer. If Jake were armed, he would have shot by now, wouldn't he?

Then Jake came into view, prompting the colonel to move out of the alley and glance toward Jake. It gave Beau the chance to run, maybe even to knock him down, but it might make him shoot Jake. Why had Jake shown up now, putting himself at risk?

"Colonel, why did you ever get involved in this? It's not what I expected of you." Jake's voice was full of concern and a little disappointment.

The gun wavered slightly and the old man's face softened for a moment. Then he regained control. "My wife needed treatments. Experimental treatments our insurance wouldn't authorize. We sold everything we could, then she got worse. When General Graham approached me, it seemed like a miracle. If there had been any other way…."

Beau took a step forward and the colonel raised the gun on him again. When Jake spoke, the colonel didn't turn toward him.

"At the expense of your career, your integrity, and at risk to the national security of everyone in the United States?"

"I didn't know about the connection to the Chinese. I never asked questions, only followed General Graham's requests."

"You had to know it wasn't all about money. These contracts weren't particularly lucrative."

"I didn't want to know. Jake, one day you'll understand. I couldn't let her go without trying everything."

"I already understand."

"You're willing to sacrifice yourself for Beau?" His voice rose, and the gun wavered again.

Beau didn't want to hear Jake's answer. Jake was the kind of man who would put himself on the line to save someone else. But Beau couldn't let him do that. He raised his trash can shield and rushed the colonel, but the gun was already in motion.

One shot echoed off the brick walls of the alley.

Chapter 24

JAKE SAT in the waiting room of another hospital, gripping the arms of the wood and plastic chair with white-knuckled fingers. Blood had dried on another uniform shirt, and he leaned back, wishing he'd had another option. Would this have ended differently if he'd been armed? Maybe it would have been worse.

"Coffee?"

Jake looked up and smiled at Beau. "Thanks."

"Any word?" Beau handed him the cup, then sat down and put a hand on Jake's arm.

"Not yet."

"Jake, Beau." Lieutenant Colonel Monroe joined them. "He's going to make it. Shot his ear off. Bleeds like a motherfucker." He turned to Beau. "Sorry."

"I've heard worse. Said worse too." Beau mustered a weak smile. "Just the head wound?"

"And a broken arm from where you tackled him with the trash can lid. That's what kept him from blowing his head off."

Beau looked like he wanted to climb under his chair, but Monroe smiled as he continued.

"That was quick thinking, Beau. It's what we teach new recruits. Anything can be a weapon. Has Jake been coaching you?"

"No, sir."

"You don't have to call me sir." The lieutenant colonel clapped his hand on Beau's upper arm a couple of times, and Beau looked to Jake with a mix of fear and pain.

Jake threw Beau a nod of understanding. "If he'd been gunning for me, Beau, you would have knocked his aim off."

"Now I just feel like I battered an old guy."

"He was asking for it—and it sure as hell beats the alternative of him shooting one of us." Jake slid an arm carefully around Beau's shoulders. "Thank you." He'd thank Beau properly when they were finally alone again. How long had that been?

"Jake, I have an update on your flight status," Monroe said with a far more casual tone than Jake expected.

"Sir?" Jake swallowed.

Beau raised his eyebrows and tactfully grabbed a magazine from the table in front of them.

Would Monroe give him bad news now, in front of Beau?

"It seems the samples got lost at the lab that processes the piss tests."

"Lost?"

"Lost. And it's too late to try again now. But I don't recommend getting your hair cut on base for a while."

Jake let out a long pent-up breath. "No, sir." So Monroe had seen the results and found a way to protect Jake from what could be a disciplinary nightmare.

"Hair cut?" Beau asked.

"Most of the substances we test for are undetectable in urine after about five days. But they can be detected in hair for about three months. If they're present in the first place." Monroe turned to Jake. "But you didn't hear any of that from me."

More grateful than he could express in words, Jake just nodded. He'd be able to keep flying in the Corps, maybe even stay in HMX-1.

Mike and Laney arrived and made their way across the waiting room. They looked suspiciously chummy.

"We have to stop meeting like this," Jake said. This time he really meant it. He was tired of hospitals and ERs and waiting rooms and blood. He thought he'd put those behind him when he'd taken the posting to HMX-1.

Monroe stood. "Everyone's going to need to give statements to the MPs and possibly the Pentagon PD. I better get over to the base and see how the squadron's doing. The rest of the crew will have a lot of questions to answer. Jake, you take the next two days off from duty, unless you're required to come in for statements. Beau, keep him occupied so he won't come to work. That's an order for both of you." He nodded at everyone and left.

"Let's get out of here," Jake said. "No reason to stick around."

"Do you want to see him?" Beau asked.

"Not on your life. Or mine."

OVER THE next few days, Mike and Beau finished writing their story. Beau took particular care not to ask Jake to reveal classified information. He'd seen enough on his own and found other sources to prove his suspicions. With proper legal representation and the safety of military whistleblower protection statutes, Jake made the necessary statements to Pentagon officials.

Beau and Mike had their own firsthand information, along with meticulous research supplemented by a variety of information Zany provided as an "unnamed Pentagon source."

The *Daily* editor knew they'd obtained some of the information under extralegal conditions, but he wasn't prosecuting the case in a court of law. As long as the legal department didn't have an issue with the veracity of the information, the editor was prepared to protect the sources. All he expected was for the powers that be to get wind of the scandal and clean house. Any prosecutions were up to Justice and the Department of Defense.

Jake had a contact in the White House who let him know the president had made sure the Pentagon and Treasury were following up on the money trails, shutting down Green Dynamics, and determining how much information had been passed to the Chinese. Given the limited progress on the projects, it appeared they'd avoided losing any critical technology. Had Jake waited longer to start asking questions, the national security risk might have been greater.

General Graham was arrested and taken to the same interrogation room where Jake spent those frantic hours until Lieutenant Colonel Monroe arrived and helped get him released. The Marine Corps Judge Advocate and the Justice Department allowed Colonel Lewis to spend the few remaining days or weeks with his wife before being formally charged and prosecuted. He wasn't considered a flight risk because he would never leave her alone.

The Pentagon and the Senate didn't waste any time once their investigations supported the accusations, starting a shake-up at the highest levels of the Department of Defense and the Senate Armed Services Committee.

It took another couple of weeks for the fallout from the story to settle. Mike and Beau made the rounds of radio and television shows covering politics.

When Mrs. Lewis passed away shortly after, Colonel Lewis turned himself in voluntarily. He'd never intended to put national security at risk and felt he deserved whatever punishment awaited him. He was allowed to go to his wife's funeral, which was well attended. Jake and Beau paid their respects, as did most of the HMX-1 Squadron. For Jake it was a mark of esteem for a woman who had treated all of them like family until she'd fallen ill.

Jake sat with the squadron at the graveside ceremony and watched Beau from a distance. For the first time in his life, he understood how love could lead someone to make such poor choices. The recent adultery and sex scandals in the military seemed polar opposites to the mistakes of a man who loved his wife so much.

Despite the upheaval, the core mission of HMX-1 went on. Lieutenant Colonel Monroe was acting CO, awaiting the paperwork that would put him in charge officially, along with a much-deserved promotion to full colonel. He'd competently run the squadron in the colonel's absence, so not much changed.

Or so Jake thought until the day the lieutenant colonel called after him as he left the AOM.

"Captain Woodley, are you ready to take the final exam?"

"Sir?" Jake didn't think he'd heard correctly. And now with blood pounding in his ears, he was certain he'd misunderstood.

"Get back in the simulator and up to speed. I'm having you pilot the South Lawn run on Friday. For real this time."

"Yes, sir."

"You think you can do it without crashing into the Washington Monument?" Monroe laughed.

The sound put Jake at ease. He hadn't realized Major Landau had told anyone about his crash in the simulator. "Definitely!"

ON FRIDAY, Beau stood on the South Lawn of the White House along with Mike, Laney, and as many of the staffers from the Eisenhower Executive Office Building and the White House as they could round up.

"I can't see very well, Beau."

Beau nodded and shifted position so Toby could stand in the front row. Someone else stepped back so Beau could regain his original spot between Laney and Toby. Jenna couldn't get the time off work, but Beau didn't want Toby to miss this.

Everyone waved little American flags and squinted in the early spring sunshine as the *thump-thump* of helicopters grew closer. Then the shiny green aircraft with the familiar white tops came into view, and Beau thought his heart would explode.

He watched as one of the big aircraft hovered and then landed on the three white disks set into the lawn about twenty meters from the entrance to the White House.

"He did it! Great job, Jake!" Beau stood on his toes and tried to catch a glimpse of Jake as the crew chief opened the side door and lowered the steps. From the right-hand seat in the cockpit, Jake gave him a thumbs-up, and Beau waved his little flag like his life depended on it.

Toby, Mike, and Laney cheered and shouted Jake's name as they also waved.

A moment later President Bergen emerged from the White House, waving and smiling at the crowd, then moved toward the row of press photographers. He saluted the crew chief, then climbed inside *Marine One*. Beau saw him stop and greet Jake and Lieutenant Colonel Monroe, who was copiloting this lift.

Once the door was closed and Jake lifted off, a little melancholy settled over Beau. He was so excited for Jake to reach this professional goal, but now he'd be away for a few days on this trip. And with the president scheduled to head to Asia for two weeks, Jake would be gone for nearly a month between the advance visit and post-trip arrangements. But Beau was never more proud of Jake's achievement.

Later Beau was at Jake's, keeping Daisy company. Jenna and Toby came over for dinner. Toby couldn't stop talking about the thrill of seeing Jake at the White House. He didn't mention the president.

"How's my hero doing?" Beau asked when Jake called late that night.

"I guess that depends who your hero is."

"Lieutenant Colonel Monroe, of course. You looked pretty good yourself today. How did it feel?"

"The winds were bad as I was landing. But it looked okay?"

"Perfect."

"You're pretty easy to please."

"That's not what you usually say." Beau smoothed a hand across Jake's empty pillow, picturing him there and not hundreds of miles away. "What did the president think?"

"He gave me a thumbs-up. He says hi."

"Shut up."

"No, really. I've got another message from him."

"Jake Woodley, you are so full of shit." But nothing could make Beau feel happier, except having Jake next to him again.

"He said he's got your name on the top of the press list for the Asia trip."

Beau hadn't applied for the trip. The spot should go to Mike or someone on the *Daily*'s international desk. "You ass, don't tease like that!"

"It's the truth." Jake paused. "So, what are you going to wear on the trip?"

"Now that's why you're my hero." But Beau was already planning a shopping trip.

Chapter 25

Two months later

"I SUPPOSE you think you're really some big shot now, don't you?" Beau was pressed up against Jake's side, and he rolled away slightly to get some air.

"Just as big as I was last week." Jake treated Beau to his irresistible grin.

Beau smiled and slid his hand along Jake's firm cock to check the veracity of his statement. "Mmmm."

"But you're much bigger than you were last week."

"Am I?" Beau looked down at himself. "How much bigger?"

"Sadly, not there." Jake leaned down to give Beau's cock a kiss, then snuggled up close to him so their erections fit together nicely. "Here." He put a finger to Beau's temple.

"I've got a big head?"

"Well, I didn't mean it that way... but then again...."

Beau grabbed a pillow and threatened Jake with it.

"Getting all those job offers. I have to admit, I like how you decided to check out the *Miami Herald* in person. Smart move."

"Who would say no to an all-expenses-paid trip to Miami?" But Beau's mind hadn't been solely on business or pleasure when he'd insisted Jake accompany him. Back in DC, "Brett" had just been allowed to plead guilty to sexually assaulting Jake in return for a deal on some of the other charges. This trip was a welcome distraction for both of them.

Beau let out a sigh and relaxed in the huge bed in their hotel room. He could smell the ocean's salty tang outside the window. The paper put them up in a lovely place near the gayest part of South Beach, and after only two days Beau already loved the place so much, he was seriously considering the job offer.

"It's a good offer, Beau. You know that."

"I know." It was too. The *Herald* wanted him to cover national politics, meaning he'd be in DC most of the time. He could get a place here, and the paper would pay his rent on a place in Washington. It didn't really get much better. "I'm not sure I'd want to deal with the travel back and forth." It was just an excuse. He still had his heart set on being asked back to the *Washington Post*, but if they had been impressed by his story, no one had told him yet.

"But I'm already picturing myself coming down here on my time off." Jake shimmied to the rhythm of Cuban salsa floating in through the open window.

"I don't like having to fight off the competition on the beach down here. I want you all to myself."

"Don't you like knowing you have what the other guys want?" Jake made a ridiculous "blue-steel" model face, making Beau crack up.

Still, he wondered whether some other guy might get Jake's attention. "Maybe I'm a little more jealous than I'd like to admit."

"You have nothing to worry about." Jake pulled Beau in and gave him a gentle kiss. "You're too important for me to fuck that up. Don't you know that by now?"

"Maybe. But a guy likes hearing it on a regular basis."

"Beau Beaumont, I love you so much." He held Beau's face in his hands and pulled him in for another sweet, loving kiss. He stroked Beau's cheek and his hair before kissing one of his hands, first the fingers and then the palm. He looked up at Beau with a mischievous grin. "Besides, you had me at 'Would you be interested in a blowjob?'"

EM LYNLEY has worked in finance, the wine industry, and high-tech, though she'd rather be writing hot man-on-man romance. She spent ten years as an economist and financial analyst, including a year as a White House Staff Economist, but only because all the intern positions were filled. Tired of boring herself and others with dry business reports and articles, her creative muse is back and naughtier than ever. She has lived and worked in London, Tokyo and Washington, D.C., but the San Francisco Bay Area is home for now.

Contact EM:
Website: http://www.emlynley.com
Blog: http://emlynley.livejournal.com
Twitter: @emlynley
Facebook: http://www.facebook.com/emlynley

Daniel "Deke" Kane is a broken man, facing the end of his career in the FBI. He's on desk duty after a botched drug raid left the suspects and two children dead. He's got one chance to prove himself, or the only thing he'll be investigating is the Help Wanted ads.

Ryan Griffiths has been on the run for ten years. Forced onto the streets when his father kicked him out, Ryan earns his living in other men's beds. Finding his john dead in a hotel room drives him under the radar until a favorite client gives him a chance at a safe, clean life. But Ryan's relatively stable new world shatters when Deke Kane catches up with him.

When Deke's tasked to take down a drug dealer with terrorist ties and a taste for the dark side of BDSM, his only chance to get close is the suspect's interest in Ryan, and he convinces Ryan to become a confidential informant. In return, Deke offers Ryan immunity from his past. As Ryan falls under the drug lord's domination, Deke finds himself falling for Ryan.

Now Deke has to choose between Ryan's safety and his own future.

www.dreamspinnerpress.com

Jeremy Linden's a PhD student researching an HIV vaccine. He's always short of money, and when biotech startup PharmaTek reduces funding for his fellowship, he's tempted to take a job at a men's dining club as a serving boy. The uniforms are skimpy, and he's expected to remove an item of clothing after each course. He can handle that, but he soon discovers there's more on the menu here than fine cuisine. How far will he go to pay his tuition, and will money get in the way when he realizes he's interested in more from one of his gentlemen?

Brice Martin is an attorney for a Silicon Valley venture capital firm. When he's asked to take a client to the infamous Dinner Club, he finds himself unexpectedly turned on by the atmosphere and especially by his server, Remy. He senses there's more to the sexy young man than meets the eye. The paradox fascinates him, and he can't get enough of Remy.

Their relationship quickly extends beyond the club and sex. But the trust and affection they've worked to achieve may crumble when Jeremy discovers Brice's VC firm is the one that pulled the plug on PharmaTek—and Jeremy's research grant.

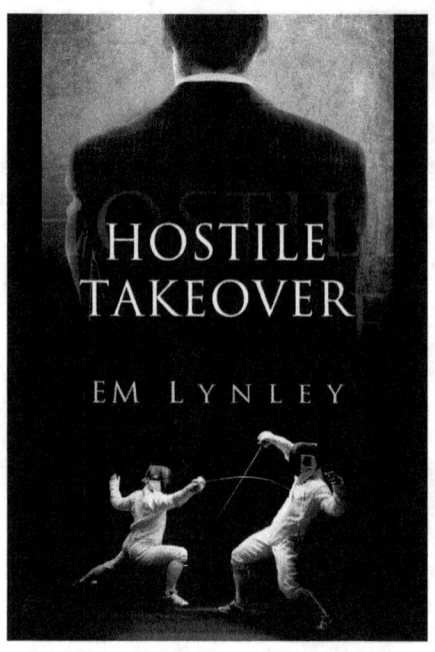

Years ago, Chase Richards and Mathias Tobler fell in love while training for the US Olympic fencing team. Afterward, they even attended the same business school so they could be together. Then Chase left Mathias alone and heartbroken in Italy. But all of that is ancient history by the time Chase thunders back into Mathias's safe, settled life with a business deal.

There's no way Mathias is going to do business with Chase. He spent nine years picking up the pieces and has moved on in life—and love. But Chase won't give up without a fight: he concocts a scheme to manipulate the market and take over the Tobler family business. If Mathias wants to save it, he'll have to face off against Chase over crossed sabers.

Chase has a reputation as an unscrupulous corporate raider, but the Tobler business holds little interest for him. In reality, he wants Mathias. Chase must win him back—by any means necessary—before Mathias gives his heart to someone else. But how does a cold-blooded corporate raider convince the man he loves that his heart really isn't made of stone?

www.dreamspinnerpress.com

OUT
OF THE
GATE

EM LYNLEY

British actor Wesley Tremayne thinks he's close to hitting the big time—a film career—with his role as a hunky explorer on a popular American TV show. Success should be just around the corner, as long as he keeps his sexual orientation a secret. Wes's best friend and beard, Julia Compton, forms the other half of a glamorous Hollywood couple that's merely a façade.

Evan Taylor left his acting career behind five years ago without looking back. He's always been more comfortable around horses than people—especially Hollywood types. His new life training racehorses is a dream come true, but increasing financial problems and an abusive boyfriend have him doubting himself and his choices.

Then Wes and his friends buy a third-rate racehorse—partially for publicity—and send him to Evan's stable. Wes's friendship with Evan soon develops into an overpowering attraction he can't act on. He's never met a man like Evan, but if there's any chance for a future together, Wes must choose between a career he loves and the man he adores.

Of all the tiny towns, in all the world, he walks into mine.

Texas native Kieran Quinn has hit the big time, working in Manhattan as a columnist for Gloss, a national literary magazine. He's well-known for his snarky, sardonic columns, but deep down he's more interested in exploring what makes people tick than his editor would like. He keeps his desire to find his own Mr. Right hidden under a sexy, carefree persona that favors champagne and underwear models of the male variety.

Jaxon Lang loves being the high school principal in tiny Buckwheat Springs, Texas after relocating from Austin to pursue his relationship with Danetta Archer, despite her reputation for leaving grooms at the altar. So far, he's avoided examining the questions he has about himself, certain that marriage will put them to rest. Then Kieran arrives in town. Kieran's charm and unique attitudes about sex and attraction soon challenge Jaxon's concept of what—and who—he wants.

While covering the latest wedding of a real-life "runaway bride," Kieran falls hard for the gorgeous—and supposedly straight—groom, Jaxon Lang, despite that ridiculous X. Then Kieran discovers the bride's hiding a shocking secret.

www.dreamspinnerpress.com

When artisan ice cream maker Jay Brown first meets food writer Cameron Clay at a charity tasting event, they get along like strawberries and chocolate sauce. Jay's unique flavors thrill more than Cameron's jaded palate, but after a delicious encounter in Jay's delivery truck, where extra-creamy frozen treats are not the only delights sampled, Cameron loses Jay's contact info—and any hope of a real date.

Desperate, Cameron convinces his editor to host an artisanal ice cream contest in hopes of drawing out the elusive genius. But more complications threaten to intervene. Will Jay even enter the contest? Or will the chance of a happily ever after melt away?

www.dreamspinnerpress.com

a novella in the *Delectable* series

Gingerbread *Palace*

E M LYNLEY

A week before Christmas, Alex Bancroft's bakery goes up in flames. When he runs back inside after a dog, firefighter Kevin Flint has to rescue Alex—and Quincy—from the smoldering building, endangering them and inflaming Kevin's resentment.

Now Alex can't create the elaborate gingerbread house he donates to a foster-kids charity each year. Fire Station 7 again comes to his rescue, offering their kitchen and their manpower.

Everyone but Kevin Flint, that is. A third-generation firefighter, he's fearful of stepping too far out of the closet. So when his powerful physical attraction for Alex ends in a sizzling secret encounter in the firehouse, Kevin can't push Alex far enough away, and Alex returns the cold shoulder.

After a change of heart, Kevin risks his life to prove he's worthy of Alex's affection, but without a Christmas miracle, their chances at sweet romance might go up in smoke.

www.dreamspinnerpress.com

a Delectable novel

an Intoxicating Crush

EM LYNLEY

Simon Ford's success is hard-won. He grew up in Napa and resents the rich people who have moved into the valley, changing the culture by opening boutique wineries and pricing the locals out of the market.

Austin Kelvin runs an award-winning winery his father started after making a fortune on Wall Street. He lives the posh lifestyle Simon resents but secretly longs to attain. However, Austin's world isn't as luxurious and privileged as it seems: he didn't inherit his father's business savvy, and his winery is going under.

When Simon's boss sends him to covertly scope out Kelvin Cellars for a possible takeover bid, Simon sees it as a step toward attaining his financial dreams. Until he falls hard for Austin. The feeling is mutual, but when Austin learns the real reason for Simon's initial interest, he suspects Simon's seduction is merely a means to procure the winery at a bargain price. If there's any hope of winning Austin's heart, Simon will have to risk it all to prove Austin is more than just an intoxicating crush.

www.dreamspinnerpress.com

World-class chef Joshua Golden is homesick for Paris before he even arrives in New York, but he'll endure it—his parents need him to help run the family restaurant while his mother recovers from surgery. Running a place so far beneath his talents is bad enough, but bad turns to worse when Josh discovers his former best friend and lover, Micah Solomon, is living at his parents' house with his ten-year-old son, Ethan.

For ten years, Josh has done his best to forget how Micah shattered his heart into tiny pieces. Now Micah's back, fresh out of prison, and helping out at the restaurant. Micah may not be the kind of sous chef Josh is used to, but he is more helpful and supportive than any of the other employees. But Josh finds it hard to keep his distance when, time after time, Micah proves himself a better man than Josh thought. Reluctantly, Josh realizes there is more to Micah than his lousy life choices… but that doesn't mean Josh is ready to forgive him.

www.dreamspinnerpress.com

Spaghetti Western

a novel in the
Delectable series

Cordon Bleu-trained chef Riley Emerson arrives in Aspen, Colorado for a summer at the best restaurant in town, only to discover his jerk of a boyfriend has dumped him, leaving his heart and his plans in tatters. Doubting himself and longing for a change of pace, he takes a low-paying position at the Rocking Z guest ranch, though he expects nature up close and personal won't hold a candle to his exciting Paris lifestyle.

When born-and-bred cattle rancher Colby Zane spots a newcomer being pawed at by a passel of horny cowboys at Aspen's Club Rawhide, he rushes in, throws the guy over his shoulder, and rescues him. Sober, Riley Emerson is sweet and sexy, but not interested in more than a one-night stand. Still, Colby's over the moon when Riley later arrives as the new cook on his family's ranch.

But all's not well at the Rocking Z. Unsurmountable financial problems force them to seek a cash infusion from outside investor Fitz Wellington. Fitz is hot for Colby, and he won't sign on the dotted line without some very personal incentives. The future of the ranch is at stake, and Colby's just that desperate, but saving the Z might mean losing Riley.

www.dreamspinnerpress.com

When Trent Copeland runs into Reed Acton at a Bangkok airport, he thinks the handsome American is too good to be true. Why would someone like Reed be interested in a quiet, introverted gay-romance writer? After all, even an obvious tourist like Trent can see that there is more to Reed's constant unexplained appearances in his path than meets the eye.

Reed Acton has one mission and one mission only—he needs to get the map that was accidentally slipped into Trent's bag and keep the mobsters who want the priceless artifact from taking deadly revenge. Trent Copeland is a delicious and damned near irresistible diversion, but Reed can't afford distractions right now, especially if he wants to keep Trent safe.

From Bangkok's seediest back alleys to the sacred north, the two men will fight to stay one step ahead of the bad guys and learn that the only treasure worth finding is... each other.

www.dreamspinnerpress.com

In this exciting sequel to *Rarer Than Rubies*, gay romance author Trent Copeland and former FBI agent Reed Action head to Italy for a Roman holiday. What should be a relaxing and romantic vacation is interrupted when Reed's not-so-former boss asks for his help with a case. Trent's shocked to discover in the six months they've been living together in LA, Reed hasn't been completely honest about his "retirement."

Reed heads for Sicily on the trail of a suspected antiquities-smuggling ring and to find Peter Isett—a former FBI partner he also hasn't been completely truthful about. Stung by Reed's dishonesty, Trent questions what else Reed might be hiding. But when he overhears something that tells him Reed's life is in danger, Trent follows Reed to a remote chain of ancient volcanic islands off Sicily's northern coast. Soon Trent is caught up in the smugglers' web, and Reed must decide between his heart and his mission—a decision complicated by his past with Peter. Reed's position is perilous: unless he can learn to put the past behind him, he risks destroying everything he's built with Trent.

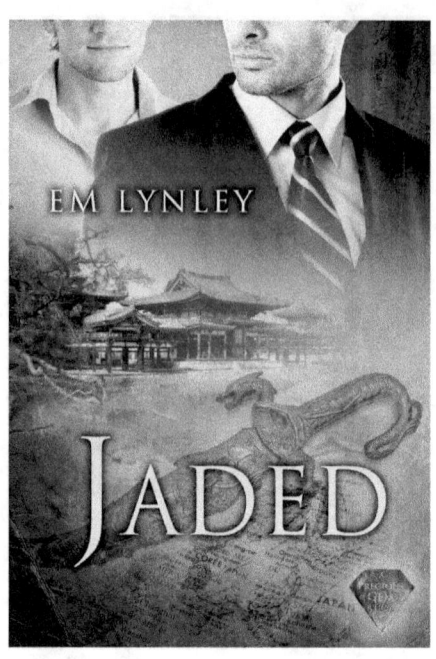

Gay-romance writer Trent Copeland finds his life in a rut while his boyfriend, Special Agent Reed Acton, is away on an undercover mission. After attending a special course at FBI headquarters in Quantico, Trent's eager for another challenge. He jumps at the opportunity for a trip to Japan to oversee appraisals of two art collections to be sold at the gallery he co-owns. But the trip isn't all cherry blossoms and Hello Kitty. When one of the collectors he meets—rumored to be the head of a Yakuza gang—turns up dead, Trent is accused of the murder and thrown in jail.

Reed drops everything to help find out who really committed the crime. He's in unknown territory in Japan, forced to navigate Tokyo's sex underworld to unravel the truth and save Trent. He poses as a "host" at a seedy late-night club. When Reed's undercover activities place him at a ruthless Yakuza leader's sex party, he must be willing to go to any lengths to secure Trent's safety and freedom. But trusting the wrong people brings both Reed and Trent to the Yakuza leader's attention. If they're ever to have a happy ever after, they'll first have to call on every skill just to stay alive.

www.dreamspinnerpress.com

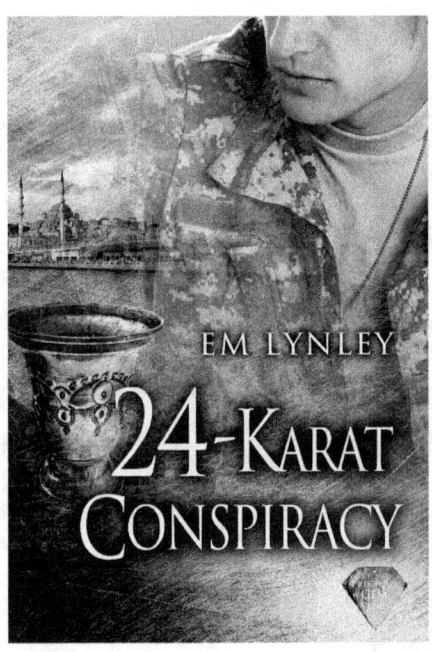

Former Ranger turned FBI agent Reed Acton faces his biggest challenge yet: a Christmas visit from partner Trent Copeland's parents. He's less equipped to handle hugs and holidays than the Taliban or international art thieves. When he's assigned to track down a set of gold Babylonian artifacts looted from the Iraqi National Museum after the fall of Baghdad, things start to look up.

This time, Trent's part of the mission, which takes them to exotic Istanbul. The crowded streets and labyrinthine markets fascinate Trent, but soon murder is on their trail. The investigation continues as Reed goes undercover at a US Army base, with Trent masquerading as his spouse. Surprisingly, fastidious and ever-fashionable Trent fits into base life right away and soon takes one of the suspects' wives under his wing when domestic abuse rears its head.

Their faux marriage leads Reed to appreciate Trent in ways he never expected, strengthening their bond—until Reed has to confront the worst demons from his past: his relationship with his estranged family.

www.dreamspinnerpress.com